NIGHTSHADE

Books By Robert Phillips

Fiction

The Land of Lost Content
Public Landing Revisited

Poetry

Inner Weather
The Pregnant Man
Running on Empty
Personal Accounts: New & Selected Poems, 1966–86
The Wounded Angel (*Limited Edition*)
Face to Face (*Limited Edition*)
Breakdown Lane
Spinach Days

Criticism & Biography

Denton Welch
William Goyen
The Confessional Poets

Anthologies

Aspects of Alice: Lewis Carroll's Dreamchild
Moonstruck: An Anthology of Lunar Poetry
Triumph of the Night: Tales of Terror & the Supernatural
Nightshade: 20th-Century Ghost Stories

Editions

William Goyen: Selected Letters from a Writer's Life
Delmore Schwartz & James Laughlin: Selected Letters
Letters of Delmore Schwartz
The Ego Is Always at the Wheel: Bagatelles by Delmore Schwartz
Shenandoah and Other Verse Plays, by Delmore Schwartz
Last and Lost Poems of Delmore Schwartz
The Stories of Denton Welch
Collected Stories of Noel Coward
New Selected Poems of Marya Zaturenska

NIGHTSHADE

20TH CENTURY
GHOST STORIES
EDITED BY ROBERT PHILLIPS

Carroll & Graf Publishers, Inc.
New York

Collection copyright © 1999 by Robert Phillips

First Carroll & Graf cloth edition 1999
First Carroll & Graf trade paperback edition 2000

Carroll & Graf Publishers, Inc.
A Division of Avalon Publishing Group
19 West 21st Street
New York, NY 10010-6805

Library of Congress Cataloging-in-Publication Data is available.
ISBN: 0-7867-0808-5

Manufactured in the United States of America

Permissions

FOR MY NIECE AND NEPHEW,
KATE ALLEN CUBBAGE
&
BENJAMIN DAVID CUBBAGE

Acknowledgments

Thanks to Kathleen Manwaring, George Arents Research Library for Special Collections, Syracuse University; and Rob House and Mary Lou Panez, University of Houston, for tracking down certain elusive stories. Also thanks to my beloved wife, Judith Bloomingdale, for her help assembling the final manuscript.

Contents

INTRODUCTION

Sir Osbert Sitwell informed Edith Wharton in the 1930s that ghosts went out when electricity came in. And in his 1944 "A Treatise on Tales of Horror," Edmund Wilson raised the question why one would read ghost stories in an age of electric light, radios, and the telephone. (One could now add, in an age of the FAX machine, the cell phone, computer E-Mail, and the Internet.) Wilson, like Sir Osbert, reasoned that electric light, unlike candles and gaslight, would have killed off any ghosts lurking in the corners and hallways of the house.

Yet, Wilson argues, there are two reasons to continue reading ghost stories in our time. The first is "a longing for mystic experience which seems always to manifest itself in periods of social confusion . . . as soon as we feel that our world has failed us, we try to find evidence for another world." (This may explain the large number of flying saucer "sightings" as well.) Wilson's second reason is "the instinct to inoculate ourselves against panic at the real horrors loose on the earth." As examples he mentions the Gestapo and airplane bombings.[1]

It seems true that ghosts are not as prevalent in twentieth-century literature as they were in Victorian letters. Still, there are many, and they have been created by very gifted writers. Mrs. Wharton prefaced her own collected ghost stories with a celebrated exchange: "Do you believe in ghosts?" To which the reply was given, "No, I don't believe in ghosts, but I'm afraid of them." This is far more than the cheap paradox it first appears to be. Many of us, it seems, are still afraid of ghosts—at least as they appear on the printed page.

The ghosts in this anthology are of two varieties—the visible and the invisible. Some, such as the ghost of the little girl in Ellen Glasgow's story, are visible only to those who believe in them. Some clearly are symbolic, such as those in Rudyard Kipling's "They" and William Trevor's "Mrs. Acland's Ghosts," which are totally artificial. These are stories in which an obsession can manifest itself concretely. The same is true of Henry James's "The Turn of the Screw," not included here for reasons of length; it is 130-odd pages long—and I do mean "odd." In some post-modern ghost tales, such as L. P. Hartley's "W.S.," the ghost becomes human and dread completely displaces reality. The Hartley story is unique also in that the ghost is a writer's own wretched literary creation, come to life to take revenge on him.

Of the visible ghosts presented here, some are very active and busy. Aichinger's makes a motorboat run perpetually. Aiken's patrols the halls of an office building while riding a bicycle. Goyen's carries a lantern at night, and Herlihy's makes mail deliveries in an audible truck. Wharton's writes and delivers ghostly letters to her widower. Others are rather passive, like that of the father in Tilghman's gentle tale, in which the ghost wants nothing more than to sit in his accustomed place on the front porch. Some of the ghosts aren't even people: Oates's and Jackson's are the ghost of a childhood doll, and Lurie's a malevolent piece of furniture. Kafka's are two bouncing balls that appear to a lonely man who really wants, but will not get, a dog.

Others are unconventional in different ways. One such appears in Muriel Spark's "The Leaf-Sweeper," in which the ghost is that of a living man—which, the author tells us, is far more repulsive than the ghost of a dead man! Another haunts Max Eberts's "Lost Lives," in which the ghost appears only in the visions and dreams of a reincarnated individual.

To be sure, there are more conventional ghost stories here as well. García Márquez gives us an old-fashioned haunted house, while Jean Rhys presents a haunted fourth-floor flat in Paris. "The Friends of the Friends" is a perfect example of a Henry James ghost story. It is told from a single point of view, in the form of a diary recounting events which either can be accepted as truthful or not. As a psychological portrait of a lady, the protagonist depicted is a forerunner of James's governess in the better-known "The Turn of the Screw."

Ten of the stories are told by a first-person narrator, while another includes a letter in the first person. This is part of the tradition dating back to Edgar Allan Poe, whose tales nearly always were told by a narrator so as to garner credibility. James's supernatural tales were filtered through a central character's consciousness. As James wrote, "We want it clear, goodness knows, but we also want it thick, and we get thickness in the human consciousness that entertains and records, that amplifies and interprets it."[2] Three of the stories may not be ghost stories at all, but rather tales of supernatural events. I include them out of personal fondness, and let the reader interpret them as he or she will.

Unlike many ghost story anthologies, all included here adhere to a high literary standard. Many are written by literary artists with whom we do not usually associate ghost stories or genre fiction. I would like to think the book fulfills Edmund Wilson's suggestion that "an anthology of considerable interest and power could be compiled by assembling horror stories by really first-rate modern writers, in which they have achieved their effects not merely by attempting to transpose into terms of contemporary life the old fairy-tales of goblins and phantoms, but by probing psychological caverns where the constraints of that life itself have engendered disquieting obsessions."[3]

Of the various kinds of ghost stories, I have omitted examples of the humorous. First, I personally find nothing funny about the topic. Secondly, the best of that genre are well known, from Brander Matthews' "The Rival Ghosts" to "The Open Window" by Saki (Hector Hugh Munro) to Donald Barthelme's "The Death of Edward Lear."

This is my second anthology of ghost stories. The first, originally titled *Triumph of the Night,* was published in 1989 by Carroll and Graf and reissued as a paperback retitled *The Omnibus of 20th Century Ghost Stories* in 1991. It since has been published in English, German, Italian, and Russian editions. It has been used in literature classrooms. And I have been flattered by having it imitated. When Larry Dark edited his *The Literary Ghost: Great Contemporary Ghost Stories* (Atlantic Monthly Press, 1991), he included no less than five stories which had appeared in my selection (those by Graham Greene, Joyce Carol Oates, Muriel Spark, Mavis Gallant, and William Goyen).

My first anthology contained only stories by American, English, Irish, and Welsh writers. For this second selection I have cast a wider net to include twentieth-century writers from other countries as well.

For the record, I cannot claim to have seen a ghost, but I as well as my wife, Judith, and son, Graham, believe we may have heard one. In 1970 we returned from New York City to my hometown in Delaware to attend my sister Elinor's wedding to James Stephenson Cubbage. (Their two children are this book's dedicatees.) My parents' home was so filled with wedding guests that we were placed overnight in my grandparents' house, which at the time was unoccupied. My grandmother, with whom I had been very close, had died in 1964. My grandfather, in failing health, resided in a nursing home. In the middle of the night in that empty house we were awakened by the most other-worldly, high-pitched sound. It was almost electronic, almost a cry. It went on endlessly. We searched the house for its source but found none. We went outside, but the sound was not apparent there. It interrupted our sleep all night. Finally, at daybreak it ceased. We asked neighbors on both sides if they'd heard the noise. They'd heard nothing. We called the local power and electric utility company—nothing. My family and I were quite willing to entertain the possibility that my maternal grandmother, Katie May Phillips, had attempted to communicate with us while we occupied the guest rooms of what had been her home for many decades. Today I'm not so sure.

Bennett Cerf tells the story of the timid soul hurrying down a long, dark corridor who collides with a shadowy personage he had not seen approaching. "You gave me a start! For a moment I could have sworn you were a ghost!" "What, my friend," answers the other, "makes you believe I'm not?"—and promptly disappears.[4]

ROBERT PHILLIPS
Houston, Texas
January 1999

NOTES

[1]Edmund Wilson, "A Treatise on Tales of Horror," *Classics and Commercials: A Literary Chronicle of the Forties* (New York: Farrar, Straus and Company, 1950), p. 173.

[2]Henry James, *The Art of the Novel* (New York: Scribner's, 1953), p. 256.

[3]Wilson, *op. cit,* p. 175.

[4]*Famous Ghost Stories,* ed. Bennett Cerf (New York: Vintage Books, 1944), p. xi.

Some are Born to sweet delight
Some are Born to Endless Night
—William Blake, AUGERIES OF INNOCENCE

NIGHTSHADE

GHOSTS
ON THE LAKE

Ilse Aichinger

During the summer people take little notice of them or think them no different from themselves, and those who leave the lake at the end of summer never notice them at all. Only towards autumn do they begin to become perceptible. Visitors who come later or stay longer, who end by not being sure whether they themselves are guests or ghosts, are able to pick them out. For there are days in early autumn when a sharp demarcation is to be observed.

There is the man who was coming in to land in his motor-boat when he discovered that he could not switch off his engine. At first he thought that this was no great calamity, and fortunately the lake was large. So he turned away from the east bank and went back towards the west bank, where the mountains rise steeply and the big hotels are. It was a fine evening, and his children waved to him from the landing stage, but still he could not switch off his engine. He acted as if he had no intention of landing and went back towards the other shore again. He passed a number of sailing boats and swans which had ventured a long way out, and when he reached the east bank again, which was reddened by the glow of the setting sun, sweat started pouring from his brow, for still he could not stop his engine. He called out cheerfully to his friends, who were sitting over coffee on the hotel terrace, that he proposed to stay out a little longer, as it was

1

such a fine evening, and they called back cheerfully that he was quite right and should certainly do so. When he appeared for the third time he called out that he was going back again to fetch his children, and he called out to his children that he was going back to fetch his friends. Soon afterwards both friends and children had disappeared from both banks, so he did not have to call out anything.

He had discovered a leak in the tank, and all the petrol had long since run out, but his engine kept on running on lake water. He no longer thought this a misfortune, and fortunately the lake was large. The last steamer passed, and people on board called out cheerfully to him, but he did not answer. If only no more boats come, he thought to himself; and no more boats came. The yachts lay in the inlets with lowered sails, and the lights in the hotel windows were reflected in the lake. Mist began to rise, he crossed the lake diagonally, and then went along the shore. At one point a girl was still bathing. She dived into the wave set up by the boat, and then she went ashore too.

But he could not repair the leaky tank while the engine was running, so he kept going. He felt relief at the thought that the day would come when his engine had used up all the water of the lake, and it struck him that sucking up the whole lake and being stranded on the muddy bottom would be a remarkable way of sinking. Soon afterwards it started to rain, and he gave up that idea. When he next passed the house from which the girl had bathed he noticed that there was still a light in the window, but farther along, when he passed his children's windows, the lights were out. When he turned back soon afterwards the girl had turned her light out too. The rain stopped, but he found this no consolation.

Next morning his friends having breakfast on the terrace were surprised to see that he was out in his boat so early. He cheerfully called out to them that the summer was nearly over, and that one shouldn't waste a moment of it, and he called out the same to his children, who had been waiting on the landing-stage since early morning; and next morning, when they wanted to send out a rescue party to bring him back, he vigorously declined it, because, after insisting for two whole days on how much he was enjoying himself, he could not possibly agree to being taken off by a rescue party, particularly in view of the girl who waited for the wave made by his boat every evening. On the fourth day he began to be afraid that people would start making fun of him, but consoled himself with the thought that this would turn out to be merely a passing phase, as indeed it did.

When the weather grew cooler his friends left the lake, and his children went home too, because the holidays were over and they had to go back to school. The noise of motor-cars on the road by the lake died away, and the only noise was now the sound of his engine on the lake. Every day the mist between the wood and the mountains grew thicker, and smoke from the chimneys hung about in the tree-tops.

The last to leave was the girl. From his boat he saw her piling her luggage into the car. She blew him a kiss, and said to herself that if he had been bewitched she might have stayed longer, but that he was too pleasure-seeking for her.

Soon afterwards he ran his boat aground at this spot out of sheer desperation. The stones made a long gash in the hull, and henceforward the boat was fuelled on air. During the autumn nights the villagers still hear the whine of his engine overhead.

Then there is the woman who starts fading away as soon as she takes off her sun-glasses.

She was not always like that. There was a time when she played in the sand without wearing sun-glasses, and later there was a time when she put on her sun-glasses as soon as the sun shone on her face and took them off as soon as the sun disappeared without starting to disappear herself. But that was a long time ago; if she had been asked, she would not have known how long ago it was herself, and in any case she would not have permitted such a question.

This unhappy state of affairs seems to have dated from the time when she started not taking off her sun-glasses in the shade, from one particular motor-ride in early summer when it suddenly became overcast, and all the others took off their dark glasses, but she kept hers on. Sun-glasses should never be worn in the shade; if they are, they get their own back.

One day not long afterwards, when she took her sun-glasses off for a moment while sailing in a friend's yacht, she suddenly felt herself fading away; her arms and legs just started vanishing into the east wind, which was raising white horses on the lake and would certainly have blown her away and caused her to disappear altogether if she had not had sufficient presence of mind quickly to put on her glasses again. However, the east wind fortunately brought good weather, sun and great heat, so for the next few weeks nobody noticed anything peculiar about her. When she danced in the evening she told everybody who wanted to know that she wore her sun-glasses to protect her eyes from the strong light of the arc-lamps, and a lot of people soon started imitating her. True, nobody knew that she kept her sun-glasses on even in bed at night by her open window, having no desire to be blown out of it, or to wake in the morning and find that she simply was not there.

When a spell of rain and bad weather came she tried taking her sun-glasses off again, but the same process of dissolution set in, and she noticed that the west wind was just as liable to blow her away as the east wind. After that she did not risk taking them off again. When the weather was bad she kept out of the way and waited for the sun to come out again, as it eventually did. Indeed, it kept on coming out again throughout the summer. Then she went sailing in her friends' yachts, played tennis, and even swam some way out into the lake with her sun-glasses on her nose. She was even kissed by various men without taking off her sun-glasses. She discovered that most things in this world can be done while wearing sun-glasses—as long as summer lasts.

Summer, however, slowly turned into autumn. Most of her friends went back to town, and only a few remained. But how could she go back to town wearing sun-glasses? Here by the lake her plight could be interpreted as a personal idiosyncrasy, and as long as there were still sunny days and the last of her friends remained things could go on as they were. But every day the wind was stronger, and sunny days grew fewer and farther between, and there was no likelihood that she would ever be able to take off her sun-glasses again.

What was to happen when winter came?

There were also the three girls in the stern of the steamer who kept giggling and poking fun at the single deck-hand on board. They came on board on the flat shore to cross over to have coffee on the hilly shore, and then they came back to the flat shore again.

The deck-hand noticed them giggling as soon as he saw them. They were saying things to each other behind their hands which he could not make out because of the loud chugging of the little steamer, but he had a definite suspicion that they were giggling at him and at the steamer; and when he climbed down from his seat beside the skipper to punch the tickets and approached the girls they giggled more than ever, which confirmed his suspicions. He went up to them and asked whether they had tickets, and, as they had, all he could do was to punch them. One of the girls asked him whether he did another job in the winter, and when he said no it set them giggling again.

After this he felt as if he had lost the badge from his cap, and he found it hard to go on punching passengers' tickets. He climbed back to his seat beside the skipper, but this time he did not take any excursionists' children with him, as he generally did; and he looked down at the calm, green lake and the prow cutting sharply through the water. An ocean liner could not have cut through it more sharply, but today the sight gave him no satisfaction. Instead he found himself irritated by the notice over the entrance to the cabin saying "Mind your head!" and the smoke from the funnel which blackened the flag flapping at the stern, as though it were his fault.

No, he had no other job in winter. The next time he went near them they asked whether the steamer plied in winter too. "Yes," he said, "because of the post." He saw them talking to each other quietly for a little while, and for some time that made him feel better. But when the steamer approached the little landing-stage and he threw the rope over the bollard they started giggling again, though his aim was perfect; and they went on giggling as long as he could see them.

An hour later they came on board again, but meanwhile the sky had become overcast, and when they were in the middle of the lake a storm broke out. The steamer started to rock, and the deck-hand seized the opportunity to show the girls what he could do. He climbed round the outside of the steamer in his oilskins more often than was necessary, and then came back again. Meanwhile it had started raining harder than ever, and he slipped on the wet wood and fell into the lake; and as one of the things that he had in common with sailors in ocean liners was that he could not swim, and as one of the things that the lake had in common with the ocean was that it was possible to drown in it, he was drowned.

He rests in peace, as is stated on his tombstone, because his body was pulled out of the water. But the three girls still go backwards and forwards on the steamer and giggle behind their hands. Those who see them should make no mistake; they are always the same.

—Translated by Eric Mosbacher

SONATA

FOR HARP

AND BICYCLE

Joan Aiken

"No one is allowed to remain in the building after five o'clock," Mr. Manaby told his new assistant, showing him into the little room that was like the inside of a parcel.

"Why not?"

"Directorial policy," said Mr. Manaby. But that was not the real reason.

Gaunt and sooty, Grimes Buildings lurched up the side of a hill toward Clerkenwell. Every little office within its dim and crumbling exterior owned one tiny crumb of light—such was the proud boast of the architect—but toward evening the crumbs were collected as by an immense vacuum cleaner, absorbed and demolished, yielding to an uncontrollable mass of dark that came tumbling in through windows and doors to take their place. Darkness infested the building like a flight of bats returning willingly to roost.

"Wash hands, please. Wash hands, please," the intercom began to bawl in the passages at a quarter to five. Without much need of prompting, the staff hustled like lemmings along the corridors to green- and blue-tiled washrooms that mocked with an illusion of cheerfulness the encroaching dusk.

"All papers into cases, please," the voice warned, five minutes later. "Look at your desks, ladies and gentlemen. Any documents left lying about? Kindly put them away. Desks must be left clear and tidy. Drawers must be shut."

7

A multitudinous shuffling, a rustling as of innumerable bluebottle flies might have been heard by the attentive ear after this injunction, as the employees of Moreton Wold and Company thrust their papers into cases, hurried letters and invoices into drawers, clipped statistical abstracts together and slammed them into filing cabinets, dropped discarded copy into wastepaper baskets. Two minutes later, and not a desk throughout Grimes Buildings bore more than its customary coating of dust.

"Hats and coats on, please. Hats and coats on, please. Did you bring an umbrella? Have you left any shopping on the floor?" At three minutes to five the homegoing throng was in the lifts and on the stairs; a clattering, staccato-voiced flood darkened momentarily the great double doors of the building, and then as the first faint notes of St. Paul's came echoing faintly on the frosty air, to be picked up near at hand by the louder chimes of St. Biddulph's-on-the-Wall, the entire premises of Moreton Wold stood empty.

"But why is it?" Jason Ashgrove, the new copywriter, asked his secretary one day. "Why are the staff herded out so fast? Not that I'm against it, mind you; I think it's an admirable idea in many ways, but there is the liberty of the individual to be considered, don't you think?"

"Hush!" Miss Golden, the secretary, gazed at him with large and terrified eyes. "You mustn't ask that sort of question. When you are taken onto the Established Staff you'll be told. Not before."

"But I want to know *now,*" Jason said in discontent. "Do you know?"

"Yes, I do," Miss Golden answered tantalizingly. "Come on, or we shan't have finished the Oat Crisp layout by a quarter to." And she stared firmly down at the copy in front of her, lips folded, candyfloss hair falling over her face, lashes hiding eyes like peridots, a girl with a secret.

Jason was annoyed. He rapped out a couple of rude and witty rhymes which Miss Golden let pass in a withering silence.

"What do you want for your birthday, Miss Golden? Sherry? Fudge? Bubble bath?"

"I want to go away with a clear conscience about Oat Crisps,"

Miss Golden retorted. It was not true; what she chiefly wanted was Mr. Jason Ashgrove, but he had not realised this yet.

"Come on, don't tease! I'm sure you haven't been on the Established Staff all that long," he coaxed her. "What happens when one is taken on, anyway? Does the Managing Director have us up for a confidential chat? Or are we given a little book called *The Awful Secret of Grimes Buildings?*"

Miss Golden wasn't telling. She opened her drawer and took out a white towel and a cake of rosy soap.

"Wash hands, please! Wash hands, please!"

Jason was frustrated. "You'll be sorry," he said. "I shall do something desperate."

"Oh no, you mustn't!" Her eyes were large with fright. She ran from the room and was back within a couple of moments, still drying her hands.

"If I took you out for a coffee, couldn't you give me just a tiny hint?"

Side by side Miss Golden and Mr. Ashgrove ran along the green-floored passages, battled down the white marble stairs among the hundred other employees from the tenth floor, the nine hundred from the floors below.

He saw her lips move as she said something, but in the clatter of two thousand feet the words were lost.

"—fire escape," he heard, as they came into the momentary hush of the carpeted entrance hall. And "—it's to do with a bicycle. A bicycle and a harp."

"I don't understand."

Now they were in the street, chilly with the winter dusk smells of celery on carts, of swept-up leaves heaped in faraway parks, and cold layers of dew sinking among the withered evening prim-roses in the bombed areas. London lay about them wreathed in twilit mystery and fading against the barred and smoky sky. Like a ninth wave the sound of traffic overtook and swallowed them.

"Please tell me!"

But, shaking her head, she stepped onto a scarlet homebound bus and was borne away from him.

Jason stood undecided on the pavement, with the crowds dividing around him as around the pier of a bridge. He scratched his head, looked about him for guidance.

An ambulance clanged, a taxi hooted, a drill stuttered, a siren wailed on the river, a door slammed, a brake squealed, and close beside his ear a bicycle bell tinkled its tiny warning.

A bicycle, she had said. A bicycle and a harp.

Jason turned and stared at Grimes Buildings.

Somewhere, he knew, there was a back way in, a service entrance. He walked slowly past the main doors, with their tubs of snowy chrysanthemums, and up Glass Street. A tiny furtive wedge of darkness beckoned him, a snicket, a hacket, an alley carved into the thickness of the building. It was so narrow that at any moment, it seemed, the overtopping walls would come together and squeeze it out of existence.

Walking as softly as an Indian, Jason passed through it, slid by a file of dustbins, and found the foot of the fire escape. Iron treads rose into the mist, like an illustration to a Gothic fairy tale.

He began to climb.

When he had mounted to the ninth story he paused for breath. It was a lonely place. The lighting consisted of a dim bulb at the foot of every flight. A well of gloom sank beneath him. The cold fingers of the wind nagged and fluttered at the tails of his jacket, and he pulled the string of the fire door and edged inside.

Grimes Buildings were triangular, with the street forming the base of the triangle, and the fire escape the point. Jason could see two long passages coming toward him, meeting at an acute angle where he stood. He started down the left-hand one, tiptoeing in the cavelike silence. Nowhere was there any sound, except for the faraway drip of a tap. No night watchman would stay in the building; none was needed. Burglars gave the place a wide berth.

Jason opened a door at random; then another. Offices lay everywhere about him, empty and forbidding. Some held lipstick-stained tissues, spilled powder, and orange peels; others were still foggy with cigarette smoke. Here was a Director's suite of rooms—a desk like half an acre of frozen lake, inch-thick carpet, roses, and the smell of cigars. Here was a conference room with scattered squares of doodled blotting paper. All equally empty.

He was not sure when he first began to notice the bell. Telephone, he thought at first, and then he remembered that all the outside lines were disconnected at five. And this bell, anyway, had not the regularity of a telephone's double ring: there was a tinkle, and then silence; a long ring, and then silence; a whole volley of rings together, and then silence.

Jason stood listening, and fear knocked against his ribs and shortened his breath. He knew that he must move or be paralyzed by it. He ran up a flight of stairs and found himself with two more endless green corridors beckoning him like a pair of dividers.

Another sound now: a waft of ice-thin notes, riffling up an arpeggio like a flurry of snowflakes. Far away down the passage it echoed. Jason ran in pursuit, but as he ran the music receded. He circled the building, but it always outdistanced him, and when he came back to the stairs he heard it fading away to the story below.

He hesitated, and as he did so heard again the bell; the bicycle bell. It was approaching him fast, bearing down on him, urgent, menacing. He could hear the pedals, almost see the shimmer of an invisible wheel. Absurdly, he was reminded of the insistent clamor of an ice-cream vendor, summoning children on a sultry Sunday afternoon.

There was a little fireman's alcove beside him, with buckets and pumps. He hurled himself into it. The bell stopped beside him, and then there was a moment while his heart tried to shake itself loose in his chest. He was looking into two eyes carved out of expressionless air; he was held by two hands knotted together out of the width of dark.

"Daisy, Daisy?" came the whisper. "Is that you, Daisy? Have you come to give me your answer?"

Jason tried to speak, but no words came.

"It's not Daisy! Who are *you?*" The sibilants were full of threat. "You can't stay here. This is private property."

He was thrust along the corridor. It was like being pushed by a whirlwind—the fire door opened ahead of him without a touch, and he was on the openwork platform, clutching the slender railing. Still the hands would not let him go.

"How about it?" the whisper mocked him. "How about jumping? It's an easy death compared with some."

Jason looked down into the smoky void. The darkness nodded to him like a familiar.

"You wouldn't be much loss, would you? What have you got to live for?"

Miss Golden, Jason thought. She would miss me. And the syllables Berenice Golden lingered in the air like a chime. Drawing on some unknown deposit of courage he shook himself loose from the holding hands and ran down the fire escape without looking back.

Next morning when Miss Golden, crisp, fragrant, and punctual, shut the door of Room 492 behind her, she stopped short of the hat-pegs with a horrified gasp.

"Mr. Ashgrove, your hair!"

"It makes me look more distinguished, don't you think?" he said.

It had indeed this effect, for his impeccable dark cut had turned to a stippled silver which might have been envied by many a diplomat.

"How did it happen? You've not—" her voice sank to a whisper—*"you've not been in Grimes Buildings after dark?"*

"Miss Golden—Berenice," he said earnestly. "Who was Daisy? Plainly you know. Tell me the story."

"Did you see him?" she asked faintly.

"Him?"

"William Heron—The Wailing Watchman. Oh," she exclaimed in terror, "I can see you did. Then you are doomed—doomed!"

"If I'm doomed," said Jason, "let's have coffee, and you tell me the story quickly."

"It all happened over fifty years ago," said Berenice, as she spooned out coffee powder with distracted extravagance. "Heron was the night watchman in this building, patrolling the corridors from dusk to dawn every night on his bicycle. He fell in love with a Miss Bell who taught the harp. She rented a room—this room—and gave lessons in it. She began to reciprocate his love, and they used to share a picnic supper every night at eleven, and she'd stay on a while to keep him company. It was an idyll, among the fire buckets and the furnace pipes.

"On Halloween he had summoned up the courage to propose to her. The day before he had told her he was going to ask her a very important question, and he came to the Buildings with a huge bunch of roses and a bottle of wine. But Miss Bell never turned up.

"The explanation was simple. Miss Bell, of course, had been losing a lot of sleep through her nocturnal romance, and so she used to take a nap in her music room between seven and ten, to save going home. In order to make sure that she would wake up, she persuaded her father, a distant relative of Graham Bell, to attach an alarm-waking fixture to her telephone which called her every night at ten. She was too modest and shy to let Heron know that she spent those hours in the building, and to give him the pleasure of waking her himself.

"Alas! On this important evening the line failed, and she never woke up. The telephone was in its infancy at that time, you must remember.

"Heron waited and waited. At last, mad with grief and jealousy, having called her home and discovered that she was not there, he concluded that she had betrayed him; he ran to the fire escape, and cast himself off it, holding the roses and the bottle of wine.

"Daisy did not long survive him but pined away soon after. Since that day their ghosts have haunted Grimes Buildings, he vainly patrolling the corridors on his bicycle, she playing her harp in the room she rented. *But they never meet.* And anyone who meets the ghost of William Heron will himself, within five days, leap down from the same fatal fire escape."

She gazed at him with tragic eyes.

"In that case we must lose no time," said Jason, and he enveloped her in an embrace as prompt as it was ardent. Looking down at the gossamer hair sprayed across his pin-stripe, he

added, "Just the same it is a preposterous situation. Firstly, I have
no intention of jumping off the fire escape—" here, however, he
repressed a shudder as he remembered the cold, clutching hands
of the evening before—"and secondly, I find it quite nonsensical
that those two inefficient ghosts have spent fifty years in this
building without coming across each other. We must remedy the
matter, Berenice. We must not begrudge our new-found happiness to others."

He gave her another kiss so impassioned that the electric type-
writer against which they were leaning began chattering to itself
in a frenzy of enthusiasm.

"This very evening," he went on, looking at his watch, "we
will put matters right for that unhappy couple and then, if I really
have only five more days to live, which I don't for one moment
believe, we will proceed to spend them together, my bewitching
Berenice, in the most advantageous manner possible."

She nodded, spellbound.

"Can you work a switchboard?" he added. She nodded again.
"My love, you are perfection itself. Meet me in the switchboard
room then, at ten this evening. I would say, have dinner with me,
but I shall need to make one or two purchases and see an old
R.A.F. friend. You will be safe from Heron's curse in the switchboard room if he always keeps to the corridors."

"I would rather meet him and die with you," she murmured.

"My angel, I hope that won't be necessary. Now," he said,
sighing, "I suppose we should get down to our day's work."

Strangely enough the copy they wrote that day, although engendered from such agitated minds, sold more packets of Oat
Crisps than any other advertising matter before or since.

That evening when Jason entered Grimes Buildings he was carrying two bottles of wine, two bunches of red roses, and a large
canvas-covered bundle. Miss Golden, who had concealed herself
in the switchboard room before the offices closed for the night,
eyed these things with surprise.

"Now," said Jason, after he had greeted her, "I want you first
to ring our own extension."

"No one will reply, surely?"

"I think *she* will reply."

Sure enough, when Berenice rang Extension 170 a faint, sleepy voice, distant and yet clear, whispered, "Hullo?"

"Is that Miss Bell?"

"Yes."

Berenice went a little pale. Her eyes sought Jason's and, prompted by him, she said formally, "Switchboard here, Miss Bell. Your ten o'clock call."

"Thank you," the faint voice said. There was a click and the line went blank.

"Excellent," Jason remarked. He unfastened his package and slipped its straps over his shoulders. "Now plug into the intercom."

Berenice did so, and then said, loudly and clearly, "Attention. Night watchman on duty, please. Night watchman on duty. You have an urgent summons to Room 492. You have an urgent summons to Room 492." The intercom echoed and reverberated through the empty corridors, then coughed itself to silence.

"Now we must run. You take the roses, sweetheart, and I'll carry the bottles."

Together they raced up eight flights of stairs and along the passages to Room 492. As they neared the door a burst of music met them—harp music swelling out, sweet and triumphant. Jason took a bunch of roses from Berenice, opened the door a little way, and gently deposited them, with a bottle, inside the door. As he closed it again Berenice said breathlessly, "Did you see anyone?"

"No," he said. "The room was too full of music." She saw that his eyes were shining.

They stood hand in hand, reluctant to move away, waiting for they hardly knew what. Suddenly the door opened again. Neither Berenice nor Jason, afterward, would speak of what they saw but each was left with a memory, bright as the picture on a Salvador Dali calendar, of a bicycle bearing on its saddle a harp, a bottle of wine, and a bouquet of red roses, sweeping improbably down the corridor and far, far away.

*　　*　　*

"We can go now," Jason said.

He led Berenice to the fire door, tucking the bottle of Médoc in his jacket pocket. A black wind from the north whistled beneath them as they stood on the openwork platform, looking down.

"We don't want our evening to be spoiled by the thought of a curse hanging over us," he said, "so this is the practical thing to do. Hang onto the roses." And holding his love firmly, Jason pulled the rip cord of his R.A.F. friend's parachute and leaped off the fire escape.

A bridal shower of rose petals adorned the descent of Miss Golden, who was possibly the only girl to be kissed in midair in the district of Clerkenwell at ten minutes to midnight on Hallow-een.

ENOCH
SOAMES

Max Beerbohm

When a book about the literature of the eighteen-nineties was given by Mr. Holbrook Jackson to the world, I looked eagerly in the index for SOAMES, ENOCH. I had feared he would not be there. He was not there. But everybody else was. Many writers whom I had quite forgotten, or remembered but faintly, lived again for me, they and their work, in Mr. Holbrook Jackson's pages. The book was as thorough as it was brilliantly written. And thus the omission found by me was an all the deadlier record of poor Soames' failure to impress himself on his decade.

I daresay I am the only person who noticed the omission. Soames had failed so piteously as all that! Nor is there a counter-poise in the thought that if he had had some measure of success he might have passed, like those others, out of my mind, to return only at the historian's beck. It is true that had his gifts, such as they were, been acknowledged in his lifetime, he would never have made the bargain I saw him make—that strange bargain whose results have kept him always in the foreground of my memory. But it is from those very results that the full piteousness of him glares out.

Not my compassion, however, impels me to write of him. For his sake, poor fellow, I should be inclined to keep my pen out of the ink. It is ill to deride the dead. And how can I write about Enoch Soames without making him ridiculous? Or rather, how am I to hush up the horrid fact that he *was* ridiculous? I shall not

17

be able to do that. Yet, sooner or later, write about him I must. You will see, in due course, that I have no option. And I may as well get the thing done now.

In the Summer Term of '93 a bolt from the blue flashed down on Oxford. It drove deep, it hurtlingly embedded itself in the soil. Dons and undergraduates stood around, rather pale, discussing nothing but it. Whence came it, this meteorite? From Paris. Its name? Will Rothenstein. Its aim? To do a series of twenty-four portraits in lithograph. These were to be published from the Bodley Head, London. The matter was urgent. Already the Warden of A, and the Master of B, and the Regius Professor of C, had meekly "sat." Dignified and doddering old men, who had never consented to sit to any one, could not withstand this dynamic little stranger. He did not sue: he invited; he did not invite: he commanded. He was twenty-one years old. He wore spectacles that flashed more than any other pair ever seen. He was a wit. He was brimful of ideas. He knew Whistler. He knew Edmond de Goncourt. He knew every one in Paris. He knew them all by heart. He was Paris in Oxford. It was whispered that, so soon as he had polished off his selection of dons, he was going to include a few undergraduates. It was a proud day for me when I—I—was included. I liked Rothenstein not less than I feared him; and there arose between us a friendship that has grown ever warmer, and been more and more valued by me, with every passing year.

At the end of Term he settled in—or rather, meteoritically into—London. It was to him I owed my first knowledge of that forever enchanting little world-in-itself, Chelsea, and my first acquaintance with Walter Sickert and other august elders who dwelt there. It was Rothenstein that took me to see, in Cambridge Street, Pimlico, a young man whose drawings were already famous among the few—Aubrey Beardsley, by name. With Rothenstein I paid my first visit to the Bodley Head. By him I was inducted into another haunt of intellect and daring, the domino room of the Café Royal.

There, on that October evening—there, in that exuberant vista of gilding and crimson velvet set amidst all those opposing mirrors and upholding caryatids, with fumes of tobacco ever rising to the painted and pagan ceiling, and with the hum of presumably cynical conversation broken into so sharply now and again by the clatter of dominoes shuffled on marble tables, I drew a deep breath, and "This indeed," said I to myself, "is life!"

It was the hour before dinner. We drank vermouth. Those who knew Rothenstein were pointing him out to those who knew him only by name. Men were constantly coming in through the swing-doors and wandering slowly up and down in search of vacant tables, or of tables occupied by friends. One of these rovers interested me because I was sure he wanted to catch Rothenstein's eye. He had twice passed our table, with a hesitating look; but Rothenstein, in the thick of a disquisition on Puvis de Chavannes, had not seen him. He was a stooping, shambling person, rather tall, very pale, with longish and brownish hair. He had a thin vague beard—or rather, he had a chin on which a large number of hairs weakly curled and clustered to cover its retreat. He was an odd-looking person; but in the 'nineties odd apparitions were more frequent, I think, than they are now. The young writers of that era—and I was sure this man was a writer—strove earnestly to be distinct in aspect. This man had striven unsuccessfully. He wore a soft black hat of clerical kind but of Bohemian intention, and a grey waterproof cape which, perhaps because it was waterproof, failed to be romantic. I decided that "dim" was the *mot juste* for him. I had already essayed to write, and was immensely keen on the *mot juste,* that Holy Grail of the period.

The dim man was now again approaching our table, and this time he made up his mind to pause in front of it. "You don't remember me," he said in a toneless voice.

Rothenstein brightly focused him. "Yes, I do," he replied after a moment, with pride rather than effusion—pride in a retentive memory. "Edwin Soames."

"Enoch Soames," said Enoch.

"Enoch Soames," repeated Rothenstein in a tone implying that it was enough to have hit on the surname. "We met in Paris two or three times when you were living there. We met at the Café Groche."

"And I came to your studio once."

"Oh yes; I was sorry I was out."

"But you were in. You showed me some of your paintings, you know. . . . I hear you're in Chelsea now."

"Yes."

I almost wondered that Mr. Soames did not, after this monosyllable, pass along. He stood patiently there, rather like a dumb animal, rather like a donkey looking over a gate. A sad figure, his. It occurred to me that "hungry" was perhaps the *mot juste* for him; but—hungry for what? He looked as if he had little appetite for anything. I was sorry for him; and Rothenstein, though he had not invited him to Chelsea, did ask him to sit down and have something to drink.

Seated, he was more self-assertive. He flung back the wings of his cape with a gesture which—had not those wings been waterproof—might have seemed to hurl defiance at things in general. And he ordered an absinthe. *"Fe me tiens toujours fidèle,"* he told Rothenstein, *"à la sorcière glauque."*

"It is bad for you," said Rothenstein drily.

"Nothing is bad for one," answered Soames. *"Dans ce monde il n'y a ni de bien ni de mal."*

"Nothing good and nothing bad? How do you mean?"

"I explained it all in the preface to *Negations.*"

"Negations?"

"Yes; I gave you a copy of it."

"Oh yes, of course. But did you explain—for instance—that there was no such thing as bad or good grammar?"

"N-no," said Soames. "Of course in Art there is the good and the evil. But in Life—no." He was rolling a cigarette. He had weak white hands, not well washed, and with finger-tips much stained by nicotine. "In Life there are illusions of good and evil, but"— his voice trailed away to a murmur in which the words *"vieux jeu"* and *"rococo"* were faintly audible. I think he felt he was not doing himself justice, and feared that Rothenstein was going to point out fallacies. Anyway, he cleared his throat and said *"Parlons d'autre chose."*

It occurs to you that he was a fool? It didn't to me. I was young, and had not the clarity of judgment that Rothenstein already had. Soames was quite five or six years older than either of us. Also, he had written a book.

It was wonderful to have written a book.

If Rothenstein had not been there, I should have revered Soames. Even as it was, I respected him. And I was very near indeed to reverence when he said he had another book coming out soon. I asked if I might ask what kind of book it was to be.

"My poems," he answered. Rothenstein asked if this was to be the title of the book. The poet meditated on this suggestion, but said he rather thought of giving the book no title at all. "If a book is good in itself—" he murmured, waving his cigarette.

Rothenstein objected that absence of title might be bad for the sale of a book. "If," he urged, "I went into a bookseller's and said simply 'Have you got?' or 'Have you a copy of?' how would they know what I wanted?"

"Oh, of course I should have my name on the cover," Soames answered earnestly. "And I rather want," he added, looking hard at Rothenstein, "to have a drawing of myself as frontispiece." Rothenstein admitted that this was a capital idea, and mentioned that he was going into the country and would be there for some time. He then looked at his watch, exclaimed at the hour, paid the waiter, and went away with me to dinner. Soames remained at his post of fidelity to the glaucous witch.

"Why were you so determined not to draw him?" I asked.

"Draw him? Him? How can one draw a man who doesn't exist?"

"He is dim," I admitted. But my *mot juste* fell flat. Rothenstein repeated that Soames was non-existent.

Still, Soames had written a book. I asked if Rothenstein had read "Negations." He said he had looked into it, "but," he added crisply, "I don't profess to know anything about writing." A reservation very characteristic of the period! Painters would not then allow that any one outside their own order had a right to any opinion about painting. This law (graven on the tablets brought down by Whistler from the summit of Fujiyama) imposed certain limitations. If other arts than painting were not

ınintelligible to all but the men who practiced them, the
... .ered—the Monroe Doctrine, as it were, did not hold
good. Therefore no painter would offer an opinion of a book
without warning you at any rate that his opinion was worthless.
No one is a better judge of literature than Rothenstein; but it
wouldn't have done to tell him so in those days; and I knew that I
must form an unaided judgment on "Negations."

Not to buy a book of which I had met the author face to face
would have been for me in those days an impossible act of self-
denial. When I returned to Oxford for the Christmas Term I had
duly secured *Negations.* I used to keep it lying carelessly on the
table in my room, and whenever a friend took it up and asked
what it was about I would say "Oh, it's rather a remarkable book.
It's by a man whom I know." Just "what it was about" I never
was able to say. Head or tail was just what I hadn't made of that
slim green volume. I found in the preface no clue to the exiguous
labyrinth of contents, and in that labyrinth nothing to explain the
preface.

Lean near to life. Lean very near—nearer.
Life is web, and therein nor warp nor woof is, but web only.
*It is for this I am Catholick in church and in thought, yet do
let swift Mood weave there what the shuttle of Mood wills.*

These were the opening phrases of the preface, but those
which followed were less easy to understand. Then came "Stark:
A *Conte,*" about a midinette who, so far as I could gather, murdered, or was about to murder, a mannequin. It seemed to me
like a story by Catulle Mendès in which the translator had either
skipped or cut out every alternate sentence. Next, a dialogue
between Pan and St. Ursula—lacking, I rather felt, in "snap."
Next, some aphorisms (entitled ἀφορίσματα). Throughout, in
fact, there was a great variety of form; and the forms had evidently been wrought with much care. It was rather the substance
that eluded me. Was there, I wondered, any substance at all? It
did now occur to me: suppose Enoch Soames was a fool! Up
cropped a rival hypothesis: suppose *I* was! I inclined to give

Soames the benefit of the doubt. I had read *"L'Après-midi d'un Faune"* without extracting a glimmer of meaning. Yet Mallarmé—of course—was a Master. How was I to know that Soames wasn't another? There was a sort of music in his prose, not indeed arresting, but perhaps, I thought, haunting, and laden perhaps with meanings as deep as Mallarmé's own. I awaited his poems with an open mind.

And I looked forward to them with positive impatience after I had had a second meeting with him. This was on an evening in January. Going into the aforesaid domino room, I passed a table at which sat a pale man with an open book before him. He looked from his book to me, and I looked back over my shoulder with a vague sense that I ought to have recognized him. I returned to pay my respects. After exchanging a few words, I said with a glance to the open book, "I see I am interrupting you," and was about to pass on, but "I prefer," Soames replied in his toneless voice, "to be interrupted," and I obeyed his gesture that I should sit down.

I asked him if he often read here. "Yes; things of this kind I read here," he answered, indicating the title of his book—*The Poems of Shelley*.

"Anything that you really"—and I was going to say "admire?" But I cautiously left my sentence unfinished, and was glad that I had done so, for he said, with unwonted emphasis, "Anything second-rate."

I had read little of Shelley, but "Of course," I murmured, "he's very uneven."

"I should have thought evenness was just what was wrong with him. A deadly evenness. That's why I read him here. The noise of this place breaks the rhythm. He's tolerable here." Soames took up the book and glanced through the pages. He laughed. Soames' laugh was a short, single and mirthless sound from the throat, unaccompanied by any movement of the face or brightening of the eyes. "What a period!" he uttered, laying the book down. And "What a country!" he added.

I asked rather nervously if he didn't think Keats had more or less held his own against the drawbacks of time and place. He admitted that there were "passages in Keats," but did not specify them. Of "the older men," as he called them, he seemed to like only Milton. "Milton," he said, "wasn't sentimental." Also, "Milton had a dark insight." And again, "I can always read Milton in the reading-room."

"The reading-room?"

"Of the British Museum. I go there every day."

"You do? I've only been there once. I'm afraid I found it rather a depressing place. It—it seemed to sap one's vitality."

"It does. That's why I go there. The lower one's vitality, the more sensitive one is to great art. I live near the Museum. I have rooms in Dyott Street."

"And you go round to the reading-room to read Milton?"

"Usually Milton." He looked at me. "It was Milton," he certificatively added, "who converted me to Diabolism."

"Diabolism? Oh yes? Really?" said I, with that vague discomfort and that intense desire to be polite which one feels when a man speaks of his own religion. "You—worship the Devil?"

Soames shook his head. "It's not exactly worship," he qualified, sipping his absinthe. "It's more a matter of trusting and encouraging."

"Ah, yes. . . . But I had rather gathered from the preface to 'Negations' that you were a—a Catholic."

"*Fe l'étais à cette époque.* Perhaps I still am. Yes, I'm a Catholic Diabolist."

This profession he made in an almost cursory tone. I could see that what was upmost in his mind was the fact that I had read "Negations." His pale eyes had for the first time gleamed. I felt as one who is about to be examined, *viva voce,* on the very subject in which he is shakiest. I hastily asked him how soon his poems were to be published. "Next week," he told me.

"And are they to be published without a title?"

"No. I found a title, at last. But I shan't tell you what it is," as though I had been so impertinent as to inquire. "I am not sure that it wholly satisfies me. But it is the best I can find. It does suggest something of the quality of the poems. . . . Strange growths, natural and wild; yet exquisite," he added, "and many-hued, and full of poisons."

I asked him what he thought of Baudelaire. He uttered the snort that was his laugh, and "Baudelaire," he said, "was a *bourgeois malgré lui.*" France had had only one poet: Villon; "and two-thirds of Villon were sheer journalism." Verlaine was "an *épicier malgré lui.*" Altogether, rather to my surprise, he rated French literature lower than English. There were "passages" in Villiers de l'Isle-Adam. But "I," he summed up, "owe nothing to France." He nodded at me. "You'll see," he predicted.

I did not, when the time came, quite see that. I thought the author of *Fungoids* did—unconsciously, no doubt—owe something to the young Parisian décadents, or to the young English ones who owed something to *them.* I still think so. The little book—bought by me in Oxford—lies before me as I write. Its pale grey buckram cover and silver lettering have not worn well. Nor have its contents. Through these, with a melancholy interest, I have again been looking. They are not much. But at the time of their publication I had a vague suspicion that they *might* be. I suppose it is my capacity for faith, not poor Soames' work, that is weaker than it once was. . . .

To a Young Woman

Thou art, who hast not been!
    Pale tunes irresolute
    And traceries of old sounds
    Blown from a rotted flute
Mingle with noise of cymbals rouged with rust,
Nor not strange forms and epicene
    Lie bleeding in the dust,
      Being wounded with wounds.
      For this it is
    That is thy counterpart
      Of age-long mockeries
Thou hast not been nor art!

There seemed to me a certain inconsistency as between the first and last lines of this. I tried, with bent brows, to resolve the discord. But I did not take my failure as wholly incompatible with a meaning in Soames' mind. Might it not rather indicate the depth of his meaning? As for the craftsmanship, "rouged with rust" seemed to me a fine stroke, and "nor not" instead of "and" had a curious felicity. I wondered who the Young Woman was, and what she had made of it all. I sadly suspect that Soames could not have made more of it than she. Yet, even now, if one doesn't try to make any sense at all of the poem, and reads it just for the sound, there is a certain grace of cadence. Soames was an artist—in so far as he was anything, poor fellow!

It seemed to me, when first I read *Fungoids*, that, oddly enough, the Diabolistic side of him was the best. Diabolism seemed to be a cheerful, even a wholesome, influence in his life.

Nocturne

Round and round the shutter'd Square
I stroll'd with the Devil's arm in mine.
No sound but the scrape of his hoofs was there
And the ring of his laughter and mine.
    We had drunk black wine.

I scream'd "I will race you, Master!"
"What matter," he shriek'd, "to-night
Which of us runs the faster?
There is nothing to fear to-night
    In the foul moon's light!"

Then I look'd him in the eyes,
And I laugh'd full shrill at the lie he told
And the gnawing fear he would fain disguise.
It was true, what I'd time and again been told:
    He was old—old.

There was, I felt, quite a swing about that first stanza—a joyous and rollicking note of comradeship. The second was slightly hysterical perhaps. But I liked the third: it was so bracingly unorthodox, even according to the tenets of Soames' peculiar sect in the faith. Not much "trusting and encouraging" here! Soames triumphantly exposing the Devil as a liar, and laughing "full shrill," cut a quite heartening figure, I thought—then! Now, in the light of what befell, none of his poems depresses me so much as "Nocturne."

I looked out for what the metropolitan reviewers would have to say. They seemed to fall into two classes: those who had little to say and those who had nothing. The second class was the larger, and the words of the first were cold; insomuch that

Strikes a note of modernity throughout. . . . These tripping numbers.—*Preston Telegraph.*

was the sole lure offered in advertisements by Soames' publisher. I had hoped that when next I met the poet I could congratulate him on having made a stir; for I fancied he was not so sure of his intrinsic greatness as he seemed. I was but able to say, rather coarsely, when next I did see him, that I hoped *Fungoids* was "selling splendidly." He looked at me across his glass of absinthe and asked if I had bought a copy. His publisher had told him that three had been sold. I laughed, as at a jest.

"You don't suppose I *care,* do you?" he said, with something like a snarl. I disclaimed the notion. He added that he was not a tradesman. I said mildly that I wasn't, either, and murmured that an artist who gave truly new and great things to the world had always to wait long for recognition. He said he cared not a *sou* for recognition. I agreed that the act of creation was its own reward.

His moroseness might have alienated me if I had regarded myself as a nobody. But ah! hadn't both John Lane and Aubrey Beardsley suggested that I should write an essay for the great new venture that was afoot—*The Yellow Book?* And hadn't Henry Harland, as editor, accepted my essay? And wasn't it to be in the very first number? At Oxford I was still *in statu pupillari.* In London I regarded myself as very much indeed a graduate now—one whom no Soames could ruffle. Partly to show off, partly in sheer good-will, I told Soames he ought to contribute to *The Yellow Book*. He uttered from the throat a sound of scorn for that publication.

Nevertheless, I did, a day or two later, tentatively ask Harland if he knew anything of the work of a man called Enoch Soames. Harland paused in the midst of his characteristic stride around the room, threw up his hands towards the ceiling, and groaned aloud: he had often met "that absurd creature" in Paris, and this very morning had received some poems in manuscript from him.

"Has he *no* talent?" he asked.

"He has an income. He's all right." Harland was the most joyous of men and most generous of critics, and he hated to talk of anything about which he couldn't be enthusiastic. So I dropped the subject of Soames. The news that Soames had an income did take the edge off solicitude. I learned afterwards that he was the son of an unsuccessful and deceased bookseller in Preston, but had inherited an annuity of £300 from a married aunt, and had no surviving relatives of any kind. Materially, then, he was "all right." But there was still a spiritual pathos about him, sharpened for me now by the possibility that even the praises of the *Preston Telegraph* might not have been forthcoming had he not been the son of a Preston man. He had a sort of weak doggedness which I could not but admire. Neither he nor his work received the slightest encouragement; but he persisted in behaving as a personage: always he kept his dingy little flag flying. Wherever congregated the *jeunes féroces* of the arts, in whatever Soho restaurant they had just discovered, in whatever music-hall they were most frequenting, there was Soames in the midst of them, or rather on the fringe of them, a dim but inevitable figure. He never sought to propitiate his fellow-writers, never bated a jot of his arrogance about his own work or of his contempt for theirs. To the painters he was respectful, even humble; but for the poets and prosaists of *The Yellow Book,* and later of *The Savoy,* he had never a word but of scorn. He wasn't resented. It didn't occur to anybody that he or his Catholic Diabolism mattered. When, in the autumn of

'96, he brought out (at his own expense, this time) a third book, his last book, nobody said a word for or against it. I meant, but forgot, to buy it. I never saw it, and am ashamed to say I don't even remember what it was called. But I did, at the time of its publication, say to Rothenstein that I thought poor old Soames was really a rather tragic figure, and that I believed he would literally die for want of recognition. Rothenstein scoffed. He said I was trying to get credit for a kind heart which I didn't possess; and perhaps this was so. But at the private view of the New English Art Club, a few weeks later, I beheld a pastel portrait of "Enoch Soames, Esq." It was very like him, and very like Rothenstein to have done it. Soames was standing near it, in his soft hat and his waterproof cape, all through the afternoon. Anybody who knew him would have recognized the portrait at a glance, but nobody who didn't know him would have recognized the portrait from its bystander: it "existed" so much more than he; it was bound to. Also, it had not that expression of faint happiness which on this day was discernible, yes, in Soames' countenance. Fame had breathed on him. Twice again in the course of the month I went to the New English, and on both occasions Soames himself was on view there. Looking back, I regard the close of that exhibition as having been virtually the close of his career. He had felt the breath of Fame against his cheek—so late, for such a little while; and at its withdrawal he gave in, gave up, gave out. He, who had never looked strong or well, looked ghastly now—a shadow of the shade he had once been. He still frequented the domino room, but, having lost all wish to excite curiosity, he no longer read books there. "You read only at the Museum now?" asked I, with attempted cheerfulness. He said he never went there now. "No absinthe there," he muttered. It was the sort of thing that in the old days he would have said for effect; but it carried conviction now. Absinthe, erst but a point in the "personality" he had striven so hard to build up, was solace and necessity now. He no longer called it *"la sorcière glauque."* He had shed away all his French phrases. He had become a plain, unvarnished, Preston man.

Failure, if it be a plain, unvarnished, complete failure, and even though it be a squalid failure, has always a certain dignity. I avoided Soames because he made me feel rather vulgar. John Lane had published, by this time, two little books of mine, and they had had a pleasant little success of esteem. I was a—slight but definite—"personality." Frank Harris had engaged me to kick up my heels in *The Saturday Review,* Alfred Harmsworth was letting me do likewise in *The Daily Mail.* I was just what Soames wasn't. And he shamed my gloss. Had I known that he really and firmly believed in the greatness of what he as an artist had achieved, I might not have shunned him. No man who hasn't lost his vanity can be held to have altogether failed. Soames' dignity was an illusion of mine. One day in the first week of June, 1897, that illusion went. But on the evening of that day Soames went too.

I had been out most of the morning, and, as it was too late to reach home in time for luncheon, I sought "the *Vingtième.*" This little place—*Restaurant du Vingtième Siècle,* to give it its full title—had been discovered in '96 by the poets and prosaists, but had now been more or less abandoned in favor of some later find. I don't think it lived long enough to justify its name; but at that time there it still was, in Greek Street, a few doors from Soho Square, and almost opposite to that house where, in the first years of the century, a little girl, and with her a boy named De Quincey, made nightly encampment in darkness and hunger among dust and rats and old legal parchments. The *Vingtième* was but a small whitewashed room, leading out into the street at one end and into a kitchen at the other. The proprietor and cook was a Frenchman, known to us as Monsieur Vingtième; the waiters were his two daughters, Rose and Berthe; and the food, according to faith, was good. The tables were so narrow, and were set so close together, that there was space for twelve of them, six jutting from either wall.

Only the two nearest to the door, as I went in, were occupied. On one side sat a tall, flashy, rather Mephistophelian man whom I had seen from time to time in the domino room and elsewhere. On the other side sat Soames. They made a queer contrast in that sunlit room—Soames sitting haggard in that hat and cape which nowhere at any season had I seen him doff, and this other, this keenly vital man, at sight of whom I more than ever wondered whether he were a diamond merchant, a conjurer, or the head of a private detective agency. I was sure Soames didn't want my company; but I asked, as it would have seemed brutal not to, whether I might join him, and took the chair opposite to his. He was smoking a cigarette, with an untasted salmi of something on his plate and a half-empty bottle of Sauterne before him; and he was quite silent. I said that the preparations for the Jubilee made London impossible. (I rather liked them, really.) I professed a wish to go right away till the whole thing was over. In vain did I attune myself to his gloom. He seemed not to hear me nor even to see me. I felt that his behavior made me ridiculous in the eyes of the other man. The gangway between the two rows of tables at the *Vingtième* was hardly more than two feet wide (Rose and Berthe, in their ministrations, had always to edge past each other, quarreling in whispers as they did so), and any one at the table abreast of yours was practically at yours. I thought our neighbor was amused at my failure to interest Soames, and so, as I could not explain to him that my insistence was merely charitable, I became silent. Without turning my head, I had him well within my range of vision. I hoped I looked less vulgar than he in contrast with Soames. I was sure he was not an Englishman, but what *was* his nationality? Though his jet-black hair was *en brosse,* I did not think he was French. To Berthe, who waited on him, he spoke French fluently, but with a hardly native idiom and accent. I gathered that this was his first visit to the *Vingtième*; but Berthe was off-hand in her manner to him: he had not made a good impression. His eyes were handsome, but—like the *Vingtième*'s tables—too narrow and set too close together. His nose was predatory, and the points of his moustache, waxed up beyond his nostrils, gave a fixity to his smile. Decidedly, he was sinister. And my sense of discomfort in his presence was intensified by the scarlet waistcoat which tightly, and so unseasonably in June, sheathed his ample chest. This waistcoat wasn't wrong merely because of the heat, either. It was somehow all wrong in itself. It wouldn't have done on Christmas morning. It would have struck a jarring note at the first night of "Hernani." I was trying to account for its wrongness when Soames suddenly and strangely broke silence. "A hundred years hence!" he murmured, as in a trance.

"We shall not be here!" I briskly but fatuously added.

"We shall not be here. No," he droned, "but the Museum will still be just where it is. And the reading-room, just where it is. And people will be able to go and read there." He inhaled sharply, and a spasm as of actual pain contorted his features.

I wondered what train of thought poor Soames had been following. He did not enlighten me when he said, after a long pause, "You think I haven't minded."

"Minded what, Soames?"

"Neglect. Failure."

"Failure?" I said heartily. "Failure?" I repeated vaguely. "Neglect—yes, perhaps; but that's quite another matter. Of course you haven't been—appreciated. But what then? Any artist who—who gives—" What I wanted to say was, "Any artist who gives truly new and great things to the world has always to wait long for recognition"; but the flattery would not out: in the face of his misery, a misery so genuine and so unmasked, my lips would not say the words.

And then—he said them for me. I flushed. "That's what you were going to say, isn't it?" he asked.

"How did you know?"

"It's what you said to me three years ago, when *Fungoids* was published." I flushed the more. I need not have done so at all, for "It's the only important thing I ever heard you say," he continued. "And I've never forgotten it. It's a true thing. It's a horrible truth. But—d'you remember what I answered? I said 'I don't care a sou for recognition.' And you believed me. You've gone on believing I'm above that sort of thing. You're shallow. What should *you* know of the feelings of a man like me? You imagine that a great artist's faith in himself and in the verdict of posterity is enough to keep him happy. . . . You've never guessed at the bitterness and loneliness, the"—his voice broke; but presently he resumed, speaking with a force that I had never known in him.

"Posterity! What use is it to *me?* A dead man doesn't know that people are visiting his grave—visiting his birthplace—putting up tablets to him—unveiling statues of him. A dead man can't read the books that are written about him. A hundred years hence! Think of it! If I could come back to life *then*—just for a few hours—and go to the reading-room, and *read!* Or better still: if I could be projected, now, at this moment, into that future, into that reading-room, just for this one afternoon! I'd sell myself body and soul to the devil, for that! Think of the pages and pages in the catalogue: 'SOAMES, ENOCH' endlessly—endless editions, commentaries, prolegomena, biographies"—but here he was interrupted by a sudden loud creak of the chair at the next table. Our neighbor had half risen from his place. He was leaning towards us, apologetically intrusive.

"Excuse—permit me," he said softly. "I have been unable not to hear. Might I take a liberty? In this little *restaurant-sans-façon*"—he spread wide his hands—"might I, as the phrase is, 'cut in'?"

I could but signify our acquiescence. Berthe had appeared at the kitchen door, thinking the stranger wanted his bill. He waved her away with his cigar, and in another moment had seated himself beside me, commanding a full view of Soames.

"Though not an Englishman," he explained, "I know my London well, Mr. Soames. Your name and fame—Mr. Beerbohm's too—very known to me. Your point is: who am *I?*" He glanced quickly over his shoulder, and in a lowered voice said "I am the Devil."

I couldn't help it: I laughed. I tried not to, I knew there was nothing to laugh at, my rudeness shamed me, but—I laughed with increasing volume. The Devil's quiet dignity, the surprise and disgust of his raised eyebrows, did but the more dissolve me. I rocked to and fro, I lay back aching. I behaved deplorably.

"I am a gentleman, and," he said with intense emphasis, "I thought I was in the company of *gentlemen.*"

"Don't!" I gasped faintly. "Oh, don't!"

"Curious, *nicht wahr?*" I heard him say to Soames. "There is a type of person to whom the very mention of my name is—oh-so-awfully-funny! In your theatres the dullest *comédien* needs only to say 'The Devil!' and right away they give him 'the loud laugh that speaks the vacant mind.' Is it not so?''

I had now just breath enough to offer my apologies. He accepted them, but coldly, and readdressed himself to Soames.

"I am a man of business," he said, "and always I would put things through 'right now,' as they say in the States. You are a poet. *Les affaires*—you detest them. So be it. But with me you will deal, eh? What you have said just now gives me furiously to hope."

Soames had not moved, except to light a fresh cigarette. He sat crouched forward, with his elbows squared on the table, and his head just above the level of his hands, staring up at the Devil. "Go on," he nodded. I had no remnant of laughter in me now.

"It will be the more pleasant, our little deal," the Devil went on, "because you are—I mistake not?—a Diabolist."

"A Catholic Diabolist," said Soames.

The Devil accepted the reservation genially. "You wish," he resumed, "to visit now—this afternoon as-ever-is—the reading-room of the British Museum, yes? but of a hundred years hence, yes? *Parfaitement.* Time—an illusion. Past and future—they are as ever-present as the present, or at any rate only what you call 'just-round-the-corner.' I switch you on to any date. I project you—pouf! You wish to be in the reading-room just as it will be on the afternoon of June 3rd, 1997? You wish to find yourself standing in that room, just past the swing-doors, this very minute, yes? and to stay there till closing time? Am I right?"

Soames nodded.

The Devil looked at his watch. "Ten past two," he said. "Closing time in summer same then as now: seven o'clock. That will give you almost five hours. At seven o'clock—pouf!—you find yourself again here, sitting at this table. I am dining to-night *dans le monde—dans le higlif.* That concludes my present visit to your great city. I come and fetch you here, Mr. Soames, on my way home."

"Home?" I echoed.

"Be it never so humble!" said the Devil lightly.

"All right," said Soames.

"Soames!" I entreated. But my friend moved not a muscle.

The Devil had made as though to stretch forth his hand across the table and touch Soames' forearm; but he paused in his gesture.

"A hundred years hence, as now," he smiled, "no smoking allowed in the reading-room. You would better therefore—"

Soames removed the cigarette from his mouth and dropped it into his glass of Sauterne.

"Soames!" again I cried. "Can't you"—but the Devil had now stretched forth his hand across the table. He brought it slowly down on—the table-cloth. Soames' chair was empty. His cigarette floated sodden in his wine-glass. There was no other trace of him.

For a few moments the Devil let his hand rest where it lay, gazing at me out of the corners of his eyes, vulgarly triumphant.

A shudder shook me. With an effort I controlled myself and rose from my chair. "Very clever," I said condescendingly. "But—*The Time Machine* is a delightful book, don't you think? So entirely original!"

"You are pleased to sneer," said the Devil, who had also risen, "but it is one thing to write about a not possible machine; it is a quite other thing to be a Supernatural Power." All the same, I had scored.

Berthe had come forth at the sound of our rising. I explained to her that Mr. Soames had been called away, and that both he and I would be dining here. It was not until I was out in the open air that I began to feel giddy. I have but the haziest recollection of what I did, where I wandered, in the glaring sunshine of that endless afternoon. I remember the sound of carpenters' hammers all along Piccadilly, and the bare chaotic look of the half-erected "stands." Was it in the Green Park, or in Kensington Gardens, or *where* was it that I sat on a chair beneath a tree, trying to read an evening paper? There was a phrase in the leading article that went on repeating itself in my fagged mind—"Little is hidden from this august Lady full of the garnered wisdom of sixty years of Sovereignty." I remember wildly conceiving a letter (to reach Windsor by express messenger told to await answer):

"MADAM,—Well knowing that your Majesty is full of the garnered wisdom of sixty years of Sovereignty, I venture to ask your advice in the following delicate matter. Mr. Enoch Soames, whose poems you may or may not know," . . .

Was there *no* way of helping him—saving him? A bargain was a bargain, and I was the last man to aid or abet any one in wriggling out of a reasonable obligation. I wouldn't have lifted a little finger to save Faust. But poor Soames!—doomed to pay without respite an eternal price for nothing but a fruitless search and a bitter disillusioning. . . .

Odd and uncanny it seemed to me that he, Soames, in the flesh, in the waterproof cape, was at this moment living in the last decade of the next century, poring over books not yet written, and seeing and seen by men not yet born. Uncannier and odder still, that to-night and evermore he would be in Hell. Assuredly, truth was stranger than fiction.

Endless that afternoon was. Almost I wished I had gone with Soames—not indeed to stay in the reading-room, but to sally forth for a brisk sight-seeing walk around a new London. I wandered restlessly out of the Park I had sat in. Vainly I tried to imagine myself an ardent tourist from the eighteenth century. Intolerable was the strain of the slow-passing and empty minutes. Long before seven o'clock I was back at the *Vingtième*.

I sat there just where I had sat for luncheon. Air came in listlessly through the open door behind me. Now and again Rose or Berthe appeared for a moment. I had told them I would not order any dinner till Mr. Soames came. A hurdy-gurdy began to play, abruptly drowning the noise of a quarrel between some Frenchmen further up the street. Whenever the tune was changed I heard the quarrel still raging. I had bought another evening paper on my way. I unfolded it. My eyes gazed ever away from it to the clock over the kitchen door. . . .

Five minutes, now, to the hour! I remembered that clocks in restaurants are kept five minutes fast. I concentrated my eyes on the paper. I vowed I would not look away from it again. I held it upright, at its full width, close to my face, so that I had no view of anything but it. . . . Rather a tremulous sheet? Only because of the draught, I told myself.

My arms gradually became stiff; they ached; but I could not drop them—now. I had a suspicion, I had a certainty. Well, what then? . . . What else had I come for? Yet I held tight that barrier of newspaper. Only the sound of Berthe's brisk footstep from the kitchen enabled me, forced me, to drop it, and to utter:

"What shall we have to eat, Soames?"

"Il est souffrant, ce pauvre Monsieur Soames?" asked Berthe.

"He's only—tired." I asked her to get some wine—Burgundy— and whatever food might be ready. Soames sat crouched forward against the table, exactly as when last I had seen him. It was as though he had never moved—he who had moved so unimaginably far. Once or twice in the afternoon it had for an instant occurred to me that perhaps his journey was not to be fruitless— that perhaps we had all been wrong in our estimate of the works of Enoch Soames. That we had been horribly right was horribly clear from the look of him. But "Don't be discouraged," I falteringly said. "Perhaps it's only that you—didn't leave enough time. Two, three centuries hence, perhaps—"

"Yes," his voice came. "I've thought of that."

"And now—now for the more immediate future! Where are you going to hide? How would it be if you caught the Paris express from Charing Cross? Almost an hour to spare. Don't go on to Paris. Stop at Calais. Live in Calais. He'd never think of looking for you in Calais."

"It's like my luck," he said, "to spend my last hours on earth with an ass." But I was not offended. "And a treacherous ass," he strangely added, tossing across to me a crumpled bit of paper which he had been holding in his hand. I glanced at the writing on it—some sort of gibberish, apparently. I laid it impatiently aside.

"Come, Soames! Pull yourself together! This isn't a mere matter of life and death. It's a question of eternal torment, mind you! You don't mean to say you're going to wait limply here till the Devil comes to fetch you?"

"I can't do anything else. I've no choice."

"Come! This is 'trusting and encouraging' with a vengeance! This is Diabolism run mad!" I filled his glass with wine. "Surely, now that you've *seen* the brute—"

"It's no good abusing him."

"You must admit there's nothing Miltonic about him, Soames."

"I don't say he's not rather different from what I expected."

"He's a vulgarian, he's a swell-mobsman, he's the sort of man who hangs about the corridors of trains going to the Riviera and steals ladies' jewel-cases. Imagine eternal torment presided over by *him!*"

"You don't suppose I look forward to it, do you?"

"Then why not slip quietly out of the way?"

Again and again I filled his glass, and always, mechanically, he emptied it; but the wine kindled no spark of enterprise in him. He did not eat, and I myself ate hardly at all. I did not in my heart believe that any dash for freedom could save him. The chase would be swift, the capture certain. But better anything than this passive, meek, miserable waiting. I told Soames that for the honor of the human race he ought to make some show of resistance. He asked what the human race had ever done for him. "Besides," he said, "can't you understand that I'm in his power? You saw him touch me, didn't you? There's an end of it. I've no will. I'm sealed."

I made a gesture of despair. He went on repeating the word "sealed." I began to realize that the wine had clouded his brain. No wonder! Foodless he had gone into futurity, foodless he still was. I urged him to eat at any rate some bread. It was maddening to think that he, who had so much to tell, might tell nothing. "How was it all," I asked, "yonder? Come! Tell me your adventures."

"They'd make first-rate 'copy,' wouldn't they?"

"I'm awfully sorry for you, Soames, and I make all possible allowances; but what earthly right have you to insinuate that I should make 'copy,' as you call it, out of you?"

The poor fellow pressed his hands to his forehead. "I don't know," he said. "I had some reason, I'm sure. . . . I'll try to remember."

"That's right. Try to remember everything. Eat a little more bread. What did the reading-room look like?"

"Much as usual," he at length muttered.

"Many people there?"

"Usual sort of number."

"What did they look like?"

Soames tried to visualise them. "They all," he presently remembered, "looked very like one another."

My mind took a fearsome leap. "All dressed in Jaeger?"

"Yes. I think so. Greyish-yellowish stuff."

"A sort of uniform?" He nodded. "With a number on it, perhaps?—a number on a large disc of metal sewn on to the left sleeve? DKF 78,910—that sort of thing?" It was even so. "And all of them—men and women alike—looking very well-cared-for? very Utopian? and smelling rather strongly of carbolic? and all of them quite hairless?" I was right every time. Soames was only not sure whether the men and women were hairless or shorn. "I hadn't time to look at them very closely," he explained.

"No, of course not. But—"

"They stared at *me*, I can tell you. I attracted a great deal of attention." At last he had done that! "I think I rather scared them. They moved away whenever I came near. They followed me about at a distance, wherever I went. The men at the round desk in the middle seemed to have a sort of panic whenever I went to make inquiries."

"What did you do when you arrived?"

Well, he had gone straight to the catalogue, of course—to the S volumes, and had stood long before SN-SOF, unable to take this volume out of the shelf, because his heart was beating so. . . . At first, he said, he wasn't disappointed—he only thought there was some new arrangement. He went to the middle desk and asked where the catalogue of *twentieth*-century books was kept. He gathered that there was still only one catalogue. Again he looked up his name, stared at the three little pasted slips he had known so well. Then he went and sat down for a long time. . . .

"And then," he droned, "I looked up the *Dictionary of National Biography* and some encyclopedias. . . . I went back to the middle desk and asked what was the best modern book on late nineteenth-century literature. They told me Mr. T. K. Nupton's book was considered the best. I looked it up in the catalogue and filled in a form for it. It was brought to me. My name wasn't in the index, but— Yes!" he said with a sudden change of tone. "That's what I'd forgotten. Where's that bit of paper? Give it me back."

I, too, had forgotten that cryptic screed. I found it fallen on the floor, and handed it to him.

He smoothed it out, nodding and smiling at me disagreeably. "I found myself glancing through Nupton's book," he resumed. "Not very easy reading. Some sort of phonetic spelling. . . . All the modern books I saw were phonetic."

"Then I don't want to hear any more, Soames, please."

"The proper names seemed all to be spelt in the old way. But for that, I mightn't have noticed my own name."

"Your own name? Really? Soames, I'm *very* glad."

"And yours."

"No!"

"I thought I should find you waiting here to-night. So I took the trouble to copy out the passage. Read it."

I snatched the paper. Soames' handwriting was characteristically dim. It, and the noisome spelling, and my excitement, made me all the slower to grasp what T. K. Nupton was driving at.

The document lies before me at this moment. Strange that the words I here copy out for you were copied out for me by poor Soames just seventy-eight years hence. . . .

From p. 234 of *Inglish Littracher 1890–1900*, bi T. K. Nupton, published bi th Stait, 1992:

"Fr. egzarmpl, a riter ov th time, naimd Max Beerbohm, hoo woz stil alive in th twentieth senchri, rote a stauri in wich e pautraid an immajnari karrakter kauld 'Enoch Soames'—a thurd-rait poit hoo beleevz imself a grate jeneus an maix a bargin with th Devvl in auder ter no wot posterriti thinx ov im! It iz a sumwot labud sattire but not without

vallu az showing hou seriusli the yung men ov th aiteen-
ninetiz took themselvz. Nou that the littreri profeshn haz bin
auganized az a department of publik servis, our riters hav
found their levvl an hav lernt ter doo their duti without thort
ov th morro. 'Th laibrer iz werthi ov hiz hire,' an that iz aul.
Thank hevvn we hav no Enoch Soameses amung us to-dai!"

I found that by murmuring the words aloud (a device which I
commend to my reader) I was able to master them, little by little.
The clearer they became, the greater was my bewilderment, my
distress and horror. The whole thing was a nightmare. Afar, the
great grisly background of what was in store for the poor dear art
of letters; here, at the table, fixing on me a gaze that made me hot
all over, the poor fellow whom—whom evidently . . . but no:
whatever down-grade my character might take in coming years, I
should never be such a brute as to—

Again I examined the screed. "Immajnari"—but here Soames
was, no more imaginary, alas! than I. And "labud"—what on
earth was that? (To this day, I have never made out that word.)
"It's all very—baffling," I at length stammered.

Soames said nothing, but cruelly did not cease to look at me.

"Are you sure," I temporized, "quite sure you copied the thing
out correctly?"

"Quite."

"Well, then it's this wretched Nupton who must have made—
must be going to make—some idiotic mistake. . . . Look here,
Soames! you know me better than to suppose that I . . . After
all, the name 'Max Beerbohm' is not at all an uncommon one, and
there must be several Enoch Soameses running around—or
rather, 'Enoch Soames' is a name that might occur to any one
writing a story. And I don't write stories: I'm an essayist, an
observer, a recorder. . . . I admit that it's an extraordinary coincidence. But you must see—"

"I see the whole thing," said Soames quietly. And he added,
with a touch of his old manner, but with more dignity than I had
ever known in him, *"Parlons d'autre chose."*

I accepted that suggestion very promptly. I returned straight to the more immediate future. I spent most of the long evening in renewed appeals to Soames to slip away and seek refuge somewhere. I remember saying at last that if indeed I was destined to write about him, the supposed "stauri" had better have at least a happy ending. Soames repeated those last three words in a tone of intense scorn. "In Life and in Art," he said, "all that matters is an *inevitable* ending."

"But," I urged, more hopefully than I felt, "an ending that can be avoided *isn't* inevitable."

"You aren't an artist," he rasped. "And you're so hopelessly not an artist that, so far from being able to imagine a thing and make it seem true, you're going to make even a true thing seem as if you'd made it up. You're a miserable bungler. And it's like my luck."

I protested that the miserable bungler was not I—was not going to be I—but T. K. Nupton; and we had a rather heated argument, in the thick of which it suddenly seemed to me that Soames saw he was in the wrong: he had quite physically cowered. But I wondered why—and now I guessed with a cold throb just why—he stared so, past me. The bringer of that "inevitable ending" filled the doorway.

I managed to turn in my chair and to say, not without a semblance of lightness, "Aha, come in!" Dread was indeed rather blunted in me by his looking so absurdly like a villain in a melodrama. The sheen of his tilted hat and of his shirtfront, the repeated twists he was giving to his mustache, and most of all the magnificence of his sneer, gave token that he was there only to be foiled.

He was at our table in a stride. "I am sorry," he sneered witheringly, "to break up your pleasant party, but—"

"You don't: you complete it," I assured him. "Mr. Soames and I want to have a little talk with you. Won't you sit? Mr. Soames got nothing—frankly nothing—by his journey this afternoon. We don't wish to say that the whole thing was a swindle—a common swindle. On the contrary, we believe you meant well. But of course the bargain, such as it was, is off."

The Devil gave no verbal answer. He merely looked at Soames

and pointed with rigid forefinger to the door. Soames was wretchedly rising from his chair when, with a desperate quick gesture, I swept together two dinner-knives that were on the table, and laid their blades across each other. The Devil stepped sharp back against the table behind him, averting his face and shuddering.

"You are not superstitious!" he hissed.

"Not at all," I smiled.

"Soames!" he said as to an underling, but without turning his face, "put those knives straight!"

With an inhibitive gesture to my friend, "Mr. Soames," I said emphatically to the Devil, "is a *Catholic* Diabolist"; but my poor friend did the Devil's bidding, not mine; and now, with his master's eyes again fixed on him, he arose, he shuffled past me. I tried to speak. It was he that spoke. "Try," was the prayer he threw back at me as the Devil pushed him roughly out through the door, *"try* to make them know that I did exist!"

In another instant I too was through that door. I stood staring all ways—up the street, across it, down it. There was moonlight and lamplight, but there was not Soames nor that other.

Dazed, I stood there. Dazed, I turned back, at length, into the little room; and I suppose I paid Berthe or Rose for my dinner and luncheon, and for Soames': I hope so, for I never went to the *Vingtième* again. Ever since that night I have avoided Greek Street altogether. And for years I did not set foot even in Soho Square, because on that same night it was there that I paced and loitered, long and long, with some such dull sense of hope as a man has in not straying far from the place where he has lost something. . . . "Round and round the shutter'd Square"—that line came back to me on my lonely beat, and with it the whole stanza, ringing in my brain and bearing in on me how tragically different from the happy scene imagined by him was the poet's actual experience of that prince in whom of all princes we should put not our trust.

But—strange how the mind of an essayist, be it never so stricken, roves and ranges!—I remember pausing before a wide doorstep and wondering if perchance it was on this very one that

the young De Quincey lay ill and faint while poor Ann flew as fast
as her feet would carry her to Oxford Street, the "stony-hearted
stepmother" of them both, and came back bearing that "glass of
port wine and spices" but for which he might, so he thought,
actually have died. Was this the very doorstep that the old De
Quincey used to revisit in homage? I pondered Ann's fate, the
cause of her sudden vanishing from the ken of her boy-friend;
and presently I blamed myself for letting the past over-ride the
present. Poor vanished Soames!

And for myself, too, I began to be troubled. What had I better
do? Would there be a hue and cry—Mysterious Disappearance of
an Author, and all that? He had last been seen lunching and dining in my company. Hadn't I better get a hansom and drive
straight to Scotland Yard? . . . They would think I was a lunatic.
After all, I reassured myself, London was a very large place, and
one very dim figure might easily drop out of it unobserved—now
especially, in the blinding glare of the near Jubilee. Better say
nothing at all, I thought.

And I was right. Soames' disappearance made no stir at all. He
was utterly forgotten before any one, so far as I am aware, noticed
that he was no longer hanging around. Now and again some poet
or prosaist may have said to another, "What has become of that
man Soames?" but I never heard any such question asked. The
solicitor through whom he was paid his annuity may be presumed to have made inquiries, but no echo of these resounded.
There was something rather ghastly to me in the general uncon-
sciousness that Soames had existed, and more than once I caught
myself wondering whether Nupton, that babe unborn, were going to be right in thinking him a figment of my brain.

In that extract from Nupton's repulsive book there is one point
which perhaps puzzles you. How is it that the author, though I
have here mentioned him by name and have quoted the exact
words he is going to write, is not going to grasp the obvious
corollary that I have invented nothing? The answer can but be
this: Nupton will not have read the later passages of this memoir.
Such lack of thoroughness is a serious fault in any one who un-
dertakes to do scholar's work. And I hope these words will meet

the eye of some contemporary rival to Nupton and be the undo-
ing of Nupton.

I like to think that some time between 1992 and 1997 somebody will have looked up this memoir, and will have forced on
the world his inevitable and startling conclusions. And I have
reasons for believing that this will be so. You realise that the
reading-room into which Soames was projected by the Devil was
in all respects precisely as it will be on the afternoon of June 3rd,
1997. You realize, therefore, that on that afternoon, when it
comes round, there the self-same crowd will be, and there
Soames too will be, punctually, he and they doing precisely what
they did before. Recall now Soames' account of the sensation he
made. You may say that the mere difference of his costume was
enough to make him sensational in that uniformed crowd. You
wouldn't say so if you had ever seen him. I assure you that in no
period could Soames be anything but dim. The fact that people
are going to stare at him, and follow him around, and seem afraid
of him, can be explained only on the hypothesis that they will
somehow have been prepared for his ghostly visitation. They will
have been awfully waiting to see whether he really would come.
And when he does come the effect will of course be—awful.

An authentic, guaranteed, proven ghost, but—only a ghost,
alas! Only that. In his first visit, Soames was a creature of flesh
and blood, whereas the creatures into whose midst he was projected were but ghosts, I take it—solid, palpable, vocal, but unconscious and automatic ghosts, in a building that was itself an
illusion. Next time, that building and those creatures will be real.
It is of Soames that there will be but the semblance. I wish I
could think him destined to revisit the world actually, physically,
consciously. I wish he had this one brief escape, this one small
treat, to look forward to. I never forget him for long. He is where
he is, and forever. The more rigid moralists among you may say
he has only himself to blame. For my part, I think he has been
very hardly used. It is well that vanity should be chastened; and
Enoch Soames' vanity was, I admit, above the average, and called
for special treatment. But there was no need for vindictiveness.
You say he contracted to pay the price he is paying; yes; but I

maintain that he was induced to do so by fraud. Well-informed in all things, the Devil must have known that my friend would gain nothing by his visit to futurity. The whole thing was a very shabby trick. The more I think of it, the more detestable the Devil seems to me.

Of him I have caught sight several times, here and there, since that day at the *Vingtième*. Only once, however, have I seen him at close quarters. This was in Paris. I was walking, one afternoon, along the Rue d'Antin, when I saw him advancing from the opposite direction—over-dressed as ever, and swinging an ebony cane, and altogether behaving as though the whole pavement belonged to him. At thought of Enoch Soames and the myriads of other sufferers eternally in this brute's dominion, a great cold wrath filled me, and I drew myself up to my full height. But—well, one is so used to nodding and smiling in the street to anybody whom one knows, that the action becomes almost independent of oneself: to prevent it requires a very sharp effort and great presence of mind. I was miserably aware, as I passed the Devil, that I nodded and smiled to him. And my shame was the deeper and hotter because he, if you please, stared straight at me with the utmost haughtiness.

To be cut—deliberately cut—by *him!* I was, I still am, furious at having had that happen to me.

THE
HAPPY AUTUMN
FIELDS

Elizabeth Bowen

The family walking party, though it comprised so many, did not deploy or straggle over the stubble but kept in a procession of threes and twos. Papa, who carried his Alpine stick, led, flanked by Constance and little Arthur. Robert and Cousin Theodore, locked in studious talk, had Emily attached but not quite abreast. Next came Digby and Lucius, taking, to left and right, imaginary aim at rooks. Henrietta and Sarah brought up the rear.

It was Sarah who saw the others ahead on the blond stubble, who knew them, knew what they were to each other, knew their names and knew her own. It was she who felt the stubble under her feet, and who heard it give beneath the tread of the others a continuous different more distant soft stiff scrunch. The field and all these outlying fields in view knew as Sarah knew that they were Papa's. The harvest had been good and was now in: he was satisfied—for this afternoon he had made the instinctive choice of his most womanly daughter, most nearly infant son. Arthur, whose hand Papa was holding, took an anxious hop, a skip and a jump to every stride of the great man's. As for Constance—Sarah could often see the flash of her hat-feather as she turned her head, the curve of her close bodice as she turned her torso. Constance gave Papa her attention but not her thoughts, for she had already been sought in marriage.

The landowner's daughters, from Constance down, walked with their beetle-green, mole or maroon skirts gathered up and

47

carried clear of the ground, but for Henrietta, who was still ankle-free. They walked inside a continuous stuffy sound, but left silence behind them. Behind them, rooks that had risen and circled, sun striking blue from their blue-black wings, planed one by one to the earth and settled to peck again. Papa and the boys were dark-clad as the rooks but with no sheen, but for their white collars.

It was Sarah who located the thoughts of Constance, knew what a twisting prisoner was Arthur's hand, felt to the depths of Emily's pique at Cousin Theodore's inattention, rejoiced with Digby and Lucius at the imaginary fall of so many rooks. She fell back, however, as from a rocky range, from the converse of Robert and Cousin Theodore. Most she knew that she swam with love at the nearness of Henrietta's young and alert face and eyes which shone with the sky and queried the afternoon.

She recognized the color of valediction, tasted sweet sadness, while from the cottage inside the screen of trees wood-smoke rose melting pungent and blue. This was the eve of the brothers' return to school. It was like a Sunday; Papa had kept the late afternoon free; all (all but one) encircling Robert, Digby and Lucius, they walked the estate the brothers would not see again for so long. Robert, it could be felt, was not unwilling to return to his books; next year he would go to college like Theodore; besides, to all this they saw he was not the heir. But in Digby and Lucius aiming and popping hid a bodily grief, the repugnance of victims, though these two were further from being heirs than Robert.

Sarah said to Henrietta: "To think they will not be here tomorrow!"

"*Is* that what you are thinking about?" Henrietta asked, with her subtle taste for the truth.

"More, I was thinking that you and I will be back again by one another at table . . ."

"You know we are always sad when the boys are going, but we are never sad when the boys have gone." The sweet reciprocal guilty smile that started on Henrietta's lips finished on those of Sarah. "Also," the young sister said, "we know this is only something happening again. It happened last year, and it will happen next. But oh how should I feel, and how should you feel, if it were something that had not happened before?"

"For instance, when Constance goes to be married?"

"Oh, I don't mean *Constance!*" said Henrietta.

"So long," said Sarah, considering, "as, whatever it is, it happens to both of us?" She must never have to wake in the early morning except to the birdlike stirrings of Henrietta, or have her cheek brushed in the dark by the frill of another pillow in whose hollow did not repose Henrietta's cheek. Rather than they should cease to lie in the same bed she prayed they might lie in the same grave. "You and I will stay as we are," she said, "then nothing can touch one without touching the other."

"So you say; so I hear you say!" exclaimed Henrietta, who then, lips apart, sent Sarah her most tormenting look. "But I cannot forget that you chose to be born without me; that you would not wait—" But here she broke off, laughed outright and said: "Oh, *see!*"

Ahead of them there had been a dislocation. Emily took advantage of having gained the ridge to kneel down to tie her bootlace so abruptly that Digby all but fell over her, with an exclamation. Cousin Theodore had been civil enough to pause beside Emily, but Robert, lost to all but what he was saying, strode on, head down, only just not colliding into Papa and Constance, who had turned to look back. Papa, astounded, let go of Arthur's hand, whereupon Arthur fell flat on the stubble.

"Dear me," said the affronted Constance to Robert.

Papa said. "What is the matter there? May I ask, Robert, where you are going, sir? Digby, remember that is your sister Emily."

"Cousin Emily is in trouble," said Cousin Theodore.

Poor Emily, telescoped in her skirts and by now scarlet under her hatbrim, said in a muffled voice: "It is just my bootlace, Papa."

"Your bootlace, Emily?"

"I was just tying it."

"Then you had better tie it.—Am I to think," said Papa, looking round them all, "that you must all go down like a pack of ninepins because Emily has occasion to stoop?"

At this Henrietta uttered a little whoop, flung her arms round Sarah, buried her face in her sister and fairly suffered with laughter. She could contain this no longer; she shook all over. Papa, who found Henrietta so hopelessly out of order that he took no notice of her except at table, took no notice, simply giving the signal for the others to collect themselves and move on. Cousin Theodore, helping Emily to her feet, could be seen to see how her heightened color became her, but she dispensed with his hand chillily, looked elsewhere, touched the brooch at her throat and said: "Thank you, I have not sustained an accident." Digby apologized to Emily, Robert to Papa and Constance. Constance righted Arthur, flicking his breeches over with her handkerchief. All fell into their different steps and resumed their way.

Sarah, with no idea how to console laughter, coaxed, "Come, come, come," into Henrietta's ear. Between the girls and the others the distance widened; it began to seem that they would be left alone.

"And why not?" said Henrietta, lifting her head in answer to Sarah's thought.

They looked around them with the same eyes. The shorn uplands seemed to float on the distance, which extended dazzling to tiny blue glassy hills. There was no end to the afternoon, whose light went on ripening now they had scythed the corn. Light filled the silence which, now Papa and the others were out of hearing, was complete. Only screens of trees intersected and knolls made islands in the vast fields. The mansion and the home farm had sunk for ever below them in the expanse of woods, so that hardly a ripple showed where the girls dwelled.

The shadow of the same rook circling passed over Sarah then over Henrietta, who in their turn cast one shadow across the stubble. "But, Henrietta, we cannot stay here for ever."

Henrietta immediately turned her eyes to the only lonely plume of smoke, from the cottage. "Then let us go and visit the poor old man. He is dying and the others are happy. One day we shall pass and see no more smoke; then soon his roof will fall in, and we shall always be sorry we did not go today."

"But he no longer remembers us any longer."

"All the same, he will feel us there in the door."

"But can we forget this is Robert's and Digby's and Lucius's goodbye walk? It would be heartless of both of us to neglect them."

"Then how heartless Fitzgeorge is!" smiled Henrietta.

"Fitzgeorge is himself, the eldest and in the Army. Fitzgeorge I'm afraid is not an excuse for us."

A resigned sigh, or perhaps the pretense of one, heaved up Henrietta's still narrow bosom. To delay matters for just a moment more she shaded her eyes with one hand, to search the distance like a sailor looking for a sail. She gazed with hope and zeal in every direction but that in which she and Sarah were bound to go. Then—"Oh, but Sarah, here *they* are, coming—they are!" she cried. She brought out her handkerchief and began to fly it, drawing it to and fro through the windless air.

In the glass of the distance, two horsemen came into view, cantering on a grass track between the fields. When the track dropped into a hollow they dropped with it, but by now the drumming of hoofs was heard. The reverberation filled the land, the silence and Sarah's being; not watching for the riders to reappear she instead fixed her eyes on her sister's handkerchief which, let hang limp while its owner intently waited, showed a bitten corner as well as a damson stain. Again it became a flag, in furious motion.—"Wave too, Sarah, wave too! Make your bracelet flash!"

"They must have seen us if they will ever see us," said Sarah, standing still as a stone.

Henrietta's waving at once ceased. Facing her sister she crunched up her handkerchief, as though to stop it acting a lie. "I can see you are shy," she said in a dead voice. "So shy you won't even wave to *Fitzgeorge?*"

Her way of not speaking the *other* name had a hundred meanings; she drove them all in by the way she did not look at Sarah's face. The impulsive breath she had caught stole silently out again, while her eyes—till now at their brightest, their most speaking—dulled with uncomprehending solitary alarm. The ordeal of awaiting Eugene's approach thus became for Sarah, from moment to moment, torture.

Fitzgeorge, Papa's heir, and his friend Eugene, the young neighboring squire, struck off the track and rode up at a trot with their hats doffed. Sun striking low turned Fitzgeorge's flesh to coral and made Eugene blink his dark eyes. The young men reined in; the girls looked up at the horses. "And my father, Constance, the others?" Fitzgeorge demanded, as though the stubble had swallowed them.

"Ahead, on the way to the quarry, the other side of the hill."

"We heard you were all walking together," Fitzgeorge said, seeming dissatisfied.

"We are following."

"What, alone?" said Eugene, speaking for the first time.

"Forlorn!" glittered Henrietta, raising two mocking hands.

Fitzgeorge considered, said "Good" severely, and signified to Eugene that they would ride on. But too late: Eugene had dismounted. Fitzgeorge saw, shrugged and flicked his horse to a trot; but Eugene led his slowly between the sisters. Or rather, Sarah walked on his left hand, the horse on his right and Henrietta the other side of the horse. Henrietta, acting like somebody quite alone, looked up at the sky, idly holding one of the empty stirrups. Sarah, however, looked at the ground, with Eugene inclined as though to speak but not speaking. Enfolded, dizzied, blinded as though inside a wave, she could feel his features carved in brightness above her. Alongside the slender stepping of his horse, Eugene matched his naturally long free step to hers. His elbow was through the reins; with his fingers he brushed back the lock that his bending to her had sent falling over his forehead. She recorded the sublime act and knew what smile shaped his lips. So each without looking trembled before an image, while slow color burned up the curves of her cheeks. The consummation would be when their eyes met.

At the other side of the horse, Henrietta began to sing. At once her pain, like a scientific ray, passed through the horse and Eugene to penetrate Sarah's heart.

We surmount the skyline: the family come into our view, we

into theirs. They are halted, waiting, on the decline to the quarry. The handsome statufied group in strong yellow sunshine, aligned by Papa and crowned by Fitzgeorge, turn their judging eyes on the laggards, waiting to close their ranks round Henrietta and Sarah and Eugene. One more moment and it will be too late; no further communication will be possible. Stop oh stop Henrietta's heartbreaking singing! Embrace her close again! Speak the only possible word! Say—oh, say what? Oh, the word is lost!

"Henrietta . . ."

A shock of striking pain in the knuckles of the outflung hand—Sarah's? The eyes, opening, saw that the hand had struck, not been struck: there was a corner of a table. Dust, whitish and gritty, lay on the top of the table and on the telephone. Dull but piercing white light filled the room and what was left of the ceiling; her first thought was that it must have snowed. If so, it was winter now.

Through the calico stretched and tacked over the window came the sound of a piano: someone was playing Tchaikowsky badly in a room without windows or doors. From somewhere else in the hollowness came a cascade of hammering. Close up, a voice: "Oh, *awake,* Mary?" It came from the other side of the open door, which jutted out between herself and the speaker—he on the threshold, she lying on the uncovered mattress of a bed. The speaker added: "I had been going away."

Summoning words from somewhere she said: "Why? I didn't know you were here."

"Evidently—Say, who is 'Henrietta'?"

Despairing tears filled her eyes. She drew back her hurt hand, began to suck at the knuckle and whimpered, "I've hurt myself."

A man she knew to be "Travis," but failed to focus, came round the door saying: "Really I don't wonder." Sitting down on the edge of the mattress he drew her hand away from her lips and held it: the act, in itself gentle, was accompanied by an almost hostile stare of concern. "Do listen, Mary," he said. "While you've slept I've been all over the house again, and I'm less than ever satisfied that it's safe. In your normal senses you'd never attempt to stay here. There've been alerts, and more than alerts, all day; one more bang anywhere near, which may happen at any moment, could bring the rest of this down. You keep telling me that you have things to see to—but do you know what chaos the rooms are in? Till they've gone ahead with more clearing, where can you hope to start? And if there *were* anything you could do, you couldn't do it. Your own nerves know that, if you don't: it was almost frightening, when I looked in just now, to see the way you were sleeping—you've shut up shop.''

She lay staring over his shoulder at the calico window. He went on: "You don't like it here. Your self doesn't like it. Your will keeps driving your self, but it can't be driven the whole way—it makes its own get-out: sleep. Well, I want you to sleep as much as you (really) do. But *not* here. So I've taken a room for you in a hotel; I'm going now for a taxi; you can practically make the move without waking up.''

"No, I can't get into a taxi without waking.''

"Do you realise you're the last soul left in the terrace?''

"Then who is that playing the piano?''

"Oh, one of the furniture-movers in Number Six. I didn't count the jaquerie; of course *they're* in possession—unsupervised, teeming, having a high old time. While I looked in on you in here ten minutes ago they were smashing out that conservatory at the other end. Glass being done in in cold blood—it was brutalizing. You never batted an eyelid; in fact, I thought you smiled.'' He listened. "Yes, the piano—they are highbrow all right. You know there's a workman downstairs lying on your blue sofa looking for pictures in one of your French books?''

"No,'' she said, "I've no idea who is there.''

"Obviously. With the lock blown off your front door anyone who likes can get in and out.''

"Including you.''

"Yes. I've had a word with a chap about getting that lock back before tonight. As for you, you don't know what is happening.''

"I did,'' she said, locking her fingers before her eyes.

The unreality of this room and of Travis's presence preyed on her as figments of dreams that one knows to be dreams can do.

This environment's being in semi-ruin struck her less than its being some sort of device or trap; and she rejoiced, if anything, in its decrepitude. As for Travis, he had his own part in the conspiracy to keep her from the beloved two. She felt he began to feel he was now unmeaning. She was struggling not to contemn him, scorn him for his ignorance of Henrietta, Eugene, her loss. His possessive angry fondness was part, of course, of the story of him and Mary, which like a book once read she remembered clearly but with indifference. Frantic at being delayed here, while the moment awaited her in the cornfield, she all but afforded a smile at the grotesquerie of being saddled with Mary's body and lover. Rearing up her head from the bare pillow, she looked, as far as the crossed feet, along the form inside which she found herself trapped: the irrelevant body of Mary, weighted down to the bed, wore a short black modern dress, flaked with plaster. The toes of the black suède shoes by their sickly whiteness showed Mary must have climbed over fallen ceilings; dirt engraved the fate-lines in Mary's palms.

This inspired her to say: "But I've made a start; I've been pulling out things of value or things I want."

For answer Travis turned to look down, expressively, at some object out of her sight, on the floor close by the bed. *"I* see," he said, "a musty old leather box gaping open with God knows what—junk, illegible letters, diaries, yellow photographs, chiefly plaster and dust. Of all things, Mary!—after a missing will?"

"Everything one unburies seems the same age."

"Then what are these, where do they come from—family stuff?"

"No idea," she yawned into Mary's hand. "They may not even be mine. Having a house like this that had empty rooms must have made me store more than I knew, for years. I came on these, so I wondered. Look if you like."

He bent and began to go through the box—it seemed to her, not unsuspiciously. While he blew grit off packets and fumbled with tapes she lay staring at the exposed laths of the ceiling, calculating. She then said: "Sorry if I've been cranky, about the hotel and all. Go away just for two hours, then come back with a taxi, and I'll go quiet. Will that do?''

"Fine—except why not now?"

"Travis . . ."

"Sorry. It shall be as you say . . . You've got some good morbid stuff in this box, Mary—so far as I can see at a glance. The photographs seem more your sort of thing. Comic but lyrical. All of one set of people—a beard, a gun and a pot hat, a schoolboy with a moustache, a phaeton drawn up in front of mansion, a group on steps, a *carte de visite* of two young ladies hand-in-hand in front of a painted field—"

"Give that to me!"

She instinctively tried and failed, to unbutton the bosom of Mary's dress: it offered no hospitality to the photograph. So she could only fling herself over on the mattress, away from Travis, covering the two faces with her body. Racked by that oblique look of Henrietta's she recorded, too, a sort of personal shock at having seen Sarah for the first time.

Travis's hand came over her, and she shuddered. Wounded, he said: "Mary . . ."

"Can't you leave *me* alone?"

She did not move or look till he had gone out saying: "Then, in two hours." She did not therefore see him pick up the dangerous box, which he took away under his arm, out of her reach.

They were back. Now the sun was setting behind the trees, but its rays passed dazzling between the branches into the beautiful warm red room. The tips of the ferns in the jardinière curled gold, and Sarah, standing by the jardinière, pinched at a leaf of scented geranium. The carpet had a great center wreath of pomegranates, on which no tables or chairs stood, and its whole circle was between herself and the others.

No fire was lit yet, but where they were grouped was a hearth. Henrietta sat on a low stool, resting her elbow above her head on the arm of Mamma's chair, looking away intently as though into a fire, idle. Mamma embroidered, her needle slowed down by her thoughts; the length of tatting with roses she had already done overflowed stiffly over her supple skirts. Stretched on the rug at Mamma's feet, Arthur looked through an album of Swiss views, not liking them but vowed to be very quiet. Sarah, from where she stood, saw fuming cataracts and null eternal snows as poor Arthur kept turning over the pages, which had tissue paper between.

Against the white marble mantelpiece stood Eugene. The dark red shadows gathering in the drawing-room as the trees drowned more and more of the sun would reach him last, perhaps never: it seemed to Sarah that a lamp was lighted behind his face. He was the only gentleman with the ladies: Fitzgeorge had gone to the stables, Papa to give an order; Cousin Theodore was consulting a dictionary; in the gunroom Robert, Lucius and Digby went through the sad rites, putting away their guns. All this was known to go on but none of it could be heard.

This particular hour of subtle light—not to be fixed by the clock, for it was early in winter and late in summer and in spring and autumn now, about Arthur's bed-time—had always, for Sarah, been Henrietta's. To be with her indoors or out, upstairs or down, was to share the same crepitation. Her spirit ran on past yours with a laughing shiver into an element of its own. Leaves and branches and mirrors in empty rooms became animate. The sisters rustled and scampered and concealed themselves where nobody else was in play that was full of fear, fear that was full of play. Till, by dint of making each other's hearts beat violently, Henrietta so wholly and Sarah so nearly lost all human reason that Mamma had been known to look at them searchingly as she sat instated for evening among the calm amber lamps.

But now Henrietta had locked the hour inside her breast. By spending it seated beside Mamma, in young imitation of Constance the Society daughter, she disclaimed for ever anything else. It had always been she who with one fierce act destroyed any toy that might be outgrown. She sat with straight back, poising her cheek remotely against her finger. Only by never looking at Sarah did she admit their eternal loss.

Eugene, not long returned from a foreign tour, spoke of travel, addressing himself to Mamma, who thought but did not speak of her wedding journey. But every now and then she had to ask Henrietta to pass the scissors or tray of carded wools, and Eugene seized every such moment to look at Sarah. Into eyes always brilliant with melancholy he dared begin to allow no other expression. But this in itself declared the conspiracy of still undeclared love. For her part she looked at him as though he, transfigured by the strange light, were indeed a picture, a picture who could not see her. The wallpaper now flamed scarlet behind his shoulder. Mamma, Henrietta, even unknowing Arthur were in no hurry to raise their heads.

Henrietta said: "If I were a man I should take my bride to Italy."

"There are mules in Switzerland," said Arthur.

"Sarah," said Mamma, who turned in her chair mildly, "where are you, my love; do you never mean to sit down?"

"To Naples," said Henrietta.

"Are you not thinking of Venice?" said Eugene.

"No," returned Henrietta, "why should I be? I should like to climb the volcano. But then I am not a man, and am still less likely ever to be a bride."

"Arthur . . ." Mamma said.

"Mamma?"

"Look at the clock."

Arthur sighed politely, got up and replaced the album on the circular table, balanced upon the rest. He offered his hand to Eugene, his cheek to Henrietta and to Mamma; then he started towards Sarah, who came to meet him. "Tell me, Arthur," she said, embracing him, "what did you do today?"

Arthur only stared with his button blue eyes. "You were there too; we went for a walk in the cornfield, with Fitzgeorge on his horse, and I fell down." He pulled out of her arms and said: "I must go back to my beetle." He had difficulty, as always, in turning the handle of the mahogany door. Mamma waited till he had left the room, then said: "Arthur is quite a man now; he no longer comes running to me when he has hurt himself. Why, I did not even know he had fallen down. Before we know, he will be going away to school too." She sighed and lifted her eyes to Eugene. "Tomorrow is to be a sad day."

Eugene with a gesture signified his own sorrow. The sentiments of Mamma could have been uttered only here in the drawing-room, which for all its size and formality was lyrical and almost exotic. There was a look like velvet in darker parts of the air; somber window draperies let out gushes of lace; the music on the piano-forte bore tender titles, and the harp though unplayed gleamed in a corner, beyond sofas, whatnots, armchairs, occasional tables that all stood on tottering little feet. At any moment a tinkle might have been struck from the lusters' drops of the brighter day, a vibration from the musical instruments, or a quiver from the fringes and ferns. But the towering vases upon the consoles, the albums piled on the tables, the shells and figurines on the flights of brackets, all had, like the alabaster Leaning Tower of Pisa, an equilibrium of their own. Nothing would fall or change. And everything in the drawing-room was muted, weighted, pivoted by Mamma. When she added: "We shall not feel quite the same," it was to be understood that she would not have spoken thus from her place at the opposite end of Papa's table.

"Sarah," said Henrietta curiously, "what made you ask Arthur what he had been doing? Surely you have not forgotten today?"

The sisters were seldom known to address or question one another in public; it was taken that they knew each other's minds. Mamma, though untroubled, looked from one to the other. Henrietta continued: "No day, least of all today, is like any other—Surely that must be true?" she said to Eugene. "You will never forget my waving my handkerchief?"

Before Eugene had composed an answer, she turned to Sarah: "Or *you*, them riding across the fields?"

Eugene also slowly turned his eyes on Sarah, as though awaiting with something like dread her answer to the question he had not asked. She drew a light little gold chair into the middle of the wreath of the carpet, where no one ever sat, and sat down. She said: "But since then I think I have been asleep."

"Charles the First walked and talked half an hour after his head was cut off," said Henrietta mockingly. Sarah in anguish pressed the palms of her hands together upon a shred of geranium leaf.

"How else," she said, "could I have had such a bad dream?"

"That must be the explanation!" said Henrietta.

"A trifle fanciful," said Mamma.

However rash it might be to speak at all, Sarah wished she knew how to speak more clearly. The obscurity and loneliness of her trouble was not to be borne. How could she put into words the feeling of dislocation, the formless dread that had been with her since she found herself in the drawing-room? The source of both had been what she must call her dream. How could she tell the others with what vehemence she tried to attach her being to each second, not because each was singular in itself, each a drop condensed from the mist of love in the room, but because she apprehended that the seconds were numbered? Her hope was that the others at least half knew. Were Henrietta and Eugene able to understand how completely, how nearly for ever, she had been swept from them, would they not without fail each grasp one of her hands?—She went so far as to throw her hands out, as though alarmed by a wasp. The shred of geranium fell to the carpet.

Mamma, tracing this behavior of Sarah's to only one cause, could not but think reproachfully of Eugene. Delightful as his conversation had been, he would have done better had he paid this call with the object of interviewing Papa. Turning to Henrietta she asked her to ring for the lamps, as the sun had set.

Eugene, no longer where he had stood, was able to make no gesture towards the bell-rope. His dark head was under the tide of dusk; for, down on one knee on the edge of the wreath, he was feeling over the carpet for what had fallen from Sarah's hand. In the inevitable silence rooks on the return from the fields could be heard streaming over the house; their sound filled the sky and even the room, and it appeared so useless to ring the bell that Henrietta stayed quivering by Mamma's chair. Eugene rose, brought out his fine white handkerchief and, while they watched, enfolded carefully in it what he had just found, then returning the handkerchief to his breast pocket. This was done so deep in the reverie that accompanies any final act that Mamma instinctively murmured to Henrietta: "But you will be my child when Arthur has gone."

The door opened for Constance to appear on the threshold. Behind her queenly figure globes approached, swimming in their own light: these were the lamps for which Henrietta had not rung, but these first were put on the hall tables. "Why, Mamma," exclaimed Constance, "I cannot see who is with you!"

"Eugene is with us," said Henrietta, "but on the point of asking if he may send for his horse."

"Indeed?" said Constance to Eugene. "Fitzgeorge has been asking for you, but I cannot tell where he is now."

The figures of Emily, Lucius and Cousin Theodore criss-crossed the lamplight there in the hall, to mass behind Constance's in the drawing-room door. Emily, over her sister's shoulder, said: "Mamma, Lucius wishes to ask you whether for once he may take his guitar to school."—"One objection, however," said Cousin Theodore, "is that Lucius's trunk is already locked and strapped." "Since Robert is taking his box of inks," said Lucius, "I do not see why I should not take my guitar."—"But Robert," said Constance, "will soon be going to college."

Lucius squeezed past the others into the drawing-room in order to look anxiously at Mamma, who said: "You have thought of this late; we must go and see." The others parted to let Mamma, followed by Lucius, out. Then Constance, Emily and Cousin Theodore deployed and sat down in different parts of the drawing-room, to await the lamps.

"I am glad the rooks have done passing over," said Emily, "they make me nervous."—"Why?" yawned Constance haughtily, "what do you think could happen?" Robert and Digby silently came in.

Eugene said to Sarah: "I shall be back tomorrow."

"But, oh—" she began. She turned to cry: "Henrietta!"

"Why, what is the matter?" said Henrietta, unseen at the back of the gold chair. "What could be sooner than tomorrow?"

"But something terrible may be going to happen."

"There cannot fail to be tomorrow," said Eugene gravely.

"*I* will see that there is tomorrow," said Henrietta.

"You will never let me out of your sight?"

Eugene, addressing himself to Henrietta, said: "Yes, promise her what she asks."

Henrietta cried: "She *is* never out of my sight. Who are you to ask me that, you Eugene? Whatever tries to come between me and Sarah becomes nothing. Yes, come tomorrow, come sooner, come—when you like, but no one will ever be quite alone with Sarah. You do not even know what you are trying to do. It is *you* who are making something terrible happen.—Sarah, tell him that this is true! Sarah—"

The others, in the dark on the chairs and sofas, could be felt to turn their judging eyes upon Sarah, who, as once before, could not speak—

—The house rocked: simultaneously the calico window split and more ceiling fell, though not on the bed. The enormous dull sound of the explosion died, leaving a minor trickle of dissolution still to be heard in parts of the house. Until the choking stinging plaster dust had had time to settle, she lay with lips pressed close, nostrils not breathing and eyes shut. Remembering the box, Mary wondered if it had been again buried. No, she found, looking over the edge of the bed: that had been unable to happen because the box was missing. Travis, who must have taken it, would when he came back no doubt explain why. She looked at her watch, which had stopped, which was not surprising; she did not remember winding it for the last two days, but then she could not remember much. Through the torn window appeared the timelessness of an impermeably clouded late summer afternoon.

There being nothing left, she wished he would come to take her to the hotel. The one way back to the fields was barred by Mary's surviving the fall of ceiling. Sarah was right in doubting that there would be tomorrow: Eugene, Henrietta were lost in time to the woman weeping there on the bed, no longer reckoning who she was.

At last she heard the taxi, then Travis hurrying up the littered stairs. "Mary, you're all right, Mary—*another?*" Such a helpless white face came round the door that she could only hold out her arms and say: "Yes, but where have *you* been?"

"You said two hours. But I wish—"

"I have missed you."

"Have you? Do you know you are crying?"

"Yes. How are we to live without natures? We only know inconvenience now, not sorrow. Everything pulverizes so easily because it is rot-dry; one can only wonder that it makes so much noise. The source, the sap must have dried up, or the pulse must have stopped, before you and I were conceived. So much flowed through people; so little flows through us. All we can do is imitate love or sorrow.—Why did you take away my box?"

He only said: "It is in my office."

She continued: "What has happened is cruel: I am left with a fragment torn out of a day, a day I don't even know where or when; and now how am I to help laying that like a pattern against the poor stuff of everything else?—Alternatively, I am a person drained by a dream. I cannot forget the climate of those hours. Or life at that pitch, eventful—not happy, no, but strung like a harp. I have had a sister called Henrietta."

"And I have been looking inside your box. What else can you expect?—I have had to write off this day, from the work point of view, thanks to you. So could I sit and do nothing for the last two hours? I just glanced through this and that—still, I know the family."

"You said it was morbid stuff."

"Did I? I still say it gives off something."

She said: "And then there was Eugene."

"Probably. I don't think I came on much of his except some notes he must have made for Fitzgeorge from some book on scientific farming. Well, there it is: I have sorted everything out and put it back again, all but a lock of hair that tumbled out of a letter I could not trace. So I've got the hair in my pocket."

"What color is it?"

"Ash-brown. Of course, it is a bit—desiccated. Do you want it?"

"No," she said with a shudder. "Really, Travis, what revenges you take!"

"I didn't look at it that way," he said puzzled.

"Is the taxi waiting?" Mary got off the bed and, picking her way across the room, began to look about for things she ought to take with her, now and then stopping to brush her dress. She took the mirror out of her bag to see how dirty her face was. "Travis—" she said suddenly.

"Mary?"

"Only, I—"

"That's all right. Don't let us imitate anything just at present."

In the taxi, looking out of the window, she said: "I suppose, then, that I am descended from Sarah?"

"No," he said, "that would be impossible. There must be some reason why you should have those papers, but that is not the one. From all negative evidence Sarah, like Henrietta, remained unmarried. I found no mention of either, after a certain date, in the letters of Constance, Robert or Emily, which makes it seem likely both died young. Fitzgeorge refers, in a letter to Robert written in his old age, to some friend of their youth who was thrown from his horse and killed, riding back after a visit to their home. The young man, whose name doesn't appear, was alone; and the evening, which was in autumn, was fine though late. Fitzgeorge wonders, and says he will always wonder, what made the horse shy in those empty fields."

OH FATHER, FATHER, WHY HAVE YOU COME BACK?

John Cheever

The trouble began one afternoon when Coverly Wapshot swung down off the slow train, the only south-bound train that still stopped at the village of St. Botolphs. It was in the late winter, just before dark. The snow was gone but the grass was dead and the place seemed not to have rallied from the February storms. He shook hands with Mr. Jowett and asked about his family. He waved to the bartender in the Viaduct House, waved to Berry Freeman in the feed store and called hello to Miles Howland, who was coming out of the bank. The late sky was brilliant and turbulent but it shed none of its operatic lights and fires onto the darkness of the green. This awesome performance was contained within the air. Between the buildings he could see the West River with its, for him, enormous cargo of pleasant memory and he took away from this brightness the unlikely impression that the river's long history had been a purifying force, leaving the water fit to drink. He turned right at Boat Street. Mrs. Williams was sitting in her parlor, reading the paper. The only light at the Brattles' was in the kitchen. The Dummers' house was dark. Mrs. Bretaigne, who was saying good-bye to a caller, welcomed him home. Then he turned up the walk to Cousin Honora's.

Maggie answered the door and he gave her a kiss. "They ain't nothing but dried beef," Maggie said. "You'll have to kill a chicken." He went down the long hall past the seven views of Rome into the Library, where he found his old cousin with an open book on her lap. Here was home-sweet-home, the polished brass, the applewood fire. "Coverly dear," Honora said in an impulse of love and kissed him on the lips. "Honora," Coverly said, taking her in his arms. Then they separated and scrutinized one another cannily to see what changes had been made.

Her white hair was still full, her face leonine, but her new false teeth were not well fitted and they made her look like a cannibal. This hinted savagery reminded Coverly of the fact that his cousin had never been photographed. In all the family albums she appeared either with her back to the camera as she ran away or with her face concealed by her hands, her handbag, her hat or a newspaper. Any stranger looking at the albums would have thought she was wanted for murder. Honora thought Coverly looked underfed and she said so. "You're skinny," she said.

"Yes."

"I'll have Maggie bring you some port."

"I'd rather have a whisky."

"You don't drink whisky," Honora said.

"I didn't used to," Coverly said, "but I do now."

"Will wonders never cease?" Honora asked.

"If you're going to kill a chicken," Maggie said from the doorway, "you'd better kill it now or you won't get supper much before midnight."

"I'll kill the chicken now," Coverly said.

"You'll have to speak louder," Honora said. "She can't hear."

Coverly followed Maggie back through the house to the kitchen. "She's crazier than ever," Maggie said. "Now she claims she can't sleep. She claims she ain't slept for years. Well, so I come into the parlor one afternoon with her tea and there she is. Sound asleep. Snoring. So I say, 'Wake up, Miss Wapshot. Here's your tea.' She says, 'What do you mean, wake up? I wasn't asleep,' she says. 'I was just lost in deep meditation.' And now she's thinking of buying an automobile. Dear Jesus, it would be like setting a hungry lion loose in the streets. She'll be running over and killing innocent little children if she don't kill herself first."

The relationship between the old women stood foursquare on

a brand of larcenous backbiting that appeared to contain so little in the way of truth that it could be passed off as comical. Maggie's hearing was perfect but for some years Honora had told everyone she was deaf. Honora was eccentric but Maggie told everyone in the village that she was mad. The physical and mental infirmities they invented for one another had a pristine quality that made it nearly impossible to believe there was any grimness in the contest.

Coverly found a hatchet in the back pantry and went down the wooden steps to the garden. Somewhere in the distance he could hear children's voices, distinctly accented with the catarrhal pronunciations of that part of the world. There was a gaggle of sound from the hen house beyond the hedge. He felt uncommonly happy in this sparsely populated place; felt some marked loosening of his discontents. It was the hour, he knew, when the pinochle players would be drifting across the green to the firehouse and when the yearnings of adolescence, exacerbated by the smallness of the village, would be approaching a climax. He could remember sitting himself on the back steps of the house on River Street, racked with a yearning for love, for friendship and renown, that had made him howl.

He went on through the hedge to the hen house. The laying hens had retired but four or five cockerels were feeding in their yard. He chased them into their house and after an undignified scuffle caught one by its yellow legs. The bird squawked for mercy and Coverly spoke to it soothingly, he hoped, as he lay its neck on the block and chopped off its head. He held the struggling body down and away from him to let the blood drain into the ground. Maggie brought him a bucket of scalding water and an old copy of the St. Botolphs *Enterprise* and he plucked and eviscerated the bird, losing his taste for chicken, step by step. He brought the carcass back to the kitchen and joined his old cousin in the library, where Maggie had set out whisky and water.

"Can we talk now?" Coverly asked.

"I guess so," Honora said. She put her elbows on her knees and leaned forward. "You want to talk about the house on River Street?"

"Yes."

"Well, nobody'll rent it and nobody'll buy it and it would break my heart to see it torn down."

"What is the matter?"

"The Whitehalls rented it in October. They moved in and moved right out again. Then the Haverstraws took it. They lasted a week. Mrs. Haverstraw told everybody in the stores that the house was haunted. But who," she asked, raising her face, "would there be to haunt the place? Our family has always been a very happy family. None of us have ever paid any attention to ghosts. But just the same it's all over town."

"What did Mrs. Haverstraw say?"

"Mrs. Haverstraw spread it around that it's the ghost of your father."

"Leander," Coverly said.

"But what would Leander want to come back and trouble people for?" Honora asked. "It wasn't that he didn't believe in ghosts. He just never had any use for them. I've heard him say many times that he thought ghosts kept low company. And you know how kind he was. He used to escort flies and moth millers out the door as if they were guests. What would he come back for except to eat a bowl of crackers and milk? Of course he had his faults."

"Were you with us," Coverly asked, "the time he smoked a cigarette in church?"

"You must have made that up," Honora said, fending for the past.

"No," Coverly said. "It was Christmas Eve and we went to Holy Communion. I remember that he seemed very devout. He was up and down, crossing himself and roaring out the responses. Then before the Benediction he took a cigarette out of his pocket and lighted it. I saw then that he was terribly drunk. I told him, 'You can't smoke in church, Daddy,' but we were in one of the front pews and a lot of people had seen him. What I wanted then was to be the son of Mr. Pluzinski the farmer. I don't know why, except that the Pluzinskis were all very serious. It seemed to me that if I could only be the son of Mr. Pluzinski I would be happy."

"You ought to be ashamed of yourself," Honora said. Then she sighed, changed her tone and added uneasily: "There was something else."

"What."

"You remember how he used to give away nickels on the Fourth of July."

"Oh, yes." Coverly then saw the front of their house in many colors. A large flag hung from the second floor, its crimson stripes faded to the color of old blood. His father stood on the porch, after the parade and before the ball game, passing out new nickels to a line of children that reached up River Street. The trees were all leafed out and in his reverie the light was quite green.

"Well, as you may remember he kept the nickels in a cigar box. He had painted it black. When I was going through the house I found the box. There were still some nickels in it. Many of them were not real. I believe he made them himself."

"You mean . . ."

"Shhhh," said Honora.

"Supper's ready," said Maggie.

Honora seemed tired after supper so he kissed her good night in the hallway and walked to his own home on the other side of town. The place had been empty since fall. There was a key on the windowsill and the door swung open onto a strong smell of must. This was the place where he had been conceived and born, where he had awakened to the excellence of life, and there was some keen chagrin at finding the scene of so many dazzling memories smelling of decay; but this, he knew, was the instinctual foolishness that leads us to love permanence when there is none. He turned on the lights in the hall and the parlor and got some logs from the shed. He was absorbed in laying and lighting a fire but when the fire was set he began to feel, surrounded by so many uninhabited rooms, an unreasonable burden of apprehension, as if his presence there were an intrusion.

It was his and his brother's house, by contract, inheritance and memory. Its leaks and other infirmities were his responsibility. It was he who had broken the vase on the mantelpiece and burned a hole in the sofa. He did not believe in ghosts, shades, spirits or any other forms of unquietness on the part of the dead. He was a man of twenty-eight, happily married, the father of a son. He weighed one hundred and thirty-eight pounds, enjoyed perfect health and had eaten some chicken for dinner. These were the facts. He took a copy of *Tristram Shandy* down from the shelf and began to read. There was a loud noise in the kitchen that so startled him the sweat stood out on his hands. He raised his head long enough to embrace this noise in the realm of hard fact. It could be a shutter, a loose piece of firewood, an animal or one of those legendary tramps who were a part of local demonology and who were supposed to inhabit the empty farms, leaving traces of fire, empty snuff cans, a dry cow and a frightened spinster. But he was strong and young and even if he should encounter a tramp in the dark hallway he could take care of himself. Why should he feel so intensely uncomfortable? He went to the telephone intending to ask the operator the time of night but the telephone was dead.

He went on reading. There was noise from the dining room. He said something loud and vigorous to express his impatience with his apprehensions but the effect of this was to convince him overwhelmingly that he had been heard. Someone was listening. There was a cure for this foolishness. He went directly to the empty room and turned on the light. There was nothing there and yet the beating of his heart was accelerated and painful and sweat ran off his palms. Then the dining room door slowly closed of itself. This was only natural since the old house sagged badly and while half the doors closed themselves, the other half wouldn't close at all. He went through the swinging door on into the pantry and the kitchen. Here again he saw nothing but felt again that there had been someone in the room when he turned on the light. There were two sets of facts—the empty room and the alarmed condition of his skin. He was determined to scotch this and he went out of the kitchen into the hallway and climbed the stairs.

All the bedroom doors stood open, and here, in the dark, he

seemed to yield to the denseness of the lives that had been lived here for nearly two centuries. The burden of the past was palpable; the utterances and groans of conception, childbirth and death, the singing at the family reunion in 1893, the dust raised by a Fourth of July parade, the shock of lovers meeting by chance in the hallway, the roar of flames in the fire that gutted the west wing in 1900, the politeness at christenings, the joy of a young husband bringing his wife back after their marriage, the hardships of a cruel winter all took on some palpableness in the dark air. But why was the atmosphere in this darkness distinctly one of trouble and failure? Ebenezer had made a fortune. Lorenzo had introduced child-welfare legislation into the state laws. Alice had converted hundreds of Polynesians to Christianity. Why should none of these ghosts and shades seem contented with their work? Was it because they had been mortal, was it because for every last one of them the pain of death had been bitter?

He returned to the fire. Here was the physical world, firelit, stubborn and beloved, and yet his physical response was not to the parlor but to the darkness in the rooms around him. Why, sitting so close to the fire, did he feel a chill slide down his left shoulder and a moment later coarsen with cold the skin of his chest, as if a hand had been placed there? If there were ghosts, he believed with his father that they kept low company. They consorted with the poorhearted and the faint. He knew that we sometimes leave after us, in a room, a stir of love or rancor when we are gone. He believed that whatever we pay for our loves in money, venereal disease, scandal or ecstasy, we leave behind us, in the hotels, motels, guest rooms, meadows and fields where we discharge this much of ourselves, either the scent of goodness or the odor of evil, to influence those who come after us. Thus it was possible that this passionate and eccentric cast had left behind them some ambiance that made his presence seem like an intrusion. It was time to go to bed and he got some blankets out of a closet and made up a bed in the spare room, nearest the stairs.

He woke at three. There was enough radiance from the moon

or the night sky itself to light the room. What had waked him, he knew immediately, was not a dream, a reverie or an apprehension; it was something that moved, something that he could see, something strange and unnatural. The terror began with his optic nerves and reverberated through his whole person but it was in the beam of his eye that the terror had begun. He was able to trace the disturbance back through his nervous system to his pupil. The eye counted on reality and what he had seen or thought he had seen was the ghost of his father. The chaos set into motion by this hallucination was horrendous and he shook with psychic and physical cold, he shook with terror, and sitting up in bed he roared: "Oh, Father, Father, Father, why have you come back?"

The loudness of his voice was some consolation. The ghost seemed to leave the room. He thought he could hear stair lifts give. Had he come back to look for a bowl of crackers and milk, to read some Shakespeare, come back because he felt like all the others that the pain of death was bitter? Had he come back to relive that moment when he had relinquished the supreme privileges of youth—when he had waked feeling less peckery than usual and realized that the doctor had no cure for autumn, no medicine for the north wind? The smell of his green years would still be in his nose—the reek of clover, the fragrance of women's breasts, so like the land-wind, smelling of grass and trees—but it was time for him to leave the field for someone younger. Spavined, gray, he had wanted no less than any youth to chase the nymphs. Over hill and dale. Now you see them; now you don't. The world a paradise, a paradise! Father, Father, why have you come back?

There was the noise of something falling in the next room. The knowledge that this was a squirrel, as it was, would not have brought Coverly to his senses. He was too far gone. He grabbed his clothing, flew down the stairs and left the front door standing open. He stopped on the sidewalk long enough to draw on his underpants. Then he ran to the corner. Here he put on his trousers and shirt but he ran the rest of the way to Honora's barefoot.

He scribbled a farewell note, left it on her hall table and caught the milk train north, a little after dawn, past the Markhams', past the Wilton Trace, past the Lowells', who had changed the sign on their barn from BE KIND TO ANIMALS to GOD ANSWERS PRAYERS, past the house where old Mr. Sturgis used to live and repair watches.

DEAD
WOMEN'S
THINGS

Kathy Chwedyk

Linda ran away from her only living relative when she was 17, and spent the next 10 years waiting for the old bat to die.

It's about time, she thought when Aunt Eunice's attorney phoned to give her the news. Linda brushed aside his expressions of sympathy and asked how soon she could have access to her great-aunt's bank account. Linda had gone from one minimum-wage job to another for the past decade because slaving eight hours a day for somebody else was not her style.

Now, at last, she would inherit the big Queen Anne house and her aunt's huge inventory of vintage clothes and furniture. She called her aunt's chief rival in the antique business and offered to sell him the house and its contents. She was meeting him at six o'clock to show him the stock.

Linda hoped Aunt Eunice was turning over in her grave.

As a frightened, newly orphaned five-year-old, Linda refused to leave her bed at night—no matter how badly she had to go to the bathroom—because she knew the dead women in the portraits could see her in the darkness. She would wake up screaming from nightmares in which the dead women captured her and held her prisoner between the walls. In these dreams, she could feel her own eyes grow stiff and cold. Her eyelids wouldn't close over them! She would scream and scream, but no one could hear her.

Aunt Eunice had no patience with Linda's childish fears. When there were customers in the shop, she would take pearls yellowed with age and place them around Linda's neck because she knew how much Linda hated to have the dead women's things touch her skin. Linda was forced to smile at the customer and try not to throw up.

Linda had imagined the gloves plumped out with dead fingers, and the monogrammed silver hairbrushes being wielded by ghostly hands. She had shuddered when Eunice placed dark velvet pillboxes on her head and pulled the wispy veils over her eyes. The soft, limp net had reminded Linda of cobwebs, and she couldn't stop shuddering until she had shampooed her hair and scrubbed her face.

But all that had been when she was an impressionable kid, Linda thought as she opened the door with the keys the attorney had given her that morning. After today, she promised herself, she would never come here again.

Once she sold the dump, she would buy a condo somewhere warm, like Florida, and fill it with shiny chrome and Plexiglas furniture. She would find a husband there, and never have to work again. Linda was pushing 30, but she still looked good. The bills might not get paid, but Linda—a born-again-blonde—always managed to come up with the money to get her roots done.

Linda felt a chill up her back as she walked into the little sitting room off the foyer. It looked exactly the same as it did all those years ago. The place still gave her the creeps.

She paced the room impatiently, uncomfortably aware that it was growing dark outside. She felt the dead women's eyes on her.

She tried to call the antique dealer's shop to reschedule the appointment so she could get out of the house and into the welcome, anonymous safety of the run-down motel at the edge of town, but the phone didn't work. Apparently the service had been shut off.

Linda jumped when she heard a shuffling sound coming from between the walls, then gave a nervous laugh. Just mice, she told herself. God, I can't wait to get out of this rodent-infested dump!

* * *

The antique dealer knocked on the door several times, then let himself in. The door had been left open.

He stopped in the sitting room before a portrait of an attractive young woman in contemporary dress and wondered at her identity. Perhaps she was a relative of Eunice's. She had her chin.

He waited for half an hour, but Eunice's niece never showed up. Reflecting upon the beastly manners of the younger generation, he finally left.

From her prison on the wall, Linda watched him go. And screamed and screamed and screamed.

THE
UPPER
BERTH

F. Marion Crawford

CHAPTER I

Somebody asked for the cigars. We had talked long, and the conversation was beginning to languish; the tobacco smoke had got into the heavy curtains, the wine had got into those brains which were liable to become heavy, and it was already perfectly evident that, unless somebody did something to rouse our oppressed spirits, the meeting would soon come to its natural conclusion, and we, the guests, would speedily go home to bed, and most certainly to sleep. No one had said anything very remarkable; it may be that no one had anything very remarkable to say. Jones had given us every particular of his last hunting adventure in Yorkshire. Mr. Tompkins of Boston, had explained at elaborate length those working principles, by the due and careful maintenance of which the Atchison, Topeka, and Santa Fé Railroad not only extended its territory, increased its departmental influence, and transported live stock without starving them to death before the day of actual delivery, but, also, had for years succeeded in deceiving those passengers who bought its tickets into the fallacious belief that the corporation aforesaid was really able to transport human life without destroying it. Signor Tombola had endeavored to persuade us, by arguments which we took no trouble to oppose, that the unity of his country in no way resembled the average modern torpedo, carefully planned, constructed with all the skill of the greatest European arsenals, but, when constructed, destined to be directed by feeble hands into a region where it must undoubtedly explode, unseen, unfeared, and unheard, into the illimitable wastes of political chaos.

It is unnecessary to go into further details. The conversation had assumed proportions which would have bored Prometheus on his rock, which would have driven Tantalus to distraction, and which would have impelled Ixion to seek relaxation in the simple but instructive dialogues of Herr Ollendorff, rather than submit to the greater evil of listening to our talk. We had sat at table for hours; we were bored, we were tired, and nobody showed signs of moving.

Somebody called for cigars. We all instinctively looked towards the speaker. Brisbane was a man of five-and-thirty years of age, and remarkable for those gifts which chiefly attract the attention of men. He was a strong man. The external proportions of his figure presented nothing extraordinary to the common eye, though his size was about the average. He was a little over six feet in height, and moderately broad in the shoulder; he did not appear to be stout, but, on the other hand, he was certainly not thin; his small head was supported by a strong and sinewy neck; his broad, muscular hands appeared to possess a peculiar skill in breaking walnuts without the assistance of the ordinary cracker, and seeing him in profile, one could not help remarking the extraordinary breadth of his sleeves, and the unusual thickness of his chest. He was one of those men who are commonly spoken of among men as deceptive; that is to say, that though he looked exceedingly strong, he was in reality very much stronger than he looked. Of his features I need say little. His head is small, his hair is thin, his eyes are blue, his nose is large, he has a small moustache and a square jaw. Everybody knows Brisbane, and when he asked for a cigar everybody looked at him.

"It is a very singular thing," said Brisbane.

Everybody stopped talking. Brisbane's voice was not loud, but possessed a peculiar quality of penetrating general conversation, and cutting it like a knife. Everybody listened. Brisbane, perceiving that he had attracted their general attention, lit his cigar with great equanimity.

"It is very singular," he continued, "that thing about ghosts. People are always asking whether anybody has seen a ghost. I have."

"Bosh! What, you? You don't mean to say so, Brisbane? Well, for a man of his intelligence!"

A chorus of exclamations greeted Brisbane's remarkable statement. Everybody called for cigars, and Stubbs, the butler, suddenly appeared from the depths of nowhere with a fresh bottle of dry champagne. The situation was saved; Brisbane was going to tell a story.

I am an old sailor, said Brisbane, and as I have to cross the Atlantic pretty often, I have my favorites. Most men have their favorites. I have seen a man wait in a Broadway bar for three-quarters of an hour for a particular car which he liked. I believe the bar-keeper made at least one-third of his living by that man's preference. I have a habit of waiting for certain ships when I am obliged to cross that duck-pond. It may be a prejudice, but I was never cheated out of a good passage but once in my life. I remember it very well; it was a warm morning in June, and the Custom House officials, who were hanging about waiting for a steamer already on her way up from the Quarantine, presented a peculiarly hazy and thoughtful appearance. I had not much luggage—I never have. I mingled with a crowd of passengers, porters, and officious individuals in blue coats and brass buttons, who seemed to spring up like mushrooms from the deck of a moored steamer to obtrude their unnecessary services upon the independent passenger. I have often noticed with a certain interest the spontaneous evolution of these fellows. They are not there when you arrive; five minutes after the pilot has called "Go ahead!" they, or at least their blue coats and brass buttons, have disappeared from deck and gangway as completely as though they had been consigned to that locker which tradition unanimously ascribes to Davy Jones. But, at the moment of starting, they are there, clean shaved, blue coated, and ravenous for fees. I hastened on board. The *Kamtschatka* was one of my favorite ships. I say was, because she emphatically no longer is. I cannot conceive of any inducement which could entice me to make another voyage in her. Yes, I know what you are going to say. She is uncommonly clean in the run aft, she has enough bluffing off in the bows to keep her dry, and the lower berths are most of them double. She has a lot of advantages, but I won't cross in her again. Excuse the digression. I got on board. I hailed a steward, whose red nose and redder whiskers were equally familiar to me.

"One hundred and five, lower berth," said I, in the businesslike tone peculiar to men who think no more of crossing the Atlantic than taking a whiskey cocktail at down-town Delmonico's.

The steward took my portmanteau, greatcoat, and rug. I shall never forget the expression of his face. Not that he turned pale. It is maintained by the most eminent divines that even miracles cannot change the course of nature. I have no hesitation in saying that he did not turn pale; but, from his expression, I judged that he was either about to shed tears, to sneeze, or to drop my portmanteau. As the latter contained two bottles of particularly fine old sherry presented to me for my voyage by my old friend Snigginson van Pickyns, I felt extremely nervous. But the steward did none of these things.

"Well, I'm d—d!" said he in a low voice, and led the way.

I supposed my Hermes, as he led me to the lower regions, had had a little grog, but I said nothing and followed him. 105 was on the port side, well aft. There was nothing remarkable about the state-room. The lower berth, like most of those upon the *Kamtschatka,* was double. There was plenty of room; there was the usual washing apparatus, calculated to convey an idea of luxury to the mind of a North American Indian; there were the usual inefficient racks of brown wood, in which it is more easy to hang a large-sized umbrella than the common tooth-brush of commerce. Upon the uninviting mattresses were carefully folded together those blankets which a great modern humorist has aptly compared to cold buckwheat cakes. The question of towels was left entirely to the imagination. The glass decanters were filled with a transparent liquid faintly tinged with brown, but from which an odor less faint, but not more pleasing, ascended to the nostrils, like a far-off seasick reminiscence of oily machinery. Sad-colored curtains half closed the upper berth. The hazy June daylight shed a faint illumination upon the desolate little scene. Ugh! how I hate that state-room!

The steward deposited my traps and looked at me as though he wanted to get away—probably in search of more passengers and more fees. It is always a good plan to start in favor with those functionaries, and I accordingly gave him certain coins there and then.

"I'll try and make yer comfortable all I can," he remarked, as he put the coins in his pocket. Nevertheless, there was a doubtful intonation in his voice which surprised me. Possibly his scale of fees had gone up, and he was not satisfied; but on the whole I was inclined to think that, as he himself would have expressed it, he was "the better for a glass." I was wrong, however, and did the man injustice.

CHAPTER II

Nothing especially worthy of mention occurred during that day. We left the pier punctually, and it was very pleasant to be fairly under way, for the weather was warm and sultry, and the motion of the steamer produced a refreshing breeze. Everybody knows what the first day at sea is like. People pace the decks and stare at each other, and occasionally meet acquaintances whom they did not know to be on board. There is the usual uncertainty as to whether the food will be good, bad, or indifferent, until the first two meals have put the matter beyond a doubt; there is the usual uncertainty about the weather, until the ship is fairly off Fire Island. The tables are crowded at first, and then suddenly thinned. Pale-faced people spring from their seats and precipitate themselves towards the door, and each old sailor breathes more freely as his seasick neighbor rushes from his side, leaving him plenty of elbow-room and an unlimited command over the mustard.

One passage across the Atlantic is very much like another, and we who cross very often do not make the voyage for the sake of novelty. Whales and icebergs are indeed always objects of interest, but, after all, one whale is very much like another whale, and one rarely sees an iceberg at close quarters. To the majority of us the most delightful moment of the day on board an ocean steamer is when we have taken our last turn on deck, have smoked our last cigar, and having succeeded in tiring ourselves, feel at liberty to turn in with a clear conscience. On that first night of the voyage I felt particularly lazy, and went to bed in 105 rather earlier than I usually do. As I turned in, I was amazed to see that I was to have a companion. A portmanteau, very like my own, lay in the opposite corner, and in the upper berth had been deposited a neatly folded rug, with a stick and umbrella. I had hoped to be alone, and I was disappointed; but I wondered who my room-mate was to be, and I determined to have a look at him.

Before I had been long in bed he entered. He was, as far as I could see, a very tall man, very thin, very pale, with sandy hair and whiskers and colorless grey eyes. He had about him, I thought, an air of rather dubious fashion; the sort of man you might see in Wall Street, without being able precisely to say what he was doing there—the sort of man who frequents the Café Anglais, who always seems to be alone and who drinks champagne; you might meet him on a racecourse, but he would never appear to be doing anything there either. A little over-dressed—a little odd. There are three or four of his kind on every ocean steamer. I made up my mind that I did not care to make his acquaintance, and I went to sleep saying to myself that I would study his habits in order to avoid him. If he rose early, I would rise late; if he went to bed late I would go to bed early. I did not care to know him. If you once know people of that kind, they are always turning up. Poor fellow! I need not have taken the trouble to come to so many decisions about him, for I never saw him again after that first night in 105.

I was sleeping soundly when I was suddenly waked by a loud noise. To judge from the sound, my room-mate must have sprung with a single leap from the upper berth to the floor. I heard him fumbling with the latch and bolt of the door, which opened almost immediately, and then I heard his footsteps as he ran at full speed down the passage, leaving the door open behind him. The ship was rolling a little, and I expected to hear him stumble or fall, but he ran as though he were running for his life. The door swung on its hinges with the motion of the vessel, and the sound annoyed me. I got up and shut it, and groped my way back to my berth in the darkness. I went to sleep again; but I have no idea how long I slept.

When I awoke it was still quite dark, but I felt a disagreeable sensation of cold, and it seemed to me that the air was damp. You know the peculiar smell of a cabin which has been wet with sea-water. I covered myself up as well as I could and dozed off again, framing complaints to be made the next day, and selecting the most powerful epithets in the language. I could hear my room-mate turn over in the upper berth. He had probably returned while I was asleep. Once I thought I heard him groan, and I argued that he was sea-sick. That is particularly unpleasant when one is below. Nevertheless I dozed off and slept till early daylight.

The ship was rolling heavily, much more than on the previous evening, and the grey light which came in through the porthole changed in tint with every movement according as the angle of the vessel's side turned the glass seawards or skywards. It was very cold—unaccountably so for the month of June. I turned my head and looked at the porthole, and saw to my surprise that it was wide open and hooked back. I believe I swore audibly. Then I got up and shut it. As I turned back I glanced at the upper berth. The curtains were drawn close together; my companion had probably felt cold as well as I. It struck me that I had slept enough. The state-room was uncomfortable, though, strange to say, I could not smell the dampness which had annoyed me in the night. My room-mate was still asleep—excellent opportunity for avoiding him, so I dressed at once and went on deck. The day was warm and cloudy, with an oily smell on the water. It was seven o'clock as I came out—much later than I had imagined. I came across the doctor, who was taking his first sniff of the morning air. He was a young man from the West of Ireland—a tremendous fellow, with black hair and blue eyes, already inclined to be stout; he had a happy-go-lucky, healthy look about him which was rather attractive.

"Fine morning," I remarked, by way of introduction.

"Well," said he, eyeing me with an air of ready interest, "it's a fine morning and it's not a fine morning. I don't think it's much of a morning."

"Well, no—it is not so very fine," said I.

"It's just what I call fuggly weather," replied the doctor.

"It was very cold last night, I thought," I remarked. "However, when I looked about, I found that the porthole was wide open. I had not noticed it when I went to bed. And the state-room was damp, too."

"Damp!" said he. "Whereabouts are you?"

"One hundred and five—"

To my surprise the doctor started visibly, and stared at me.

"What is the matter?" I asked.

"Oh—nothing," he answered; "only everybody has complained of that state-room for the last three trips."

"I shall complain, too," I said. "It has certainly not been properly aired. It is a shame!"

"I don't believe it can be helped," answered the doctor. "I believe there is something—well, it is not my business to frighten passengers."

"You need not be afraid of frightening me," I replied. "I can stand any amount of damp. If I should get a bad cold, I will come to you."

I offered the doctor a cigar, which he took and examined very critically.

"It is not so much the damp," he remarked. "However, I dare say you will get on very well. Have you a room-mate?"

"Yes; a deuce of a fellow, who bolts out in the middle of the night, and leaves the door open."

Again the doctor glanced curiously at me. Then he lit the cigar and looked grave.

"Did he come back?" he asked presently.

"Yes. I was asleep, but I waked up, and heard him moving.

Then I felt cold and went to sleep again. This morning I found the porthole open."

"Look here," said the doctor quietly, "I don't care much for this ship. I don't care a rap for her reputation. I tell you what I will do. I have a good-sized place up here. I will share it with you, though I don't know you from Adam."

I was very much surprised at the proposition. I could not imagine why he should take such a sudden interest in my welfare. However, his manner, as he spoke of the ship, was peculiar.

"You are very good, doctor," I said. "But, really, I believe even now the cabin could be aired, or cleaned out, or something. Why do you not care for the ship?"

"We are not superstitious in our profession, sir," replied the doctor, "but the sea makes people so. I don't want to prejudice you, and I don't want to frighten you, but if you will take my advice you will move in here. I would as soon see you overboard," he added earnestly, "as know that you or any other man was to sleep in 105."

"Good gracious! Why?" I asked.

"Just because on the three last trips the people who have slept there actually have gone overboard," he answered gravely.

The intelligence was startling and exceedingly unpleasant, I confess. I looked hard at the doctor to see whether he was making game of me, but he looked perfectly serious. I thanked him warmly for his offer, but told him I intended to be the exception to the rule by which every one who slept in that particular state-room went overboard. He did not say much, but looked as grave as ever, and hinted that, before we got across, I should probably reconsider his proposal. In the course of time we went to breakfast, at which only an inconsiderable number of passengers assembled. I noticed that one or two of the officers who breakfasted with us looked grave. After breakfast I went into my state-room in order to get a book. The curtains of the upper berth were still closely drawn. Not a sound was to be heard. My room-mate was probably still asleep.

As I came out I met the steward whose business it was to look after me. He whispered that the captain wanted to see me, and then scuttled away down the passage as if very anxious to avoid any questions. I went toward the captain's cabin, and found him waiting for me.

"Sir," said he, "I want to ask a favor of you."

I answered that I would do anything to oblige him.

"Your room-mate has disappeared," he said. "He is known to have turned in early last night. Did you notice anything extraordinary in his manner?"

The question, coming as it did in exact confirmation of the fears the doctor had expressed half an hour earlier staggered me:

"You don't mean to say he has gone overboard?" I asked.

"I fear he has," answered the captain.

"This is the most extraordinary thing—" I began.

"Why?" he asked.

"He is the fourth, then?" I explained. In answer to another question from the captain, I explained, without mentioning the doctor, that I had heard the story concerning 105. He seemed very much annoyed at hearing that I knew of it. I told him what had occurred in the night.

"What you say," he replied, "coincides almost exactly with what was told me by the room-mates of two of the other three. They bolt out of bed and run down the passage. Two of them were seen to go overboard by the watch; we stopped and lowered boats, but they were not found. Nobody, however, saw or heard the man who was lost last night—if he is really lost. The steward, who is a superstitious fellow, perhaps, and expected something to go wrong, went to look for him this morning, and found his berth empty, but his clothes lying about, just as he had left them. The steward was the only man on board who knew him by sight, and he has been searching everywhere for him. He has disappeared! Now, sir, I want to beg you not to mention the circumstance to any of the passengers; I don't want the ship to get a bad name, and nothing hangs about an ocean-goer like stories of suicides. You shall have your choice of any one of the officers' cabins you like, including my own, for the rest of the passage. Is that a fair bargain?"

"Very," said I; "and I am much obliged to you. But since I am alone, and have the state-room to myself, I would rather not move. If the steward will take out that unfortunate man's things, I would as lief stay where I am. I will not say anything about the matter, and I think I can promise you that I will not follow my room-mate."

The captain tried to dissuade me from my intention, but I preferred having a state-room alone to being the chum of any officer on board. I do not know whether I acted foolishly, but if I had taken his advice I should have had nothing more to tell. There would have remained the disagreeable coincidence of several suicides occurring among men who had slept in the same cabin, but that would have been all.

That was not the end of the matter, however, by any means. I obstinately made up my mind that I would not be disturbed by such tales, and I even went so far as to argue the question with the captain. There was something wrong about the state-room, I said. It was rather damp. The porthole had been left open last night. My room-mate might have been ill when he came on board, and he might have become delirious after he went to bed. He might even now be hiding somewhere on board, and might be found later. The place ought to be aired and the fastening of the port looked to. If the captain would give me leave, I would see that what I thought necessary were done immediately.

"Of course you have a right to stay where you are if you please," he replied, rather petulantly; "but I wish you would turn out and let me lock the place up, and be done with it."

I did not see it in the same light, and left the captain, after promising to be silent concerning the disappearance of my companion. The latter had had no acquaintances on board, and was not missed in the course of the day. Towards evening I met the doctor again, and he asked me whether I had changed my mind. I told him I had not.

"Then you will before long," he said, very gravely.

CHAPTER III

We played whist in the evening, and I went to bed late. I will confess now that I felt a disagreeable sensation when I entered my state-room. I could not help thinking of the tall man I had seen on the previous night, who was now dead, drowned, tossing about in the long swell, two or three hundred miles astern. His face rose very distinctly before me as I undressed, and I even went so far as to draw back the curtains of the upper berth, as though to persuade myself that he was actually gone. I also bolted the door of the state-room. Suddenly I became aware that the porthole was open, and fastened back. This was more than I could stand. I hastily threw on my dressing-gown and went in search of Robert, the steward of my passage. I was very angry, I remember, and when I found him I dragged him roughly to the door of 105, and pushed him towards the open porthole.

"What the deuce do you mean, you scoundrel, by leaving that port open every night? Don't you know it is against the regulations? Don't you know that if the ship heeled and the water began to come in, ten men could not shut it? I will report you to the captain, you blackguard, for endangering the ship!"

I was exceedingly wroth. The man trembled and turned pale, and then began to shut the round glass plate with the heavy brass fittings.

"Why don't you answer me?" I said roughly.

"If you please, sir," faltered Robert, "there's nobody on board as can keep this 'ere port shut at night. You can try it yourself, sir. I ain't a-going to stop hany longer on board o' this vessel, sir; I ain't, indeed. But if I was you, sir, I'd just clear out and go and sleep with the surgeon, or something, I would. Look 'ere, sir, is that fastened what you may call securely, or not, sir? Try it, sir, see if it will move a hinch."

I tried the port, and found it perfectly tight.

"Well, sir," continued Robert, triumphantly, "I wager my reputation as an A1 steward that in 'arf an hour it will be open again; fastened back, too, sir, that's the horful thing—fastened back!"

I examined the great screw and the looped nut that ran on it.

"If I find it open in the night, Robert, I will give you a sovereign. It is not possible. You may go."

"Soverin' did you say, sir? Very good, sir. Thank ye, sir. Good-night, sir. Pleasant reepose, sir, and all manner of hinchantin' dreams, sir."

Robert scuttled away, delighted at being released. Of course, I thought he was trying to account for his negligence by a silly story, intended to frighten me, and I disbelieved him. The consequence was that he got his sovereign, and I spent a very peculiarly unpleasant night.

I went to bed, and five minutes after I had rolled myself up in my blankets the inexorable Robert extinguished the light that burned steadily behind the ground-glass pane near the door. I lay quite still in the dark trying to go to sleep, but I soon found that impossible. It had been some satisfaction to be angry with the steward, and the diversion had banished that unpleasant sensation I had at first experienced when I thought of the drowned man who had been my chum; but I was no longer sleepy, and I lay awake for some time, occasionally glancing at the porthole, which I could just see from where I lay, and which, in the darkness, looked like a faintly luminous soup-plate suspended in blackness. I believe I must have lain there for an hour, and, as I remember, I was just dozing into sleep when I was roused by a draught of cold air, and by distinctly feeling the spray of the sea blown upon my face. I started to my feet, and not having allowed in the dark for the motion of the ship, I was instantly thrown violently across the state-room upon the couch which was placed beneath the porthole. I recovered myself immediately, however, and climbed upon my knees. The porthole was again wide open and fastened back!

Now these things are facts. I was wide awake when I got up, and I should certainly have been waked by the fall had I still been dozing. Moreover, I bruised my elbows and knees badly, and the bruises were there on the following morning to testify to the fact, if I myself had doubted it. The porthole was wide open and fastened back—a thing so unaccountable that I remember very well feeling astonishment rather than fear when I discovered it. I at once closed the plate again, and screwed down the loop nut with all my strength. It was very dark in the state-room. I reflected that the port had certainly been opened within an hour after Robert had at first shut it in my presence, and I determined to watch it, and see whether it would open again. Those brass fittings are very heavy and by no means easy to move; I could not believe that the clump had been turned by the shaking of the screw. I stood peering out through the thick glass at the alternate white and grey streaks of the sea that foamed beneath the ship's side. I must have remained there a quarter of an hour.

Suddenly, as I stood, I distinctly heard something moving behind me in one of the berths, and a moment afterwards, just as I turned instinctively to look—though I could, of course, see nothing in the darkness—I heard a very faint groan. I sprang across the state-room, and tore the curtains of the upper berth aside, thrusting in my hands to discover if there were any one there. There was some one.

I remember that the sensation as I put my hands forward was as though I were plunging them into the air of a damp cellar, and from behind the curtains came a gust of wind that smelled horribly of stagnant sea-water. I laid hold of something that had the shape of a man's arm, but was smooth, and wet, and icy cold. But suddenly, as I pulled, the creature sprang violently forward against me, a clammy, oozy mass, as it seemed to me, heavy and wet, yet endowed with a sort of supernatural strength. I reeled across the state-room, and in an instant the door opened and the thing rushed out. I had not had time to be frightened, and quickly recovering myself, I sprang through the door and gave chase at the top of my speed, but I was too late. Ten yards before me I could see—I am sure I saw it—a dark shadow moving in the dimly lighted passage, quickly as the shadow of a fast horse thrown before a dog-cart by the lamp on a dark night. But in a moment it had disappeared, and I found myself holding on to the polished rail that ran along the bulkhead where the passage turned towards the companion. My hair stood on end, and the cold perspiration rolled down my face. I am not ashamed of it in the least: I was very badly frightened.

Still I doubted my senses, and pulled myself together. It was absurd, I thought. The Welsh rarebit I had eaten had disagreed with me. I had been in a nightmare. I made my way back to my state-room, and entered it with an effort. The whole place smelled of stagnant sea-water, as it had when I had waked on the previous evening. It required my utmost strength to go in, and grope among my things for a box of wax lights. As I lighted a railway reading lantern which I always carry in case I want to read after the lamps are out, I perceived that the porthole was again open, and a sort of creeping horror began to take possession of me which I never felt before, nor wish to feel again. But I got a light and proceeded to examine the upper berth, expecting to find it drenched with sea-water.

But I was disappointed. The bed had been slept in, and the smell of the sea was strong; but the bedding was as dry as a bone. I fancied that Robert had not had the courage to make the bed after the accident of the previous night—it had all been a hideous dream. I drew the curtains back as far as I could and examined the place very carefully. It was perfectly dry. But the porthole was open again. With a sort of dull bewilderment of horror I closed it and screwed it down, and thrusting my heavy stick through the brass loop, wrenched it with all my might, till the thick metal began to bend under the pressure. Then I hooked my reading lantern into the red velvet at the head of the couch, and sat down to recover my senses if I could. I sat there all night, unable to think of rest—hardly able to think at all. But the port-hole remained closed, and I did not believe it would now open again without the application of a considerable force.

The morning dawned at last, and I dressed myself slowly, thinking over all that had happened in the night. It was a beautiful day and I went on deck, glad to get out into the early, pure sunshine, and to smell the breeze from the blue water, so different from the noisome, stagnant odor of my state-room. Instinctively I turned aft, towards the surgeon's cabin. There he stood, with a pipe in his mouth, taking his morning airing precisely as on the preceding day.

"Good-morning," said he quietly, but looking at me with evident curiosity.

"Doctor, you were quite right," said I. "There is something wrong about that place."

"I thought you would change your mind," he answered, rather triumphantly. "You have had a bad night, eh? Shall I make you a pick-me-up? I have a capital recipe."

"No, thanks," I cried. "But I would like to tell you what happened."

I then tried to explain as clearly as possible precisely what had occurred, not omitting to state that I had been scared as I had never been scared in my whole life before. I dwelt particularly on the phenomenon of the porthole, which was a fact to which I could testify, even if the rest had been an illusion. I had closed it twice in the night, and the second time I had actually bent the brass in wrenching it with my stick. I believe I insisted a good deal on this point.

"You seem to think I am likely to doubt the story," said the doctor, smiling at the detailed account of the state of the porthole. "I do not doubt it in the least. I renew my invitation to you. Bring your traps here, and take half my cabin."

"Come and take half of mine for one night," I said. "Help me to get at the bottom of this thing."

"You will get to the bottom of something else if you try," answered the doctor.

"What?" I asked.

"The bottom of the sea. I am going to leave this ship. It is not canny."

"Then you will not help me to find out—"

"Not I," said the doctor, quickly. "It is my business to keep my wits about me—not to go fiddling about with ghosts and things."

"Do you really believe it is a ghost?" I enquired, rather contemptuously. But as I spoke I remembered very well the horrible sensation of the supernatural which had got possession of me during the night. The doctor turned sharply on me.

"Have you any reasonable explanation of these things to offer?" he asked. "No; you have not. Well, you say you will find an explanation. I say that you won't, sir, simply because there is not any."

"But, my dear sir," I retorted, "do you, a man of science, mean to tell me that such things cannot be explained?"

"I do," he answered stoutly. "And, if they could, I would not be concerned in the explanation."

I did not care to spend another night alone in the state-room, and yet I was obstinately determined to get at the root of the disturbances. I do not believe there are many men who would have slept there alone, after passing two such nights. But I made up my mind to try it, if I could not get any one to share a watch with me. The doctor was evidently not inclined for such an experiment. He said he was a surgeon, and that in case any accident occurred on board he must be always in readiness. He could not afford to have his nerves unsettled. Perhaps he was quite right, but I am inclined to think that his precaution was prompted by his inclination. On enquiry, he informed me that there was no one on board who would be likely to join me in my investigations, and after a little more conversation I left him. A little later I met the captain, and told him my story. I said that, if no one would spend the night with me, I would ask leave to have the light burning all night, and would try it alone.

"Look here," said he, "I will tell you what I will do. I will share your watch myself, and we will see what happens. It is my belief that we can find out between us. There may be some fellow skulking on board, who steals a passage by frightening the passengers. It is just possible that there may be something queer in the carpentering of that berth."

I suggested taking the ship's carpenter below and examining the place; but I was overjoyed at the captain's offer to spend the night with me. He accordingly sent for the workman and ordered him to do anything I required. We went below at once. I had all the bedding cleared out of the upper berth, and we examined the place thoroughly to see if there was a board loose anywhere, or a panel which could be opened or pushed aside. We tried the planks everywhere, tapped the flooring, unscrewed the fittings of the lower berth and took it to pieces—in short, there was not a square inch of the state-room which was not searched and tested. Everything was in perfect order, and we put everything back in its place. As we were finishing our work, Robert came to the door and looked in.

"Well, sir—find anything, sir?" he asked, with a ghastly grin.

"You were right about the porthole, Robert," I said, and I gave him the promised sovereign. The carpenter did his work silently and skillfully, following my directions. When he had done he spoke.

"I'm a plain man, sir," he said. "But it's my belief you had better just turn out your things, and let me run half a dozen four-inch screws through the door of this cabin. There's no good never came o' this cabin yet, sir, and that's all about it. There's been four lives lost out o' here to my own remembrance, and that in four trips. Better give it up, sir—better give it up!"

"I will try it for one night more," I said.

"Better give it up, sir—better give it up! It's a precious bad job," repeated the workman, putting his tools in his bag and leaving the cabin.

But my spirits had risen considerably at the prospect of having the captain's company, and I made up my mind not to be prevented from going to the end of the strange business. I abstained from Welsh rarebits and grog that evening, and did not even join in the customary game of whist. I wanted to be quite sure of my nerves, and my vanity made me anxious to make a good figure in the captain's eyes.

CHAPTER IV

The captain was one of those splendidly tough and cheerful specimens of seafaring humanity whose combined courage, hardihood, and calmness in difficulty leads them naturally into high positions of trust. He was not the man to be led away by an idle tale, and the mere fact that he was willing to join me in the investigation was proof that he thought there was something seriously wrong, which could not be accounted for on ordinary theories, nor laughed down as a common superstition. To some extent, too, his reputation was at stake, as well as the reputation of the ship. It is no light thing to lose passengers overboard, and he knew it.

About ten o'clock that evening, as I was smoking a last cigar, he came up to me, and drew me aside from the beat of the other passengers who were patrolling the deck in the warm darkness.

"This is a serious matter, Mr. Brisbane," he said. "We must make up our minds either way—to be disappointed or to have a pretty rough time of it. You see I cannot afford to laugh at the affair, and I will ask you to sign your name to a statement of whatever occurs. If nothing happens to-night, we will try it again to-morrow and next day. Are you ready?"

So we went below, and entered the state-room. As we went in I could see Robert the steward, who stood a little further down the passage, watching us, with his usual grin, as though certain that something dreadful was about to happen. The captain closed the door behind us and bolted it.

"Supposing we put your portmanteau before the door," he suggested. "One of us can sit on it. Nothing can get out then. Is the port screwed down?"

I found it as I had left it in the morning. Indeed, without using a lever, as I had done, no one could have opened it. I drew back the curtains of the upper berth so that I could see well into it. By the captain's advice I lighted my reading lantern, and placed it so that it shone upon the white sheets above. He insisted upon sitting on the portmanteau, declaring that he wished to be able to swear that he had sat before the door.

Then he requested me to search the state-room thoroughly, an operation very soon accomplished, as it consisted merely in looking beneath the lower berth and under the couch below the porthole. The spaces were quite empty.

"It is impossible for any human being to get in," I said, "or for any human being to open the port."

"Very good," said the captain, calmly. "If we see anything now, it must be either imagination or something supernatural."

I sat down on the edge of the lower berth.

"The first time it happened," said the captain, crossing his legs and leaning back against the door, "was in March. The passenger who slept here, in the upper berth, turned out to have been a lunatic—at all events, he was known to have been a little touched, and he had taken his passage without the knowledge of his friends. He rushed out in the middle of the night, and threw himself overboard, before the officer who had the watch could stop him. We stopped and lowered a boat; it was a quiet night, just before that heavy weather came on; but we could not find him. Of course his suicide was afterwards accounted for on the ground of his insanity."

"I suppose that often happens?" I remarked, rather absently.

"Not often—no," said the captain; "never before in my experience, though I have heard of it happening on board of other ships. Well, as I was saying, that occurred in March. On the very next trip— What are you looking at?" he asked, stopping suddenly in his narration.

I believe I gave no answer. My eyes were riveted upon the porthole. It seemed to me that the brass loop-nut was beginning to turn very slowly upon the screw—so slowly, however, that I was not sure it moved at all. I watched it intently, fixing its position in my mind, and trying to ascertain whether it changed. Seeing where I was looking, the captain looked too.

"It moves!" he exclaimed, in a tone of conviction. "No, it does not," he added, after a minute.

"If it were the jarring of the screw," said I, "it would have opened during the day; but I found it this evening jammed tight as I left it this morning."

I rose and tried the nut. It was certainly loosened, for by an effort I could move it with my hands.

"The queer thing," said the captain, "is that the second man who was lost is supposed to have got through that very port. We had a terrible time over it. It was in the middle of the night, and the weather was very heavy; there was an alarm that one of the ports was open and the sea running in. I came below and found everything flooded, the water pouring in every time she rolled, and the whole port swinging from the top bolts—not the port-hole in the middle. Well, we managed to shut it, but the water did some damage. Ever since that the place smells of sea-water from time to time. We supposed the passenger had thrown himself out, though the Lord only knows how he did it. The steward kept telling me that he cannot keep anything shut here. Upon my word—I can smell it now, cannot you?" he enquired, sniffing the air suspiciously.

"Yes—distinctly," I said, and I shuddered as that same odor of stagnant sea-water grew stronger in the cabin. "Now, to smell like this, the place must be damp," I continued, "and yet when I examined it with the carpenter this morning everything was per-fectly dry. It is most extraordinary—hallo!"

My reading lantern, which had been placed in the upper berth, was suddenly extinguished. There was still a good deal of light from the pane of ground glass near the door, behind which loomed the regulation lamp. The ship rolled heavily, and the cur-tain of the upper berth swung far out into the state-room and back again. I rose quickly from my seat on the edge of the bed, and the captain at the same moment started to his feet with a loud cry of surprise. I had turned with the intention of taking down the lantern to examine it, when I heard his exclamation, and immediately afterwards his call for help. I sprang towards him. He was wrestling with all his might with the brass loop of the port. It seemed to turn against his hands in spite of all his efforts. I caught up my cane, a heavy oak stick I always used to carry, and thrust it through the ring and bore on it with all my strength. But the strong wood snapped suddenly, and I fell upon the couch. When I rose again the port was wide open, and the captain was standing with his back against the door, pale to the lips.

"There is something in that berth!" he cried, in a strange voice, his eyes almost starting from his head. "Hold the door, while I look—it shall not escape us, whatever it is!"

But instead of taking his place, I sprang upon the lower bed, and seized something which lay in the upper berth.

It was something ghostly, horrible beyond words, and it moved in my grip. It was like the body of a man long drowned, and yet it moved, and had the strength of ten men living; but I gripped it with all my might—the slippery, oozy, horrible thing—the dead white eyes seemed to stare at me out of the dusk; the putrid odor of rank sea-water was about it, and its shiny hair hung in foul wet curls over its dead face. I wrestled with the dead thing; it thrust itself upon me and forced me back and nearly broke my arms; it wound its corpse's arms about my neck, the living death, and overpowered me, so that I, at last, cried aloud and fell, and left my hold.

As I fell the thing sprang across me, and seemed to throw itself upon the captain. When I last saw him on his feet his face was white and his lips set. It seemed to me that he struck a violent blow at the dead being, and then he, too, fell forward upon his face, with an inarticulate cry of horror.

The thing paused an instant, seeming to hover over his prostrate body, and I could have screamed again for very fright, but I had no voice left. The thing vanished suddenly, and it seemed to my disturbed senses that it made its exit through the open port, though how that was possible, considering the smallness of the aperture, is more than any one can tell. I lay a long time upon the floor, and the captain lay beside me. At last I partially recovered my senses and moved, and instantly I knew that my arm was broken—the small bone of the left forearm near the wrist.

I got upon my feet somehow, and with my remaining hand I tried to raise the captain. He groaned and moved, and at last came to himself. He was not hurt, but he seemed badly stunned.

Well, do you want to hear any more? There is nothing more. That is the end of my story. The carpenter carried out his scheme of running half a dozen four-inch screws through the door of 105; and if ever you take a passage in the *Kamtschatka*, you may ask for a berth in that state-room. You will be told that it is engaged—yes—it is engaged by that dead thing.

I finished the trip in the surgeon's cabin. He doctored my broken arm, and advised me not to "fiddle about with ghosts and things'' any more. The captain was very silent, and never sailed again in that ship, though it is still running. And I will not sail in her either. It was a very disagreeable experience, and I was very badly frightened, which is a thing I do not like. That is all. That is how I saw a ghost—if it was a ghost. It was dead, anyhow.

THE
SUPPER
AT ELSINORE

Isak Dinesen

Upon the corner of a street of Elsinore, near the harbor, there stands a dignified old gray house, built early in the eighteenth century, and looking down reticently at the new times grown up around it. Through the long years it has been worked into a unity, and when the front door is opened on a day of north-north-west the door of the corridor upstairs will open out of sympathy. Also when you tread upon a certain step of the stair, a board of the floor in the parlor will answer with a faint echo, like a song.

It had been in the possession of the family De Coninck for many years, but after the state bankruptcy of 1813 and simultaneous tragic happenings within the family itself, they gave it up and moved to their house in Copenhagen. An old woman in a white cap looked after the old house for them, with a man to assist her, and, living in the old rooms, would think and talk of old days. The two daughters of the house had never married, and were now too old for it. The son was dead. But in summers of long ago—so Madam Bæk would recount—on Sunday afternoons when the weather was fine, the Papa and Mamma De Coninck, with the three children, used to drive in a landaulet to the country house of the old lady, the grandmother, where they would dine, as the custom was then, at three o'clock, outside on the lawn under a large elm tree which, in June, scattered its little round and flat brown seeds thickly upon the grass. They would partake of duck with green peas and of strawberries with cream, and the little boy would run to and fro, in white nankeens, to feed his grand-mother's Bolognese dogs.

The two young sisters used to keep, in cages, the many birds presented to them by their seafaring admirers. When asked if they did not play the harp, old Madam Bæk would shrug her shoulders over the impossibility of giving any account of the many perfections of the young ladies. As to their adorers, and the proposals which had been made them, this was a hopeless theme to enter upon. There was no end to it.

Old Madam Bæk, who had herself been married for a short time to a sailor, and had, when he was drowned, reentered the service of the De Coninck family as a widow, thought it a great pity that neither of the lovely sisters had married. She could not quite get over it. Toward the world she held the theory that they had not been able to find any man worthy of them, except their brother. But she herself felt that her doctrine would not hold water. If this had been the two sisters' trouble, they ought to have put up with less than the ideal. She herself, on their behalf, would have done so, although it would have cost her much. Also, in her heart she knew better. She was seventeen years older than the elder sister, Fernande, whom they called Fanny, and eighteen years older than the younger, Eliza, who was born on the day of the fall of the Bastille, and she had been with them for the greater part of her life. Even if she was unable to put it into words, she felt keenly enough, as with her own body and soul, the doom which hung over the breed, and which tied these sisters and this brother together and made impossible for them any true relation to other human beings.

While they had been young, no event in the social world of Elsinore had been a success without the lovely De Coninck sisters. They were the heart and soul of all the gayety of the town. When they entered its ballrooms, the ceilings of sedate old merchants' houses seemed to lift a little, and the walls to spring out in luminous Ionian columns, bound with vine. When one of them opened the ball, light as a bird, bold as a thought, she consecrated the gathering to the gods of true joy of life, from whose presence care and envy are banished. They could sing duets like a pair of nightingales in a tree, and imitate without effort and without the slightest malice the voices of all the *beau monde* of Elsinore, so as to make the paunches of their father's friends, the matadors of the town, shake with laughter around their card tables. They could make up a charade or a game of forfeits in no time, and when they had been out for their music lessons, or to the Promenade, they came back brimful of tales of what had happened, or of tales out of their own imaginations, one whim stumbling over the other.

And then, within their own rooms, they would walk up and down the floor and weep, or sit in the window and look out over the harbor and wring their hands in their laps, or lie in bed at night and cry bitterly, for no reason in the world. They would talk, then, of life with the black bitterness of two Timons of Athens, and give Madam Bæk an uncanny feeling, as in an atmosphere of corrodent rust. Their mother, who did not have the curse in her blood, would have been badly frightened had she been present at these moments, and would have suspected some unhappy love affair. Their father would have understood them, and have grieved on their behalf, but he was occupied with his affairs, and did not come into his daughters' rooms. Only this elderly female servant, whose temperament was as different as possible from theirs, would understand them in her way, and would keep it all within her heart, as they did themselves, with mingled despair and pride. Sometimes she would try to comfort them. When they cried out, "Hanne, is it not terrible that there is so much lying, so much falsehood, in the world?" she said, "Well, what of it? It would be worse still if it were actually true, all that they tell."

Then again the girls would get up, dry their tears, try on their new bonnets before the glass, plan their theatricals and sleighing parties, shock and gladden the hearts of their friends, and have the whole thing over again. They seemed as unable to keep from one extremity as from the other. In short, they were born melancholiacs, such as make others happy and are themselves helplessly unhappy, creatures of playfulness, charm and salt tears, of fine fun and everlasting loneliness.

Whether they had ever been in love, old Madam Bæk herself could not tell. They used to drive her to despair by their hard skepticism as to any man being in love with them, when she, indeed, knew better, when she saw the swains of Elsinore grow pale and worn, go into exile or become old bachelors from love of them. She also felt that could they ever have been quite convinced of a man's love of them, that would have meant salvation to these young flying Dutchwomen. But they stood in a strange, distorted relation to the world, as if it had been only their reflection in a mirror which they had been showing it, while in the background and the shadow the real woman remained a looker-on. She would follow with keen attention the movements of the lover courting her image, laughing to herself at the impossibility of the consummation of their love, when the moment should come for it, her own heart hardening all the time. Did she wish that the man would break the glass and the lovely creature within it, and turn around toward herself? Oh, that she knew to be out of the question. Perhaps the lovely sisters derived a queer pleasure out of the adoration paid to their images in the mirror. They could not do without it in the end.

Because of this particular turn of mind they were predestined to be old maids. Now that they were real old maids, of fifty-two and fifty-three, they seemed to have come to better terms with life, as one bears up with a thing that will soon be over. That they were to disappear from the earth without leaving any trace whatever did not trouble them, for they had always known that it would be so. It gave them a certain satisfaction to feel that they were disappearing gracefully. They could not possibly putrefy, as would most of their friends, having already been, like elegant spiritual mummies, laid down with myrrh and aromatic herbs. When they were in their sweet moods, and particularly in their relations with the younger generation, the children of their friends, they even exhaled a spiced odor of sanctity, which the young people remembered all their lives.

The fatal melancholy of the family had come out in a different manner in Morten, the boy, and in him had fascinated Madam Bæk even to possession. She never lost patience with him, as she sometimes did with the girls, because of the fact that he was male and she female, and also by reason of the true romance which surrounded him as it had never surrounded his sisters. He had been, indeed, in Elsinore, as another highborn young dandy before him, the observed of all observers, the glass of fashion and the mold of form. Many were the girls of the town who had remained unmarried for his sake, or who had married late in life one having a likeness, perhaps not quite *en face* and not quite in profile, to that god-like young head which had, by then, forever disappeared from the horizon. And there was even the girl who had been, in the eyes of all the world, engaged to be married to Morten, herself married now, with children—*aber frage nur nicht wie!* She had lost that radiant fairness which had in his day given her the name, in Elsinore, of "golden lambkin," so that where that fairy creature had once pranced in the streets a pale and quiet lady now trod the pavement. But still this was the girl whom, when he had stepped out of his barge on a shining March day at the pier of Elsinore, with the whole population of the town waving and shouting to him, he had lifted from the ground and held in his arms, while all the world had swung up and down around her, had whirled fans and long streamers in all the hues of the rainbow.

Morten De Coninck had been more reticent of manner than his sisters. He had no need to exert himself. When he came into a room, in his quiet way, he owned and commanded it. He had all the beauty of limb and elegance of hands and feet of the ladies of the family, but not their fineness of feature. His nose and mouth seemed to have been cut by a rougher hand. But he had the most striking, extraordinarily noble and serene forehead. People talking to him lifted their eyes to that broad pure brow as if it had been radiant with the diamond tiara of a young emperor, or the halo of a saint. Morten De Coninck looked as if he could not possibly know either guilt or fear. Very likely he did not. He played the part of a hero to Elsinore for three years.

This was the time of the Napoleonic wars, when the world was trembling on its foundations. Denmark, in the struggle of the Titans, had tried to remain free and to go her own ways, and had

had to pay for it. Copenhagen had been bombarded and burned. On that September night, when the sky over the town had flamed red to all Sealand, the great chiming bells of Frue Kirke, set going by the fire, had played, on their own, Luther's hymn, *Ein fester Burg ist unser Gott,* just before the tall tower fell into ruins. To save the capital the government had had to surrender the fleet. The proud British frigates had led the warships of Denmark—the apples of her eye, a string of pearls, a flight of captive swans—up through the Sound. The empty ports cried to heaven, and shame and hatred were in all hearts.

It was in the course of the struggles and great events of the following years of 1807 and 1808 that the flotilla of privateers sprang up, like live sparks from a smoking ruin. Driven forth by patriotism, thirst of revenge, and hope of gain, the privateers came from all the coasts and little islands of Denmark, manned by gentlemen, ferrymen and fishermen, idealists and adventurers— gallant seamen all of them. As you took out your letter of marque you made your own cause one with that of the bleeding country; you had the right to strike a blow at the enemy whenever you had the chance, and you might come out of the rencounter a rich man. The privateer stood in a curious relationship to the state: it was a sort of acknowledged maritime love-affair, a left-handed marriage, carried through with passionate devotion on both sides. If she did not wear the epaulets and sanctifying bright metal of legitimate union, she had at least the burning red kiss of the crown of Denmark on her lips, and the freedom of the concubine to enchant her lord by these wild whims which queens do not dream of. The royal navy itself—such as was left of it in those ships which had been away from Copenhagen that fatal September week—took a friendly view of the privateer flotilla and lived with it on congenial terms; on such terms, probably, as those on which Rachel lived with her maid Bilhah, who accomplished what she could not do herself. It was a great time for grave men. There were cannons singing once more in the Danish fairways, here and there, and where they were least expected, for the privateers very rarely worked together; every one of them was out on its own. Incredible, heroic deeds were performed, great prizes were snatched away under the very guns of the conveying frigates and were brought into port, by the triumphant wild little boats with their rigging hanging down in rags, amid shouts of exultation. Songs were made about it all. There can rarely have been a class of heroes who appealed more highly and deeply to the heart and imagination of the common people, and to all the boys, of a nation.

It was soon found that the larger type of ship did not do well for this traffic. The ferryboat or snow, with a station bill of twelve to twenty men, and with six to ten swivel guns, handy and quick in emergencies, was the right bird for the business. The nautical skill of the captain and his knowledge of the seaways played a great part, and the personal bravery of the crew, their artfulness with the guns, and, in boarding, with hand weapons, carried the point. Here were the honors of war to be won; and not only honor, but gold; and not gold alone, but revenge upon the violator, sweet to the heart. And when they came in, these old and young sea dogs, covered with snow, their whole rigging sometimes coated with ice until the ship looked as if it were drawn with chalk upon a dark sea, they had their hour of glory behind them, but a great excitement in front, for they made a tremendous stir in the little seaport towns. Then came the judgment of the prize, and the sale of the salved goods, which might be of great value. The government took its share, and each man on board came in for his, from the captain, gunner, and mate to the boys, who received one-third of a man's share. A boy might have gone to sea possessing nothing but his shirt, trousers and trouserstrap, and come back with those badly torn and red-stained, and a tale of danger and high seas to tell his friends, and might be jingling five hundred riksdaler in his pocket a fortnight later, when the sale was over. The Jews of Copenhagen and Hamburg, each in three tall hats, one on top of the other, made their appearance upon the spot quickly, to play a great rôle at the sale, or, beforehand, to coax the prize-marks out of the pockets of impatient combatants.

Soon there shot up, like new comets, the names of popular heroes and their boats, around whose fame myths gathered daily.

There was Jens Lind, of the *Cort Adeler,* the one they called "Velvet" Lind because he was such a swell, and who played the rôle of a great nabob for some years, and then, when all gain was spent, finished up as a bear-leader. There was Captain Raaber, of *The Revenger,* who was something of a poet; the brothers Wulff-sen, of *The Mackerel* and the *Madame Clark,* who were gentle-men of Copenhagen; and Christen Kock, of the *Æolus,* whose entire crew—every single man—was killed or wounded in her fight with a British frigate off Læssø; and there was young Morten De Coninck, of the *Fortuna II.*

When Morten first came to his father and asked him to equip a privateer for him, the heart of old Mr. De Coninck shrank a little from the idea. There were many rich and respectable shipowners of Copenhagen, some of them greater merchants than he, who had in these days launched their privateers, and Mr. De Coninck, who yielded to no one in patriotic feeling, had himself suffered heavy losses at the hands of the British. But the business was painful to him. There was to his mind something revolting in the idea of attacking merchant ships, even if they did carry contra-band. It seemed to him like assaulting ladies or shooting alba-trosses. Morten had to turn for support to his father's cousin, Fernand De Coninck, a rich old bachelor of Elsinore whose mother was French and who was an enthusiastic partisan of the Emperor Napoleon. Morten's two sisters masterfully assisted him in getting around Uncle Fernand, and in November, 1807, the young man put to sea in his own boat. The uncle never regretted his generosity. The whole business rejuvenated him by twenty years, and he possessed, in the end, a collection of souvenirs from the ships of the enemy that gave him great pleasure.

The *Fortuna II* of Elsinore, with a crew of twelve and four swivel guns, received her letter of marque on the second of No-vember—was not this date, and the dates of exploits following it, written in Madam Bæk's heart, like the name of Calais in Queen Mary's, now, thirty-three years after? Already on the fourth the *Fortuna II* surprised an English brig off Hveen. An English man-of-war, hastening to the spot, shot at the privateer, but her crew managed to cut the cables of the prize and bring her into safety under the guns of Kronborg.

On the twentieth of November the boat had a great day. From a convoy she cut off the British brig, *The William,* and the snow, *Jupiter,* which had a cargo of sail cloth, stoneware, wine, spirits, coffee, sugar and silks. The cargo was unloaded at Elsinore, but both prizes were brought to Copenhagen, where they were condemned. Two hundred Jews came to Elsinore to bid at the auction sale of the *Jupiter*'s cargo, on the thirtieth of December. Morten himself bought in a piece of white brocade which was said to have been made in China and sent from England for the wedding dress of the Czar's sister. At this time Morten had just become engaged, and all Elsinore laughed and smiled at him as he walked away with the parcel under his arm.

Many times he was pursued by the enemy's men-of-war. Once, on the twenty-seventh of May, in flight from a British frigate, he ran ashore near Aarhus, but escaped by throwing his ballast of iron overboard, and got in under the guns of the Danish batteries. The burghers of Aarhus provided the illustrious young privateersman with new iron for his ballast, free of charge. It was said that the little seamstresses brought him their pressing-irons, and kissed them in parting with them, to bring him luck.

On the fifteenth of January the *Fortuna* had, together with the privateer *Three Friends,* captured six of the enemy's ships, and with these was bearing in with Drogden, to have them realized in Copenhagen, when one of the prizes ran ashore on the Middelgrund. It was a big British brig loaded with sail cloth, valued at 100,000 riksdaler, which the privateers had, on the morning of the same day, cut off from an English convoy. The British men-of-war were still pursuing them. At the sight of the accident the pursuing ships instantly dispatched a strong detachment of six longboats to recapture their brig. The privateers, on their side, were not disposed to give her up, and beat up against the British, who were driven away by a fire of grape-shot and had to give up the recapture. But the ship was to be lost all the same. The prizemaster on board her, at the sight of the enemy's boats with their greatly superior forces, had put fire to the brig so that she should not fall again into the hands of the British. The fire spread so violently that the ship could not be saved, and all night the people of Copenhagen watched the tall, terrible beacon to the north. The five remaining prizes were taken to Copenhagen.

It was in the summer of the same year that the *Fortuna II* came in for a life-and-death fight off Elsinore. She had by then become a thorn in the flesh of the British, and on a dark night in August they made ready, from the men-of-war stationed on the Swedish coast, to capture her. Two big launches were sent off, their holes bound with wool. The crew of the privateer had turned in, and only young Morten himself and his balker were on deck when the launches, manned by thirty-five sailors, grated against the *Fortuna*'s sides, and the boarding pikes were planted in her boards. From the launches shots were fired, but on board the privateer there was neither time nor room for using the guns. It became a struggle of axes, broadswords and knives. The enemy swarmed on deck from all sides; men were cutting at the chain-cable and hanging in the figurehead. But it did not last long. The *Fortuna*'s men put up a desperate fight, and in twenty minutes the deck was cleared. The enemy jumped into its boats and pushed off. The guns were used then, and three canister shots were fired after the retreating British. They left twelve dead and wounded men on the deck of the *Fortuna II.*

At Elsinore the people had heard the musketry fire from the longboats, but no reply from the *Fortuna.* They gathered at the harbor and along the ramparts of Kronborg, but the night was dark, and although the sky was just reddening in the east, no one could see what was happening. Then, just as the first light of morning was filling the dull air, three shots rang out, one after another, and the boys of Elsinore said that they could see the white smoke run along the dark waves. The *Fortuna II* bore in with Elsinore half an hour later. She looked black against the eastern sky. It was apparent that her rigging had been badly crippled, and gradually the people on land were able to distinguish the little dark figures on board, and the red on the deck. It was said that there was not a single broadsword or knife on board that was not red, and all the netting from stern to main chains had been soaked with blood. There was not one man on board, either, who had not been wounded, but only one was badly hurt. This was a West-Indian Negro, from the Danish colonies there— "black in skin but a Dane in heart," the newspapers of Elsinore said the next day. Morten himself, fouled with gunpowder, a bandage down over one eye, white in the morning light and wild still from the fight, lifted both his arms high in the air to the cheering crowd on shore.

In the autumn of that same year the whole privateer trade was suddenly prohibited. It was thought that it drew the enemy's frigates to the Danish seas, and constituted a danger to the country. Also, it was on many sides characterized as a wild and inhuman way of fighting. This broke the hearts of many gallant sailors, who left their decks to wander all over the world, unable to settle down again to their work in the little towns. The country grieved over her birds of prey.

To Morten De Coninck, all people agreed, the new order came conveniently. He had gathered his laurels and could now marry and settle down in Elsinore.

He was then engaged to Adrienne Rosenstand, the falcon to the white dove. She was the bosom friend of his sisters, who treated her much as if they had created her themselves, and took pleasure in dressing up her loveliness to its greatest advantage. They had refined and decided tastes, and spent as much time on the choice of her trousseau as if it had been their own. Between themselves they were not always so lenient to their frail sister-in-law, but would passionately deplore to one another the mating of their brother with a little *bourgeoise,* an ornamental bird out of the poultry yard of Elsinore. Had they thought the matter over a little, they ought to have congratulated themselves. The timidity and conventionality of Adrienne still allowed them to shine unrivaled within their sphere of daring and fantasy; but what figures would the falcon's sisters have cut, had he, as might well have happened, brought home a young eagle-bride?

The wedding was to take place in May, when the country around Elsinore is at its loveliest, and all the town was looking forward to the day. But it did not come off in the end. On the morning of the marriage the bridegroom was found to be missing, and he was never seen again in Elsinore. The sisters, dissolved in tears of grief and shame, had to take the news to the bride, who fell down in a swoon, lay ill for a long time, and never quite recovered. The whole town seemed to have been struck dumb by the blow, and to wrap up its head in sorrow. No one made much out of this unique opportunity for gossip. Elsinore felt the loss its own, and the fall.

No direct message from Morten De Coninck ever reached Elsinore. But in the course of the years strange rumors of him drifted in from the West. He was a pirate, it was said first of all, and that was not an unheard-of fate for a homeless privateer. Then it was rumored that he was in the wars in America, and had distinguished himself. Later it was told that he had become a great planter and slave-owner in the Antilles. But even these rumors were lightly handled by the town. His name was hardly ever mentioned, until, after long years, he could be talked about as a figure out of a fairy tale, like Bluebeard or Sindbad the Sailor. In the drawing-rooms of the De Coninck house he ceased to exist after his wedding-day. They took his portrait down from the wall. Madame De Coninck took her death over the loss of her son. She had a great deal of life in her. She was a stringed instrument from which her children had many of their high and clear notes. If it were never again to be used, if no waltz, serenade, or martial march were ever to be played upon it again, it might as well be put away. Death was no more unnatural to her than silence.

To Morten's sisters the infrequent news of their brother was manna on which they kept their hearts alive in a desert. They did not serve it to their friends, nor to their parents; but within the distillery of their own rooms they concocted it according to many recipes. Their brother would come back an admiral in a foreign fleet, his breast covered with unknown stars, to marry the bride waiting for him, or come back wounded, broken in health, but highly honored, to die in Elsinore. He would land at the pier. Had he not done so, and had they not seen it with their own eyes? But even this spare food came in time to be seasoned with much pungent bitterness. They themselves, in the end, would rather have starved than have swallowed it, had they had the choice. Morten, it was told, far from being a distinguished naval officer or a rich planter, had indeed been a pirate in the waters around Cuba and Trinidad—one of the last of the breed. But, pursued by the ships *Albion* and *Triumph,* he had lost his ship near Port of Spain, and himself had a narrow escape. He had tried to make his living in many hard ways and had been seen by somebody in New Orleans, very poor and sick. The last thing that his sisters heard of him was that he had been hanged.

From Morten's wedding day, Madam Bæk had carried her wound in silence for thirty years. The sophistries of his sisters she never chose to make use of; she let them go in at one ear and out at the other. She was very humble and attentive to the deserted bride, when she again visited the family, yet she never showed her much sympathy. Also she knew, as was ever the case in the house, more than any other inhabitant of it. It cannot be said that she had seen the catastrophe approach, but she had had strange warnings in her dreams. The bridegroom had been in the habit, from childhood, of coming and sitting with her in her little room from time to time. He had done that while they were making great preparations for his happiness. Over her needlework and her glasses she had watched his face. And she, who often worked late at night, and who would be up in the linen-room before the early summer sun was above the Sound, was aware of many comings and goings unknown to the rest of the household. Something had happened to the engaged people. Had he begged her to take him and hold him, so that it should no longer be in his power to leave her? Madam Bæk could not believe that any girl could refuse Morten anything. Or had she yielded, and found the magic ineffective? Or had she been watching him, daily slipping away from her, and still had not the strength to offer the sacrifice which might have held him?

Nobody would ever know, for Adrienne never talked of these things; indeed, she could not have done so if she had wanted to. Ever since her recovery from her long illness she seemed to be a little hard of hearing. She could only hear the things which could be talked about very loudly, and finished her life in an atmosphere of high-shrickcd platitudes.

For fifteen years the lovely Adrienne waited for her bridegroom, then she married.

The two sisters De Coninck attended the wedding. They were magnificently attired. This was really the last occasion upon which they appeared as the belles of Elsinore, and although they were then in their thirties, they swept the floor with the young girls of the town. Their wedding present to the bride was no less imposing. They gave her their mother's diamond earrings and brooch, a *parure* unique in Elsinore. They had likewise robbed the windows of their drawing-rooms of all their flowers to adorn the altar, this being a December wedding. All the world thought that the two proud sisters were doing these honors to their friend to make amends for what she had suffered at their brother's hands. Madam Bæk knew better. She knew that they were acting out of deep gratitude, that the diamond *parure* was a thank-offering. For now the fair Adrienne was no longer their brother's virgin widow, and held no more the place next to him in the eyes of all the world. When the gentle intruder now walked out of their house, the least they could do was to follow her to the door with deep courtesies. To her children, later in life, they also for the same reason showed the most excessive kindness, leaving them, in the end, most of their worldly goods; and to all this they were driven by their thankfulness to that pretty brood of ornamental chickens out of the poultry yard of Elsinore, because they were not their brother's children.

Madam Bæk herself had been asked to the wedding, and had a pleasant evening. When the ice was being served, she suddenly thought of the icebergs in the great black ocean, of which she had read, and of a lonely young man gazing at them from the deck of a ship, and at that moment her eyes met those of Miss Fanny, at the other end of the table. These dark eyes were all ablaze, and shone with tears. With all her De Coninck strength the distinguished old maid was suppressing something: a great longing, or shame, or triumph.

But there was another girl of Elsinore whose story may rightly be told, very briefly, in this place. That was an innkeeper's daughter of Sletten, by the name of Katrine, of the blood of the charcoal burners who live near Elsinore and are in many ways like gypsies. She was a big, handsome, dark and red-cheeked girl, and was said to have been, at a time, the sweetheart of Morten De Coninck. This young woman had a sad fate. She was thought to have gone a little out of her head. She took to drink and to worse ways, and died young. To this girl, Eliza, the younger of the sisters, showed great kindness. Twice she started her in a little milliner's shop, for the girl was talented and had an eye for elegance, and advertised it herself by wearing no bonnets but hers, and to the end of her life she gave her money. When, after many scandals in Elsinore, Katrine moved to Copenhagen, and took up her residence in the street of Dybensgade, where, in general, the ladies of the town never set foot, Eliza De Coninck still went to see her, and seemed to come back having gathered strength and a secret joy from her visits. For this was the way in which a girl beloved and deserted by Morten De Coninck ought to behave. This plain ruin, misery and degradation were the only harmonious accompaniment to the happenings, which might resound in and rejoice the heart of the sister while she stopped her ears to the words of comfort of the world. Eliza sat at Katrine's deathbed like a witch attentively observing the working of the deadly potion, holding her breath for the fulfillment of it.

The winter of 1841 was unusually severe. The cold began before Christmas, but in January it turned into a deadly still, continuous frost. A little snow in spare hard grains came down from time to time, but there was no wind, no sun, no movement in air or water. The ice was thick upon the Sound, so that people could walk from Elsinore to Sweden to drink coffee with their friends, the fathers of whom had met their own fathers to the roar of cannons on the same waters, when the waves had gone high. They looked like little rows of small black tin soldiers upon the infinite gray plane. But at night, when the lights from the houses and the dull street lamps reached only a little way out on the ice, this flatness and whiteness of the sea was very strange, like the breath of death over the world. The smoke from the chimneys went straight up in the air. The oldest people did not remember another such winter.

Old Madam Bæk, like other people, was very proud of this extraordinarily cold weather, and much excited about it, but during these winter months she changed. She probably was near her end, and was going off quickly. It began by her fainting in the dining-room one morning when she had been out by herself to buy fish, and for some time she could hardly move. She became very silent. She seemed to shrink, and her eyes grew pale. She went about in the house as before, but now it seemed to her that she had to climb an endless steep hill when in the evenings, with her candlestick and her shadow, she walked up the stair; and she seemed to be listening to sounds from far away when, with her knitting, she sat close to the crackling tall porcelain stove. Her friends began to think that they should have to cut out a square hole for her in that iron ground before the thaw of spring would set in. But she still held on, and after a time she seemed to become stronger again, although more rigid, as if she herself had frozen in the hard winter with a frost that would not thaw. She never got back that gay and precise flow of speech which, during seventy years, had cheered so many people, kept servants in order, and promoted or checked the gossip of Elsinore.

One afternoon she confided to the man who assisted her in the house her decision to go to Copenhagen to see her ladies. The next day she went out to arrange for her trip with the hackney man. The news of her project spread, for the journey from Elsinore to Copenhagen is no joke. On a Thursday morning she was up by candlelight and descended the stone steps to the street, her carpetbag in her hand, while the morning light was still dim.

The journey was no joke. It is more than twenty-six miles from Elsinore to Copenhagen, and the road ran along the sea. In many places there was hardly any road; only a track that went along the seashore. Here the wind, blowing onto the land, had swept away the snow, so that no sledges could pass, and the old woman went in a carriage with straw on the floor. She was well wrapped up, still, as the carriage drove on and the winter day came up and showed all the landscape so silent and cold, it was as if nothing at all could keep alive here, least of all an old woman all by herself in a carriage. She sat perfectly quiet, looking around her. The plane of the frozen Sound showed gray in the gray light. Here and there seaweed strewn upon the beach marked it with brown and black. Near the road, upon the sand, the crows were marching martially about, or fighting over a dead fish. The little fishermen's houses along the road had their doors and windows carefully shut. Sometimes she would see the fishermen themselves, in high boots that came above their knees, a long way out on the ice, where they were cutting holes to catch cod with a tin bait. The sky was the color of lead, but low along the horizon ran a broad stripe the color of old lemon peel or very old ivory.

It was many years since she had come along this road. As she drove on, long-forgotten figures came and ran alongside the carriage. It seemed strange to her that the indifferent coachman in a fur cap and the small bay horses should have it in their power to drive her into a world of which they knew nothing.

They came past Rungsted, where, as a little girl, she had served in the old inn, red-tiled, close to the road. From here to town the road was better. Here had lived, for the last years of his life, in sickness and poverty, the great poet Ewald, a genius, the swan of the North. Broken in health, deeply disappointed in his love for the faithless Arendse, badly given to drink, he still radiated a rare vitality, a bright light that had fascinated the little girl. Little Hanne, at the age of ten, had been sensitive to the magnetism of the great mysterious powers of life, which she did not understand. She was happy when she could be with him. Three things, she had learned from the talk of the landlady, he was always begging for: to get married, since to him life without women seemed unbearably cold and waste: alcohol of some sort—although he was a fine connoisseur of wine, he could drink down the crass gin of the country as well: and, lastly, to be taken to Holy Communion. All three were firmly denied him by his mother and stepfather, who were rich people of Copenhagen, and even by his friend, Pastor Schoenheyder, for they did not want him to be happy in either of the first two ways, and they considered that he must alter his ways before he could be made happy in the third. The landlady and Hanne were sorry for him. They would have married him and given him wine and taken him to Holy Communion, had it lain with them. Often, when the other children had been playing, Hanne had left them to pick early spring violets for him in the grass with cold fingers, looking forward to the sight of his face when he smelled the little bunches of flowers. There was something here which she could not understand, and which still held all her being strongly—that violets could mean so much. Generally he was very gay with her, and would take her on his knees and warm his cold hands on her. His breath sometimes smelled of gin, but she never told anybody. Even three years later, when she was confirmed, she imagined the Lord Jesus with his long hair in a queue, and with that rare, wild, broken and arrogant smile of the dying poet.

Madam Bæk came through the East Gate of Copenhagen just as people were about to light their lamps. She was held up and questioned by the toll collectors, but when they found her to be an honest woman in possession of no contraband they let her pass. So she would appear at the gate of heaven, ignorant of what was wanted of her, but confident that if she behaved correctly, according to her lights, others would behave correctly, according to theirs.

She drove through the streets of Copenhagen, looking around—for she had not been there for many years—as she would look around to form an opinion of the new Jerusalem. The streets here were not paved with gold or chrysoprase, and in places there was a little snow; but such as they were she accepted them. She likewise accepted the stables, where she was to get out, and the walk in the icy-cold blue evening of Copenhagen to Gammeltorv, where lay the house of her ladies.

Nevertheless she felt, as she took her way slowly through the streets, that she was an intruder and did not belong. She was not even noticed, except by two young men, deep in a political discussion, who had to separate to let her pass between them, and by a couple of boys, who remarked upon her bonnet. She did not like this sort of thing, it did not take place in Elsinore.

The windows of the first floor of the Misses De Conincks'

house were brightly lighted. Remembering it to be Fernande's birthday, Madam Bæk, down in the square, reasoned that the ladies would be having a party.

This was the case, and while Madam Bæk was slowly ascending the stair, dragging her heavy feet and her message from step to step, the sisters were merrily entertaining their guests in their warm and cozy gray parlor with its green carpet and shining mahogany furniture.

The party was characteristic of the two old maids by being mostly composed of gentlemen. They existed, in their pretty house in Gammeltorv, like a pair of prominent spiritual courtesans of Copenhagen, leading their admirers into excesses and seducing them into scattering their spiritual wealth and health upon their charms. As a couple of corresponding young courtesans of the flesh would be out after the great people and princes of this world, so were they ever spreading their snares for the *honoratiori* of the world spiritual, and tonight could lay on the table no meaner acquisition than the Bishop of Sealand, the director of the Royal Theater of Copenhagen, who was himself a distinguished dramatic and philosophical scribe, and a famous old painter of animals, just back from Rome, where he had been shown great honor. An old commodore with a fresh face, who had carried a wound since 1807, and a lady-in-waiting to the Dowager Queen, elegant and a good listener, who looked as if her voluminous skirt was absolutely massive, from her waist down, completed the party, all of whom were old friends, but were there chiefly to hold the candle.

If these sisters could not live without men, it was because they had the firm conviction, which, as an instinct, runs in the blood of seafaring families, that the final word as to what you are really worth lies with the other sex. You may ask the members of your own sex for their opinion and advice as to your compass and crew, your cuisine and garden, but when it comes to the matter of what you yourself are worth, the words of even your best friends are void and good for nothing, and you must address yourself to the opposite sex. Old white skippers, who have been round the Horn and out in a hundred hurricanes, know the law.

They may be highly respected on the deck or in the mess, and honored by their staunch gray contemporaries, but it is, finally the girls who have the say as to whether they are worth keeping alive or not. The old sailors' women are aware of this fact, and will take a good deal of trouble to impress even the young boys toward a favorable judgment. This doctrine, and this quick estimating eye is developed in sailors' families because there the two sexes have the chance to see each other at a distance. A sailor, or a sailor's daughter, judges a person of the other sex as quickly and surely as a hunter judges a horse; a farmer, a head of cattle; and a soldier, a rifle. In the families of clergymen and scribes, where the men sit in their houses all their days, people may judge each other extremely well individually, but no man knows what a woman is, and no woman what a man is; they cannot see the wood for trees.

The two sisters, in caps with lace streamers, were doing the honors of the house gracefully. In those days, when gentlemen did not smoke in the presence of ladies, the atmosphere of an evening party remained serene to the end, but a very delicate aromatic and exotic stream of steam rose from the tumblers of rare old rum with hot water, lemon and sugar, upon the table in the soft glow of the lamp. None of the company was quite uninfluenced by this nectar. They had a moment before been conjuring forth their youth by the singing of old songs which they themselves remembered their fathers' friends singing over their wine in the really good old days. The Bishop, who had a very sweet voice, had been holding up his glass while giving the ancient toast to the old generation:

Let the old ones be remembered now; they once were gay and free. And that they knew to love, my dear, the proof thereof are we!

The echo of the song—for she now declared that it was a five-minutes' course from her ear to her mind—was making Miss Fanny De Coninck thoughtful and a little absentminded. What a strange proof, she thought, are these dry old bodies here tonight of the fact that young men and women, half a century ago, sighed and shivered and lost themselves in ecstasies. What a curious proof is this gray hand of the follies of young hands upon a night in May long, long ago.

As she was standing, her chin, in this intensive dreaming, pressed down a little upon the black velvet ribbon around her throat, it would have been difficult for anyone who had not known her in her youth to find any trace of beauty in Fanny's face. Time had played a little cruelly with her. A slight wryness of feature, which had been an adorable piquantry once, was now turned into an uncanny little disfigurement. Her birdlike lightness was caricatured into abrupt little movements in fits and starts. But she had her brilliant dark eyes still, and was, all in all, a distinguished, and slightly touching, figure.

After a moment she took up again the conversation with the Bishop as animatedly as before. Even the little handkerchief in her fingers and the small crystal buttons down her narrow silk bosom seemed to take part in the argument. No pythoness on her tripod, her body filled with inspiring fumes, could look more prophetic. The theme under discussion was the question whether, if offered a pair of angel's wings which could not be removed, one would accept or refuse the gift.

"Ah, Your Right Worshipfulness," said Miss Fanny, "in walking up the aisle you would convert the entire congregation with your back. There would not be a sinner left in Copenhagen. But remember that even you descend from the pulpit at twelve o'clock every Sunday. It must be difficult enough for you as it is, but how would you, in a pair of white angel's wings, get out of—" What she really wanted to say was, "get out of using a chamber-pot?" Had she been forty years younger she would have said it. The De Coninck sisters had not been acquainted with sailors all of their lives for nothing. Very vigorous expressions, and oaths even, such as were never found in the mouths of the other young ladies of Elsinore, came naturally to their rosy lips, and used to charm their admirers into idolatry. They knew a good many names for the devil, and in moments of agitation would say, "Hell—to hell!" Now the long practice of being a lady and a hostess prevented

Fanny, and she said instead very sweetly, "of eating a roast white turkey?" For that was what the Bishop had been doing at dinner with obvious delight. Still, her imagination was so vividly at work that it was curious that the prelate, gazing, at close quarters, with a fatherly smile into her clear eyes, did not see there the picture of himself, in his canonicals, making use of a chamber-pot in a pair of angel's wings.

The old man was so enlivened by the debate that he spilled a few drops from his glass onto the carpet. "My dear charming Miss Fanny," he said, "I am a good Protestant and flatter myself that I have not quite failed in making things celestial and terrestrial go well together. In that situation I should look down and see, in truth, my celestial individuality reflected in miniature, as you see yours every day in the little bit of glass in your fair hand."

The old professor of painting said: "When I was in Italy I was shown a small, curiously shaped bone, which is found only in the shoulder of the lion, and is the remains of a wing bone, from the time when lions had wings, such as we still see in the lion of St. Mark. It was very interesting."

"Ah, indeed, a fine monumental figure on that column," said the Bishop, who had also been in Italy, and who knew that he had a leonine head.

"Oh, if I had a chance of those wings," said Miss Fanny, "I should not care a hang about my fine or monumental figure, but, by St. Anne, I should fly."

"Allow me," said the Bishop, "to hope, Miss Fanny, that you would not. We may have our reasons to mistrust a flying lady. You have, perhaps, heard of Adam's first wife, Lilith? She was in contradistinction to Eve, made all out of earth, like himself. What was the first thing that she did? She seduced two angels and made them betray to her the secret word which opens heaven, and so she flew away from Adam. That goes to teach us that where there is too much of the earthly element in a woman, neither husband nor angels can master her.

"Indeed," he went on, warming to his subject, his glass still in his hand, "in woman, the particularly heavenly and angelic attributes, and those which we most look up to and worship, all go to weigh her down and keep her on the ground. The long tresses, the veils of pudicity, the trailing garments, even the adorable womanly forms in themselves, the swelling bosom and hip, are as little as possible in conformity with the idea of flying. We, all of us, willingly grant her the title of angel, and the white wings, and lift her up on our highest pedestal, on the one inevitable condition that she must not dream of, must even have been brought up in absolute ignorance of, the possibility of flight.''

"Ah, la la," said Fanny, "we are aware of that, Bishop, and so it is ever the woman whom you gentlemen do not love or worship, who possesses neither the long lock nor the swelling bosom, and who has had to truss up her skirts to sweep the floor, who chuckles at the sight of the emblem of her very thralldom, and anoints her broomstick upon the eve of Walpurgis.''

The director of the Royal Theater rubbed his delicate hands gently against each other. "When I hear the ladies complain of their hard task and restrictions in life," he said, "it sometimes reminds me of a dream that I once had. I was at the time writing a tragedy in verse. It seemed to me in my dream that the words and syllables of my poem made a rebellion and protested, 'Why must we take infinite trouble to stand, walk and behave according to difficult and painful laws which the words of your prose do not dream of obeying?' I answered, 'Mesdames, because you are meant to be poetry. Of prose we think, and demand, but little. It must exist, if only for the police regulations and the calendar. But a poem which is not lovely has no *raison d'être.'* God forgive me if I have ever made poems which had in them no loveliness, and treated ladies in a manner which prevented them from being perfectly lovely—my remaining sins I can shoulder easily then.''

"How," said the old commodore, "could I entertain any doubts as to the reality of wings, who have grown up amongst sailing ships and amongst the ladies of the beginning of our century? The beastly steamships which go about these days may well be a species of witches of the sea—they are like self-supporting women. But if you ladies are contemplating giving up being white-sailed ships and poems—well, we must be perfectly lovely poems ourselves, then, and leave you to make up the police regulations. Without poetry no ship can be sailed. When I was a cadet, on the way to Greenland, and in the Indian Ocean, I used to console myself, on the middle watch, by thinking, in consecutive order, of all the women I knew, and by quoting poetry that I had learned by heart."

"But you have always been a poem, Julian," said Eliza, "a roundel." She felt tempted to put her arms round her cousin, they had always been great friends.

"Ah, in talking about Eve and Paradise," said Fanny, "you all still remain a little jealous of the snake."

"When I was in Italy," said the professor, "I often thought what a curious thing it is that the serpent, which, if I understand the Scripture, opened the eyes of man to the arts, should be, in itself, an object impossible to get into a picture. A snake is a lovely creature. At Naples they had a large reptile house, and I used to study the snakes there for many hours. They have skins like jewels, and their movements are wonderful performances of art. But I have never seen a snake done successfully in a picture. I could not paint it myself."

"Do you remember," said the commodore, who had been following his own thoughts, "the swing that I put up for you, at Øregaard, on your seventeenth birthday, Eliza? I made a poem about it."

"Yes, I do, Julian," said Eliza, her face brightening, "it was made like a ship."

It was a curious thing about the two sisters, who had been so unhappy as young women, that they should take so much pleasure in dwelling upon the past. They could talk for hours of the most insignificant trifles of their young days, and these made them laugh and cry more heartily than any event of the present day. Perhaps to them the first condition for anything having real charm was this: that it must not really exist.

It was another curious phenomenon about them that they, to whom so very little had happened, should talk of their married friends who had husbands, children and grandchildren with pity and slight contempt, as of poor timid creatures whose lives had been dull and uneventful. That they themselves had had no husbands, children or lovers did not restrain them from feeling that they had chosen the more romantic and adventurous part. The explanation was that to them only possibilities had any interest; realities carried no weight. They had themselves had all possibilities in hand, and had never given them away in order to make a definite choice and come down to a limited reality. They might still take part in elopements by rope-ladder, and in secret marriages, if it came to that. No one could stop them. Thus their only intimate friends were old maids like themselves, or unhappily married women, dames of the round table of possibilities. For their happily married friends, fattened on realities, they had, with much kindness, a different language, as if these had been of a slightly lower caste, with whom intercourse had to be carried on with the assistance of interpreters.

Eliza's face had brightened, like a fine, pure jar of alabaster behind which a lamp is lighted, at mention of the swing, made like a boat, which had been given her for her seventeenth birthday. She had always been by far the loveliest of the De Coninck children. When they were young their old French aunt had named them *la Bonté, la Beauté* and *l'Esprit,* Morten being *la Bonté.*

She was as fair as her sister was dark, and in Elsinore, where at the time a fashion for surnames had prevailed, they had called her "Ariel," or "The Swan of Elsinore." There had been that particular quality about her beauty that it seemed to hold promise, to be only the first step of the ladder of some extraordinary career. Here was this exceptional young female creature who had had the inspiration to be, from head to foot, strikingly lovely. But that was only the beginning of it. The next step was perhaps her clothes, for Eliza had always been a great swell, and had run up heavy debts—for which at times her brother had taken the responsibility before their father—on brocades, cashmeres, and plumes ordered from Copenhagen and Hamburg, and even from Paris. But that was also only the beginning of something. Then came the way in which she moved, and danced. There was about it an atmosphere of suspense which caused onlookers to hold their breaths. What was this extraordinary girl to do next? If at this time she had indeed unfolded a pair of large white wings, and had soared from the pier of Elsinore up into the summer air, it would have surprised no one. It was clear that she must do something extraordinary with such an abundance of gifts. "There is more strength in that girl," said the old boatswain of *La Fortuna,* when upon a spring day she came running down to the harbor, bareheaded, "than in all *Fortuna's* crew." Then in the end she had done nothing at all.

At Grammeltorv she was quietly, as if intentionally, fading day by day, into an even more marble-like loveliness. She could still span her waist with her two long slim hands, and moved with much pride and lightness, like an old Arab mare a little stiff, but unmistakably noble, at ease in the sphere of war and fantasias. And there was still that about her which kept open a perspective, the feeling that somewhere there were reserves and it was not out of the question that extraordinary things might happen.

"God, that swing, Eliza!" said the commodore. "You had been so hard on me in the evening that I actually went out into the garden of Øregaard, on that early July morning, resolved to hang myself. And as I was looking up into the crown of the great elm, I heard you saying behind me: 'That would be a good branch.' That, I thought, was cruelly said. But as I turned around there you were, your hair still done up in curling papers, and I remembered that I had promised you a swing. I could not die, in any case, till you had had it. When I got it up, and saw you in it, I thought: If it shall be my lot in life to be forever only ballast to the white sails of fair girls, I still bless my lot."

"That is what we have loved you for all your life," said Eliza.

An extremely pretty young maid, with pale blue ribbons on her cap—kept by the pair of old spiritual courtesans to produce an equilibrium in the establishment, in the way in which two worldly young courtesans might have kept, to the same end, an ugly and misshapen servant, a dwarf with wit and imagination—brought in a tray filled with all sorts of delicacies: Chinese ginger, tangerines, and crystallized fruit. In passing Miss Fanny's chair she said softly, "Madam Bæk has come from Elsinore, and waits in the kitchen."

Fanny's color changed, she could never receive calmly the news that anybody had arrived, or had gone away. Her soul left her and flew straight to the kitchen, from where she had to drag it back again.

"In that summer of 1806," she said, "the *Odyssey* had been translated into Danish for the first time, I believe. Papa used to read it to us in the evenings. Ha, how we played the hero and his gallant crew, braved the Cyclops and cruised between the island of the Læstrygones and the Phæacian shores! I shall never be made to believe that we did not spend that summer in our ships, under brown sails."

Shortly after this the party broke up, and the sisters drew up the blinds of their window to wave to the four gentlemen who helped Miss Bardenfleth into her court carriage and proceeded in a gayly talking group across the little iron-gray desert of nocturnal Gammeltorv, remarking, in the midst of philosophical and poetic discussions, upon the extraordinary cold.

This moment at the end of their parties always went strangely to the sisters' hearts. They were happy to get rid of their guests; but a little silent, bitter minute accompanied the pleasure. For they could still make people fall in love with them. They had the radiance in them which could refract little rainbow effects in the atmosphere of Copenhagen existence. But who could make them feel in love? That glass of mental and sentimental alcohol which made for warmth and movement within the old phlebolitic veins of their guests—from where were they themselves to get it? From each other, they knew, and in general they were content with the fact. Still, at this moment, the *tristesse* of the eternal hostess stiffened them a little.

Not so tonight, for no sooner had they lowered the blind again than they were off to the kitchen, making haste to send their pretty maid to bed, as if they knew the real joy of life to be found solely amongst elderly women. They made Madam Bæk and themselves a fresh cup of coffee, lifting down the old copper kettle from the wall. Coffee, according to the women of Denmark, is to the body what the word of the Lord is to the soul.

Had it been in the old days that the sisters and their servant met again after a long separation, the girls would have started at once to entertain the widow with accounts of their admirers. The theme was ever fascinating to Madam Bæk, and dear to the sisters by reason of the opportunity it gave them of shocking her. But these days were past. They gave her the news of the town—an old widower had married again, and another had gone mad—also a little gossip of the Court, such as she would understand, which they had heard from Miss Bardenfleth. But there was something in Madam Bæk's face which caught their attention. It was heavy with fate; she brought news herself. Very soon they paused to let her speak.

Madam Bæk allowed the pause to wax long.

"Master Morten," she said at last, and at the sound of her own thoughts of these last long days and nights she herself grew very pale, "is at Elsinore. He walks in the house."

At this news a deadly silence filled the kitchen. The two sisters felt their hair stand on end. The terror of the moment lay, for them, in this: that it was Madam Bæk who had recounted such news to them. They might have announced it to her, out of perversity and fancies, and it would not have meant much. But that Hanne, who was to them the principle of solidity and equilibrium for the whole world, should open her mouth to throw at them the end of all things—that made these seconds in their kitchen feel to the two younger women like the first seconds of a great earthquake.

Madam Bæk herself felt the unnatural in the situation, and all which was passing through the heads of her ladies. It would have terrified her as well, had she still had it in her to be terrified. Now she felt only a great triumph.

"I have seen him," she said, "seven times."

Here the sisters took to trembling so violently that they had to put down their coffee cups.

"The first time," said Madam Bæk, "he stood in the red dining-room, looking at the big clock. But the clock had stopped. I had forgotten to wind it up."

Suddenly a rain of tears sprang out of Fanny's eyes, and bathed her pale face. "Oh, Hanne, Hanne," she said.

"Then I met him once on the stair," said Madam Bæk. "Three times he has come and sat with me. Once he picked up a ball of wool for me, which had rolled onto the floor, and threw it back in my lap."

"How did he look to you?" asked Fanny, in a broken, cracked voice, evading the glance of her sister, who sat immovable.

"He looks older than when he went away," said Madam Bæk. "He wears his hair longer than people do here; that will be the American fashion. His clothes are very old, too. But he smiled at me just as he always did. The third time that I saw him, before he went—for he goes in his own way, and just as you think he is there, he is gone—he blew me a kiss exactly as he used to do when he was a young man and I had scolded him a little."

Eliza lifted her eyes, very slowly, and the eyes of the two sisters met. Never in all their lives had Madam Bæk said anything to them which they had for a moment doubted.

"But," said Madam Bæk, "this last time I found him standing before your two pictures for a long time. And I thought that he wanted to see you, so I have come to fetch you to Elsinore."

At these words the sisters rose up like two grenadiers at parade. Madam Bæk herself, although terribly agitated, sat where she had sat, as ever the central figure of their gatherings.

"When was it that you saw him?" asked Fanny.

"The first time," said Madam Bæk, "was three weeks ago to-day. The last time was on Saturday. Then I thought: 'Now I must go and fetch the ladies.' "

Fanny's face was suddenly all ablaze. She looked at Madam Bæk with a great tenderness, the tenderness of their young days. She felt that this was a great sacrifice, which the old woman was bringing out of her devotion to them and her sense of duty. For these three weeks, during which she had been living with the ghost of the outcast son of the De Coninck house, all alone, must have been the great time of Madam Bæk's life, and would remain so for her forever. Now it was over.

It would have been difficult to say if, when she spoke, she came nearest to laughter or tears. "Oh, we will go, Hanne," she said, "we will go to Elsinore."

"Fanny, Fanny," said Eliza, "he is not there; it is not he."

Fanny made a step forward toward the fire, so violently that the streamers of her cap fluttered. "Why not, Lizzie?" she said. "God means to do something for you and me after all. And do you not remember, when Morten was to go back to school after the holiday, and did not want to go, that he made us tell Papa that he was dead? We made a grave under the apple tree, and laid him down in it. Do you remember?" The two sisters at this moment saw, with the eyes of their minds, exactly the same picture of the little ruddy boy, with earth in his curls, who had been lifted out of his grave by their angry young father, and of themselves, with their small spades and soiled muslin frocks, following the procession home like disappointed mourners. Their brother might play a trick on them this time.

As they turned to each other their two faces had the same expression of youthful waggishness. Madam Bæk, in her chair, felt at the sight like a happily delivered lady-in-the-straw. A weight and a fullness had been taken from her, and her importance had gone with it. That was ever the way of the gentry. They would lay their hands on everything you had, even to the ghosts.

Madam Bæk would not let the sisters come back with her to Elsinore. She made them stay behind for a day. She wanted to see for herself that the rooms were warm to receive them, and that there would be hot water bottles in those maiden beds in which they had not slept for so long. She went the next day, leaving them in Copenhagen till the morrow.

It was good for them that they had been given these hours in which to make up their minds and prepare themselves to meet the ghost of their brother. A storm had broken loose upon them, and their boats, which had been becalmed in back waters, were whirled in a blizzard, amongst waves as high as houses. Still they were, in their lappets of lace, no landlubbers in the tempests of life. They were still able to maneuver, and they held their sheets. They did not melt into tears either. Tears were never a solution for them. They came first and were a weakness only; now they were past them, out in the great dilemma. They were themselves acquainted with the old sailors' rule:

Comes wind before rain—Topsail down and up again.
Comes rain before wind—Topsail down and all sails in.

They did not speak together much while waiting for admission
to their Elsinore house. Had the day been Sunday they would
have gone to church, for they were keen churchgoers, and critics
of the prominent preachers of the town, so that they generally
came back holding that they could have done it better themselves. In the church they might have joined company; the house
of the Lord alone of all houses might have held them both. Now
they had to wander in opposite parts of the town, in snowy
streets and parks, their small hands in muffs, gazing at cold naked
statues and frozen birds in the trees.

How were two highly respected, wealthy, popular and petted
ladies to welcome again the hanged boy of their own blood?
Fanny walked up and down the linden avenue of the Royal Rose
Gardens of Rosenborg. She could never revisit it later, not even in
summer time, when it was a green and golden bower, filled like
an aviary with children's voices. She carried with her, from one
end of it to the other, the picture of her brother, looking at the
clock, and the clock stopped and dead. The picture grew upon
her. It was upon his mother's death from grief of him that he was
gazing, and upon the broken heart of his bride. The picture still
grew. It was upon all the betrayed and broken hearts of the
world, all the sufferings of weak and dumb creatures, all injustice
and despair on earth, that he was gazing. And she felt that it was
all laid upon her shoulders. The responsibility was hers. That the
world suffered and died was the fault of the De Conincks. Her
misery drove her up and down the avenue like a dry leaf before
the wind—a distinguished lady in furred boots, in her own heart
a great, mad, wing-clipped bird, fluttering in the winter sunset.
Looking askance she could see her own large nose, pink under
her veil, like a terrible, cruel beak. From time to time a question
came into her mind: What is Eliza thinking now? It was strange
that the elder sister should feel thus, with bitterness and fear, that
her younger sister had deserted her in her hour of need. She had
herself fled her company, and yet she repeated to herself: "What,

could she not watch with me one hour?" It had been so even in the old De Coninck home. If things began to grow really difficult, Morten and the Papa and Mamma De Coninck would turn to the quiet younger girl, so much less brilliant than herself: "What does Eliza think?"

Toward evening, as it grew dark, and as she reflected that Madam Bæk must by now be at home in Elsinore, Fanny suddenly stopped and thought, Am I to pray to God? Several of her friends, she knew, had found comfort in prayer. She herself had not prayed since she had been a child. Upon the occasions of her Sundays in church, which were visits of courtesy to the Lord, her little silences of bent head had been gestures of civility. Her prayer now, as she began to form it, did not please her either. She used, as a girl, to read out his correspondence to her papa, so she was well acquainted with the jargon of mendicant letters— ". . . Feeling deeply impressed with the magnificence of your noble and well-known loving-kindness . . ." She herself had had many mendicant letters in her days; also many young men had begged her, on their knees, for something. She had been highly generous to the poor, and hard on the lovers. She had not begged herself, nor would she begin it now on behalf of her proud young brother. As her prayer took on a certain likeness to a mendicant letter or to a proposal, she stopped it. "He shall not be ashamed," she thought, "for he has called upon me. He shall not be afraid of ten thousands of people that have set themselves against him round about." Upon this she walked home.

When upon Saturday afternoon the sisters arrived at the house in Elsinore, they went through much deep agitation of the heart. Even the air—even the smell in the hall, that atmosphere of salt and seaweed which ever braces up old seaside houses—went straight through them. They say, thought Miss Fanny, sniffing, that your body is changed completely within the course of seven years. How I have changed, and how I have forgotten! But my nose must be the same. My nose I have still kept and it remembers all. The house was as warm as a box, and this struck them as a sweet compliment, as if an old admirer had put on his gala uniform for them. Many people, in revisiting old places, sigh at the sight of change and age. The De Coninck sisters, on the contrary, felt that the old house might well have deplored the signs of age and decay at this meeting again of theirs, and have cried: Heavens, heavens! Are these the damask-cheeked, silver-voiced girls in dancing sandals who used to slide down the banisters of my stairs?—sighing down its long chimneys, Oh, God! Fare away, fare away! When, then, it chose to pass over its feelings and pretend that they were the same, it was a fine piece of courtesy on its part.

Old Madam Bæk's great and ceremonious delight in their visit was also bound to touch them. She stood out on the steps to receive them; she changed their shoes and stockings for them, and had warm drinks ready. If we can make her happy so easily, they thought, how is it that we never came till now? Was it that the house of their childhood and young days had seemed to them a little empty and cold, a little grave-like, until it had a ghost in it?

Madam Bæk took them around to show them the spots where Morten had stood, and she repeated his gestures many times. The sisters did not care a pin what gestures he would make to anybody but themselves, but they valued the old woman's love of their brother, and listened patiently. In the end Madam Bæk felt very proud, as if she had been given a sacred relic out of the boy's beloved skeleton, a little bone that was hers to keep.

The room in which supper was made ready was a corner room. It turned two windows to the east, from which there was a view of the old gray castle of Kronborg, copper-spired, like a clenched fist out in the Sound. Above the ramparts departed commandants of the fortress had made a garden, in which, in their winter bareness, lindens now showed the world what loosely built trees they are when not drilled to walk, militarily, two by two. Two windows looked south out upon the harbor. It was strange to find the harbor of Elsinore motionless, with sailors walking back from their boats on the ice.

The walls of the room had once been painted crimson, but with time the color had faded into a richness of hues, like a glassful of dying red roses. In the candlelight these flat walls blushed and shone deeply, in places glowing like little pools of dry, burning, red lacquer. On one wall hung the portraits of the two young De Coninck sisters, the beauties of Elsinore. The third portrait, of their brother, had been taken down so long ago that only a faint shadow on the wall showed where it had once been. Some potpourri was being burned on the tall stove, on the sides of which Neptune, with a trident, steered his team of horses through high waves. But the dried rose-petals dated from summers of long ago. Only a very faint fragrance now spread from their funeral pile, a little rank, like the bouquet of fine claret kept too long. In front of the stove the table was laid with a white tablecloth and delicate Chinese cups and plates.

In this room the sisters and the brother De Coninck had in the old days celebrated many secret supper-parties, when preparing some theatrical or fancy-dress show, or when Morten had returned very late at night from an expedition in his sailing boat, of which their parents must know nothing. The eating and drinking at such times had to be carried on in a subdued manner, so as not to wake up the sleeping house. Thirty-five years ago the red room had seen much merriment caused by this precaution.

Faithful to tradition, the Misses De Coninck now came in and took their seats at table, opposite each other, on either side of the stove, and in silence. To these indefatigable old belles of a hundred balls, age and agitation all the same began to assert themselves. Their eyelids were heavy, and they could not have held out much longer if something had not happened.

They did not have to wait long. Just as they had poured out their tea, and were lifting the thin cups to their lips, there was a slight rustle in the quiet room. When they turned their heads a little, they saw their brother standing at the end of the table.

He stood there for a moment and nodded to them, smiling at them. Then he took the third chair and sat down, between them. He placed his hands upon the edge of the table, gently moving them sideward and back again, exactly as he always used to do.

Morten was poorly dressed in a dark gray coat that looked faded and much worn. Still it was clear that he had taken pains about his appearance for the meeting, he had on a white collar and a carefully tied high black stock, and his hair was neatly brushed back. Perhaps he had been afraid, Fanny for a moment thought, that after having lived so long in rough company he should impress his sisters as less refined and well mannered than before. He need not have worried; he would have looked a gentleman on the gallows. He was older than when they had seen him last, but not as old as they. He looked a man of forty.

His face was somehow coarser than before, weather-beaten and very pale. It had, with the dark, always somewhat sunken eyes, that same divine play of light and darkness which had long ago made maidens mad. His large mouth also had its old frankness and sweetness. But to his pure forehead a change had come. It was not that it was now crossed by a multitude of little horizontal lines, for the marble of it was too fine to be marred by such superficial wear. But time had revealed its true character. It was not the imperial tiara, that once had caught all eyes, above his dark brows. It was the grave and noble likeness to a skull. The radiance of it belonged to the possessor, not of the world, but of the grave and of eternity. Now, as his hair had withdrawn from it, it gave out the truth frankly and simply. Also, as you got, from the face of the brother, the key of understanding to this particular type of family beauty, you would recognize it at once in the appearance of the sisters, even in the two youthful portraits on the wall. The most striking characteristic in the three heads was the generic resemblance to the skull.

All in all, Morten's countenance was quiet, considerate, and dignified, as it had always been.

"Good evening, little sisters; well met, well met," he said, "it was very sweet and sisterly of you to come and see me here. You had a—" he stopped a moment, as if searching for his word, as if not in the habit of speaking much with other people—"a nice fresh drive to Elsinore, I should say," he concluded.

His sisters sat with their faces toward him, as pale as he. Morten had always been wont to speak very lowly, in contrast to themselves. Thus a discussion between the sisters might be carried on with the two speaking at the same time, on the chance of the one shrill voice drowning the other. But if you wanted to hear what Morten said, you had to listen. He spoke in just the same way now, and they had been prepared for his appearance, more or less, but not for his voice.

They listened then as they had done before. But they were longing to do more. As they had set eyes on him they had turned their slim torsos all around in their chairs. Could they not touch him? No, they knew that to be out of the question. They had not been reading ghost stories all their lives for nothing. And this very thing recalled to them the old days, when, for these private supper-parties of theirs, Morten had come in at times, his large cloak soaked with rain and sea water, shining, black and rough like a shark's skin, or glazed over with snow, or freshly tarred, so that they had, laughing, held him at arm's length off their frocks. Oh, how thoroughly had the tunes of thirty years ago been transposed from a major to a minor key! From what blizzards had he come in tonight? With what sort of tar was he tarred?

"How are you, my dears?" he asked. "Do you have as merry a time in Copenhagen as in the old days at Elsinore?"

"And how are you yourself, Morten?" asked Fanny, her voice a full octave higher than his. "You are looking a real, fine privateer captain. You are bringing all the full, spiced, trade winds into our nunnery of Elsinore."

"Yes, those are fine winds," said Morten.

"How far away you have been, Morten!" said Eliza, her voice trembling a little. "What a multitude of lovely places you have visited, that we have never seen! How I have wished, how I have wished that I were you."

Fanny gave her sister a quick strong glance. Had their thoughts gone up in a parallel motion from the snowy parks and streets of Copenhagen? Or did this quiet sister, younger than she, far less brilliant, speak the simple truth of her heart?

"Yes, Lizzie, my duck," said Morten. "I remember that. I have thought of that—how you used to cry and stamp your little feet and wring your hands shouting, 'Oh, I wish I were dead.' "

"Where do you come from, Morten?" Fanny asked him.

"I come from hell," said Morten. "I beg your pardon," he added, as he saw his sister wince. "I have come now, as you see, because the Sound is frozen over. I can come then. That is a rule.''

Oh, how the heart of Fanny flew upward at his words. She felt it herself, as if she had screamed out, in a shout of deliverance, like a woman in the final moment of childbirth. When the Emperor, from Elba, set foot on the soil of France he brought back the old time with him. Forgotten was red-hot Moscow, and the deadly white and black winter marches. The tricolor was up in the air, unfolded, and the old grenadiers threw up their arms and cried once more: *Vive l'empereur!* Her soul, like they, donned the old uniform. It was for the benefit of onlookers only, and for the fun of the thing, from now, that she was dressed up in the body of an old woman.

"Are we not looking a pair of old scarecrows, Morten?" she asked, her eyes shining at him. "Were not our old aunts right when they preached to us about our vanity, and the vanity of all things? Indeed, the people who impress on the young that they should purchase, in time, crutches and an ear-trumpet, do carry their point in the end."

"No, you are looking charming, Fanny," he said, his eyes shining gently back. "Like a bumblebee-hawkmoth." For they used to collect butterflies together in their childhood. "And if you were really looking like a pair of old ladies I should like it very much. There have been few of them where I have been, for many years. Now when grandmamma had her birthday parties at Øregaard, that was where you would see a houseful of fine old ladies. Like a grand aviary, and grandmamma amongst them like a proud cockatoo."

"Yet, you once said," said Fanny, "that you would give a year of your existence to be free from spending the afternoon with the old devils."

"Yes, I did that," said Morten, "but my ideas about a year of my existence have changed since then. But tell me, seriously, do they still tie weights to *billets-doux,* and throw them into your carriage when you drive home from the balls?"

"Oh!" said Eliza, drawing in her breath.

Was klaget aus dem dunkeln Thal
Die Nachtigall?
Was seufzt darein der Erlenbach
Mit manchem Ach?

She was quoting a long-forgotten poem by a long-forgotten lover.

"You are not married, my dears, are you?" said Morten, suddenly frightened at the absurd possibility of a stranger belonging to his sisters.

"Why should we not be married?" asked Fanny. "We both of us have husbands and lovers at each finger-tip. I, I married the Bishop of Sealand—he lost his balance a little in our bridal bed because of his wings." She could not prevent a delicate thin little laughter coming out of her in small puffs, like steam from a kettle-spout. The Bishop looked, at the distance of forty-eight hours, ridiculously small, like a little doll seen from a tower. "Lizzie married—" she went on, and then stopped herself. When they were children the young De Conincks had lived under a special superstition, which they had from a marionette comedy. It came to this: that the lies which you tell are likely to become truth. On this account they had always been careful in their choice of what lies they would tell. Thus they would never say that they could not pay a Sunday visit to their old aunts because they had a toothache, for they would be afraid that Nemesis might be at their heels, and that they would indeed have a toothache. But they might safely say that their music master had told them not to practice their gavottes any longer, as they already played them with masterly art. The habit was still in their blood.

"No, to speak the truth, Morten," Fanny said, "we are old maids, all on your account. Nobody would have us. The De Conincks have had a bad name as consorts since you went off and took away the heart and soul and innocence of Adrienne."

She looked at him to see what he would say to this. She had followed his thoughts. They had been faithful, but he—what had he done? He had encumbered them with a lovely and gentle sister-in-law.

Their uncle, Fernand De Coninck, he who had helped Morten to get his ship, had in the old days lived in France during the Revolution. That was the place and the time for a De Coninck to live in. Also he had never got quite out of them again, not even when he had been an old bachelor in Elsinore, and he never felt quite at home in a peaceful life. He had been full of anecdotes and songs of the period, and when they had been children the brother and the sisters had known them by heart from him. After a moment Morten slowly and in a low voice began to quote one of Uncle Fernand's ditties. This had been made on a special occasion, when the old aunts of the King of France had been leaving the country, and the revolutionary police had ordered all their boxes to be opened and examined at the frontier, for fear of treachery.

He said:

> *ivez-vous ses chemises,*
> *à Marat?*
> *Avez-vous ses chemises?*
> *C'est pour vous un tres villain cas*
> *si vous les avez prises.*

Fanny's face immediately reflected the expression of her brother's. Without searching her memory more than a moment she followed him with the next verse of the song. This time it is the King's old aunts speaking:

> *Avait-il de chemises,*
> *à Marat?*
> *Avait-il de chemises?*
> *Moi je crois qu'il n'en avait pas.*
> *Ou les avait-il prises?*

And Eliza took up the thread after her, laughing a little:

> *Il en avait trois grises,*
> *à Marat.*

Il en avait trois grises.
Avec l'argent de son mandat
sur le Pont Neuf acquises.

With these words the brother and the sisters lightened their hearts and washed their hands forever of fair, unhappy Adrienne Rosenstand.

"But you were married, Morten?" said Eliza kindly, the laughter still in her voice.

"Yes," said Morten, "I had five wives. The Spanish are lovely women, you know, like a mosaic of jewels. One of them was a dancer, too. When she danced it was really like a swarm of butterflies whirling round, and being drawn into, the little central flame; you did not know what was up and what was down, and that seemed to me then, when I was young, a charming quality in a wife. One was an English skipper's daughter, an honest girl, and she will never have forgotten me. One was the young widow of a rich planter. She was a real lady. All her thoughts had some sort of long train trailing after them. She bore me two children. One was a Negress, and her I liked best."

"Did they go on board your ship?" Eliza asked.

"No, none of them ever came on board my ship," said Morten.

"And tell us," said Fanny, "which, out of all the things that you had, you liked the best?"

Morten thought her question over for a moment. "Out of all lives," he said, "the life of a pirate is the best."

"Finer than that of a privateer captain in the Sound?" asked Fanny.

"Yes, it is that," said Morten, "inasmuch as you are in the open sea."

"But what made you decide to become a pirate?" asked Fanny, much intrigued, for this was really like a book of romance and adventure.

"The heart, the heart," said Morten, "that which throws us into all our disasters. I fell in love. It was the *coup de foudre* of which Uncle Fernand spoke so much. He himself knew it to be no laughing matter. And she was somebody else's, so I could not have her without cheating law and order a little. She was built in Genoa, had been used by the French as a dispatch-carrier, and was known to be the quickest schooner that ever flew over the Atlantic. She was run ashore at the coast of the island of St. Martin, which is half French and half Dutch, and was sold by the Dutch at Philippsburg. Old Van Zandten, the ship-owner, who employed me then and loved me as a son, sent me to Philippsburg to buy her for him. She was the loveliest, yes, by far the loveliest thing I ever saw. She was like a swan. When she came along, carrying the press of her sails, she was light, gallant, noble, a great lady—like one of grandmamma's swans at Øregaard, when we teased them—pure, loyal, like a Damascene blade. And then, my dears, she was a little like *Fortuna II.* She had, like her, a very small foresail with an unusually large mainsail and high boom.

"I took all old Van Zandten's money then and bought her for myself, and after that we had, she and I, to keep off the respectable people of the country. What are you to do when love sets to at you? I made her a faithful lover, and she had a fine time with her loyal crew, adored and petted like a dainty lady who has her toenails polished with henna. With me she became the fear of the Caribbean Sea, the little sea-eaglet who kept the tame birds on the stir. So I do not know for certain whether I did right or wrong. Shall not he have the fair woman who loves her most?"

"And was she in love with you as well?" asked Eliza, laughing.

"But who shall ask a woman if she is in love with him?" said Morten. "The question to ask about woman is this: 'What is her price, and will you pay it?' We should not cheat them, but should ask them courteously and pay with a good grace, whether it be cash, love, marriage, or our life or honor which they charge us; or else, if we are poor people and cannot pay, take off our hats to them and leave them for the wealthier man. That has been sound moral Latin with men and women since the world began. As to their loving us—for one thing, Can they love us?"

"And what of the women who have no price?" said Eliza, laughing still.

"What of those indeed, dear?" said Morten. "Whatever they ought to have been, they should not have been women. God may have them, and he may know what to do with them. They drive men into bad places, and afterward they cannot get us out even when they want to."

"What was the name of your ship?" asked Eliza, her eyes cast down.

Morten looked up at her, laughing. "The name of my ship was *La Belle Eliza*," he answered. "Did you not know?"

"Yes, I knew," said Eliza, her voice full of laughter once more. "A merchant captain of Papa's told me, many years ago in Copenhagen, how his crew had gone mad with fear and had made him turn back into port when, off St. Thomas, they spied the topsails of a pirate ship. They were as afraid of her, he said, as of Satan himself. And he told me that the name of the ship was *La Belle Eliza*. I thought then that she would be your boat."

So this was the secret which the old maid had guarded from all the world. She had not been marble all through. Somewhere within her this little flame of happiness had been kept alive. To this purpose—for it had been to no other—had she grown up so lovely in Elsinore. A ship was in blue water, as in a bed of hyacinths, in winds and warm air, her full white sails like to a bold chalk-cliff, baked by the sun, with much sharp steel in boards, not one of the broadswords or knives not red, and the name of the ship fairly and truly *La Belle Eliza*. Oh, you burghers of Elsinore, did you see me dance the minuet once? To those same measures did I tread the waves.

While he had been speaking the color had mounted to her face. She looked once more like a girl, and the white streamers of her cap were no longer the finery of an old lady, but the attire of a chaste, flaming bride.

"Yes, she was like a swan," Morten said, "sweet, sweet, like a song."

"Had I been in that merchant ship," said Eliza, "and you had boarded her, your ship should have been mine by right, Morten."

"Yes," said he, smiling at her, "and my whole *matelotage*. That was our custom when we took young women. You would have had an adoring seraglio."

"I lost her," he said, "through my own fault, at a river mouth of Venezuela. It is a long story. One of my men betrayed her anchoring place to the British governor of Port of Spain, in Trinidad. I was not with her then. I had gone myself the sixty miles to Port of Spain in a fishing boat, to get information about a Dutch cargo boat. I saw all my crew hanged there, and saw her for the last time.

"It was after that," he said after a pause, "that I never slept well again. I could not get down into sleep. Whenever I tried to dive down into it I was shoved upward again, like a piece of flotsam. From that time I began to lose weight, for I had thrown overboard my ballast. It was with her. I had become too light for anything. From that time on I was somehow without body. Do you remember how Papa and Uncle Fernand used to discuss, at dinner, the wines which they had bought together, and to talk of some of them having a fine enough bouquet, but no body to them? That was the case with me, then, my dears: a bouquet I should say that I may still have had, but no body. I could not sink into friendship, or fear, or any real delight any longer. And still I could not sleep."

The sisters had no need to pretend sympathy with this misfortune. It was their own. All the De Conincks suffered from sleeplessness. When they had been children they had laughed at their father and his sisters when they greeted one another in the morning first of all with minute inquiries and accounts of how they had slept at night. Now they did not laugh; the matter meant much to them also now.

"But when you cannot sleep at night," said Fanny, sighing, "is it that you wake up very early, or is it that you cannot fall asleep at all?"

"Nay, I cannot fall asleep at all," said Morten.

"Is it not, then," asked Fanny, "because you are—" She would have said "cold," but remembering where he had said he came from, she stopped herself.

"And I have known all the time," said Morten, who did not seem to have heard what she said to him, "that I shall never lay me down to rest until I can sleep once more on her, in her, *La Belle Eliza*."

"But you lived ashore, too," said Fanny, her mind running after his, for she felt as if he were about to escape her.

"Yes, I did," said Morten. "I had for some time a tobacco plantation in Cuba. And that was a delightful place. I had a white house with pillars which you would have liked very much. The air of those islands is fine, delicate, like a glass of true rum. It was there that I had the lovely wife, the planter's widow, and two children. There were women to dance with there, at our balls, light like the trade winds—like you two. I had a very pretty pony to ride there, named Pegasus; a little like Papa's Zampa. Do you remember him?"

"And you were happy there?" Fanny asked.

"Yes, but it did not last," said Morten. "I spent too much money. I lived beyond my means, something which Papa had always warned me against. I had to clear out of it." He sat silent for a little while.

"I had to sell my slaves," he said.

At these words he grew so deadly pale, so ashen gray, that had they not known him to be dead for long they would have been afraid that he might be going to die. His eyes, all his features, seemed to sink into his face. It became the face of a man upon the stake, when the flames take hold.

The two women sat pale and rigid with him, in deep silence. It was as if the breath of the hoarfrost had dimmed three windows. They had no word of comfort for their brother in this situation. For no De Coninck had ever parted with a servant. It was a code to them that whoever entered their service must remain there and be looked after by them forever. They might make an exception with regard to marriage or death, but unwillingly. In fact it was the opinion of their circle of friends that in their old age the sisters had come to have only one real object in life, which was to amuse their servants.

Also they felt that secret contempt for all men, as beings unable to raise money at any fatal moment, which belongs to fair women with their consciousness of infinite resources. The sisters De Coninck, in Cuba, would never have allowed things to come to such a tragic point. Could they not easily have sold themselves three hundred times, and made three hundred Cubans happy, and so saved the welfare of their three hundred slaves? There was, therefore, a long pause.

"But the end," said Fanny finally, drawing in her breath deeply, "that was not yet, then?"

"No, no," said Morten, "not till quite a long time after that. When I had no more money I started an old brig in the carrying trade, from Havana to New Orleans first, and then from Havana to New York. Those are difficult seas." His sister had succeeded in turning his mind away from his distress, and as he began to explain to her the various routes of his trade he warmed to his subject. Altogether he had, during the meeting, become more and more sociable and had got back all his old manner of a man who is at ease in company and is in really good understanding with the minds of his convives. "But nothing would go right for me," he went on. "I had one run of bad luck after another. No, in the end, you see, my ship foundered near the Cay Sal bank, where she ran full of water and sank in a dead calm; and with one thing and another, in the end, if you do not mind my saying so, in Havana I was hanged. Did you know that?"

"Yes," said Fanny.

"Did you mind that, I wondered, you two?" he asked.

"No!" said his sisters with energy.

They might have answered him with their eyes turned away, but they both looked back at him. And they thought that this might perhaps be the reason why he was wearing his collar and stock so unusually high; there might be a mark on that strong and delicate neck around which they had tied the cambric with great pains when they had been going to balls together.

There was a moment's silence in the red room, after which Fanny and Morten began to speak at the same time.

"I beg your pardon," said Morten.

"No," said Fanny, "no. What were you going to say?"

"I was asking about Uncle Fernand," said Morten. "Is he still alive?"

"Oh, no, Morten, my dear," said Fanny, "he died in 'thirty. He was an old man then. He was at Adrienne's wedding, and made a speech, but he was very tired. In the evening he took me aside and said to me: 'My dear, it is a *gênante fête.*' And he died only three weeks later. He left Eliza his money and furniture. In a drawer we found a little silver locket, set with rose diamonds, with a curl of fair hair, and on it was written, 'The hair of Charlotte Corday.' "

"I see," said Morten. "He had a fine figure, Uncle Fernand. And Aunt Adelaide, is she dead too?"

"Yes, she died even before he did," said Fanny. She meant to tell him something of the death of Madame Adelaide De Coninck, but did not go on. She felt depressed. These people were dead; he ought to have known of them. The loneliness of her dead brother made her a little sick at heart.

"How she used to preach to us, Aunt Adelaide," he said. "How many times did she say to me: 'This melancholy of yours, Morten, this dissatisfaction with life which you and the girls allow yourselves, makes me furious. What is good enough for me is good enough for you. You all ought to be married and have large families to look after; that would cure you.' And you, Fanny, said to her: 'Yes, little Aunt, that was the advice, from an auntie of his, which our Papa did follow.' "

"Toward the end," Eliza broke in, "she would not hear or think of anything that had happened since the time when she was thirty years old and her husband died. Of her grandchildren she said: 'These are some of the new-fangled devices of my young children. They will soon find out how little there is to them.' But she could remember all the religious scruples of Uncle Theodore, her husband, and how he had kept her awake at night with meditations upon the fall of man and original sin. Of those she was still proud."

"You must think me very ignorant," Morten said. "You know so many things of which I know nothing."

"Oh, dear Morten," said Fanny, "you surely know of a lot of things of which we know nothing at all."

"Not many, Fanny," said Morten. "One or two, perhaps."

"Tell us one or two," said Eliza.

Morten thought over her demand for a little while.

"I have come to know of one thing," he said, "of which I myself had no idea once. *C'est une invention très fine, très spirituelle, de la part de Dieu,* as Uncle Fernand said of love. It is this: that you cannot eat your cake and have it. I should never have hit upon that on my own. It is indeed an original idea. But then, you see, he is really *très fin, très spirituel,* the Lord."

The two sisters drew themselves up slightly, as if they had received a compliment. They were, as already said, keen church-goers, and their brother's words had ever carried great weight with them.

"But do you know," said Morten suddenly, "that little snappy pug of Aunt Adelaide's, Fingal—him I have seen."

"How was that?" Fanny asked. "Tell us about that."

"That was when I was all alone," said Morten, "when my ship had foundered at the Cay Sal bank. We were three who got away in a boat, but we had no water. The others died, and in the end I was alone."

"What did you think of then?" Fanny asked.

"Do you know, I thought of you," said Morten.

"What did you think of us?" Fanny asked again in a low voice.

Morten said, "I thought: we have been amateurs in saying no, little sisters. But God can say no. Good God, how he can say no. We think that he can go on no longer, not even he. But he goes on, and says no once more.

"I had thought of that before, quite a good deal," Morten said, "at Elsinore, during the time before my wedding. And now I kept on thinking upon it. I thought of those great, pure, and beautiful things which say no to us. For why should they say yes to us, and tolerate our insipid caresses? Those who say yes, we get them under us, and we ruin them and leave them, and find when we have left them that they have made us sick. The earth says yes to our schemes and our work, but the sea says no; and we, we love the sea ever. And to hear God say no, in the stillness, in his own voice, that to us is very good. The starry sky came up, there, and said no to me as well. Like a noble, proud woman."

"And did you see Fingal then?" Eliza asked.

"Yes," said Morten. "Just then. As I turned my head a little,

Fingal was sitting with me in the boat. You know, he was an ill-tempered little dog always, and he never liked me because I teased him. He used to bite me every time he saw me. I dared not touch him there in the boat. I was afraid that he would snap at me again. Still, there he sat, and stayed with me all night."

"And did he go away then?" Fanny asked.

"I do not know, my dear," Morten said. "An American schooner, bound for Jamaica, picked me up in the early morning. There on board was a man who had bid against me at the sale in Philippsburg. In this way it came to pass that I was hanged—in the end, as you say—at Havana."

"Was that bad?" asked Fanny in a whisper.

"No, my poor Fanny," said Morten.

"Was there anyone with you there?" Fanny whispered.

"Yes, there was a fat young priest there," said Morten. "He was afraid of me. They probably told him some bad things about me. But still he did his best. I asked him: 'Can you obtain for me, now, one minute more to live in?' He said, 'What will you do with one minute of life, my poor son?' I said, 'I will think, with the halter around my neck, for one minute of *La Belle Eliza.*' "

While they now sat in silence for a little while, they heard some people pass in the street below the window, and talk together. Through the shutters they could follow the passing flash of their lanterns.

Morten leaned back in his chair, and he looked now to his sisters older and more worn than before. He was indeed much like their father, when the Papa De Coninck had come in from his office tired, and had taken pleasure in sitting down quietly in the company of his daughters.

"It is very pleasant in here, in this room," he said, "it is just like old days—do you not think so? With Papa and Mamma below. We three are not very old yet. We are good-looking people still."

"The circle is complete again," said Eliza gently, using one of their old expressions.

"Is completed, Lizzie," said Morten, smiling back at her.

"The vicious circle," said Fanny automatically, quoting another of their old familiar terms.

"You were always," said Morten, "such a clever lass."

At these kind direct words Fanny impetuously caught at her breath.

"And, oh, my girls," Morten exclaimed, "how we did long then, with the very entrails of us, to get away from Elsinore!"

His elder sister suddenly turned her old body all around in the chair, and faced him straight. Her face was changed and drawn with pain. The long wake and the strain began to tell on her, and she spoke to him in a hoarse and cracked voice, as if she were heaving it up from the innermost part of her chest.

"Yes," she cried, "yes, you may talk. But you mean to go away again and leave me. You! You have been to these great warm seas of which you talk, to a hundred countries. You have been married to five people. Oh, I do not know of it all! It is easy for you to speak quietly, to sit still. You have never needed to beat your arms to keep warm. You do not need to now!"

Her voice failed her. She stuttered in her speech and clasped the edge of the table. "And here," she groaned out, "I am—cold. The world is bitterly cold around me. I am so cold at night, in my bed, that my warming-pans are no good to me!"

At this moment the tall grandfather's clock started to strike, for Fanny had herself wound it up in the afternoon. It struck midnight in a grave and slow measure, and Morten looked quickly up at it.

Fanny meant to go on speaking, and to lift at last all the deadly weight of her whole life off her, but she felt her chest pressed together. She could not out-talk the clock, and her mouth opened and shut twice without a sound.

"Oh, hell," she cried out, "to hell!"

Since she could not speak she stretched out her arms to him, trembling. With the strokes of the clock his face became gray and blurred to her eyes, and a terrible panic came upon her. Was it for this that she had wound up the clock! She threw herself toward him, across the table.

"Morten!" she cried in a long wail. "Brother! Stay! Listen! Take me with you!"

As the last stroke fell, and the clock took up its ticking again, as if it meant to go on doing something, in any case, through all eternity, the chair between the sisters was empty, and at the sight Fanny's head fell down on the table.

She lay like that for a long time, without stirring. From the winter night outside, from far away to the north, came a resounding tone, like the echo of a cannon shot. The children of Elsinore knew well what it meant: it was the ice breaking up somewhere, in a long crack.

Fanny thought, dully, after a long while, What is Eliza thinking? and laboriously lifted her head, looked up, and dried her mouth with her little handkerchief. Eliza sat very still opposite her, where she had been all the time. She dragged the streamers of her cap downward and together, as if she were pulling a rope, and Fanny remembered seeing her, long, long ago, when angry or in great pain or joy, pulling in the same way at her long golden tresses. Eliza lifted her pale eyes and stared straight at her sister's face.

"To think," said she, " 'to think, with the halter around my neck, for one minute of *La Belle Eliza.*' "

LOST

LIVES

Max Eberts

I would only draw pictures of an ocean liner, a long sleek liner with four raked funnels. I was nearly five when I drew my first one. Sometimes I drew the ship sailing across the sea on a bright day, other times skimming across a calm sea at night, all the deck lights and portholes glowing bright. This went on for months. Of all those pictures, only a few had a view of the shore in the background—two of them during the day with green rolling hills miles away and one at night with city lights shimmering on the shore.

By the time I was six, I only drew pictures of the liner at night, rows of portholes glowing yellow, their lights reflecting on the calm black sea, and hundreds of stars filling the sky above. Often I drew in the tiny silhouettes of a few passengers walking along the promenade or upper decks. I got quite good. Many of them were "remarkable for a six-year-old," according to people who came to our house and saw them. "What a beautiful ship that is," or "Isn't that a wonderful drawing of an ocean liner at night?" I remember them saying. My parents also liked them. My father, a U.S. Navy Admiral, said "it was only natural that I drew ships." A family friend once remarked, "Maybe he'll be a commodore." Occasionally, someone would ask me, "Why a four-funneled ship?" or "How do you know about four-funneled liners?" I didn't know. I always shook my head with a strange feeling that suddenly made me anxious.

One day not long after my seventh birthday, I drew a picture of the four-funneled liner at night. The sea was calm, the stars bright as stars in Christmas cards of nights with shepherds and wise men. The ship's lights reflected on the dark water. But in this picture, the ship was dipping at the bow. The liner was sinking. I drew this again and again. Month after month, I labored over my drawings—always the same long liner with four funnels, always sinking at night, going down at the bow. But each new drawing emerged with more details. Passengers began to crowd the deck around the lifeboats. Some of the lifeboats began to lower. Others floated nearby, their occupants looking back at the sight—the ship a blaze of lights. I colored their reflections on the midnight water. Above I always colored in a thousand stars.

This went on for years. My father tried to interest me in navy ships, hoping I might draw them. Once I heard him tell my mother, "It won't be long before he's drawing other ships or things. Let him sink this ship, and he'll move on to drawing other things." But I continued to only draw the four-funneled ocean liner sinking at night.

My second-grade teacher, Sister Sylvia, was alarmed. My third-grade teacher, Sister Katherine, said my drawings were "an unhealthy obsession." They called my parents, who didn't know what to do. "Why do you always draw these sinking ships?" they finally asked. I had no answer.

I did things other boys did. I played baseball and dodge ball, climbed trees, rode bikes, and swam at the Officer's Club. But when I didn't play with the other boys, I came inside to draw my sinking ship. Sometimes, my mother watched me make my drawings. I know she must have been concerned. I was a quiet boy. For years, she called me her incense burner. I must have been like one—something inside me, foreign, mysterious, quietly consuming me.

My drawings became more and more elaborate. By the time I was eight, I was spending days on them. The scene was always the same: the night imbued with the deepest blues, the sky saturated with stars, the lights of the ship reflecting on the calm water as the liner's bow dipped into the navy-black sea. Some of the pictures I thought were beautiful, and so did others. One of my parents' friends offered to buy one. He finally convinced my parents that by selling it, they could use the money to buy me art supplies.

Months later my parents paid for me to have art lessons. "He has obvious talent," they told their friends, who agreed. But I know they really hoped I would draw other things. It didn't happen. Instead, I drew more sophisticated renderings of the sinking ship.

By ten, I had learned perspective, and my color drawings began to look more and more realistic. Or, as my art teacher put it, "very convincing." Yet, people who saw them said they were mysterious. By 10, I was making watercolor and oil paintings of the sinking ship—always the same liner but different views, sometimes unexpected angles that took people by surprise. In one of the paintings, seen from starboard side, the sea rushed the forward decks, while beyond, on the horizon, a strange light, as if from a distant ship, seemed to glow through a mist. Another one was from the point-of-view of a lifeboat lowering, its passengers looking up the hull of the ship, the rows of bright portholes getting smaller toward the vanishing point. Another looked from a distance toward the starboard side of the ship, the entire length of the liner a shadowy structure defined by golden lights piercing the deep blue night, the rows of lights listing toward the bow. There was also the one I painted on a huge canvas. Its point-of-view was from high above off to the port side, the liner's lights burning faintly below, the midnight sea stretching out, the stars bursting above the horizon. Everyone who saw it loved that painting the most. Even my parents liked that one and hung it in the dining room, the admiral's dining room with its rich paneled walls, mahogany table, and a captain's clock. I loved looking at that painting while I ate dinner.

Most of the other paintings were in my room. Nearly every square inch of my wall space was occupied by them. There were even two large paintings that hung flat against my ceiling. I would look at them at night lying in bed. On moonlit nights, the light streaming in my window illuminated certain paintings on the

wall, their deep blues becoming luminous. Soon there were
paintings everywhere—in the basement where I painted them,
stacked in closets, or hanging in bathrooms. Those favorites that
were not already hanging in my room, I hung on the hallway
walls leading to my room. Because my father was a Navy admiral,
we moved every so often. The months before we moved I would
give many of the paintings away. But I saved most of my favorites.
And as soon as we were settled in our new quarters, I would
begin painting again.

When I was eleven, I was looking through a book about ocean
liners and came across a picture of a painting of a great four-
funneled liner sinking. It was breathtaking. I remember how my
heart pounded and blood rushed to my head when I first saw it.
Something inside of me, inside of my heart was all at once
thrilled, fascinated, and terrified, as when one passes an automobile accident at night and the red flashing police and ambulance
lights tell you that maybe someone has died here. But this was
different because the sight of the ship was beautiful and spectac-
ular. It moved me with a power of something like a huge natural
disaster or a fantastic Biblical event. The ship was named *Titanic,*
and its sight stirred something inside of me I couldn't understand.
My eyes drank in every detail. My drawings took on the exact
details of *Titanic.*

And then there were the dreams, the recurring dreams. I'm always a boy. I don't really know how old I am—somewhere between 12 and 16. I'm always outside on a cold night, on an upper
deck of a magnificent liner—a four-funneled liner. I'm wearing a
fine wool overcoat. The sky is dense with stars—stars dense as a
dream itself—winter stars, all of them winter-blue, brighter than
Polaris. Suddenly, there are thousands of tiny ice crystals like the
finest snow floating down—a myriad of prisms reflecting the
deck lights. They vanish. The sounds of the air passing through
the ship's rigging, the sea breaking at the bow and pushing away
from the ship's sides, the steady rhythm of the ship's vibrations,
all become silent. A group of string musicians strike up lively

tunes. They are joined later by another cellist. Well-dressed passengers trickle into lifeboats.

Sometimes in the dream I'm searching for my family. Other
times, I'm alone. But always there is this other boy—15 or 16. He
tells me things about the ship, the passengers, and the crew and
leads me about the boat. He is wearing a fine wool coat like mine
and a white shirt with an Eaton collar and a silk tie. I think he has
an English accent.

Always in my dream, the serene sea creeping up the hull glows
green from the lights still burning bright in the submerged state-
rooms and saloons. Soon the water is rushing toward me, up the
forward decks. The ship's pitch steepens. Everything is crashing.
I slide into the icy water. From aft I hear the screams of a thousand people. They sound like ghostly spirits wailing. They sound
like Lucifer's angels falling.

I would always wake shivering with chills and the terror of
being alone in the cold black sea—mobs and mobs of silent stars
above. For days afterward, the images of peoples' faces filled my
head—the people I encountered in the dream, especially the boy
in the wool overcoat and the blue silk tie. "Who was he?" I
became obsessed with him. I even drew him, attempting to re-
construct every detail of his face—his boyish handsome face, his
dark eyebrows and hair, his blue eyes, blue even in the cold dark
night.

On my twelfth birthday, my crazy Aunt Polly—who had been a
nun for six years before leaving her order, and who claims she
was a nun in a past life—presented me with membership in the
Titanic Historical Society and a first edition copy of Walter
Lord's, *A Night to Remember* and said, "Perhaps, my dear, you
were on the *Titanic* in your previous life." The idea of reincarnation was very mysterious to me. Perhaps because it was considered taboo. I was, after all, a Catholic in a Catholic family, attending Catholic boy's school, and on Sundays Catholic Mass and
catechism. I was fully aware that my religion, and for that matter,
my parents or any of the nuns and priests who taught me, did not
take reincarnation seriously. Still, the notion of having lived in a
previous time and place fascinated me.

That evening I read *A Night to Remember* and was once again mesmerized. It all made sense, senseless as it was: a maiden voyage of the world's most magnificent liner, *Titanic* racing serenely across the cold calm North Atlantic, while the iceberg streamed in collision course, its icy finger buckling the steel of the ship's forward hull. The drama and spectacle of the ship upending, then plunging into the sea's cold black slip, into death's icy grip, seemed all too real. Aunt Polly was right: I was on that ship.

So many startling details—one stuck in my mind. *Titanic* sank in the wee hours of April 15. I was born at 2:25 A.M. on April 15, the exact time and date that over 1500 people drowned when *Titanic* went down.

The next day I called Aunt Polly: "Did I die that night? Which passenger was I?" She replied, "With your lineage you likely voyaged first class."

My search began. I memorized names of first-class passengers—who survived, who perished. I read numerous books about *Titanic,* hoping something would trigger a hidden memory of my past life. I wrote the president of the *Titanic* Historical Society regularly and told him of my revelation. He sent me accounts of survivors and copies of articles that had appeared in magazines and newspapers, many from 1912. I read Henry Sleeper Harper's self-absorbed account of the sinking. This was a first-class passenger who got into a lifeboat with his Egyptian manservant and his Pekingese dog. I read Colonel Gracie's *A Survivor's Story* and was amazed how he was at the launching of every lifeboat. He seemed to be everywhere on the boat deck at once. I learned endless details about the Astors, the Ryersons, the Harpers, the Carters, the Allisons, the Duff-Gordons. Though fascinated with the comings and goings of first-class passengers, I discovered nothing about me.

I kept thinking about the boy who always appears in my recurring dreams. He must have been there. Was I that boy? With his fine wool coat, silk tie, and white shirt with an Eaton collar, he must have been a first-class passenger. I continued to look for any clue that might tell me something about the boy—something about me.

I came across a 17-year-old's account of what happened that night. John Borland Thayer, Jr. was his name. He seemed familiar. I felt as if I knew or had met young Jack. The son of wealthy industrialist, John Borland Thayer, Jack was traveling with his parents in first class. That night he got separated from his parents, and in the last minutes of the ship's life, he jumped into the darkness and swam to an overturned lifeboat. He survived. Jack's story kindled something inside me. He spoke of how in the last minutes of the disaster, in the swirling chaos, he was one in "a mass of hopeless, dazed humanity, attempting as the Almighty and nature made us, to keep our breath until the last possible moment."

Giving up on the first class, I searched for clues from in the accounts of second-class passengers, and though a few teenage boys in second class drowned that night, I could find nothing that was like looking in a mirror.

I was drawn to third class, their hard lives, their high hopes, their harder luck. I was horrified to learn that more first-class men survived than third-class children. Of those who drowned in third class, it was very hard to learn their stories, which were lost with their lives. There was little interest in their stories. The steerage, as they were called, were mere immigrants lost trying to cross the border. They might as well have been a school of fallen angels with cloven feet.

The April I turned thirteen, my parents took a sailing trip. My parents loved the sea as much as I, and we often went sailing. My father, who for years before I was born was a Navy aviator, loved sailing the sea more than flying. "Walking the waters under the stars is to wander into God's country," he would say. He took us "voyaging" in his sloop, a beautiful old fifty-footer he spent years restoring, though he claimed it restored him. Her name, *Aquellos Mundos*, "Those Worlds," places we dreamed of sailing to, the Lesser Antilles, the Cyclades, New Hebrides, Polynesia—flowers scattered across the oceans. On clear nights at sea, we would gaze at the stars, my father reflecting out loud how small we are in the cosmos, my mother adding how when we're born, God sets a star afire. "People and stars," she would say, "isn't it amazing the way God brought us together?"

One night—a still moonless night—of our April voyage to a place called Porchau Mund, the wind had died and so had our engine. There wasn't even a flutter of breeze—the water a black mirror reflecting the shimmerings of stars so big the mast skimmed blooms of light. The sky was a valley of flowering clover we might fall into. We turned off the lanterns. The stars bloomed again. Was the valley or the boat drifting? The mast balanced us between two heavens. We gave ourselves to this limbo, gave up our bodies, our features, became mere voices, became black inlets jutting into splendor—the way we might have been in the world before the womb, floating in the floating, a vast dark place, the glimmer of blossoms breaking through.

Later that night, we saw a bright light appear on the horizon. Through the binoculars we watched the light become two lights, then four lights, then eight—like a living thing springing from the sea. Was it a yacht? A tanker? A destroyer? The lights swelled larger and brighter, until what we viewed with wonder suddenly was upon us, a sea-blown arrival, coming head-on. Frightening my mother, it streamed toward us on collision-course. The bow, a juggernaut of power, towered higher as it moved closer—sixty, fifty yards away. Just as we were preparing to jump, the ship veered starboard, my father shouting, "Look at the size of her!" Long and sleek, a thousand feet, it was an ocean liner lit from prow to stern. There was music, strains of strings, soft notes of clarinets and oboes floating down, weaving in and out of a saxophone's lead. Women in evening gowns, men in dinner jackets, were dancing on an aft deck. Others strolled along the promenade. I could hear their laughter, their voices, things they said. And the lights! Never had I seen such lights—deck lamps and rows of portholes like golden Japanese lanterns strung for a party, all glimmering on the water. Was it real? This floating steel phantom of people and lights, passing strange and wonderful? We rocked then drifted in its wake, a blue trail of phosphorescence churned up by the liner's turbines. I wanted to be on that ship!

We watched it disappear the way it came—a bright star on the horizon, then nothing.

That night I dreamed I can't find my family. "There aren't enough lifeboats," an officer tells a wealthy passenger. The lights from portholes and decks reflect on black water—calm, cold as a glacial lake. A sextet begins to play. Officers help women and children into boats—women in evening gowns and long cloaks, one wears chinchilla over a nightgown with silk slippers, children in mackinaws and scarves. Men in tuxedos, others in overcoats and bowlers, kiss loved ones good-by. "Get in," I'm told. "Not without my family," I say. A handsome boy of fifteen or so brings forth a child. The officer takes the child but refuses the boy. The boy's eyes are the color of his blue silk tie. The boat lowers. A newlywed yells down to his bride, "I'll beat you to New York!" We watch the boat drift away. On Upper Deck my family calls out my name. In wool coats and life jackets, we're hugging, huddling. The funnels blast with steam. A distress rocket takes off in a stream of luminous blue, lost to a galaxy. The ship pitches forward. The last lifeboat lowers. The music stops. Passengers peer out at the darkness—the lifeboats darker than the black of the sea. The night is sodden with stars never seen, like the great city of lights from the other world. The steerage class bursts from below—hundreds, women and children in waves of panic. My father is leading us. Glass and large things are crashing. A rush of sea sweeps my parents away. The black water is a slow cold ether—the cries, the stars whirling all around me.

I awoke, my breath nearly stolen from me, my heart racing, my entire body shivering with fear. The dream was so real. "It was a dream," I told myself. In my sleeping bag on the sloop's aft deck, I looked at the stars—the stars I always see in my dream before I die. It took me a moment to figure out that I wasn't still dreaming. It was cold. My parents must have placed blankets over my sleeping bag. Toward the bow, my father was holding vigil, keeping watch for any ocean traffic and waiting for a wind. My mother was asleep in a sleeping bag next to him. We were all here. We were all safe. I just lay there stunned, gazing up at the silent fire.

I fell asleep—and dreamed again.

* * *

I'm on an upper deck looking aft. From where I am, I can see three of the ship's funnels. I'm wearing my wool coat. I'm thrilled by the night, the stars, the cold air whistling through the rigging, the ship's lulling vibration, the bow slicing through the calm sea. This night only the stars are more wonderful than the ship.

I hear a bell ring three times—sharply, quickly—forward of the bridge. A minute later there is a shudder and a scraping noise. Moments after that, I see what looks like a glistening mast of a windjammer glide by. Thousands of whiskers of light like a fine snow of tiny prisms are suddenly falling all around me. They vanish. Then everything is still. Until steam begins to burst from three of the funnels.

I rise from the deck chair. Standing next to me is the dark-haired handsome boy in the blue silk tie and the wool overcoat like mine.

"They're serving brandy and port inside," he says. "Let's go have one."

"How old are you?" I ask.

"I just turned 16," he says.

"I'm not even that. Aren't we too young for brandy?"

"Not this cold night. You had better drink up," he says.

We walk down a grand stairway crowned with a glass dome that radiates soft white light that reflects off the polished oak walls and the black iron and gilt balustrade. Well-dressed people are gathered near the stairway landing. It doesn't seem like I'm on a ship, but rather a European palace or fine hotel. He leads me down a wide hallway toward music and the sound of many conversations. We enter a large room he says is the first-class lounge. It is warm and light, a stately spacious room. A small string ensemble is playing.

"They're playing 'Glow Worm'!" I say laughing. "I never knew 'Glow Worm' could sound so grand and grown-up."

"Oh, you like music?" He smiles and then looks at the crowd with delight.

Elegantly dressed people are mingling throughout the room. Some of the men are in tuxedos, others in suits. One man wears a smoking jacket. A very few people, perhaps five in the entire room, are actually wearing life jackets. A woman is calling out to Elinor, who is wearing a beautiful gown with what looks like a silk cape over her shoulders. "That's Mrs. Widener with her son Harry," he tells me with his slight English accent. "They're loaded, as you Americans would say." There is laughing. A woman enters with a fur coat over silk slippers and a silk night-gown that drags below her fur. "O Charlotte!" another woman exclaims.

"That's Mrs. Charlotte Cardeza. She's also from Philadelphia and is very wealthy."

Nearby, I overhear a pretty woman say to her friend, "I heard Charlotte brought a dozen trunks and 70 dresses on this cross-ing—and that's all she could throw together?" Her friend, who is older and nearly as pretty, replies, "Well, my dear, I can't say that I blame her. It seems we spend half our lives dressing and un-dressing. We're forever changing our clothes." They both laugh.

He takes two brandy snifters of cognac from a silver tray held by a waiter wearing a white jacket and white gloves. The waiter looks disapprovingly. "We're French," the boy says with author-ity, handing me one. "Drink up, it's the finest cognac."

"Did you feel the ship hit the iceberg, Lucille?" a man to our right in a navy-blue, three-button suit, asks an older attractive woman.

"Look. There are the Thayers."

"Where?" I ask, hoping to see young Jack.

"Over by the fireplace."

I look and see Mr. and Mrs. Thayer.

"They're from Philadelphia . . ."

"I know, and they're very wealthy," I add.

He just smiles. "Philadelphia must be beautiful."

"Do you think so? By the way, do you know their son Jack?"

"No, but I know who he is; I saw him tonight."

The room is like a party. The musicians strike up "The Merry Widow Waltz." And as the passengers talk among themselves, moving about the room—the women with their graceful ges-tures, the men standing straight holding their gloves in one hand—I see what the boy sees with his clear blue eyes: a people who may as well be the most elegant, self-assured people ever. There was a sense that being perfectly well-dressed and well-mannered gave one an inward grace and fulfillment that even religion was unable to provide.

"You know, every night of the voyage I put on my best trousers, my finest white shirt, and one of two silk ties I own, and I put on this fine wool coat that was my father's and go walking all through the first-class sections of the ship, and everyone thinks I'm one of them."

"Who are you?" I ask him.

"I'm not one of them. I wish I were. Follow me," he says.

We finish our cognacs, and as we leave the room, I notice that the ship has a definite forward list. By the door a steward hands us lifebelts. I follow the boy outside onto the promenade deck, walking aft. It's bitter cold. We enter another beautiful room that opens into another stairway, much like the grand stairway we walked down earlier. The white glass dome above is not as large.

"This is the aft grand stairway," he tells me. "In here is the first-class smoking room." We peek in. We hear the voices of men and see a table of men playing cards. "There's a revolving door on the other side. You'll have to see it," he adds with excitement.

We walk down the stairway through an arched entry door and into what has to be the most beautiful restaurant. The walls are a polished fruit wood with carved details, and throughout the room are carved wood columns. The carpet is thick and the color of red wine. The tables are set for the next day, gleaming with white table cloths, crystal, and china. Arranged around them are plushly upholstered chairs.

"This is the a la carte restaurant," he says. "I'm an assistant saucier. Messier Gatti, the owner, hired me the night before *Titanic* set sail, after he ate a meal I prepared for him. It all happened so fast; I don't know if he even has had time to report my hiring. But it doesn't matter. I don't work for White Star Line. The a la carte restaurant is private."

He tells me about how he worked as a cook in a small Southampton restaurant and about the lamb dish he made for Gatti the

night before *Titanic* sailed. He tells me of how he is all alone, his
mother and father both dead. He wears a gold ring that was his
father's. He's showing me the table Captain Smith sat at tonight
when we hear breaking glass. Things are breaking and crashing
around us.

We run up the aft grand stairway and into the promenade deck.
People are running the opposite way. He yells for me not to go
that way but to follow him. We run toward the bow, back into
the grand stairway. He lifts up a little boy—six or seven—who is
alone and crying. We run up the stairway and can see water,
swirling below, crashing and rushing in from above. The roar is
terrifying. There are people screaming from below and many others rushing along beside us. We make it out to the boat deck to
starboard side. There are no lifeboats, and no elegant people mill-
ing about. The bow is completely submerged. The ship not only
is pitching forward, it is listing to port. From the edge of the
deck, I can see rows of portholes glowing beneath the water. On
deck, the lights burn golden, then orange, then almost an eerie
red. Hundreds of desperate people are pressing around an unlaunched collapsible boat—some frantically struggling to get in.
Shots are fired. Total chaos breaks out, water lapping against the
forward end of the boat deck. The ship takes a sudden forward
plunge. A large wave suddenly lunges toward us. Everyone gathered around the unlaunched collapsible is swept away. Screams
are drowned out by the roar of the wave.

Somehow I'm now holding the little boy's hand. I don't see my
blue-eyed friend anywhere. I notice his ring on my hand—as if I
have become him. The little boy and I scramble up the deck
toward the stern. He seems too terrified to scream or cry. We run
into a wall of people. The wave swallows us and we are washed
against the boat deck wall. The little boy is swept away, his hand
pulled from mine. Complete panic is racing through me. I'm trying to find him. I'm struggling under the freezing water for at
least a minute. Someone strong has grabbed onto my leg and is
pulling me deeper. I shake loose with everything I have and swim
toward the green glow of deck lights, the icy water stinging my
eyes. I latch on to the railing above the officer's quarters and

crawl up on the roof of the grand stairway, alongside the covered dome. As I'm catching my breath, I can hear loud rattles, roars, and crashing sounds coming from within the ship. I can still feel the little boy's hand leaving mine.

The cables of the first funnel are snapping. The funnel rips from its mounting with a tearing roar and crashes into the water. I climb down to the deck where the compass platform is, between the second and third funnel. I climb up to the platform by the third funnel and then down into the second-class boat deck, between the third and fourth funnel. The ship's stern is rearing up to such an incredible angle that those climbing aft can no longer move. They can only hang on. I'm clinging to a railing and am looking down at tiny figures bobbing in the water. The lights go out. The crashing sounds feel as if they are right below me, snapping, mangling, and ripping like two trains crashing. We're going down into darkness. Something knocks me into the icy water. The screams are like the wails of thousands falling from great heights. I'm struck by a falling woman and hit by pieces of wood rising to the surface. I see the light of the stern mast slide away. Hundreds and hundreds of people are crying out. I see the black silhouette of the stern—a black finger pointing to black sky. It disappears. And there rose into the night the chilling cries coming from a thousand and a half throats of men, women, and children—people screaming for the lifeboats to come back, screaming for members of their family who were separated from them, screaming from the painful cold of the water stabbing them, screaming for help, screaming for their lives. As I swim around, I pass groups of three or four or five people joined in a circle by locking their arms. I pass one group, a family perhaps, with seven people, many of them children joined together in a circle. I pass a mother holding her child on some floating wreckage. The woman is weeping. The cries continue from those drifting about. My arms and legs ache from the planks of wood that struck me. They ache from the cold. It is getting harder to cry out, harder to breathe. I keep swimming to find a boat. No boats are coming. I raise my hand out of the water and touch the gold ring. I see a shooting star. I see the mobs of silent stars—silent as those safe in the lifeboats.

For years I had recurrences of this dream—a dream as restless as the unknown graves of lost lives. For years I am haunted by the blue-eyed boy. I search for his face in the faces of my school-mates, in the faces of boys on the playing fields, in the faces of grown-up boys—even women who might look like his mother.

There have been other related strange episodes in my life. One night, late for a Phillies baseball game, we were hurrying toward the stadium. From the distance we heard the roar of the crowd. I fell to the ground and wept uncontrollably, the sound reminding me of the horrible screams that cold April night. Another time, I prepared a dinner for my parents' wedding anniversary—rack of lamb with a pear cognac sauce. To this day it is our favorite dinner. I had never cooked before. Of course I live in Philadel-phia and even now I can still feel the small hand of the little boy slipping out of mine.

The month I turned sixteen, I received a large parcel from *Titanic* International, one of many *Titanic* Historical Societies I joined. In the parcel were photographs and information about the recovery of bodies in the aftermath of the liner's sinking. Three Canadian ships were sent on the difficult mission of recov-ering bodies of passengers and crew. The first ship out was the *Mackay-Bennett,* and one of the first bodies recovered was that of a two-year-old, blond-haired boy. Three hundred and twenty-eight floating dead were plucked from the sea, many amid wind-ing trails of wreckage. Faces of the bodies recovered were photo-graphed in an effort to later identify them.

I was stunned to see a photo of the handsome blue-eyed boy. His face was still handsome, his eyes were open—clear and blue, even though it was a black and white photo. He wore his fine wool coat and his blue silk tie. Many were buried at sea, once they were documented. His body, however, with other recovered bodies believed to be those of first-class passengers, was brought back to Halifax. Even the dead bodies of *Titanic*'s first-class pas-sengers received special treatment because they would be claimed by family. A footnote with the photo stated that the boy was fifteen or sixteen. He was well-dressed and wore a gold ring. He was never identified. He is buried at Halifax. I made a pilgrimage there.

The boy has left his mark. He was not a boy of privilege. I was, yet I feel as much an outsider among my privileged peers as he did among patrons of the a la carte restaurant. As a man I am still the boy, "the kid," easily dismissed, by colleagues who don't consider me a "major player," passed over for the big money cases at my law firm. In my legal cases, I represent those who have been exploited by the wealthy. In my dreams at night, I am always a boy, a youth wanting to be remembered, wanting people to see the courage within me. Now, when I walk along city streets, through airports, or railway stations, I look for lost lives in passing faces—those who know about death's stealth, death's icy grip, the sea's black slip.

THE
SHADOWY
THIRD

Ellen Glasgow

When the call came I remember that I turned from the telephone in a romantic flutter. Though I had spoken only once to the great surgeon, Roland Maradick, I felt on that December afternoon that to speak to him only once—to watch him in the operating-room for a single hour—was an adventure which drained the color and the excitement from the rest of life. After all these years of work on typhoid and pneumonia cases, I can still feel the delicious tremor of my young pulses; I can still see the winter sunshine slanting through the hospital windows over the white uniforms of the nurses.

"He didn't mention me by name. Can there be a mistake?" I stood, incredulous yet ecstatic, before the superintendent of the hospital.

"No, there isn't a mistake. I was talking to him before you came down." Miss Hemphill's strong face softened while she looked at me. She was a big, resolute woman, a distant Canadian relative of my mother's, and the kind of nurse I had discovered in the month since I had come up from Richmond, that Northern hospital boards, if not Northern patients, appear instinctively to select. From the first, in spite of her hardness, she had taken a liking—I hesitate to use the word "fancy" for a preference so impersonal—to her Virginia cousin. After all, it isn't every Southern nurse, just out of training, who can boast a kinswoman in the superintendent of a New York hospital.

166

"And he made you understand positively that he meant me?" The thing was so wonderful that I simply couldn't believe it.

"He asked particularly for the nurse who was with Miss Hudson last week when he operated. I think he didn't even remember that you had a name. When I asked if he meant Miss Randolph, he repeated that he wanted the nurse who had been with Miss Hudson. She was small, he said, and cheerful-looking. This, of course, might apply to one or two of the others, but none of these was with Miss Hudson."

"Then I suppose it is really true?" My pulses were tingling. "And I am to be there at six o'clock?"

"Not a minute later. The day nurse goes off duty at that hour, and Mrs. Maradick is never left by herself for an instant."

"It is her mind, isn't it? And that makes it all the stranger that he should select me, for I have had so few mental cases."

"So few cases of any kind," Miss Hemphill was smiling, and when she smiled I wondered if the other nurses would know her. "By the time you have gone through the treadmill in New York, Margaret, you will have lost a good many things besides your inexperience. I wonder how long you will keep your sympathy and your imagination? After all, wouldn't you have made a better novelist than a nurse?"

"I can't help putting myself into my cases. I suppose one ought not to?"

"It isn't a question of what one ought to do, but of what one must. When you are drained of every bit of sympathy and enthusiasm, and have got nothing in return for it, not even thanks, you will understand why I try to keep you from wasting yourself."

"But surely in a case like this—for Doctor Maradick?"

"Oh, well, of course—for Doctor Maradick." She must have seen that I implored her confidence, for, after a minute, she let fall carelessly a gleam of light on the situation: "It is a very sad case when you think what a charming man and a great surgeon Doctor Maradick is."

Above the starched collar of my uniform I felt the blood leap in bounds to my cheeks. "I have spoken to him only once," I murmured, "but he is charming, and so kind and handsome, isn't he?"

"His patients adore him."

"Oh, yes, I've seen that. Everyone hangs on his visits." Like the patients and the other nurses, I also had come by delightful, if imperceptible, degrees to hang on the daily visits of Doctor Maradick. He was, I suppose, born to be a hero to women. From my first day in his hospital, from the moment when I watched, through closed shutters, while he stepped out of his car, I have never doubted that he was assigned to the great part in the play. If I had been ignorant of his spell—of the charm he exercised over his hospital—I should have felt it in the waiting hush, like a dawn breath, which followed his ring at the door and preceded his imperious footstep on the stairs. My first impression of him, even after the terrible events of the next year, records a memory that is both careless and splendid. At that moment, when, gazing through the chinks in the shutters, I watched him, in his coat of dark fur, cross the pavement over the pale streaks of sunshine, I knew beyond any doubt—I knew with a sort of infallible pre-science—that my fate was irretrievably bound up with his in the future. I knew this, I repeat, though Miss Hemphill would still insist that my foreknowledge was merely a sentimental gleaning from indiscriminate novels. But it wasn't only first love, impres-sionable as my kinswoman believed me to be. It wasn't only the way he looked. Even more than his appearance—more than the shining dark of his eyes, the silvery brown of his hair, the dusky glow in his face—even more than his charm and his magnifi-cence, I think, the beauty and sympathy in his voice won my heart. It was a voice, I heard someone say afterwards, that ought always to speak poetry.

So you will see why—if you do not understand at the begin-ning, I can never hope to make you believe impossible things!—so you will see why I accepted the call when it came as an imperative summons. I couldn't have stayed away after he sent for me. However much I may have tried not to go, I know that in the end I must have gone. In those days, while I was still hoping to write novels, I used to talk a great deal about "destiny" (I have learned since then how silly all such talk is), and I suppose it was my "destiny" to be caught in the web of Roland Maradick's personality. But I am not the first nurse to grow love-sick about a doctor who never gave her a thought.

"I am glad you got the call, Margaret. It may mean a great deal to you. Only try not to be too emotional." I remember that Miss Hemphill was holding a bit of rose-geranium in her hand while she spoke—one of the patients had given it to her from a pot she kept in her room, and the scent of the flower is still in my nostrils—or my memory. Since then—oh, long since then—I have wondered if she also had been caught in the web.

"I wish I knew more about the case." I was pressing for light. "Have you ever seen Mrs. Maradick?"

"Oh, dear, yes. They have been married only a little over a year, and in the beginning she used to come sometimes to the hospital and wait outside while the doctor made his visits. She was a very sweet-looking woman then—not exactly pretty, but fair and slight, with the loveliest smile, I think, I have ever seen. In those first months she was so much in love that we used to laugh about it among ourselves. To see her face light up when the doctor came out of the hospital and crossed the pavement to his car, was as good as a play. We never tired of watching her—I wasn't superintendent then, so I had more time to look out of the window while I was on day duty. Once or twice she brought her little girl in to see one of the patients. The child was so much like her that you would have known them anywhere for mother and daughter."

I had heard that Mrs. Maradick was a widow, with one child, when she first met the doctor, and I asked now, still seeking an illumination I had not found, "There was a great deal of money, wasn't there?"

"A great fortune. If she hadn't been so attractive, people would have said, I suppose, that Doctor Maradick married her for her money. Only," she appeared to make an effort of memory, "I believe I've heard somehow that it was all left in trust away from Mrs. Maradick if she married again. I can't, to save my life, remember just how it was; but it was a queer will, I know, and Mrs.

Maradick wasn't to come into the money unless the child didn't live to grow up. The pity of it—"

A young nurse came into the office to ask for something—the keys, I think, of the operating-room, and Miss Hemphill broke off inconclusively as she hurried out of the door. I was sorry that she left off just when she did. Poor Mrs. Maradick! Perhaps I was too emotional, but even before I saw her I had begun to feel her pathos and her strangeness.

My preparations took only a few minutes. In those days I always kept a suitcase packed and ready for sudden calls; and it was not yet six o'clock when I turned from Tenth Street into Fifth Avenue, and stopped for a minute, before ascending the steps, to look at the house in which Doctor Maradick lived. A fine rain was falling, and I remember thinking, as I turned the corner, how depressing the weather must be for Mrs. Maradick. It was an old house, with damp-looking walls (though that may have been because of the rain) and a spindle-shaped iron railing which ran up the stone steps to the black door, where I noticed a dim flicker through the old-fashioned fanlight. Afterwards I discovered that Mrs. Maradick had been born in the house—her maiden name was Calloran—and that she had never wanted to live anywhere else. She was a woman—this I found out when I knew her better—of strong attachments to both persons and places; and though Doctor Maradick had tried to persuade her to move uptown after her marriage, she had clung, against his wishes, to the old house in lower Fifth Avenue. I dare say she was obstinate about it in spite of her gentleness and her passion for the doctor. Those sweet, soft women, especially when they have always been rich, are sometimes amazingly obstinate. I have nursed so many of them since—women with strong affections and weak intellects—that I have come to recognize the type as soon as I set eyes upon it.

My ring at the bell was answered after a little delay, and when I entered the house I saw that the hall was quite dark except for the waning glow from an open fire which burned in the library. When I gave my name, and added that I was the night nurse, the servant appeared to think my humble presence unworthy of illumination. He was an old negro butler, inherited perhaps from Mrs. Maradick's mother, who, I learned afterwards, was from South Carolina; and while he passed me on his way up the staircase, I heard him vaguely muttering that he "wa'n't gwinter tu'n on dem lights twel de chile had done playin'."

To the right of the hall, the soft glow drew me into the library, and crossing the threshold timidly, I stooped to dry my wet coat by the fire. As I bent there, meaning to start up at the first sound of a footstep, I thought how cozy the room was after the damp walls outside to which some bared creepers were clinging; and I was watching the strange shapes and patterns the firelight made on the old Persian rug, when the lamps of a slowly turning motor flashed on me through the white shades at the window. Still dazzled by the glare, I looked round in the dimness and saw a child's ball of red and blue rubber roll towards me out of the gloom of the adjoining room. A moment later, while I made a vain attempt to capture the toy as it spun past me, a little girl darted airily, with peculiar lightness and grace, through the doorway, and stopped quickly, as if in surprise at the sight of a stranger. She was a small child—so small and slight that her footsteps made no sound on the polished floor of the threshold; and I remember thinking while I looked at her that she had the gravest and sweetest face I had ever seen. She couldn't—I decided this afterwards—have been more than six or seven years old, yet she stood there with a curious prim dignity, like the dignity of an elderly person, and gazed up at me with enigmatical eyes. She was dressed in Scotch plaid, with a bit of red ribbon in her hair, which was cut in a fringe over her forehead and hung very straight to her shoulders. Charming as she was, from her uncurled brown hair to the white socks and black slippers on her little feet, I recall most vividly the singular look in her eyes, which appeared in the shifting light to be of an indeterminate color. For the odd thing about this look was that it was not the look of childhood at all. It was the look of profound experience, of bitter knowledge.

"Have you come for your ball?" I asked; but while the friendly question was still on my lips, I heard the servant returning. In my confusion I made a second ineffectual grasp at the plaything, which had rolled away from me into the dusk of the drawing-room. Then, as I raised my head, I saw that the child also had slipped from the room; and without looking after her I followed the old negro into the pleasant study above, where the great surgeon awaited me.

Ten years ago, before hard nursing had taken so much out of me, I blushed very easily, and I was aware at the moment when I crossed Doctor Maradick's study that my cheeks were the color of peonies. Of course, I was a fool—no one knows this better than I do—but I had never been alone, even for an instant, with him before, and the man was more than a hero to me, he was—there isn't any reason now why I should blush over the confession—almost a god. At that age I was mad about the wonders of surgery, and Roland Maradick in the operating-room was magician enough to have turned an older and more sensible head than mine. Added to his great reputation and his marvelous skill, he was, I am sure of this, the most splendid-looking man, even at forty-five, that one could imagine. Had he been ungracious—had he been positively rude to me, I should still have adored him; but when he held out his hand, and greeted me in the charming way he had with women, I felt that I would have died for him. It is no wonder that a saying went about the hospital that every woman he operated on fell in love with him. As for the nurses—well, there wasn't a single one of them who had escaped his spell—not even Miss Hemphill, who could have been scarcely a day under fifty.

"I am glad you could come, Miss Randolph. You were with Miss Hudson last week when I operated?"

I bowed. To save my life I couldn't have spoken without blushing the redder.

"I noticed your bright face at the time. Brightness, I think, is what Mrs. Maradick needs. She finds her day nurse depressing." His eyes rested so kindly upon me that I have suspected since that he was not entirely unaware of my worship. It was a small thing, heaven knows, to flatter his vanity—a nurse just out of a training-school—but to some men no tribute is too insignificant to give pleasure.

"You will do your best, I am sure." He hesitated an instant—just long enough for me to perceive the anxiety beneath the genial smile on his face—and then added gravely, "We wish to avoid, if possible, having to send her away."

I could only murmur in response, and after a few carefully chosen words about his wife's illness, he rang the bell and directed the maid to take me upstairs to my room. Not until I was ascending the stairs to the third story did it occur to me that he had really told me nothing. I was as perplexed about the nature of Mrs. Maradick's malady as I had been when I entered the house.

I found my room pleasant enough. It had been arranged—at Doctor Maradick's request, I think—that I was to sleep in the house, and after my austere little bed at the hospital, I was agreeably surprised by the cheerful look at the apartment into which the maid led me. The walls were papered in roses, and there were curtains of flowered chintz at the window, which looked down on a small formal garden at the rear of the house. This the maid told me, for it was too dark for me to distinguish more than a marble fountain and a fir-tree, which looked old, though I afterwards learned that it was replanted almost every season.

In ten minutes I had slipped into my uniform and was ready to go to my patient; but for some reason—to this day I have never found out what it was that turned her against me at the start—Mrs. Maradick refused to receive me. While I stood outside her door I heard the day nurse trying to persuade her to let me come in. It wasn't any use, however, and in the end I was obliged to go back to my room and wait until the poor lady got over her whim and consented to see me. That was long after dinner—it must have been nearer eleven than ten o'clock—and Miss Peterson was quite worn out by the time she came for me.

"I'm afraid you'll have a bad night," she said as we went downstairs together. That was her way, I soon saw, to expect the worst of everything and everybody.

"Does she often keep you up like this?"

"Oh, no, she is usually very considerate. I never knew a sweeter character. But she still has this hallucination—"

Here again, as in the scene with Doctor Maradick, I felt that the explanation had only deepened the mystery. Mrs. Maradick's hallucination, whatever form it assumed, was evidently a subject for evasion and subterfuge in the household. It was on the tip of my tongue to ask, "What is her hallucination?"—but before I could get the words past my lips we had reached Mrs. Maradick's door, and Miss Peterson motioned me to be silent. As the door opened a little way to admit me, I saw that Mrs. Maradick was already in bed, and that the lights were out except for a night-lamp burning on a candle-stand beside a book and a carafe of water.

"I won't go in with you," said Miss Peterson in a whisper; and I was on the point of stepping over the threshold when I saw the little girl, in the dress of Scotch plaid, slip by me from the dusk of the room into the electric light of the hall. She held a doll in her arms, and as she went by she dropped a doll's work-basket in the doorway. Miss Peterson must have picked up the toy, for when I turned in a minute to look for it I found that it was gone. I remember thinking that it was late for a child to be up—she looked delicate, too—but, after all, it was no business of mine, and four years in a hospital had taught me never to meddle in things that do not concern me. There is nothing a nurse learns quicker than not to try to put the world to rights in a day.

When I crossed the floor to the chair by Mrs. Maradick's bed, she turned over on her side and looked at me with the sweetest and saddest smile.

"You are the night nurse," she said in a gentle voice; and from the moment she spoke I knew that there was nothing hysterical or violent about her mania—or hallucination, as they called it. "They told me your name, but I have forgotten it."

"Randolph—Margaret Randolph." I liked her from the start, and I think she must have seen it.

"You look very young, Miss Randolph."

"I am twenty-two, but I suppose I don't look quite my age. People usually think I am younger."

For a minute she was silent, and while I settled myself in the chair by the bed, I thought how strikingly she resembled the little girl I had seen first in the afternoon, and then leaving her room a few moments before. They had the same small, heart-shaped faces, colored ever so faintly; the same straight, soft hair, between brown and flaxen; and the same large, grave eyes, set very far apart under arched eyebrows. What surprised me most, however, was that they both looked at me with that enigmatical and vaguely wondering expression—only in Mrs. Maradick's face the vagueness seemed to change now and then to a definite fear—a flash, I had almost said, of startled horror.

I sat quite still in my chair, and until the time came for Mrs. Maradick to take her medicine not a word passed between us. Then, when I bent over her with the glass in my hand, she raised her head from the pillow and said in a whisper of suppressed intensity:

"You look kind. I wonder if you could have seen my little girl?"

As I slipped my arm under the pillow I tried to smile cheerfully down on her. "Yes, I've seen her twice. I'd know her anywhere by her likeness to you."

A glow shone in her eyes, and I thought how pretty she must have been before illness took the life and animation out of her features. "Then I know you're good." Her voice was so strained and low that I could barely hear it. "If you weren't good you couldn't have seen her."

I thought this queer enough, but all I answered was, "She looked delicate to be sitting up so late."

A quiver passed over her thin features, and for a minute I thought she was going to burst into tears. As she had taken the medicine, I put the glass back on the candle-stand, and bending over the bed, smoothed the straight brown hair, which was as fine and soft as spun silk, back from her forehead. There was something about her—I don't know what it was—that made you love her as soon as she looked at you.

"She always had that light and airy way, though she was never sick a day in her life," she answered calmly after a pause. Then, groping for my hand, she whispered passionately, "You must not tell him—you must not tell any one that you have seen her!"

"I must not tell any one?" Again I had the impression that had come to me first in Doctor Maradick's study, and afterwards with Miss Peterson on the staircase, that I was seeking a gleam of light in the midst of obscurity.

"Are you sure there isn't any one listening—that there isn't any one at the door?" she asked, pushing aside my arm and raising herself on the pillows.

"Quite, quite sure. They have put out the lights in the hall."

"And you will not tell him? Promise me that you will not tell him." The startled horror flashed from the vague wonder of her expression. "He doesn't like her to come back, because he killed her."

"Because he killed her!" Then it was that light burst on me in a blaze. So this was Mrs. Maradick's hallucination! She believed that her child was dead—the little girl I had seen with my own eyes leaving her room; and she believed that her husband—the great surgeon we worshipped in the hospital—had murdered her. No wonder they veiled the dreadful obsession in mystery! No wonder that even Miss Peterson had not dared to drag the horrid thing out into the light! It was the kind of hallucination one simply couldn't stand having to face.

"There is no use telling people things that nobody believes," she resumed slowly, still holding my hand in a grasp that would have hurt me if her fingers had not been so fragile. "Nobody believes that he killed her. Nobody believes that she comes back every day to the house. Nobody believes—and yet you saw her—"

"Yes, I saw her—but why should your husband have killed her?" I spoke soothingly, as one would speak to a person who was quite mad. Yet she was not mad, I could have sworn this while I looked at her.

For a moment she moaned inarticulately, as if the horror of her thoughts were too great to pass into speech. Then she flung out her thin, bare arm with a wild gesture.

"Because he never loved me!" she said. "He never loved me!"

"But he married you," I urged gently while I stroked her hair. "If he hadn't loved you, why should he have married you?"

"He wanted the money—my little girl's money. It all goes to him when I die."

"But he is rich himself. He must make a fortune from his profession."

"It isn't enough. He wanted millions." She had grown stern and tragic. "No, he never loved me. He loved someone else from the beginning—before I knew him."

It was quite useless, I saw, to reason with her. If she wasn't mad, she was in a state of terror and despondency so black that it had almost crossed the border-line into madness. I thought once that I would go upstairs and bring the child down from her nursery; but, after a moment's hesitation, I realized that Miss Peterson and Doctor Maradick must have long ago tried all these measures. Clearly, there was nothing to do except soothe and quiet her as much as I could; and this I did until she dropped into a light sleep which lasted well into the morning.

By seven o'clock I was worn out—not from work but from the strain on my sympathy—and I was glad, indeed, when one of the maids came in to bring me an early cup of coffee. Mrs. Maradick was still sleeping—it was a mixture of bromide and chloral I had given her—and she did not wake until Miss Peterson came on duty an hour or two later. Then, when I went downstairs, I found the dining-room deserted except for the old housekeeper, who was looking over the silver. Doctor Maradick, she explained to me presently, had his breakfast served in the morning-room on the other side of the house.

"And the little girl? Does she take her meals in the nursery?"

She threw me a startled glance. Was it, I questioned afterwards, one of distrust or apprehension?

"There isn't any little girl. Haven't you heard?"

"Heard? No. Why, I saw her only yesterday."

The look she gave me—I was sure of it now—was full of alarm.

"The little girl—she was the sweetest child I ever saw—died just two months ago of pneumonia."

"But she couldn't have died." I was a fool to let this out, but the shock had completely unnerved me. "I tell you I saw her yesterday."

The alarm in her face deepened. "That is Mrs. Maradick's trouble. She believes that she still sees her."

"But don't you see her?" I drove the question home bluntly.

"No." She set her lips tightly. "I never see anything."

So I had been wrong, after all, and the explanation, when it came, only accentuated the terror. The child was dead—she had died of pneumonia two months ago—and yet I had seen her, with my own eyes, playing ball in the library; I had seen her slipping out of her mother's room, with her doll in her arms.

"Is there another child in the house? Could there be a child belonging to one of the servants?" A gleam had shot through the fog in which I was groping.

"No, there isn't any other. The doctors tried bringing one once, but it threw the poor lady into such a state she almost died of it. Besides, there wouldn't be any other child as quiet and sweet-looking as Dorothea. To see her skipping along in her dress of Scotch plaid used to make me think of a fairy, though they say that fairies wear nothing but white or green."

"Has any one else seen her—the child, I mean—any of the servants?"

"Only old Gabriel, the colored butler, who came with Mrs. Maradick's mother from South Carolina. I've heard that negroes often have a kind of second sight—though I don't know that that is just what you would call it. But they seem to believe in the supernatural by instinct, and Gabriel is so old and doty—he does no work except answer the door-bell and clean the silver—that nobody pays much attention to anything that he sees—"

"Is the child's nursery kept as it used to be?"

"Oh, no. The doctor had all the toys sent to the children's hospital. That was a great grief to Mrs. Maradick; but Doctor Brandon thought, and all the nurses agreed with him, that it was best for her not to be allowed to keep the room as it was when Dorothea was living."

"Dorothea? Was that the child's name?"

"Yes, it means the gift of God, doesn't it? She was named after the mother of Mrs. Maradick's first husband, Mr. Ballard. He was the grave, quiet kind—not the least like the doctor."

I wondered if the other dreadful obsession of Mrs. Maradick's had drifted down through the nurses or the servants to the housekeeper; but she said nothing about it, and since she was, I suspected, a garrulous person, I thought it wiser to assume that the gossip had not reached her.

A little later, when breakfast was over and I had not yet gone upstairs to my room, I had my first interview with Doctor Brandon, the famous alienist who was in charge of the case. I had never seen him before, but from the first moment that I looked at him I took his measure almost by intuition. He was, I suppose, honest enough—I have always granted him that, bitterly as I have felt towards him. It wasn't his fault that he lacked red blood in his brain, or that he had formed the habit, from long association with abnormal phenomena, of regarding all life as a disease. He was the sort of physician—every nurse will understand what I mean—who deals instinctively with groups instead of with individuals. He was long and solemn and very round in the face; and I hadn't talked to him ten minutes before I knew he had been educated in Germany, and that he had learned over there to treat every emotion as a pathological manifestation. I used to wonder what he got out of life—what any one got out of life who had analyzed away everything except the bare structure.

When I reached my room at last, I was so tired that I could barely remember either the questions Doctor Brandon had asked or the directions he had given me. I fell asleep, I know, almost as soon as my head touched the pillow; and the maid who came to inquire if I wanted luncheon decided to let me finish my nap. In the afternoon, when she returned with a cup of tea, she found me still heavy and drowsy. Though I was used to night nursing, I felt as if I had danced from sunset to daybreak. It was fortunate, I reflected, while I drank my tea, that every case didn't wear on one's sympathies as acutely as Mrs. Maradick's hallucination had worn on mine.

Through the day I did not see Doctor Maradick; but at seven o'clock when I came up from my early dinner on my way to take the place of Miss Peterson, who had kept on duty an hour later than usual, he met me in the hall and asked me to come into his study. I thought him handsomer than ever in his evening clothes, with a white flower in his buttonhole. He was going to some public dinner, the housekeeper told me, but, then, he was always going somewhere. I believe he didn't dine at home a single evening that winter.

"Did Mrs. Maradick have a good night?" He had closed the door after us, and turning now with the question, he smiled kindly, as if he wished to put me at ease in the beginning.

"She slept very well after she took the medicine. I gave her that at eleven o'clock."

For a minute he regarded me silently, and I was aware that his personality—his charm—was focused upon me. It was almost as if I stood in the center of converging rays of light, so vivid was my impression of him.

"Did she allude in any way to her—to her hallucination?" he asked.

How the warning reached me—what invisible waves of sense-perception transmitted the message—I have never known; but while I stood there, facing the splendor of the doctor's presence, every intuition cautioned me that the time had come when I must take sides in the household. While I stayed there I must stand either with Mrs. Maradick or against her.

"She talked quite rationally," I replied after a moment.

"What did she say?"

"She told me how she was feeling, that she missed her child, and that she walked a little every day about her room."

His face changed—how I could not at first determine.

"Have you seen Doctor Brandon?"

"He came this morning to give me his directions."

"He thought her less well today. He has advised me to send her to Rosedale."

I have never, even in secret, tried to account for Doctor Maradick. He may have been sincere. I tell you only what I know—not what I believe or imagine—and the human is sometimes as inscrutable, as inexplicable, as the supernatural.

While he watched me I was conscious of an inner struggle, as if opposing angels warred somewhere in the depths of my being. When at last I made my decision, I was acting less from reason, I knew, than in obedience to the pressure of some secret current of thought. Heaven knows, even then, the man held me captive while I defied him.

"Doctor Maradick,"I lifted my eyes for the first time frankly to his, "I believe that your wife is as sane as I am—or as you are."

He started. "Then she did not talk freely to you?"

"She may be mistaken, unstrung, piteously distressed in mind"—I brought this out with emphasis—"but she is not—I am willing to stake my future on it—a fit subject for an asylum. It would be foolish—it would be cruel to send her to Rosedale."

"Cruel, you say?" A troubled look crossed his face, and his voice grew very gentle. "You do not imagine that I could be cruel to her?"

"No, I do not think that." My voice also had softened.

"We will let things go on as they are. Perhaps Doctor Brandon may have some other suggestion to make." He drew out his watch and compared it with the clock—nervously, I observed, as if his action were a screen for his discomfiture or perplexity. "I must be going now. We will speak of this again in the morning."

But in the morning we did not speak of it, and during the month that I nursed Mrs. Maradick I was not called again into her husband's study. When I met him in the hall or on the staircase, which was seldom, he was as charming as ever; yet, in spite of his courtesy, I had a persistent feeling that he had taken my measure on that evening, and that he had no further use for me.

As the days went by Mrs. Maradick seemed to grow stronger. Never, after our first night together, had she mentioned the child to me; never had she alluded by so much as a word to her dreadful charge against her husband. She was like any woman recovering from a great sorrow, except that she was sweeter and gentler. It is no wonder that everyone who came near her loved her; for there was a mysterious loveliness about her like the mystery of light, not of darkness. She was, I have always thought, as much of an angel as it is possible for a woman to be on this earth. And yet,

angelic as she was, there were times when it seemed to me that
she both hated and feared her husband. Though he never entered
her room while I was there, and I never heard his name on her
lips until an hour before the end, still I could tell by the look of
terror in her face whenever his step passed down the hall that
her very soul shivered at his approach.

During the whole month I did not see the child again, though
one night, when I came suddenly into Mrs. Maradick's room, I
found a little garden, such as children make out of pebbles and
bits of box, on the window-sill. I did not mention it to Mrs.
Maradick, and a little later, as the maid lowered the shades, I
noticed that the garden had vanished. Since then I have often
wondered if the child were invisible only to the rest of us, and if
her mother still saw her. But there was no way of finding out
except by questioning, and Mrs. Maradick was so well and patient
that I hadn't the heart to question. Things couldn't have been
better with her than they were, and I was beginning to tell myself
that she might soon go out for an airing, when the end came so
suddenly.

It was a mild January day—the kind of day that brings the
foretaste of spring in the middle of winter, and when I came
downstairs in the afternoon, I stopped a minute by the window
at the end of the hall to look down on the box maze in the
garden. There was an old fountain, bearing two laughing boys in
marble, in the center of the graveled walk, and the water, which
had been turned on that morning for Mrs. Maradick's pleasure,
sparkled now like silver as the sunlight splashed over it. I had
never before felt the air quite so soft and springlike in January;
and I thought, as I gazed down on the garden, that it would be a
good idea for Mrs. Maradick to go out and bask for an hour or so
in the sunshine. It seemed strange to me that she was never
allowed to get any fresh air except the air that came through her
windows.

When I went into her room, however, I found that she had no
wish to go out. She was sitting, wrapped in shawls, by the open
window, which looked down on the fountain; and as I entered
she glanced up from a little book she was reading. A pot of daffo-

dils stood on the window-sill—she was very fond of flowers and we tried always to keep some growing in her room.

"Do you know what I am reading, Miss Randolph?" she asked in her soft voice; and she read aloud a verse while I went over to the candle-stand to measure out a dose of medicine.

" 'If thou hast two loaves of bread, sell one and buy daffodils, for bread nourisheth the body, but daffodils delight the soul.' That is very beautiful, don't you think so?"

I said "Yes," that it was beautiful; and then I asked her if she wouldn't go downstairs and walk about in the garden.

"He wouldn't like it," she answered; and it was the first time she had mentioned her husband to me since the night I came to her. "He doesn't want me to go out."

I tried to laugh her out of the idea; but it was no use, and after a few minutes I gave up and began talking of other things. Even then it did not occur to me that her fear of Doctor Maradick was anything but a fancy. I could see, of course, that she wasn't out of her head; but sane persons, I knew, sometimes have unaccountable prejudices, and I accepted her dislike as a mere whim or aversion. I did not understand then and—I may as well confess this before the end comes—I do not understand any better today. I am writing down the things I actually saw, and I repeat that I have never had the slightest twist in the direction of the miraculous.

The afternoon slipped away while we talked—she talked brightly when any subject came up that interested her—and it was the last hour of day—that grave, still hour when the movement of life seems to droop and falter for a few precious minutes—that brought us the thing I had dreaded silently since my first night in the house. I remember that I had risen to close the window, and was leaning out for a breath of the mild air, when there was the sound of steps, consciously softened, in the hall outside, and Doctor Brandon's usual knock fell on my ears. Then, before I could cross the room, the door opened, and the doctor entered with Miss Peterson. The day nurse, I knew, was a stupid woman; but she had never appeared to me so stupid, so armored and encased in her professional manner, as she did at that moment.

"I am glad to see that you are taking the air." As Doctor Brandon came over to the window, I wondered maliciously what devil of contradictions had made him a distinguished specialist in nervous diseases.

"Who was the other doctor you brought this morning?" asked Mrs. Maradick gravely; and that was all I ever heard about the visit of the second alienist.

"Someone who is anxious to cure you." He dropped into a chair beside her and patted her hand with his long, pale fingers. "We are so anxious to cure you that we want to send you away to the country for a fortnight or so. Miss Peterson has come to help you to get ready, and I've kept my car waiting for you. There couldn't be a nicer day for a trip, could there?"

The moment had come at last. I knew at once what he meant, and so did Mrs. Maradick. A wave of color flowed and ebbed in her thin cheeks, and I felt her body quiver when I moved from the window and put my arms on her shoulders. I was aware again, as I had been aware that evening in Doctor Maradick's study, of a current of thought that beat from the air around into my brain. Though it cost me my career as a nurse and my reputation for sanity, I knew that I must obey that invisible warning.

"You are going to take me to an asylum," said Mrs. Maradick.

He made some foolish denial or evasion; but before he had finished I turned from Mrs. Maradick and faced him impulsively. In a nurse this was flagrant rebellion, and I realized that the act wrecked my professional future. Yet I did not care—I did not hesitate. Something stronger than I was driving me on.

"Doctor Brandon," I said, "I beg you—I implore you to wait until tomorrow. There are things I must tell you."

A queer look came into his face, and I understood, even in my excitement, that he was mentally deciding in which group he should place me—to which class of morbid manifestations I must belong.

"Very well, very well, we will hear everything," he replied

soothingly; but I saw him glance at Miss Peterson, and she went over to the wardrobe for Mrs. Maradick's fur coat and hat.

Suddenly, without warning, Mrs. Maradick threw the shawls away from her, and stood up. "If you send me away," she said, "I shall never come back. I shall never live to come back."

The grey of twilight was just beginning, and while she stood there, in the dusk of the room, her face shone out as pale and flower-like as the daffodils on the window-sill. "I cannot go away!" she cried in a sharper voice. "I cannot go away from my child!"

I saw her face clearly; I heard her voice; and then—the horror of the scene sweeps back over me!—I saw the door open slowly and the little girl run across the room to her mother. I saw the child lift her little arms, and I saw the mother stoop and gather her to her bosom. So closely locked were they in that passionate embrace that their forms seemed to mingle in the gloom that enveloped them.

"After this can you doubt?" I threw out the words almost savagely—and then, when I turned from the mother and child to Doctor Brandon and Miss Peterson, I knew breathlessly—oh, there was a shock in the discovery!—that they were blind to the child. Their blank faces revealed the consternation of ignorance, not of conviction. They had seen nothing except the vacant arms of the mother and the swift, erratic gesture with which she stooped to embrace some invisible presence. Only my vision— and I have asked myself since if the power of sympathy enabled me to penetrate the web of material fact and see the spiritual form of the child—only my vision was not blinded by the clay through which I looked.

"After this can you doubt?" Doctor Brandon had flung my words back to me. Was it his fault, poor man, if life had granted him only the eyes of flesh? Was it his fault if he could see only half of the thing there before him?

But they couldn't see, and since they couldn't see I realized that it was useless to tell them. Within an hour they took Mrs. Maradick to the asylum; and she went quietly, though when the time came for parting from me she showed some faint trace of feeling. I remember that at the last, while we stood on the pavement, she lifted her black veil, which she wore for the child, and said: "Stay with her, Miss Randolph, as long as you can. I shall never come back."

Then she got into the car and was driven off, while I stood looking after her with a sob in my throat. Dreadful as I felt it to be, I didn't, of course, realize the full horror of it, or I couldn't have stood there quietly on the pavement. I didn't realize it, indeed, until several months afterwards when word came that she had died in the asylum. I never knew what her illness was, though I vaguely recall that something was said about "heart failure"—a loose enough term. My own belief is that she died simply of the terror of life.

To my surprise Doctor Maradick asked me to stay on as his office nurse after his wife went to Rosedale; and when the news of her death came there was no suggestion of my leaving. I don't know to this day why he wanted me in the house. Perhaps he thought I should have less opportunity to gossip if I stayed under his roof; perhaps he still wished to test the power of his charm over me. His vanity was incredible in so great a man. I have seen him flush with pleasure when people turned to look at him in the street, and I know that he was not above playing on the sentimental weakness of his patients. But he was magnificent, heaven knows! Few men, I imagine, have been the objects of so many foolish infatuations.

The next summer Doctor Maradick went abroad for two months, and while he was away I took my vacation in Virginia. When we came back the work was heavier than ever—his reputation by this time was tremendous—and my days were so crowded with appointments, and hurried flittings to emergency cases, that I had scarcely a minute left in which to remember poor Mrs. Maradick. Since the afternoon when she went to the asylum the child had not been in the house; and at last I was beginning to persuade myself that the little figure had been an optical illusion—the effect of shifting lights in the gloom of the old rooms—not the apparition I had once believed it to be. It does not take long for a phantom to fade from the memory—especially when one leads the active and methodical life I was forced into that winter. Perhaps—who knows?—(I remember telling myself) the doctors may have been right, after all, and the poor lady may have actually been out of her mind. With this view of the past, my judgment of Doctor Maradick insensibly altered. It ended, I think, in my acquitting him altogether. And then, just as he stood clear and splendid in my verdict of him, the reversal came so precipitately that I grow breathless now whenever I try to live it over again. The violence of the next turn in affairs left me, I often fancy, with a perpetual dizziness of the imagination.

It was in May that we heard of Mrs. Maradick's death, and exactly a year later, on a mild and fragrant afternoon, when the daffodils were blooming in patches around the old fountain in the garden, the housekeeper came into the office, where I lingered over some accounts, to bring me news of the doctor's approaching marriage.

"It is no more than we might have expected," she concluded rationally. "The house must be lonely for him—he is such a sociable man. But I can't help feeling," she brought out slowly after a pause in which I felt a shiver pass over me, "I can't help feeling that it is hard for that other woman to have all the money poor Mrs. Maradick's first husband left her."

"There is a great deal of money, then?" I asked curiously.

"A great deal." She waved her hand, as if words were futile to express the sum. "Millions and millions!"

"They will give up this house, of course?"

"That's done already, my dear. There won't be a brick left of it by this time next year. It's to be pulled down and an apartment-house built on the ground."

Again the shiver passed over me. I couldn't bear to think of Mrs. Maradick's old home falling to pieces.

"You didn't tell me the name of the bride," I said. "Is she someone he met while he was in Europe?"

"Dear me, no! She is the very lady he was engaged to before he married Mrs. Maradick, only she threw him over, so people said, because he wasn't rich enough. Then she married some lord or prince from over the water; but there was a divorce, and now she has turned again to her old lover. He is rich enough now, I guess, even for her!''

It was all perfectly true, I suppose; it sounded as plausible as a story out of a newspaper; and yet while she told me I felt, or dreamed that I felt, a sinister, an impalpable hush in the air. I was nervous, no doubt; I was shaken by the suddenness with which the housekeeper had sprung her news on me; but as I sat there I had quite vividly an impression that the old house was listening— that there was a real, if invisible, presence somewhere in the room or the garden. Yet, when an instant afterwards I glanced through the long window which opened down to the brick terrace, I saw only the faint sunshine over the deserted garden, with its maze of box, its marble fountain, and its patches of daffodils.

The housekeeper had gone—one of the servants, I think, came for her—and I was sitting at my desk when the words of Mrs. Maradick on that last evening floated into my mind. The daffodils brought her back to me; for I thought, as I watched them growing, so still and golden in the sunshine, how she would have enjoyed them. Almost unconsciously I repeated the verse she had read to me:

''If thou has two loaves of bread, sell one and buy daffodils''— and it was at this very instant, while the words were still on my lips, that I turned my eyes to the box maze, and saw the child skipping rope along the graveled path to the fountain. Quite distinctly, as clear as day, I saw her come, with what children call the dancing step, between the low box borders to the place where the daffodils bloomed by the fountain. From her straight brown hair to her frock of Scotch plaid and her little feet, which twinkled in white socks and black slippers over the turning rope, she was as real to me as the ground on which she trod or the laughing marble boys under the splashing water. Starting up from my chair, I made a single step to the terrace. If I could only reach her—only speak to her—I felt that I might at last solve the mystery. But with the first flutter of my dress on the terrace, the airy little form melted into the quiet dusk of the maze. Not a breath stirred the daffodils, not a shadow passed over the sparkling flow of the water; yet, weak and shaken in every nerve, I sat down on the brick step of the terrace and burst into tears. I must have known that something terrible would happen before they pulled down Mrs. Maradick's home.

The doctor dined out that night. He was with the lady he was going to marry, the housekeeper told me; and it must have been almost midnight when I heard him come in and go upstairs to his room. I was downstairs because I had been unable to sleep, and the book I wanted to finish I had left that afternoon in the office. The book—I can't remember what it was—had seemed to me very exciting when I began it in the morning; but after the visit of the child I found the romantic novel as dull as a treatise on nursing. It was impossible for me to follow the lines, and I was on the point of giving up and going to bed, when Doctor Maradick opened the front door with his latch-key and went up the staircase. "There can't be a bit of truth in it," I thought over and over again as I listened to his even step ascending the stairs. "There can't be a bit of truth in it." And yet, though I assured myself that "there couldn't be a bit of truth in it," I shrank, with a creepy sensation, from going through the house to my room in the third story. I was tired out after a hard day, and my nerves must have reacted morbidly to the silence and the darkness. For the first time in my life I knew what it was to be afraid of the unknown, of the unseen; and while I bent over my book, in the glare of the electric light, I became conscious presently that I was straining my senses for some sound in the spacious emptiness of the rooms overhead. The noise of a passing motor-car in the street jerked me back from the intense hush of expectancy; and I can recall the wave of relief that swept over me as I turned to my book again and tried to fix my distracted mind on its pages.

I was still sitting there when the telephone on my desk rang, with what seemed to my overwrought nerves a startling abruptness, and the voice of the superintendent told me hurriedly that Doctor Maradick was needed at the hospital. I had become so accustomed to these emergency calls in the night that I felt reassured when I had rung up the doctor in his room and had heard the hearty sound of his response. He had not yet undressed, he said, and would come down immediately while I ordered back his car, which must just have reached the garage.

"I'll be with you in five minutes!" he called as cheerfully as if I had summoned him to his wedding.

I heard him cross the floor of his room; and before he could reach the head of the staircase, I opened the door and went out into the hall in order that I might turn on the light and have his hat and coat waiting. The electric button was at the end of the hall, and as I moved towards it, guided by the glimmer that fell from the landing above, I lifted my eyes to the staircase, which climbed dimly, with its slender mahogany balustrade, as far as the third story. Then it was, at the very moment when the doctor, humming gaily, began his quick descent of the steps, that I distinctly saw—I will swear to this on my deathbed—a child's skipping rope lying loosely coiled, as if it had dropped from a careless little hand, in the bend of the staircase. With a spring I had reached the electric button, flooding the hall with light; but as I did so, while my arm was still outstretched behind me, I heard the humming voice change to a cry of surprise or terror, and the figure on the staircase tripped heavily and stumbled with groping hands into emptiness. The scream of warning died in my throat while I watched him pitch forward down the long flight of stairs to the floor at my feet. Even before I bent over him, before I wiped the blood from his brow and felt for his silent heart, I knew that he was dead.

Something—it may have been, as the world believes, a misstep in the dimness, or it may have been, as I am ready to bear witness, an invisible judgment—something had killed him at the very moment when he most wanted to live.

A SHAPE
OF LIGHT

William Goyen

So it was there that, long ago, in that town, the message was sent and lost; and it is here, many years later, in this city and in this time, that the lost message is risen and reclaimed and fixed forever in the light of so much darkness and of so many meanings.

1. *The Record*

The words he wrote down on paper, shaped in long thin skeletal characters, with a bony forefinger maneuvering his pencil, even as though the characters themselves were ghosts of the alphabet, are ghosts of a page—the page is haunted. But on this haunted page he comes back to us, his face and his look and all about him; he comes back like an old sad age yellow on a page. It is a dim ghostly line of words, his words on the page; bring a light to it: see how the words flare up to light, answering to what put them there. The page is lighted.

So the record reads: "If on an evening of a good moon you will see a lighted shape, much like a scrap of light rising like a ghost from the ground, then saddle your horse and follow it where it will go. It will lead you here and yonder, all night long until daybreak. Then you will see it vanish into the ground. Some old-timers here call this Bailey's Light and say that it is the lantern of a risen ghost of an old pioneer, Bailey was his name; and that old

191

Bailey is risen to search for something he has lost in his lifetime,
something, even as ghost, he wants to get back or to get straight,
riding on his horse to find it. So he is flashing his lantern through
the night, for this. Others have said it is a farmer's lantern, glowing as the farmer swings it down to the river to see its tide and
whether it will flood his crops. Still others say it is a ghostly
hunter hunting. At any rate, there is a ghost in my night here, and
I have studied him and finally thought to watch for him and to
follow his light if he should rise up and go abroad.''

"Oh where you agoing Boney Benson, and it nightfall? Why are
you leaving the supper table so suddenly; you have golloped your
food; your supper will get cold and I will get cold. Where you
agoing so suddenly, Boney Benson?''

Because he followed the light, lo here! lo there! time and time
again, every time he saw it, he knew where the light went, he
found its secret territory. Something was there for him to find out
and he had to endure, wait, study and study it until its buried,
difficult meaning came to him. But it didn't finally come, when it
came, like an easy vision. He had to *follow,* hard and in hardship
and torment, he had to give himself wholly, unafraid, surrendered
to it. He had to leave things behind. When he left the territory of
his meaning, his burden was to bear, understanding the meaning
at last, what he had found out, and to pass it on—and this was his
life, bearing, suffering the found-out meaning of what he was
involved in, haunted by it, grieved by it, but possessing it—and
watching it continue to grow, on and on, into deeper and larger
meaning. This, only, was all his pain.

Well, then, let me see here how to tell it, for I tell you this man
had seen a strange and most marvelous passing thing and now
has made me see it; and to fasten it in a telling and hold it recorded that way, though it itself run on, is all my aim and craving,
find I tongue to tell it. I will want to tell you how, after seeing this
light rise up and glide, a man got up to leave whatever he was
doing to follow; and how the following of this light came to be
the one gesture of his life—not to catch the light or disturb it or

claim it for himself, how could he? It belonged to all the others
before him, too, and to those after him, to whom this is told, but
just to see what he could see, shown up in the shed light of this
light where it went; and to keep himself out of it, he didn't matter, it was the light that mattered: he passed away, the light remained and went on.

Yet one must acknowledge how he loved, *required,* respected
the *idea,* the *image* of himself as alone after the light and tormented by it, wandering sometimes weeping in a cold place,
anonymous, alien, free. The times he raced through the freezing
and windy spaces, desperate, full of strange fears—*what* was he
looking for?—were often terrible; yet the idea, later in his mind,
the image of himself: that wild and terrible shape riding the land,
makes us both weep for him, as though he were some pitiful
begging stranger; and silently rejoice, because we know he was
free in his suffering and that he was surrendered to and claimed
utterly by the truth of himself, belonging to that mysteriously
beautiful and often cruel Force that wanted to use him for something. Then what did the light want to use him for? His only aim
was to find out.

So this man made covenant with himself not to ally himself
with any pattern of life or form of human activity that would
keep him from his suffering after the lighted shape in which he
sought the truth he was after. He would use this light to shine it
over all things, live and dead, to see what they were, to touch
them with light so that he could give them a name, as though
they were the first things and he the first man, to keep taking
inventory of it all, to hold it all straight and named and preserved
in the light. This task, this pursuit, seemed the best he could do
in his time, having found the light or having had the light passed
on to him by those before him and so keep it alive and so pass it
on.

For what other task was there in the world to give oneself to?
All around him roiled a giant and anxious watchlessness, the
blind conquests of men engaged in hunts to kill, plots to gain,
plans to trick to glory or increase. The little light! Sometimes only
like a speck in the eye; sometimes only a tiny bright spot at the

end of a long and dark corridor. Often he thought of all the places to be or go, of the people in places, kin and comrades and lovers, of their faces, the light in eyes, of their flesh. Then it seemed he was no more than ghost, living only a phantom life, underground, *below* life, cut-off, far away, loose and on the lightless rim of the world. Then he cried out, "O will you mock me, destroy me, ghost of light that I follow?" Those times he was tortured by his choice, he cursed his station, abused himself and finally blinded his eyes with his hands to put out the light. But there it was, shining, in his head, a miner's little lantern, going over the ground of his mind; and he could only follow it.

What put the blessing of the light upon him that turned his flesh to fire, that turned his eyes away from everything that would keep them from the path of the light? What serpent urged him to this record to get for himself this knowledge and this image which changed him into something that he could only be by himself, something which he wanted to give to others (what a mystery that what was his light became others' darkness) yet which seemed to destroy them or turn them away from him? Was the light, then, death? Was the light, then, his own image of himself which, given to others, stole their own self-image from them and left them him-imagined, without even the light to go after? What to proclaim out of this man's gesture, light or darkness?

Well, let me see how can I tell it, for I tell you he knew a most wonderful passing thing; and can I find tongue to shape it, I will leave something of us both behind, a shape of light in the darkness, a lighted shape of dust: a record.

"Why are you awatching out the kitchen window; what is there for you to see? Eat your supper and pay some 'tention to me. . . ."

"There is something live in the land, my wife Allie; and my eyes are awatching to see. But one eye is on you, my wife Allie; and one eye is watching through the window."

"You can't divide me with the outdoors; when your eye turns

from me the light is taken from me and I am left in half a shadow; why do you turn the light from me?"

"I have an eye watching for the light, you must understand."

"Oh you are going to leave me again. When you leave me so cold and in my darkness, I cannot understand, Boney Benson; I cannot understand."

Lying connected to his wife in their moist bed, melted in their sweat and simmering in their sweet civet, he thought, "I am traveler home under the hill." Yet outside he would see a light, ground ghost; and he would turn back to himself and rally up himself, draw up and rise and dismember the joining to go to it. Often it would be only a lantern hanging back in the trees, with no hand to show for it; or sometimes just the light of the brooder in the henhouse; sometimes a glowing wad of fireflies along the ground, and sometimes a nightfire on the hill. In the end, after so much of this breaking away to see could it be this light, everything, every giving of himself, every sacrifice of himself only delivered him over and back to himself and his pursuit again. There was, finally, no escape.

Then one night at supper he surely saw it, and he saddled King and went after it. They followed all night long, finding nothing but what grew out of the ground or lay upon it, grass and creature. He returned at daybreak, after it disappeared.

"Oh where you agoing and it nightfall? Why are you leaving the suppertable so suddenly, you have golloped your food. Your supper will get cold and I will go cold. Where you agoing so suddenly?"

"I have seen it, I have seen it; and I am going to saddle my horse and follow it. Wait for me till I get back, my wife Allie."

"O do not saddle the purple horse, O do not ride the purple horse King. . . . Shall I keep the sweet potatoes warm in the oven?"

"I will never eat them, my wife Allie; or eat them cold. . . ."

*   *   *

So let us go with him a little ways, a ghost of the light, following him only with our eyes, so let us come sit here under the hill with him and he will tell us so we can tell it. Circle of insects round us, grasshoppers, caterpillars, eye like the pod of green peas, ripe bursting eye, pluckable. . . . They plucked out sweet old Gloucester's eyeballs and his poor houseless poverty came wild out of the hill, and in his skins led the blind old turned-out Somebody down the road to the cliff. Come let us hold us close to all this dream of dust, of these figures of dust and light, we are a radiant bowl of light and dust shaped by the stillness of his moment of telling. . . .

"I would not be mad as they say I am, poor houseless poverty, caved in the side of this hill, the road beyond with the foot of the traveler upon it, raising the dust at his heels, see him go, Old Somebody, holding to the highway. Breathed out of this dust, I will find the first things, late I will find them, last to the first things, come let us join to find the first beginning things, they are still, even yet, here in everything: say dust, say light, see what shall we call them. Old Ancestor, rib-sprung, old dusty one seared by the light, mixture of light and dust, come under this hill a moment, stay a moment . . . Old Somebody. We have the everlasting shed blood covenant upon our flesh.

"Walking one day I found a child let down from Heaven on a piece of string, standing in a meadow of bluebonnets and paintbrush, leashed out to me. This was my lost child and I told him what he did not know, left my words with him, our covenant, and laid this charge upon him: *speak of this little species that cannot speak for itself; be gesture; and use the light and follow it wherever it may lead you, and lead others to it. And though critics may mock you, lovers leave you and the whole world fall away from you . . . follow the light into the darkness where all vanishment comes back again.*

"I gave him, this errand boy, this runner and rider, the message and it rose and was delivered, but he was cut off and left earthbound and could not rise again to where he had dropped down from, but was dismembered and cast out, untied, to be a wanderer on roads of dirt . . . *behold I am he who sold you, bound in leathern thongs, to a new master; but o my brother! I beseech you remember not my sin against you and grant me this prayer. Bind me now hand and foot; beat me with stripes, shave my head and cast me into prison: make me suffer all I inflicted on you, and then perchance the Lord will have mercy and forget my great sin that I have committed against Him and against you!* Come on wild heart, my wild wild heart, come on; for there is another country and another language. I came into my life to find it a kind of darkness until I discovered the record of this little lantern, and I will die, too, with the little light in my hand, buried with the little light in the ground.

"Riding one night, I galloped upon a flock of shining night-people under shining trees; it was a festival of some large clan of blood-kin, they all had that strong *look* about them that told they were members of blood. They were beautifully dressed, in satins and pongees; and sashes of silk were hung from the delicate trees, fragile colored lanterns hung in the trees, the moon in the trees, too, like one of the lanterns; the breeze was alive, a soft trembling hand roving under and among the silks, all in a smooth pastoral place. The feast was laid out on the ground and covered with the most translucent veil of muslin, showing beneath it the fruit and the victuals, a heaped-up pile of riches. But keep the feast from the insect that was already coming down upon it, the flies and bees already hovered in a swarming circle around the edge, and the crawling things had trailed the festival and lay in hordes on the rim of the festival. Put it under glass, save it save it, this food and this flesh shining under the passing sun. The red and golden drums lie on the ground and the flutes and winds lie lipless, ungiven; and ungiven or given, the lips will pucker and the lungs will puncture and shrivel and fingers of flesh for drums will curl and cleave to bone. Yea dazzle me dazzle me! Round me like a wheel of stars. Flash the fireworks on me, blind my eyes, dazzle me. You are all so beautiful. 'We were on a picnic,' they would tell it, 'the whole flock of us, down by the sandbank at the river, on the Fourtha July. Suddenly in the woods, walking under the trees, was a figure; and someone whispered, 'It's old Boney

Benson.' We watched him. Did he want to join us? He did not
come any closer, but hovered on the edge of our picnic, across
the bobwire fence, just looking to see. We were all, food and
person, the whole picnic, in his eye. What did he want from us?
Him—you know who—went to see what Boney Benson might
want, *he* was not afraid of Boney Benson, even took him a biscuit
and a drink of water; and when *he* tried to cross the bobwire
fence *he* fell upon it and was caught and cut there. Boney Benson
helped *him* off and went away—without the water, for the water
was spilt; but *he* did not drop the biscuit and gave it safely to
Boney Benson. The blood was on *his* trousers.

"To us arrives the unanswerable at our door and cries *answer!*
and will not stay or be there to hear when we open the door—
nor can we ever give any answer, the unanswerable is unanswerable. Nor will the unnamable, always hovering over and round us
for its name, be ever named. The patched webbed face of a ghost
floats round us, hangs and hovers in our air lodged like a becalmed kite over us, moored to our hearts that try to send messages up the string to it. Dance my pretties, laugh; and on I go, on
the road, the dust at my feet and you for a moment in the
meadow, under the silken sashes, shining in the eye of the insect
that has it all in the little mirror of his eye.

"In a grassy corner, humped upon a mossy rock, an old naked
man bent over his geometric shape and measured with long forefinger and straddled legs of his compass the secret from his brain
and his wild burning eye. He has measured the enigmatic arc, my
pretties, he has found a figure for the distance between point and
point, within the sharp corner of an angle he has found the little
meaning; come let us slide into this tiny harbor of angle under
the spread length of this old artificer's fingers, let us be measured
and encompassed by this small compass scope, come on wild
hearts, my wild wild hearts, come on, under the span of this
naked old man's fingers, safe in the shape of his sweet brain of
dust. Naked, no shoe for his foot, he has gone to his dark place to
stay and meditate until he has his meaning.

"Horse of dreams, with a bowed down head and dust-shot eye,
ride me away from this world of grief, come ride me ride me

away. Till I have grieved myself free, at last; till I have sorrowed myself free. And then where we go it will not matter. We will carry our baby in our arms, we will have our trunk and the baby-buggy, that is all we will carry, and onto the road we will go, turned back into our lives that were stolen from us. Move here, move there, hide here, break out there; O will you mock me, destroy me, ghost of light that I follow?

"So what happened was this: we came onto the wide strange region lying under a nightfall sky. It was twilight, you understand, although good dark hadn't come yet. On our right was an orchard of wild fruit trees and the trees were full of white creatures, white, you understand. The pale early moon was the color of the creatures, fowl-like, and like it was of their feather, it seemed a white fowl rising from the far bush, the moon did, in the color of distance: blue. There stood the trees abloom with white creatures, only the glimmer of last daylight lingering over the roan-colored grasses; and in the background the scrawly trees were like marks scrawled on a dark wall.

"There were four of us, you understand, on horseback: the three Tilson boys and me, I was on King's back—he was going after it, too—and riding after it, what I had seen so many times I could but finally follow it. This is what we were going after, this gentle and curious light that was now following a straight path along the ground, and tumbling on as if it was a lighted ball of weed. And if I could tell you I would regale you with telling how this light had come up tattered out of the ground and wound itself into this ball and started rolling along. And if I could de-scribe you it, I would do it, how this radiant object shed the most delicate and pure, clear illumination on little things in its path and along both sides: so that what it showed us who followed was the smallest detail of the world, the frail eternal life of the ground, the whiskers of a fieldmouse, the linked bones in the jointed feet of a hidden sleeping bird, a clear still white tincture of dew hanging like a fallen star on a blade of grass, a hairy worm on a stem like one lost eyebrow, the hued crescent of the shale of a sloughed snake like a small pale fallen rainbow.

"So following this ghostly little lamp of light, we came, of a

sudden, into this unearthly landscape, the one I have told you
about, with the white beings. We knew the country, you understand—our ancestors had broken it as wilderness and started all
their seed there, my grandfathers and their fathers, me, all my
blood-kin, children and children's children. We descendants
thought we had measured and blazed it all. But there is always
some unknown part of all that is known—and we had stumbled
into it, following this light. I knew my ancestors had followed this
light, it was that ancient a thing, this light; that they had ridden
behind it, over branch and pasture, thicket and prairie, from supper till sunrise, when they saw it sink into the ground. There are
the records to prove it, for these old men made records, stopping
to put down what happened, even as I am doing: 'Around us
were disorder, rancor, words gone sour in the mouth like persim-
mons; thoughts turned rotten in the mind, crops eaten, droughts
and floods, poorly wives and an evil chance of children; but when
we saw this light, we left the worst behind and followed to see
what it was, that it might show us what our sorrow meant.' "

The record stopped here, there was never another word written.
What had this old man seen or found that had stopped all words,
that would not take words? What had happened to this old Fol-
lower, so long gone? Had the light been his death, had he met
with mishap or evil on the route of the light? Or had he not been
able to put another word to all that he had seen and so *abandoned* the record to become the light? Think of that moment of
abandonment, that moment of realization that spirit passes *beyond* its vain laboring to make flesh or word of what is beyond
both and incapable of containing them wholly: he rose and vanished into that region, and there we must find him.

And now, after so much struggle and after so much following, I
ask, *was he the light?* Does his cry, now before eyes on a lighted
page, proclaim: *Will you follow the light that led me?* If from
your bed or through your window, on a night of a good moon,
you see a shape rise like a tatter from the ground and go along,
saddle your horse and follow it and see where it will lead you.

A tilted gravestone marks this man and his proclaiming cry; and it is said, indeed, to this very day, in that town, that a light rises from it at nights and wanders over the countryside, beckoning after it a race of the road, a race of followers. What more to say. It goes *on,* as this teller and this listener do.

2. *The Message*

Call Boney Benson from his grave. Call him from the dirt, for some one of us must disturb him so that he will rise and wander over the ground of the mind until he is followed and defined and laid away again to rest.

Suddenly he comes back, rising, called for, to his name, swinging his lantern along the railroad track. With his return comes the image of a kite. It has come slowly, this slow-footed, late-arriving image of Boney Benson and the kite . . . wait for the coming back, as image waits, too.

In a town, once, there lived this Boney Benson. He worked at the depot and, like a skeleton-headed ghost in charge of the movement of the dead, flagged the midnight freight trains with a red lantern. One night, while you waited with your kin at the depot, the children in their sleepers, for the arrival of the ten-o-six, just to watch it for a thrill—you had all been riding on the highway to cool off (it was broiling August) and had come on back to park at the depot to watch the train come in—you saw him pushing a freight cart with a casket on it and saw him help some Negroes load it onto the baggage car. You saw him make the sign of the cross. People in the car whispered of someone lately died in the town—so this was why they had come to the depot—and you heard one of the menfolks say under his breath, "Good-bye, old Stacey," and it seemed the dead person was given over to the hands of Boney Benson. People in the car said "Old Boney Benson! Doesn't he look scarey; looks worse and worse ever time you see him"; and whispered his story beyond your hearing. You related him, again, to death and phantoms and thought him in some way and sorrowfully in charge of the dead who were moved where, in what direction, towards what graveyard or judgment, on the trains that rolled into the town out of blackness of night and went on ahead into swallowing blackness.

Whether he had a wife or family or other kinfolks in the town you never heard it said, and your only information came from conversations overheard—which makes you think how impoverished a servitude is childhood and how people talked about seemed only ghosts and that it is later, when we have our own eyes and language, that we reclaim these as flesh and blood people of earth, but only when they are ghosts, and too late. But they come back to take their lost flesh. Yet you heard enough said about him to render him a haunted man of bones, crossed by his own bony fingers, crucified on the gaunt cross of his own body, two sticks nailed together. At night he hovered over you in your nightmares, his crossed face, speaking of his life; but you did not ask a question.

Where did he live in the daytime, where did he sleep, who were his folks? On the days spent in the graveyard with the women kinfolks to clean the family plot and to plant camphor and crepe-myrtle trees and hoe the weeds, shape the graves of dead kin and put out poison for armadillos, grave robbers, you imagined him somewhere in the graveyard, nursing the dead.

It was late one March afternoon when you were flying a kite in the pasture that you looked up and saw Boney Benson coming down the train tracks, where he belonged, in your mind, as any train, as though that was the natural place for him to travel, and not the road or path. You watched him coming closer, in a steam of his own kicked up dust; and when he got to where you were holding the string of your kite in the pasture, he switched off the tracks and crossed the pasture to you. You would not run; you waited; you were a kite's mooring and the kite was your responsibility in the sky and you could not abandon it or cut it adrift. He approached you ghostlike, like a dream you could have of him and so cry out, "Somebody! Somebody!" in the night until a hand touched and quietened you. Still, you were not afraid.

He stood over you, smelling of train and graveyard, as his image later hovered over you, as the kite itself hovered over you now, so long so limpbodied a man—as though he were pasted together, drawn loosely over the cross-sticks of his body, whittled arms; and he dangled there over you for a moment. Boney Benson looked up at the kite that hung over you in a gray steady wind, then down at you, and said, in his bony voice, "Have you sent a message up to it, Son?" You said no sir. And he said, "Well, then let's do it, Partner."

Now this was a kite built so carefully and with stern labor, made out of kindling wood and shoe-box tissue paper, the first built kite of yours that had ever flown: a miracle had happened, your construction had been removed a distance from you; you were no longer joined except by the most tenuous connection of thread: you the mooring on one end, on the other end the artifice, built of good stuff off the place, freed and lifted up into a life of its own, hovering over the place it had freed itself from and which had provided the materials to make it with.

Boney Benson took from his pocket a piece of barkish Indian Chief tablet paper written on in pencil and said, "Let me send the message." You gave him the tight string and stepped back—your kite was in his spidery hands. You looked up at the face of the kite, hovering over the world, and down a little to his, over you, too. It seemed both faces were in the air, lodged there over you, and his face was like the kite's: red papery face with sticks of bones. Boney Benson very carefully put the message on the kite string and it started going up. The message faltered, then moved slowly, climbing, climbing, stopped awhile as if to rest or as if afraid of so high an ascent, then went faster faster up to the kite and lay pressed close against the face of it by the wind as though there were a conversation—or the kite was reading the message. Then the kite dived, in an instant, and began falling falling. Boney Benson started pulling in the slack. But the string fell all around him. You rushed up to help, but it was no use, the string was falling, coiling all over the pasture, looping and winding round you as though there were some runaway bobbin in heaven and all the thread was raveling, unwinding down upon you in the pasture; and the kite was crashing to the earth. You saw it falling far away at the end of the pasture and you saw it headed for a crooked tree.

But the message, like a kite itself, kept the air and began flying itself. You were, for a moment, Boney Benson and you, watching kite and message, one soaring and wafting and turning in the sunlight that suddenly broke through the March clouded sky, the other falling falling. The message went traveling on, now faster faster; and then the sun had its eyes on it and was reading Boney Benson's letter; then the wind took it for a moment and read it, Braille-like, with its soft lips; the message moved on out of the lighted zone of the sun and passed into the shadow of a cloud and if there was rain up there the rain must have had the message for a moment, too.

The message went on and on, through zones and fields of air; and again in a flash of sunlight you saw it like a silver mote, then lost it among a flight of birds, it like a bird itself; then finally, just as the kite fell broken across the branches of a tree, its knotted tail, made of an old quilt, looped over the limbs, far across at the edge of the pasture, you saw the message for the last time, going on, now itself like a kite, wafting, lowering, rising again, flashing in the shuttering light, over the town and then beyond it—on away into invisibility. Boney Benson finally said, looking down at you, "Excuse me for losing your kite, Son; I'll get you another one"; and you said, "Wonder where the message went . . . ?" and for an instant he bent in a gesture that would haunt you forever and uttered a deep, stifled cry, as though something had hit him in the pit of the stomach and mashed his breath out. And then he went on away, down the railroad tracks.

Now: what you saw, Boney Benson and you, was this: fallen kite and flying message, one free, one captive. You could tell about the kite, how its corpse lay hidden all summer among the leaves of the tree, leaf itself, with only you to know about it, secretly, as though it were a bird's nest, left by Boney Benson who never came again but vanished like the message; how the wind found it, though, even hidden, and rattled it to haunt you; and how in the autumn when all the leaves had been taken by the

wind and flown away like pieces of paper or lay like fallen messages under the crossed tree or scattered like pages of lost letters
over the pasture, blowing into yards, down the roads and the
railroad track, slapped and pasted against wire fences to paper
them like walls of leaves, the whitened bones of the kite's sticks
hung like a glaring cross in the naked tree for all to see . . . until
the sticks, even, finally disappeared into birds' or squirrels' nests
or fell onto the ground and rotted into it. Thus it all vanished
away into you, as into air and into ground, until one day it would
be remade and told about, flown again. For what there is to tell
about is *what was not seen* . . . and this is all your chore. What
is not seen torments the eye as though eye were only a ball of
glass in a socket, until the brain can build an image of what is
unseen and give vision to the eye.

What happened to the message, the going-on part of the
wreckage? Even then, you spent your days trying to account for
it. Finally, you imagine, it frightened birds, slipped through the
fingers of the wind that had once had it but could not have it
again, fell, fell like a leaf. It fell over a landscape of fragile trees
like hair, animals like broken curves in the fields, into the hush of
afternoon where miraculous morning had happened and left the
landscape dazed into afternoon and where tears of dew had
dried, a weeping was over; and everything was stilled. Then the
rain fell upon the message and made it quiet, and took its words
away; or the sun drew up the words and mixed them into cloud
and the message fell as gentle rain. Children with their parents in
the fields may have looked up and said, "Yonder is something
falling out of the sky, it's raining a piece of paper." But if there
were some who saw, there were many more who did not see the
falling message—so many things fall and no eye to follow them
down, a solitary Newton watched an apple fall and who knows
who saw the ruined wings of that old father's shape come down,
on that terrible day?
What happened to the message? Upon a landscape of hushed
tumult and serenity, something was falling falling. It was no mote
or vision in the eye of any who saw it flecking the sky and flash-

ing, it was real and substantial as apple or winged son. The landscape was one of cows folded and horses cropping, of a few stones like sheep in the field, a smooth pastoral place where it seemed no violence could happen. Shimmering tresses of tree locks hung in the near distance, in the far distance some bare, scratchy trees looking like burrs in a meadow. In this landscape lay a little graveyard with graves and tilted gravestones, a gathered family; and this falling missile might have fallen among the graves.

What happened to the message, wherever it fell? It began a life of its own. Now having its own life, it could—and began to—attract life to it, involve itself in other life. A tree may have grown through it (later made a house) or a perpetual fern, eternally fertilizing itself; insects left trails and messages on it, rain melted its speech away—it was taken by all things, and finally moldered into earth and spread into everything.

What did the message say on it? Sun knew it and rain knew it, wind knew it; but not you, you had to wait. "Why did you leave me, Boney Benson; why did you go away and it nightfall?" "When you come home we will all go into Mississippi to see can we find our kinfolks." "Many a beau have I let go, because I wanted you, because I wanted you. . . ." "I have read your letter and cried and cried; and read it and cried again." "No. 5 will arrive two-fifteen, on time, carrying mail and news"; "If, at nightfall, you see a shape of light traveling over the ground, saddle your horse and follow it, to see what it will show you. . . ."

What happened to the messenger? Where had he come from, before your time; where did he vanish away to? Imagine his room: bare, curtainless, crooked window shades streaked by rain because the windows had been left open; the smell of trains in it; a crucifix on the wall at the head of the bed. In his bed, on a thin sunken mattress, his long form under the covers, his dust-covered hightop shoes toeing out from under the bed, his Hamilton white-face railroadman's watch ticking on the little marble-top table. The closet door ajar, crooked on its hinges; within, his blue striped coveralls hung from a staple on the wall like his own hanged body. No photographs, no Bible, no Western stories, no hair oil; merely the room where he lay, ungiven to it, as if stopping over to rest, having arrived there on his way to not any particular where. But can a man's life be so bare, so unpossessed? Somewhere he had left something behind.

For years his gesture and his image haunted you, hung and hovered over you like a kite in the air around you, triangular face, bony, stretched papery skin of a kite, his face, swimming and dipping and bowing and rising and darting, looking down at you . . . his kite face . . . *send up a message!* You had built kite and kite had taken his message and delivered it. Now you must shape him, like kite, and send his message back to him. For out of a wreck something is left, freed, sent on to other hands, put into the world, leaving a ghost behind until ghost and flesh be brought together again and the whole thing vanish, accounted for, to its eternal hushedness.

What to proclaim out of it all? For years the message, scrap of paper hearing what words? had been falling falling over the unstilled landscape of your mind, with no place to land, no resting place, no one to receive the cry of the message. You were pondering and brooding over dust and light, the poverty of dirt, the little speck of light the dust draws to and hovers round. You thought of that king's son, wild in his skins, the traveler lost in the hill, his old kinsman blind on the road, the joining of father and son. You were full of this kind of thought and laboring with passion and sternness to shape dust and light and poor houseless poverty into some little lasting form, shaped out of dust but held together for a little while by the light you begged for. Every day the shape of a terrible thought or idea or memory rose up in you from some opened grave to claim your mind like a presence; it was a wrestling with some visitation of ghost. You fought it out upon another body, as though you thought flesh might appease or pacify the ghost; or upon your own, as if to chasten the ghost in your flesh. To be still! hands folded, mind resting like a fallen kite, its cry gone on, and take silence in the silencing of all flesh and let the ghost ride out of the flesh.

You, kite-maker and kite-flier, were in a great city where, following some shape—was it of light or of darkness?—you had wandered into an unreal, ghost-haunted territory, into a land-scape of addict elations, hallucinations and obsessions, where it seemed you were a kite flying over the landscape—your gaze walked down the tight string that held you aloft, alienated you, separated you; and far far below you saw the fisted, gripped hand that held you—your only mooring to the ground, this vanished artificer. *Who will send the kite a message?* you cried; or can kite send *down* a message, though kite fall and lie broken and caught in a leafless tree like one torn leaf in a windless season? This cry was hidden in the thick and leafed and numberless cries of your brain, secret, lodged and hidden. You were in this city where men had lost speech and could not tell, where children had lost fathers, where childless men and womanless men searched for wife and child; homeless poverties were wild and aloose in the flumes of stone. Through holes in the walls between men, two eyes met, eye upon eye, seeing jungles in the eye, vines, a lion in the jungle, a tear. So this is what it has all led to, you thought, this ghost-grieved room where I sit, Hellstreet below, the odor of delicatessens, dogshit on the sidewalks, drunken men wheeling and calling in the street, the dirty yelling children (you sonofa-bitch you think you're a bigshot because you got a pack of ciga-rettes! motherfucker); the Cubans and the Portuguese sitting on the fire-plugs; the blown trash, the forlorn apartment houses; the caricature of a woods where human beings, moiling like insects, broke the tender night; and you wanting to make something tender and full of faith and simplicity in the midst of this tenderlessness and ugliness, this loveless, faithless, vile world of men and goods. To live in the veins until something deep deep within begins to open out and rise up, slowly slowly! It is in the veins that the purity lives and happens. It is all there, everything, the whole truth, the whole vision, in the veins, you thought. O grief! O lonely! Speech lies lodged under us like a river under slate; grief hangs over us like a becalmed kite: send messages up to it, down to it.

You thought of the messages ticking on the telegraphs at de-pots, of all the letters speaking in the mailbags and mailboxes, cries along the telephone wires, of all the people telling things, the whole world talking and telling and sending out messages; yet nobody could tell, the gesture was lost. For speech lay lodged under men like a river under slate, hung becalmed over them like a hovering kite in a windless season—send messages down to it, send messages up to it . . . try! try! The patched webbed face of a ghost floats round us, hangs lodged in our air over us, moored to our hearts that try to send messages up the string to it. *Proclaim it! Proclaim it!* But no message would rise.

Looking upon this world from your window, you saw the wind lift a scrap of paper from the dirty street and carry it high up into the air and close to your window—you could see that it was piece of a letter. *Boney Benson!* There was a cry, lifted from deep down in you up to your throat, that you could not utter. It was his cry, now covered up with dirt, that he had given to you and you had carried, long-since-silent cry the day you lost the kite and freed the message from his pocket. You turned and called out, man now and no longer child, speaker now and no longer listener, asking man's question, crying man's cry: *Boney Benson! what did the message say that day, what did the message say?* Cry cannot be left in throat or breast, unrisen and unfreed—put it into the air and let it go on, cried, freed, though falling wreckage follow and hang like ghost and ruin of cry all the long season: there is the fall and there is the rising. *Call Boney Benson from his grave!* Now Boney Benson was all your question and all your pain; and tell it.

His wife Allie had died with his unborn baby in her, as if the child had not wanted to be born—or had Boney Benson betrayed her in some way so that she would not give him his child? They said that in the last month the baby had suddenly risen in its mother's body as if climbing a tower, climbed up close to her heart and, rolled up in a ball and nestled there, it would not descend and come out into the broad world but died under the bell of her heart. They said how, as she lay dying, Allie Benson cried out to her phantom, gasping for the breath it was taking from her, "Go away, go away," and how, to try to breathe, she

craned and stretched her neck and ducked and drew back her
head as though she were nodding yes yes yes, clawing at her
heart, at the assassin within her as if it were some kind of vam-
pire creeping up the length of her. As she lay dying—and no one
knew why, what was the matter with her, was it her heart, was
she having a convulsion—the gathered kinswomen and the doctor, who finally came, tried to take the child from her, to save it at
least, but they found the child had rolled away from the opening
of its cave, like a ball, and had risen and tucked itself up close
against her heart, to stay with her, it seemed; or as if to try to save
her by giving her its breath; or perhaps to speak to her some
urgent message through the blood, tolling the bell of her heart;
but surely to take her life away. Thus they both died, mother and
child, each taking the life of the other with him. Allie Benson died
of strangled anguish and bewilderment and unearthly pain, in
terror of her death, not knowing what her death was, whether it
was Boney Benson's hands at her throat; in her terrible death's
nightmare did she think he was strangling her to death for some
blood vengeance or did she know it was this risen deathchild
within her? Will anyone ever know? For she had not been able to
make him out, this man her husband Boney Benson, and his mystery lived and thrived within her like some spreading, choking
fungus, like some mysterious inner life she questioned every day:
why he held himself apart from her, why he would suddenly
leave her in the middle of love, why he would go off and come
back, time and time again: and she could not understand, it grew
and grew so that it was Boney Benson's mystery that grew within
her, swelling her, and in the end would not come out into light of
day but rose and perished, destroying her. This little murderer
whose wet white rodent hands had seized her heart and clutched
it till it choked and stopped, what was it, of what meaning was it
that a child should murder its mother? They died together, then,
Allie and child, and then Boney Benson buried them together in
the graveyard where they lay, murderer within murdered, in a
dirt grave.

　　Boney Benson turned against himself and blamed his Self for
this ruin and loss—what did it mean? Had he been the agent of

death, was he the murderer?—and after violent days of self-abuse he chastised himself by destroying his Self, in the wildest passion, in the grove of trees behind the house he and Allie had lived in. What he spoke out when he did this, what sermon he delivered to his Self no ear ever heard but ear of tree and wind and grass, and who can ever tell that, where no tongue is? He ran to Doctor Browder and cried, "See what I have done to myself!" Doctor Browder saw blood on Boney Benson's hands and when he looked to see he saw this terrible sight. But Boney Benson was doctored and healed and became a changed strange man; he changed into this tall, towery kind of a bony man, gone all to hair, they said, because his hair sprangled out like some Apache Plume bush, wild and cottony, and he seemed as stalky as a sugar-cane pole, and so gentle. He was an odd man to have in a town, in any place in this world. But he was gentle and harmless, for his harm was gone from him into a grave.

It was further said, by boys to each other when they were separated together in their own world and life by rivers or creeks or in gins or deep green ditches, where there hovered over them always the signal of the exulting boy's life, jumping up clear of the water, in swimming naked, they cried to each other, "Look what a stake I've got!" there was this excitement, there was this pride, this swollen pride, this ready danger . . . it was further told by boys that Boney Benson buried his member in the grave. Surely he must have felt this was the only way to reach his lost child—through the way of its beginning and no other—the last, as the first, gift and sacrifice to give, it was no other's and no longer his own. He had knocked on Allie's breast and called to the child, after her death; he had laid his head on her heart and listened for sounds of it, but there was no other way to reach this child that he had given her, her death, made by him, his own artifice—of death. And certainly he said when he gave his Self to the grave, I will cry down to him with the cry of the cock and I will look upon him with the eye of the Old Ancestor, where he lies buried in his grave of her flesh of dust, our buried image that rose but would not come forth, seedling of the seed of my Self; I have given him myself through your rose of sweet flesh, I have delivered him my message through the underground tunnel of your sweet flesh. And now, he prayed, let my member turn to dust, he has no home but a house of dust, this poverty of dirt. He lay widened out over the dirt grave, imagining himself clasped to her, palm to palm, mouth to mouth, knee to knee; or thin as a line, narrow plank of flesh, he her light load; and when the curious and shamed and unbelieving people of the town came to look at the grave they saw this human shape mashed into the dirt like a butter print, or the dirt so scattered and roiled that an armadillo might have been there in the night.

The tale is told that the child was born in the grave, delivered itself of its tomb within tomb and, mole-like, began a life of its own underground, rising at nights when the Mexicans who lived in the Mexican houses round the edge of the graveyard were playing their mandolins and harmonicas and singing their passionated luted summer-heat songs in the pallid summer nights, to wander phantom over the countryside.

What rose from the grave to journey in the night time? People reported this light that seemed to rise like a ball from the grave of Allie Benson and her child and stray over the ground, as if it were some animal come out of its hole or cave at night to graze or cavort or wander, under a moon, in the night breeze, in the lunar stillness. It was the Mexicans who saw it at first from their windows and from their porches. Then night fishermen saw it along the river banks, and it was seen along the railroad tracks at night or in the woods by campers disturbed on their pallets. Boney Benson, hearing of this and knowing his own secret, came to hide in the graveyard at night to watch for this rising shape; and so it came to be known as Boney Benson's Light. This is the tale that was told.

At first he laid over the grave with his own hands and at night a piece of flat slate from the side of the river to hold down the phantom—and then under the moon the Mexicans could see him lying on the cold slab of slate, thigh against the rock, beating fists on the horizontal wall, knocking, calling down, finger-tips, lips, thighs upon the wall between him and his bereaved member.

So Boney Benson was this double man: railroadman at the depot, strange and shut-up swinging his lantern; and creature of his private room: when he opened his door to a dark room, closed it behind him and mashed the button to turn on the light, he burst into this possessed shape, haunted and spectral in a lighted box of a room, and then the light went out. He appeared at the graveyard on his horse. There his night search began; and when he saw this lighted shape rise from the grave he began to follow it, and this was his regular night-time journey, following this shape where it went.

The grave was seldom let alone or unvisited, it drew people to it to spy upon it. Three strong young men in their time of wildness that no house could hamper or hush had been hunting on their horses one night and they rode upon the grave to explore the gossip tale of Boney Benson's Light; and when their horses reared back and wailed and whinnied and their hound dogs bayed for death, cowering behind the bushes, the three young men looked to see why: the slate lid of the grave of Allie Benson and her ghostchild was broken open, there was a ragged hole in it and something had escaped. In their terror they sat fixed and gaping on their raring horses, when suddenly a figure of a man stepped out from behind the trees that circled the grave, and it was Boney Benson. "I have seen it, the light; it has risen and gone yonder. Will you follow it with me?" On their horses they went and followed, the three young men and Boney Benson.

The story, told first by the three young men, then on and on year after year by descendants and followers, kin and friend (they left the record, else how could we have known it?), is that the four followers on horseback rode and rode in the night, following the shape of light, until they came upon a field where all the little white children were, the gravechildren, misbegotten, wasted-face, cat-sucked hair grown dank to their heels, fingernails long as spurs, wan-eyed and musty smelling, of the odor of wilted cemetery roses and moldering zinnia stems, dressed in long loose-hanging little countrychild garments of faded no-color which hung limp upon them from the shoulders with only ragged holes for ragged arms; parentless, homeless, orphans of dirt, children of earth, musting among roots, in a graveyard kindergarten: pioneers! blood-kin! breakers of wilderness! homesteaders! Yet how even among these, one of them would not stay, not even among these; memberless, it orphaned itself even of orphans, and strayed away on; and they followed the light, Boney Benson and the three young men, on and on, on horseback, the hounds following, Boney Benson on his purple horse ahead and leading, all as quiet and passionate as men in love, going on away into the far night time, following the lighted shape, on away to the very rim of the world, it seemed. What they saw as they rode—was it a mockery or a blessing that grieved them or a vision that changed them or gave them a meaning of the haunted and bedeviled world they lived in? In a little glen they passed did they not see mother nursing child at laden breasts, father standing at a distance, leaning on a staff—they were resting and strengthening themselves, for they were on some journey, too; on a log did they not find woman and child, man under a tree where a lighted lantern hung; Madonnas in meadows, mothers among rocks, in caves; landscapes with martyrs, with hermits in hills and in trees, a husband leading back a back-turned wife from death, wings and limbs of a lost son falling from the sky; and once, in a broad grassy moonlit place two lovers on their backs, side touching side; and then the followers saw him turn, rise as if lifted on wings and light upon her like an insect on a flower, so airily; and arms and legs winged and flared, he gathered over her in all grace and lightness, riding aloft her as if floating over her, and where he touched her closest he pierced her in such a whirring and bumbling and trembling that he welted and blazed her and left her stung; and the followers went on.

So they went on, in their wonder, losing the light betimes and Boney Benson crying out in his breast, *out, out of this darkness, where is the light?* and then, finding the light again, going on behind it, the May night all in them, the stars, the blue naked night, the full white lips of the young moon, the silver, the blue and the sweetness of the wind's limbs, gentle and delicate as a young girl's, all in them. So they went on, into a strange and uterine country under an astral light and saw in the darkling West the white star lowering toward the horizon, lying on the rind of heaven, and thought: tell us that flesh is a cold and boned cask that drops into whatever darkness lies below the rim, that flesh sets, as star does, into darkness and never rises in the burning East again nor burns the long night through, as star does.

Somewhere along the way, in this country, the three young men turned back, their passion wearied, saying, "Where you go we cannot follow any longer," but Boney Benson went on. He died, in another country, and was brought back to this graveyard to be buried next to the grave of his wife and child. But the record was made and kept and the light did not vanish. It continued to rise, you can still see it on any night, to this very day; and who will follow it to carry on the record?

Yet what to tell? What to proclaim out of it all? That messages of words travel into territory where there are no words, into that wordless region where there is only a kind of music, a wail, or a sigh, or a stifled cry: the gesture of the inexpressible, and they carry a message there to leave it. What we must say can be discovered, whispered, in the overbreath of what lies on a piece of paper, there is a music produced out somewhere, outside and over what is put down in words. Words can only carry us, on away, to what waits so splendidly and purely and overwhelmingly unspeakable, we are delivered to that. There lies the territory, the unuttering region we are led to, that region like the deep underwater zones that house the sunken gesture: a slowly undulating worm in the lower light, the winnowing curve of a root, the glister of a tiny slime-egg, the burst and glow and glimmer-out of ooze from which all seeds break—the first and forgotten source; and to conceive the world over again in the image of the life of this territory of unutterance is all worthy enterprise. There lies, pure and breathing, the fallen unread message, the unjoined member; there lies the imperishable record of what happened.

This is what you thought and this is what happened, on that terrible day in that accursed city when a cry long-ago-uttered rose and was given back; in that city that did not know that at all moments Icarus was falling, a watched apple dropping, Eu-

*ropa raped upon a wreathed Bull across an ignorant pasture,
Orpheus leading back a lover who could be turned to stone by
the look of his eyes, a piece of paper rising in a windy street, a
ghost called back from the grave to take his name and his remembrance in a message that was given back.*

W.S.

L. P. Hartley

The first postcard came from Forfar. "I thought you might like a picture of Forfar," it said. "You have always been so interested in Scotland, and that is one reason why I am interested in you. I have enjoyed all your books, but do you really get to grips with people? I doubt it. Try to think of this as a handshake from your devoted admirer, W.S."

Like other novelists, Walter Streeter was used to getting communications from strangers. Usually they were friendly but some times they were critical. In either case he always answered them, for he was conscientious. But answering them took up the time and energy he needed for his writing, so that he was rather relieved that W.S. had given no address. The photograph of Forfar was uninteresting and he tore it up. His anonymous correspondent's criticism, however, lingered in his mind. Did he really fail to come to grips with his characters? Perhaps he did. He was aware that in most cases they were either projections of his own personality or, in different forms, the antithesis of it. The Me and the Not Me. Perhaps W.S. had spotted this. Not for the first time Walter made a vow to be more objective.

About ten days later arrived another postcard, this time from Berwick-on-Tweed. "What do you think of Berwick-on-Tweed?" it said. "Like you, it's on the Border. I hope this doesn't sound rude. I don't mean that you are a border-line case! You know how much I admire your stories. Some people call them other-worldly.

I think you should plump for one world or the other. Another firm handshake from W.S."

Walter Streeter pondered over this and began to wonder about the sender. Was his correspondent a man or a woman? It looked like a man's handwriting—commercial, unself-conscious—and the criticism was like a man's. On the other hand, it was like a woman to probe—to want to make him feel at the same time flattered and unsure of himself. He felt the faint stirrings of curiosity but soon dismissed them; he was not a man to experiment with acquaintances. Still it was odd to think of this unknown person speculating about him, sizing him up. Other-worldly, indeed! He re-read the last two chapters he had written. Perhaps they didn't have their feet firm on the ground. Perhaps he was too ready to escape, as other novelists were nowadays, into an ambiguous world, a world where the conscious mind did not have things too much its own way. But did that matter? He threw the picture of Berwick-on-Tweed into his November fire and tried to write; but the words came haltingly, as though contending with an extra-strong barrier of self-criticism. And as the days passed he became uncomfortably aware of self-division, as though someone had taken hold of his personality and was pulling it apart. His work was no longer homogeneous, there were two strains in it, unreconciled and opposing, and it went much slower as he tried to resolve the discord. Never mind, he thought: perhaps I was getting into a groove. These difficulties may be growing pains, I may have tapped a new source of supply. If only I could correlate the two and make their conflict fruitful, as many artists have!

The third postcard showed a picture of York Minster. "I know you are interested in cathedrals," it said. "I'm sure this isn't a sign of megalomania in your case, but smaller churches are sometimes more rewarding. I'm seeing a good many churches on my way south. Are you busy writing or are you looking round for ideas? Another hearty handshake from your friend W.S."

It was true that Walter Streeter was interested in cathedrals. Lincoln Cathedral had been the subject of one of his youthful fantasies and he had written about it in a travel book. And it was also true that he admired mere size and was inclined to under-value parish churches. But how could W.S. have known that? And was it really a sign of megalomania? And who was W.S. anyhow?

For the first time it struck him that the initials were his own. No, not for the first time. He had noticed it before, but they were such commonplace initials; they were Gilbert's, they were Maugham's, they were Shakespeare's—a common possession. Anyone might have them. Yet now it seemed to him an odd coin-cidence; and the idea came into his mind—suppose I have been writing postcards to myself? People did such things, especially people with split personalities. Not that he was one, of course. And yet there were these unexplained developments—the cleav-age in his writing, which had now extended from his thought to his style, making one paragraph languorous with semi-colons and subordinate clauses, and another sharp and incisive with main verbs and full-stops.

He looked at the handwriting again. It had seemed the perfec-tion of ordinariness—anybody's hand—so ordinary as perhaps to be disguised. Now he fancied he saw in it resemblances to his own. He was just going to pitch the postcard in the fire when suddenly he decided not to. I'll show it to somebody, he thought.

His friend said, "My dear fellow, it's all quite plain. The woman's a lunatic. I'm sure it's a woman. She has probably fallen in love with you and wants to make you interested in her. I should pay no attention whatsoever. People whose names are mentioned in the papers are always getting letters from lunatics. If they worry you, destroy them without reading them. That sort of person is often a little psychic, and if she senses that she's getting a rise out of you she'll go on."

For a moment Walter Streeter felt reassured. A woman, a little mouse-like creature, who had somehow taken a fancy to him! What was there to feel uneasy about in that? It was really rather sweet and touching, and he began to think of her and wonder what she looked like. What did it matter if she was a little mad? Then his subconscious mind, searching for something to torment him with, and assuming the authority of logic, said: Supposing those postcards are a lunatic's, and you are writing them to your-self, doesn't it follow that you must be a lunatic too?

He tried to put the thought away from him; he tried to destroy the postcard as he had the others. But something in him wanted to preserve it. It had become a piece of him, he felt. Yielding to an irresistible compulsion, which he dreaded, he found himself putting it behind the clock on the chimney-piece. He couldn't see it but he knew that it was there.

He now had to admit to himself that the postcard business had become a leading factor in his life. It had created a new area of thoughts and feelings and they were most unhelpful. His being was strung up in expectation of the next postcard.

Yet when it came it took him, as the others had, completely by surprise. He could not bring himself to look at the picture. "I hope you are well and would like a postcard from Coventry," he read. "Have you ever been sent to Coventry? I have—in fact you sent me there. It isn't a pleasant experience, I can tell you. I am getting nearer. Perhaps we shall come to grips after all. I advised you to come to grips with your characters, didn't I? Have I given you any new ideas? If I have you ought to thank me, for they are what novelists want, I understand. I have been re-reading your novels, living in them, I might say. Another hard handshake. As always, W.S."

A wave of panic surged up in Walter Streeter. How was it that he had never noticed, all this time, the most significant fact about the postcards—that each one came from a place geographically closer to him than the last? "I am coming nearer." Had his mind, unconsciously self-protective, worn blinkers? If it had, he wished he could put them back. He took an atlas and idly traced out W.S.'s itinerary. An interval of eighty miles or so seemed to separate the stopping-places. Walter lived in a large West Country town about ninety miles from Coventry.

Should he show the postcards to an alienist? But what could an alienist tell him? He would not know, what Walter wanted to know, whether he had anything to fear from W.S.

Better go to the police. The police were used to dealing with poison-pens. If they laughed at him, so much the better.

They did not laugh, however. They said they thought the post-cards were a hoax and that W.S. would never show up in the flesh. Then they asked if there was anyone who had a grudge against him. "No one that I know of," Walter said. They, too, took the view that the writer was probably a woman. They told him not to worry but to let them know if further postcards came.

A little comforted, Walter went home. The talk with the police had done him good. He thought it over. It was quite true what he had told them—that he had no enemies. He was not a man of strong personal feelings such feelings as he had went into his books. In his books he had drawn some pretty nasty characters. Not of recent years, however. Of recent years he had felt a reluctance to draw a very bad man or woman: he thought it morally irresponsible and artistically unconvincing, too. There was good in everyone: Iagos were a myth. Latterly—but he had to admit that it was several weeks since he laid pen to paper, so much had this ridiculous business of the postcards weighed upon his mind—if he had to draw a really wicked person he represented him as a Communist or a Nazi—someone who had deliberately put off his human characteristics. But in the past, when he was younger and more inclined to see things as black or white, he had let himself go once or twice. He did not remember his old books very well but there was a character in one, "The Outcast," into whom he had really got his knife. He had written about him with extreme vindictiveness, just as if he was a real person whom he was trying to show up. He had experienced a curious pleasure in attributing every kind of wickedness to this man. He never gave him the benefit of the doubt. He had never felt a twinge of pity for him, even when he paid the penalty for his misdeeds on the gallows. He had so worked himself up that the idea of this dark creature, creeping about brimful of malevolence, had almost frightened him.

Odd that he couldn't remember the man's name.

He took the book down from the shelf and turned the pages—even now they affected him uncomfortably. Yes, here it was, William . . . William . . . he would have to look back to find the surname. William Stainsforth.

His own initials.

Walter did not think the coincidence meant anything but it colored his mind and weakened its resistance to his obsession. So uneasy was he that when the next postcard came it came as a relief.

"I am quite close now," he read, and involuntarily he turned the postcard over. The glorious central tower of Gloucester Cathedral met his eye. He stared at it as if it could tell him something, then with an effort went on reading. "My movements, as you may have guessed, are not quite under my control, but all being well I look forward to seeing you some time this week-end. Then we can really come to grips. I wonder if you'll recognize me! It won't be the first time you have given me hospitality. My hand feels a bit cold to-night, but my handshake will be just as hearty. As always, W.S."

"P.S. Does Gloucester remind you of anything? Gloucester jail?"

Walter took the postcard straight to the police station, and asked if he could have police protection over the week-end. The officer in charge smiled at him and said he was quite sure it was a hoax; but he would tell someone to keep an eye on the premises.

"You still have no idea who it could be?" he asked.

Walter shook his head.

It was Tuesday; Walter Streeter had plenty of time to think about the week-end. At first he felt he would not be able to live through the interval, but strange to say his confidence increased instead of waning. He set himself to work as though he *could* work, and presently he found he could—differently from before, and, he thought, better. It was as though the nervous strain he had been living under had, like an acid, dissolved a layer of non-conductive thought that came between him and his subject: he was nearer to it now, and his characters, instead of obeying woodenly his stage directions, responded wholeheartedly and with all their beings to the tests he put them to. So passed the days, and the dawn of Friday seemed like any other day until something jerked him out of his self-induced trance and suddenly he asked himself, "When does a week-end begin?"

A long week-end begins on Friday. At that his panic returned. He went to the street door and looked out. It was a suburban, unfrequented street of detached Regency houses like his own. They had tall square gate-posts, some crowned with semi-circular iron brackets holding lanterns. Most of these were out of repair: only two or three were ever lit. A car went slowly down the street; some people crossed it: everything was normal.

Several times that day he went to look and saw nothing unusual, and when Saturday came, bringing no postcard, his panic had almost subsided. He nearly rang up the police station to tell them not to bother to send anyone after all.

They were as good as their word: they did send someone. Between tea and dinner, the time when week-end guests most commonly arrive, Walter went to the door and there, between two unlit gate-posts, he saw a policeman standing—the first policeman he had ever seen in Charlotte Street. At the sight, and at the relief it brought him, he realized how anxious he had been. Now he felt safer than he had ever felt in his life, and also a little ashamed at having given extra trouble to a hardworked body of men. Should he go and speak to his unknown guardian, offer him a cup of tea or a drink? It would be nice to hear him laugh at Walter's fancies. But no—somehow he felt his security the greater when its source was impersonal and anonymous. "P.C. Smith" was somehow less impressive than "police protection."

Several times from an upper window (he didn't like to open the door and stare) he made sure that his guardian was still there; and once, for added proof, he asked his housekeeper to verify the strange phenomenon. Disappointingly, she came back saying she had seen no policeman; but she was not very good at seeing things, and when Walter went a few minutes later he saw him plain enough. The man must walk about, of course, perhaps he had been taking a stroll when Mrs. Kendal looked.

It was contrary to his routine to work after dinner but to-night he did, he felt so much in the vein. Indeed, a sort of exaltation possessed him; the words ran off his pen; it would be foolish to check the creative impulse for the sake of a little extra sleep. On, on. They were right who said the small hours were the time to work. When his housekeeper came in to say good night he scarcely raised his eyes.

In the warm, snug little room the silence purred around him like a kettle. He did not even hear the door bell till it had been ringing for some time.

A visitor at this hour?

His knees trembling, he went to the door, scarcely knowing what he expected to find; so what was his relief on opening it, to see the doorway filled by the tall figure of a policeman. Without waiting for the man to speak—

"Come in, come in, my dear fellow," he exclaimed. He held his hand out, but the policeman did not take it. "You must have been very cold standing out there. I didn't know that it was snowing, though," he added, seeing the snowflakes on the policeman's cape and helmet. "Come in and warm yourself."

"Thanks," said the policeman. "I don't mind if I do."

Walter knew enough of the phrases used by men of the policeman's stamp not to take this for a grudging acceptance. "This way," he prattled on. "I was writing in my study. By Jove, it *is* cold, I'll turn the gas on more. Now won't you take your traps off, and make yourself at home?"

"I can't stay long," the policeman said, "I've got a job to do, as *you* know."

"Oh yes," said Walter, "such a silly job, a sinecure." He stopped, wondering if the policeman would know what a sinecure was. "I suppose you know what it's about—the postcards?"

The policeman nodded.

"But nothing can happen to me as long as you are here," said Walter. "I shall be as safe . . . as safe as houses. Stay as long as you can, and have a drink."

"I never drink on duty," said the policeman. Still in his cape and helmet, he looked around. "So this is where you work," he said.

"Yes, I was writing when you rang."

"Some poor devil's for it, I expect," the policeman said.

"Oh, why?" Walter was hurt by his unfriendly tone, and noticed how hard his gooseberry eyes were.

"I'll tell you in a minute," said the policeman, and then the telephone bell rang. Walter excused himself and hurried from the room.

"This is the police station," said a voice. "Is that Mr. Streeter?" Walter said it was.

"Well, Mr. Streeter, how is everything at your place? All right, I hope? I'll tell you why I ask. I'm sorry to say we quite forgot about that little job we were going to do for you. Bad co-ordination, I'm afraid."

"But," said Walter, "you did send someone."

"No, Mr. Streeter, I'm afraid we didn't."

"But there's a policeman here, here in this very house."

There was a pause, then his interlocutor said, in a less casual voice:

"He can't be one of our chaps. Did you see his number by any chance?"

"No."

A longer pause and then the voice said:

"Would you like us to send somebody now?"

"Yes, p . . . please."

"All right then, we'll be with you in a jiffy."

Walter put back the receiver. What now? he asked himself. Should he barricade the door? Should he run out into the street? Should he try to rouse his housekeeper? A policeman of any sort was a formidable proposition, but a rogue policeman! How long would it take the real police to come? A jiffy, they had said. What was a jiffy in terms of minutes? While he was debating the door opened and his guest came in.

"No room's private when the street door's once passed," he said. "Had you forgotten I was a policeman?"

"Was?" said Walter, edging away from him. "You *are* a policeman."

"I have been other things as well," the policeman said. "Thief, pimp, blackmailer, not to mention murderer. *You* should know."

The policeman, if such he was, seemed to be moving towards him and Walter suddenly became alive to the importance of small distances—the distance from the sideboard to the table, the distance from one chair to another.

"I don't know what you mean," he said. "Why do you speak like that? I've never done you any harm. I've never set eyes on you before."

"Oh, haven't you?" the man said. "But you've thought about me and"—his voice rose—"and you've written about me. You got some fun out of me, didn't you? Now I'm going to get some fun out of you. You made me just as nasty as you could. Wasn't that doing me harm? You didn't think what it would feel like to be me, did you? You didn't put yourself in my place, did you? You hadn't any pity for me, had you? Well, I'm not going to have any pity for you."

"But I tell you," cried Walter, clutching the table's edge, "I don't know you!"

"And now you say you don't know me! You did all that to me and then forgot me!" His voice became a whine, charged with self-pity. "You forgot William Stainsforth."

"William Stainsforth!"

"Yes. I was your scapegoat, wasn't I? You unloaded all your self-dislike on me. You felt pretty good while you were writing about me. You thought, what a noble, upright fellow you were, writing about this rotter. Now, as one W.S. to another, what shall I do, if I behave in character?"

"I . . . I don't know," muttered Walter.

"You don't know?" Stainsforth sneered. "You ought to know, you fathered me. What would William Stainsforth do if he met his old dad in a quiet place, his kind old dad who made him swing?"

Walter could only stare at him.

"You know what he'd do as well as I," said Stainsforth. Then his face changed and he said abruptly, "No, you don't, because you never really understood me. I'm not so black as you painted me." He paused, and a flicker of hope started in Walter's breast. "You never gave me a chance, did you? Well, I'm going to give you one. That shows you never understood me, doesn't it?"

Walter nodded.

"And there's another thing you have forgotten."

"What is that?"

"I was a kid once," the ex-policeman said.

Walter said nothing.

"You admit that?" said William Stainsforth grimly. "Well, if you can tell me of one virtue you ever credited me with—just one kind thought—just one redeeming feature—"

"Yes?" said Walter, trembling.

"Well, then I'll let you off."

"And if I can't?" whispered Walter.

"Well, then, that's just too bad. We'll have to come to grips and you know what that means. You took off one of my arms but I've still got the other. "Stainsforth of the iron hand" you called me."

Walter began to pant.

"I'll give you two minutes to remember," Stainsforth said. They both looked at the clock. At first the stealthy movement of the hand paralyzed Walter's thought. He stared at William Stainsforth's face, his cruel, crafty face, which seemed to be always in shadow, as if it was something the light could not touch. Desperately he searched his memory for the one fact that would save him; but his memory, clenched like a fist, would give up nothing. "I must invent something," he thought, and suddenly his mind relaxed and he saw, printed on it like a photograph, the last page of the book. Then, with the speed and magic of a dream, each page appeared before him in perfect clarity until the first was reached, and he realized with overwhelming force that what he looked for was not there. In all that evil there was not one hint of good. And he felt, compulsively and with a kind of exaltation, that unless he testified to this the cause of goodness everywhere would be betrayed.

"There's nothing to be said for you!" he shouted. "And you know it! Of all your dirty tricks this is the dirtiest! You want me to whitewash you, do you? The very snowflakes on you are turning black! How dare you ask me for a character? I've given you one already! God forbid that I should ever say a good word for you! I'd rather die!"

Stainsforth's one arm shot out. "Then die!" he said.

*   *   *

The police found Walter Streeter slumped across the dining-table. His body was still warm, but he was dead. It was easy to tell how he died; for it was not his hand that his visitor had shaken, but his throat. Walter Streeter had been strangled. Of his assailant there was no trace. On the table and on his clothes were flakes of melting snow. But how it came there remained a mystery, for no snow was reported from any district on the day he died.

THE ASTRAL BODY OF A U.S. MAIL TRUCK

James Leo Herlihy

Note to the person who finds this important document upon my death. I, Mrs. Dorothy Fitzpatrick, urge you, in fact I beg you, please to send a copy of it to Duke University, the Extrasensory Perception Department they have there which I've read about. Another copy please to the Institute for Studies in Spiritualism in Long Beach, California. And if the finder has half a heart to understand with, upon finishing his or her perusal of this document, he or she will undoubtedly be pleased to see to it that a copy gets into the hands of my neighbor right here in Tampa, Mrs. Malvina Cheney, who lives catty-cornered across the street. I myself have severed all relations with this person, for reasons that will become self-evident upon further perusal.

Purpose. For all I know I am breaking new ground here, and wish to bequeath my tiny bit to the great storehouse of human knowledge on certain subjects, to wit:

It is known that dogs and cats and horses and such have ghosts as well as people. That is, they have definite spirit life after decease. Surely there is ample evidence on file in the above places on that score. Cases for instance where a person and her pet, like my former neighbor Mrs. V. and her dachshund, were killed simultaneously at the same time by a speeding auto in front of a fruit market on the Tamiami Trail. And not only did Mrs. V. make an appearance to loved ones after being thus jarred loose from her physical container, but also the little dog right along with her as well.

This is common enough I have no doubt, but now I wish to add to this body of knowledge the fact that even a machine can put in an astral appearance, under certain circumstances. In my own experience, to wit, a U.S. Mail Truck.

The record: I include here certain notes of an autobiographical nature for whatever they may be worth to students of the subject. I am a lady living alone at the age of forty-eight for the better part of two years since my husband passed away in a shrimp boat that sank in a gale off Key West, and am of sound mind. Although of course his passing left me distraught for some time thereafter which I do not consider in any way an abnormalcy. Particularly not since I was able to function fine right after his death, continuing to hostess at the Two Skippers Marine Grill and Yacht Club Lounge on Caroline Street, knowing it's best to keep right on going in a time of loss for otherwise the thing can get the best of you. Naturally I took off until the funeral was over, but was there at the old stand the very next day, and cheerful too, of which I am proud, not unduly.

But this is veering from my topic.

For reasons that have nothing to do with these notes, I saw fit to retire the following year at the age of forty-seven, and take it just plain easy for a change in my lovely white cottage on Front Street. Frankly, I am a great reader in matters of metaphysics, astrology and spiritualism, and saw fit to pursue these studies in earnest during the remaining years left to me.

I do not consider forty-seven *old* by a long shot, but it seemed to me I ought to begin to develop my inner life against the cold time of old age, so as not to become a sad elder citizen with nothing to fall back on at all. Possibly my younger years had not been spent too wisely according to the standards of the average person. That is, I did not jump into marriage and have a lot of kids, etc., but instead chose to have a good time for a little while, which went on well into my thirties. And so perhaps I, a childless lady, had some regrets on that score and wanted to do better with the rest of my years now that the Captain (my husband) had made the Big Change, leaving me on my own again.

It was in this frame of mind that I settled into my widowhood in the lovely white cottage on Front Street, living on income from the Two Skippers Marine Grill and Yacht Club Lounge, which half interest in it was left me by the Captain.

The truth is, I was not too miserable. I told myself he was at sea (which of course he was) on a voyage from which he would not return to me—but one day I would join him. That was the philosophical way I looked at it, and was therefore not too miserable at all.

I turned to feminine matters such as my little garden, and began to tend it in earnest. Each morning I got up at seven or so and drank coffee in the garden while fiddling with ferns and flowers and seeds and such. Then later, after a bit of toast and an egg, perhaps I'd study for an hour or two there in the shade of the banyan tree, study my astrology charts and just plain meditate into the flowers at times. Mornings in this part of the country have excessively blue skies, and our birds here are known to sing in abundance.

Thus everything went along reasonably splendid for the first year.

Mail is delivered in our neighborhood at about eleven-thirty A.M. The mailman (who I will call Sidney as a non-diplume—not that I think he'd be ashamed, but it is of no concern to anybody else's business) was a very nice vigorous man, fairly short and perhaps a smidgeon younger than myself, with a fine smile. He used to ride up every morning on this very cute type of three-wheeled truck they give the mailmen to use for their rounds here lately.

The way I'd know he was coming was as follows: I'd hear the motor from about two blocks away. It did not make a *VVvvrrr-roooommm* sound like an ordinary car motor. I'd say it was more like a thousand putt-putts all jammed together into a very few seconds. At any rate it was just the proper sound for a fine little red white and blue truck to make, and after a while I noticed that just the mere sound of it made my heart go *putputputputput* each morning when I heard it.

All of which is not at all extraneous to the record, as students of these matters will soon see as more is revealed. For it was this kindred sounding in my own bosom that tipped me off finally as to how I felt about Mr. Sidney Ritter. (This was in the *second* year after the death of the Captain, I might chance to repeat, certainly not the first.)

I received a good deal of mail in those days. I sent for literature for my studies, plus assorted magazines, and also wrote quite a few letters and received answers from people on these topics that interest me, namely, spiritualism, metaphysics, etc., as noted above. Therefore, Sidney always had something for me, it seemed.

He also customarily had a bill or a catalog or some trifle to deliver to my catty-cornered neighbor, Mrs. Malvina Cheney. This woman was always waiting for him each morning in front of her quite ugly green-and-yellow house. It was Sidney's next stop after my own tasteful white cottage.

It was my unpleasant duty to inject here, for the purpose of accuracy, a note on Mrs. Cheney's unfortunate character. The woman is a dangerous troublemaker of the first water. She seldom leaves her front porch (even gives herself henna packs there) for fear of missing something. Usually of course there are red henna splotches all over her unfortunate face. Several months were destined to pass before Malvina Cheney would present me with evidence to support my first hunch about her, namely, that she is of a very low order of human life and deserves our sympathy.

Now I intend not to beat around the bush at all. Students of these matters will understand.

Sidney Ritter and I started in having a love affair.

Note please that Sidney was not a married man, but a widower with three good-looking but ungrateful children. When his wife died, he went back to living with his mother, a dominating (Scorpio) creature who made his life miserable. All she ever had to say to him in the way of conversation was accusing him of various faults, etc. I see no reason to go into her character, but wish to give a picture of the pathetic home life of a gentleman whose children had been alienated from him by a dominating Scorpio.

Which explains, I believe, his lonesomeness for decent human company.

Sidney began to come around in the evenings, after first of all faithfully having supper at home for the sake of his kids, even though I doubt they appreciated it. Then he would come and sit in my garden, sometimes sharing a can of beer or two with me at the most.

I don't know if two people make a symposium, but let me say right here that we had wonderful talks on all subjects, politics and love and exceedingly deep matters. And sometimes merely our own personal feelings. Out of all due respect for the Captain who was no kind of talker at all (although a fine and faithful husband in other respects) I believe Sidney's company was as excellent as any I'd ever enjoyed in my life.

Frankly, he thought the world of me as well.

"Dorothy," he said to me on that first evening, sitting in a wicker chair in my garden, "I have never taken you for just an ordinary woman with a good figure and blond hair, far from it." And then he confessed to me that even in the old days before he had the Front Street route, he used to see me now and then, crossing a street somewhere or hostessing at the Two Skippers, and admired me in a special way. He stated that I had "eyes with a capital E."

(Although I do have exceptionally large pale blue eyes, set wide apart which men like, he was undoubtedly making reference to the fact that I have second sight. For I was born with a veil.)

Let me state that I did not remember Sidney at all from those old days. First of all, I did not have the habit of looking around at other men while married to the Captain, not even when he was on a three-week trip at sea. (I have indicated that my younger years were not spent too wisely, but do not interpret this too hastily, as I have always been a one-man woman. That is, during the duration of all intimate associations, I have practiced strictest fidelity.) And second of all, a mailman looks very different out of uniform.

But it was this ability of Sidney's to look beneath the surface of a woman, to see not only the color of her eyes but some of her deepest feelings, that drew me to him from the start.

There is no need here to delve further into the extremely personal events of that night, the night he reported to me his fondness for my eyes. But let it be said that henceforward the sound of a U.S. Mail Truck was better music to me than even the finest blues record on the jukebox at the Two Skippers Marine Grill and Yacht Club Lounge on Caroline Street.

Late in the mornings from then on, whenever I heard the first faraway *putputputputput,* the effect on me was such that I was forced to cease whatever I was doing and catch my breath. At times I had to sit down altogether before regaining enough strength to go out and wait for him to turn the corner into Front Street.

(I think the government is to be profoundly saluted for giving out these little trucks, which make all the difference between night and day in the life of any mailman. For now, with all that power under him, he is like a gallant horseman on his daily rounds, instead of a beast of burden with a heavy pack on his back as in the old days, on foot. But this is veering.)

At the start of our association, Sidney always arranged to touch my fingers in a lingering way as he handed me my envelopes. And sometimes, in a whisper, he would communicate some sweet message of a personal nature. The two of us, like high school children in love, enjoyed greatly the pleasurable throes of our secret.

And then we became somewhat reckless.

Sidney took to coming back to the garden with me for a few minutes to have a cup of coffee. It seems we had forgotten altogether the hostile presence of Mrs. Malvina Cheney on the porch of her green-and-yellow, excessively tasteless house across the street.

*   *   *

Late in the summer, Sidney's mother went to the hospital for what would prove to be a nasty though not fatal operation, and for more than three weeks Sidney had to stay home every single evening to tend to his children. A neighbor woman looked after them in the daytime, but as is only proper, Sidney took over for himself in the evenings. Therefore, that August, we saw each other only at the brief two or three minute coffee sessions that Sidney could snatch from the government quite harmlessly each morning. And so it went, right into September.

On the first Tuesday of the month, it so happened there was a heavy rain going on at mail time. Certainly we could not sit in the garden, quite naturally, and so Sidney stepped into my living room.

It is only necessary to state here quite flatly that on this particular rainy morning, Sidney and I lost control of ourselves. (I'd like to add that this had never before taken place on government time. However, on that morning, it did.)

Up to this point, I had no concrete evidence on which to base my suspicion of the true depths of lowness of Malvina Cheney's nature. Previously, I had merely taken the view that she was coarse, and let it go at that.

But that rainy Tuesday morning, incredible as it may be to believe, Sidney stepped out of my front door, and there, *right on my porch,* stood this creature, dripping wet and carrying a closed umbrella.

"Don't you touch me!" she screamed. Naturally Sidney had not the slightest intention of touching that low person. On pain of death, he would not have touched her with her own closed umbrella, I might add. But she kept shouting at him, and making no sense whatever. "You're a public servant, do you hear me, and I want my mail! You're my employee, do you know that?"

Sidney tried to get past the woman, but she stood there blocking the steps and spilling out these thoughts from her very low-vibration mind, and saying, "Don't you dare touch me!"

It was hard to believe that such a nightmare was taking place right there on my own front porch in the rain. Sidney and I were both struck dumb with the horror of it.

"Don't you think the post office won't hear about this," she said. "I've known what was going on over here, for months now I've known all about it!"

Sidney was trembling understandably. He looked straight into my eyes, pleading with me for help. That did it. Knowing the high regard he had for my eyes, and seeing him look into them for guidance, my dander was up.

"Malvina Cheney," I said in a cold and frightening tone of voice. "You remove yourself from my front porch this precise second, or I'll tear you in half."

I am unable to report accurately what took place next. I do not believe I actually *handled* the woman, but somehow Sidney got past her. He flew down my front path and into his truck, Malvina Cheney right behind him broadcasting at the top of her voice. It was raining harder than ever. Poor Sidney was soaked to the bone. It looked like every front porch on the street had people on it now, mostly women, and they were all looking and listening to every foul word that came out of that mouth.

I stood on my porch and cried like an infant. Sidney had some trouble getting his motor started. He kept pumping and pumping with his foot. Somehow he got it going and went speeding away up the street at a terrible speed. Malvina Cheney went right on, marching up and down the sidewalk with her umbrella hoisted, her mouth going a mile a minute at its usual excessive volume.

I went back inside. For some reason I kept looking at the bed, at the crumpled pillow where Sidney's head had been. I remember this part very clearly. I was leaning on the doorway of the bedroom, telling myself that what I wanted most to do was to go over to the bed and take up that pillow and hold it next to my face. But I never made it to the pillow.

The accident took place then. It took place right on the corner of Front and Caroline Street. I heard it, the whole thing. Two different screeches of brakes, one of them Sidney's and the other an enormous moving van, and then the worst crashing sound I ever heard in my life.

Yes, I heard the whole thing very clearly. And I just kept looking at the pillow, wanted to go hold it, but unable to move.

The purpose of this record, as heretofore stated, is not to dwell upon my own mortal agony and such trivial emotions. These after all will pass, along with the body which is merely a dollar and a half worth of chemicals.

I intend to restrict myself to a record of the evidence pertaining to the activity of the spirit after it has stepped out of its material bonds.

The following morning, the Tampa *Sun-Times* carried a front-page story of the terrible wreck of the post office truck and the moving van. There were photographs printed with it. At the bottom of the article, it said the name of the funeral home where Sidney would be laid out.

Frankly, I laughed out loud. This may seem crusty, considering the three orphans. But having the knowledge I have acquired through my studies, the notion of death does not truly faze me at all. My only sad thought about Sidney was that he should have made the Big Change in such a violent smash-up. It seemed to me he deserved better than that, but these things alas do happen occasionally, even to very fine people when they have the misfortune of getting their paths crossed up with inferior vibrations of the sort we have on our street.

But I need not have worried for a minute. Because it turned out that Sidney himself was in fine fettle.

That morning, the morning after the crash, was fine and sunny. Of course I had not slept, for in such circumstances sleep is often withheld from a person. I was sitting in the big overstuffed chair in my living room where I had spent the night with Sidney's lovely crumpled pillow next to my face. And at eleven-forty, I heard, as usual, the most beautiful sound in the world, a faraway *putputputputput.*

My emotions of that moment may have some pertinence to the record. Therefore I report that I experienced no surprise whatever, but merely a great wave of happiness, a more tremendous joy than anything I had ever experienced in my life. And I had not one doubt that the truck I heard was Sidney's and that he himself was the driver. People's driving is just like their voices or their handwriting. Nobody could ever imitate the way Sidney Ritter took a corner in that little truck. Of if they tried, they might fool Mrs. Cheney, but not a person so sensitively attuned to the sound as myself.

Next, as on many a morning in the past, I felt the same weakness in the stomach at the sound. I caught my breath and stepped out onto the porch into the sunlight. I am pleased to report that Mrs. Cheney was nowhere in sight. I walked up my little path and stood at the sidewalk, and soon, much closer than before, I heard the *putputputputput,* and then I saw Sidney and the truck.

It was just as red white and blue as ever. If there was any change at all (and I would not *swear* to this detail), it seemed to me Sidney took that corner with even more style than I'd ever seen him do it before.

I watched him swerving zigzag up the street, stopping first on one side and then the other, until at last he reached my gate. Something told me Sidney did not want today to be different from any other day. Certainly he was not interested in a discussion of the previous day's misfortunes. He wanted to forget any reference to that altogether.

I said, Good morning, Mr. Ritter—in exactly my usual voice. And he said, G'morning, Mrs. Fitzpatrick. Then, just as on the first morning following the start of our intimate association, Sidney whispered to me, "No mail today, but I think you got my message."

Later that day a second uniformed man came by the house and put something in my mailbox. Of course the post office had to put on someone to replace Sidney Ritter.

But as far as I know I'm the only person on the block that gets two deliveries a day.

I have not seen this new man at all. And since I am busy with my studies, I seldom see anyone, even Sidney. But I always hear his truck, and sometimes I hear it at night, too, *putputputputput-*

put-ing along on its zigzag way and swerving around in colossal style through all the streets of heaven.

My final suggestion, which it occurs to me the above facts may support, is this: that anything sufficiently loved in the time of its life may achieve immortality in the astral plane.

Additional note: Upon further reconsideration, I see no reason whatsoever for sending a copy of this record to Mrs. Malvina Cheney.

THE

BUS

Shirley Jackson

Old Miss Harper was going home, although the night was wet and nasty. Miss Harper disliked traveling at any time, and she particularly disliked traveling on this dirty small bus which was her only way of getting home; she had frequently complained to the bus company about their service because it seemed that no matter where she wanted to go, they had no respectable bus to carry her. Getting away from home was bad enough—Miss Harper was fond of pointing out to the bus company—but getting home always seemed very close to impossible. Tonight Miss Harper had no choice: if she did not go home by this particular bus she could not go for another day. Annoyed, tired, depressed, she tapped irritably on the counter of the little tobacco store which served also as the bus station. Sir, she was thinking, beginning her letter of complaint, although I am an elderly lady of modest circumstances and must curtail my fondness for travel, let me point out that your bus service falls far below . . .

Outside, the bus stirred noisily, clearly not anxious to be moving; Miss Harper thought she could already hear the weary sound of its springs sinking out of shape. I just can't make this trip again, Miss Harper thought, even seeing Stephanie isn't worth it, they really go out of their way to make you uncomfortable. "Can I get my ticket, please?" she said sharply, and the old man at the other end of the counter put down his paper and gave her a look of hatred.

Miss Harper ordered her ticket, deploring her own cross voice, and the old man slapped it down on the counter in front of her and said, "You got three minutes before the bus leaves."

He'd love to tell me I missed it, Miss Harper thought, and made a point of counting her change.

The rain was beating down, and Miss Harper hurried the few exposed steps to the door of the bus. The driver was slow in opening the door and as Miss Harper climbed in she was thinking, Sir, I shall never travel with your company again. Your ticket salesmen are ugly, your drivers are surly, your vehicles indescribably filthy . . .

There were already several people sitting in the bus, and Miss Harper wondered where they could possibly be going; were there really this many small towns served only by this bus? Were there really other people who would endure this kind of trip to get somewhere, even home? I'm very out of sorts, Miss Harper thought, very out of sorts; it's too strenuous a visit for a woman of my age; I need to get home. She thought of a hot bath and a cup of tea and her own bed, and sighed. No one offered to help her put her suitcase on the rack, and she glanced over her shoulder at the driver sitting with his back turned and thought, he'd probably rather put me off the bus than help me, and then, perceiving her own ill nature, smiled. The bus company might write a letter of complaint about *me,* she told herself and felt better. She had providentially taken a sleeping pill before leaving for the bus station, hoping to sleep through as much of the trip as possible, and at last, sitting near the back, she promised herself that it would not be unbearably long before she had a bath and a cup of tea, and tried to compose the bus company's letter of complaint. Madam, a lady of your experience and advanced age ought surely to be aware of the problems confronting a poor but honest little company which wants only . . .

She was aware that the bus had started, because she was rocked and bounced in her seat, and the feeling of rattling and throbbing beneath the soles of her shoes stayed with her even when she slept at last. She lay back uneasily, her head resting on the seat back, moving back and forth with the motion of the bus, and around her other people slept, or spoke softly, or stared blankly out the windows at the passing lights and the rain.

Sometime during her sleep Miss Harper was jostled by some-one moving into the seat behind her, her head was pushed and her hat disarranged; for a minute, bewildered by sleep, Miss Harper clutched at her hat, and said vaguely, "Who?"

"Go back to sleep," a young voice said, and giggled. "I'm just running away from home, that's all."

Miss Harper was not awake, but she opened her eyes a little and looked up to the ceiling of the bus. "That's wrong," Miss Harper said as clearly as she could. "That's wrong. Go back."

There was another giggle. "Too late," the voice said. "Go back to sleep."

Miss Harper did. She slept uncomfortably and awkwardly, her mouth a little open. Sometime, perhaps an hour later, her head was jostled again and the voice said, "I think I'm going to get off here. 'By now."

"You'll be sorry," Miss Harper said, asleep. "Go back."

Then, still later, the bus driver was shaking her. "Look, lady," he was saying, "I'm not an alarm clock. Wake up and get off the bus."

"What?" Miss Harper stirred, opened her eyes, felt for her pocketbook.

"I'm not an alarm clock," the driver said. His voice was harsh and tired. "I'm not an alarm clock. Get off the bus."

"What?" said Miss Harper again.

"This is as far as you go. You got a ticket to here. You've ar-rived. And I am not an alarm clock waking up people to tell them when it's time to get off; you got here, lady, and it's not part of my job to carry you off the bus. I'm not—"

"I intend to report you," Miss Harper said, awake. She felt for her pocketbook and found it in her lap, moved her feet, straight-ened her hat. She was stiff and moving was difficult.

"Report me. But from somewhere else. I got a bus to run. Now will you please get off so I can go on my way?"

His voice was loud, and Miss Harper was sickeningly aware of faces turned toward her from along the bus, grins, amused comments. The driver turned and stamped off down the bus to his seat, saying, "She thinks I'm an alarm clock," and Miss Harper, without assistance and moving clumsily, took down her suitcase and struggled with it down the aisle. Her suitcase banged against seats, and she knew that people were staring at her; she was terribly afraid that she might stumble and fall.

"I'll certainly report you," she said to the driver, who shrugged.

"Come on, lady," he said. "It's the middle of the night and I got a bus to run."

"You ought to be *ashamed* of yourself," Miss Harper said wildly, wanting to cry.

"Lady," the driver said with elaborate patience, "please get off my bus."

The door was open, and Miss Harper eased herself and her suitcase onto the steep step. "She thinks everyone's an alarm clock, got to see she gets off the bus," the driver said behind her, and Miss Harper stepped onto the ground. Suitcase, pocketbook, gloves, hat; she had them all. She had barely taken stock when the bus started with a jerk, almost throwing her backward, and Miss Harper, for the first time in her life, wanted to run and shake her fist at someone. I'll report him, she thought, I'll see that he loses his job, and then she realized that she was in the wrong place.

Standing quite still in the rain and the darkness Miss Harper became aware that she was not at the bus corner of her town where the bus should have left her. She was on an empty crossroads in the rain. There were no stores, no lights, no taxis, no people. There was nothing, in fact, but a wet dirt road under her feet and a signpost where two roads came together. Don't panic, Miss Harper told herself, almost whispering, don't panic; it's all right, it's all right, you'll see that it's all right, don't be frightened.

She took a few steps in the direction the bus had gone, but it was out of sight and when Miss Harper called falteringly, "Come back," and, "Help," there was no answer to the shocking sound of her own voice out loud except the steady drive of the rain. I sound old, she thought, but I will not panic. She turned in a circle, her suitcase in her hand, and told herself, don't panic, it's all right.

There was no shelter in sight, but the signpost said RICKET'S LANDING; so that's where I am, Miss Harper thought, I've come to Ricket's Landing and I don't like it here. She set her suitcase down next to the signpost and tried to see down the road; perhaps there might be a house, or even some kind of a barn or shed where she could get out of the rain. She was crying a little, and lost and hopeless, saying Please, won't someone come? when she saw headlights far off down the road and realized that someone was really coming to help her. She ran to the middle of the road and stood waving, her gloves wet and her pocketbook draggled. "Here," she called, "here I am, please come and help me."

Through the sound of the rain she could hear the motor, and then the headlights caught her and, suddenly embarrassed, she put her pocketbook in front of her face while the lights were on her. The lights belonged to a small truck, and it came to an abrupt stop beside her and the window near her was rolled down and a man's voice said furiously, "You want to get killed? You trying to get killed or something? What you doing in the middle of the road, trying to get killed?" The young man turned and spoke to the driver. "It's some dame. Running out in the road like that."

"Please," Miss Harper said, as he seemed almost about to close the window again, "please help me. The bus put me off here when it wasn't my stop and I'm lost."

"Lost?" The young man laughed richly. "First I ever heard anyone getting lost in Ricket's Landing. Mostly they have trouble *finding* it." He laughed again, and the driver, leaning forward over the steering wheel to look curiously at Miss Harper, laughed too. Miss Harper put on a willing smile, and said, "Can you take me somewhere? Perhaps a bus station?"

"No bus station." The young man shook his head profoundly. "Bus comes through here every night, stops if he's got any passengers."

"Well," Miss Harper's voice rose in spite of herself; she was suddenly afraid of antagonizing these young men; perhaps they might even leave her here where they found her, in the wet and dark. "Please," she said, "can I get in with you, out of the rain?"

The two young men looked at each other. "Take her down to the old lady's," one of them said.

"She's pretty wet to get in the truck," the other one said.

"Please," Miss Harper said, "I'll be glad to pay you what I can."

"We'll take you to the old lady," the driver said. "Come on, move over," he said to the other young man.

"Wait, my suitcase." Miss Harper ran back to the signpost, no longer caring how she must look, stumbling about in the rain, and brought her suitcase over to the truck.

"That's awful wet," the young man said. He opened the door and took the suitcase from Miss Harper. "I'll just throw it in the back," he said, and turned and tossed the suitcase into the back of the truck; Miss Harper heard the sodden thud of its landing, and wondered what things would look like when she unpacked; my bottle of cologne, she thought despairingly. "Get *in,*" the young man said, and, "My God, you're wet."

Miss Harper had never climbed up into a truck before, and her skirt was tight and her gloves slippery from the rain. Without help from the young man she put one knee on the high step and somehow hoisted herself in; this cannot be happening to me, she thought clearly. The young man pulled away fastidiously as Miss Harper slid onto the seat next to him.

"You are pretty wet," the driver said, leaning over the wheel to look around at Miss Harper. "Why were you out in the rain like that?"

"The bus driver." Miss Harper began to peel off her gloves; somehow she had to make an attempt to dry herself. "He told me it was my stop."

"That would be Johnny Talbot," the driver said to the other young man. "He drives that bus."

"Well, I'm going to report him," Miss Harper said. There was a little silence in the truck, and then the driver said, "Johnny's a good guy. He means all right."

"He's a bad bus driver," Miss Harper said sharply.

The truck did not move. "You don't want to report old Johnny," the driver said.

"I most certainly—" Miss Harper began, and then stopped. Where am I? she thought, what is happening to me? "No," she said at last, "I won't report old Johnny."

The driver started the truck, and they moved slowly down the road, through the mud and the rain. The windshield wipers swept back and forth hypnotically, there was a narrow line of light ahead from their headlights, and Miss Harper thought, what is happening to me? She stirred, and the young man next to her caught his breath irritably and drew back. "She's soaking wet," he said to the driver. "I'm wet already."

"We're going down to the old lady's," the driver said. "She'll know what to do."

"What old lady?" Miss Harper did not dare to move, even turn her head. "Is there any kind of a bus station? Or even a taxi?"

"You could," the driver said consideringly, "you could wait and catch that same bus tomorrow night when it goes through. Johnny'll be driving her."

"I just want to get home as soon as possible," Miss Harper said. The truck seat was dreadfully uncomfortable, she felt steamy and sticky and chilled through, and home seemed so far away that perhaps it did not exist at all.

"Just down the road a mile or so," the driver said reassuringly.

"I've never heard of Ricket's Landing," Miss Harper said. "I can't imagine how he came to put me off there."

"Maybe somebody else was supposed to get off there and he thought it was you by mistake." This deduction seemed to tax the young man's mind to the utmost, because he said, "See, someone else might of been supposed to get off instead of you."

"Then *he's* still on the bus," said the driver, and they were both silent, appalled.

Ahead of them a light flickered, showing dimly through the rain, and the driver pointed and said, "There, that's where we're going." As they came closer Miss Harper was aware of a growing dismay. The light belonged to what seemed to be a roadhouse, and Miss Harper had never been inside a roadhouse in her life.

The house itself was only a dim shape looming in the darkness, and the light, over the side door, illuminated only a sign, hanging crooked, which read BEER *Bar & Grill.*

"Is there anywhere else I could go?" Miss Harper asked timidly, clutching her pocketbook. "I'm not at all sure, you know, that I ought—"

"Not many people here tonight," the driver said, turning the truck into the driveway and pulling up in the parking lot which had once, Miss Harper was sad to see, been a garden. "Rain, probably."

Peering through the window and the rain, Miss Harper felt, suddenly, a warm stir of recognition, of welcome; it's the house, she thought, why, of course, the house is lovely. It had clearly been an old mansion once, solidly and handsomely built, with the balance and style that belonged to a good house of an older time. "Why?" Miss Harper asked, wanting to know why such a good house should have a light tacked on over the side door, and a sign hanging crooked but saying BEER *Bar & Grill;* "Why?" asked Miss Harper, but the driver said, "This is where you wanted to go. Get her suitcase," he told the other young man.

"In here?" asked Miss Harper, feeling a kind of indignation on behalf of the fine old house, "into this saloon?" Why, I used to live in a house like this, she thought, what are they doing to our old houses?

The driver laughed. "You'll be safe," he said.

Carrying her suitcase and her pocketbook Miss Harper followed the two young men to the lighted door and passed under the crooked sign. Shameful, she thought, they haven't even bothered to take care of the place; it needs paint and tightening all around and probably a new roof, and then the driver said, "Come on, come on," and pushed open the heavy door.

"I used to live in a house like this," Miss Harper said, and the young men laughed.

"I bet you did," one of them said, and Miss Harper stopped in the doorway, staring, and realized how strange she must have sounded. Where there had certainly once been comfortable rooms, high-ceilinged and square, with tall doors and polished

floors, there was now one large dirty room, with a counter running along one side and half a dozen battered tables; there was a
jukebox in a corner and torn linoleum on the floor. "Oh, no,"
Miss Harper said. The room smelled unpleasant, and the rain
slapped against the bare windows.

Sitting around the tables and standing around the jukebox
were perhaps a dozen young people, resembling the two who
had brought Miss Harper here, all looking oddly alike, all talking
and laughing flatly. Miss Harper leaned back against the door; for
a minute she thought they were laughing about her. She was wet
and disheartened and these noisy people did not belong at all in
the old house. Then the driver turned and gestured to her.
"Come and meet the old lady," he said, and then, to the room at
large, "Look, we brought company."

"Please," Miss Harper said, but no one had given her more
than a glance. With her suitcase and her pocketbook she followed the two young men across to the counter; her suitcase
bumped against her legs and she thought, I must not fall down.

"Belle, Belle," the driver said, "look at the stray cat we found."

An enormous woman swung around in her seat at the end of
the counter, and looked at Miss Harper; looking up and down,
looking at the suitcase and Miss Harper's wet hat and wet shoes,
looking at Miss Harper's pocketbook and gloves squeezed in her
hand, the woman seemed hardly to move her eyes; it was almost
as though she absorbed Miss Harper without any particular effort.
"Hell you say," the woman said at last. Her voice was surprisingly
soft. "Hell you say."

"She's wet," the second young man said; the two young men
stood one on either side of Miss Harper, presenting her, and the
enormous woman looked her up and down. "Please," Miss
Harper said; here was a woman at least, someone who might
understand and sympathize, "please, they put me off my bus at
the wrong stop and I can't seem to find my way home. Please."

"Hell you say," the woman said, and laughed, a gentle laugh.
"She sure is wet," she said.

"Please," Miss Harper said.

"You'll take care of her?" the driver asked. He turned and

smiled down at Miss Harper, obviously waiting, and, remembering, Miss Harper fumbled in her pocketbook for her wallet. How
much, she was wondering, not wanting to ask, it was such a short
ride, but if they hadn't come I might have gotten pneumonia, and
paid all those doctor's bills; I have caught cold, she thought with
great clarity, and chose two five-dollar bills from her wallet. They
can't argue over five dollars each, she thought, and sneezed. The
two young men and the large woman were watching her with
great interest, and all of them saw that after Miss Harper took out
the two five-dollar bills there were a single and two tens left in
the wallet. The money was not wet. I suppose I should be grateful for that, Miss Harper thought, moving slowly. She handed a
five-dollar bill to each young man and felt that they glanced at one
another over her head.

"Thanks," the driver said; I could have gotten away with a
dollar each, Miss Harper thought. "Thanks," the driver said again,
and the other young man said, "Say, thanks."

"Thank *you,*" Miss Harper said formally.

"I'll put you up for the night," the woman said. "You can sleep
here. Go tomorrow." She looked Miss Harper up and down again.
"Dry off a little," she said.

"Is there anywhere else?" Then, afraid that this might seem
ungracious, Miss Harper said, "I mean, is there any way of going
on tonight? I don't want to impose."

"We got rooms for rent." The woman half turned back to the
counter. "Cost you ten for the night."

She's leaving me bus fare home, Miss Harper thought; I suppose I should be grateful. "I'd better, I guess," she said, taking
out her wallet again. "I mean, thank you."

The woman accepted the bill and half turned back to the
counter. "Upstairs," she said. "Take your choice. No one's
around." She glanced sideways at Miss Harper. "I'll see you get a
cup of coffee in the morning. I wouldn't turn a dog out without a
cup of coffee."

"Thank you." Miss Harper knew where the staircase would be,
and she turned and, carrying her suitcase and her pocketbook,
went to what had once been the front hall and there was the

staircase, so lovely in its still proportions that she caught her breath. She turned back and saw the large woman staring at her, and said, "I used to live in a house like this. Built about the same time, I guess. One of those good old houses that were made to stand forever, and where people—"

"Hell you say," the woman said, and turned back to the counter.

The young people scattered around the big room were talking; in one corner a group surrounded the two who had brought Miss Harper and now and then they laughed. Miss Harper was touched with a little sadness now, looking at them, so at home in the big ugly room which had once been so beautiful. It would be nice, she thought, to speak to these young people, perhaps even become their friend, talk and laugh with them; perhaps they might like to know that this spot where they came together had been a lady's drawing room. Hesitating a little, Miss Harper wondered if she might call "Good night," or "Thank you" again, or even "God bless you all." Then, since no one looked at her, she started up the stairs. Halfway there was a landing with a stained-glass window, and Miss Harper stopped, holding her breath. When she had been a child the stained-glass window on the stair landing in her house had caught the sunlight, and scattered it on the stairs in a hundred colors. Fairyland colors, Miss Harper thought, remembering; I wonder why we don't live in these houses now. I'm lonely, Miss Harper thought, and then she thought, but I must get out of these wet clothes; I really am catching cold.

Without thinking she turned at the top of the stairs and went to the front room on the left; that had always been her room. The door was open and she glanced in; this was clearly a bedroom for rent, and it was ugly and drab and cheap. The light turned on with a cord hanging beside the door, and Miss Harper stood in the doorway, saddened by the peeling wallpaper and the sagging floor; what have they done to the house, she thought; how can I sleep here tonight?

At last she moved to cross the room and set her suitcase on the bed. I must get dry, she told herself, I must make the best of things. The bed was correctly placed, between the two front windows, but the mattress was stiff and lumpy, and Miss Harper was frightened at the faint smell of dark couplings and a remote echo in the springs; I will not think about such things, Miss Harper thought, I will not let myself dwell on any such thing; this might be the room where I slept as a girl. The windows were almost right—two across the front, two at the side—and the door was placed correctly; how they did build these old places to a square-cut pattern, Miss Harper thought, how they did put them together; there must be a thousand houses all over the country built exactly like this. The closet, however, was on the wrong side. Some oddness of construction had set the closet to Miss Harper's right as she sat on the bed, when it ought really to have been on her left; when she was a girl the big closet had been her playhouse and her hiding place, but it had been on the left.

The bathroom was wrong, too, but that was less important. Miss Harper had thought wistfully of a hot tub before she slept, but a glance a the bathtub discouraged her; she could simply wait until she got home. She washed her face and hands, and the warm water comforted her. She was further comforted to find that her bottle of cologne had not broken in her suitcase and that nothing inside had gotten wet. At least she could sleep in a dry nightgown, although in a cold bed.

She shivered once in the cold sheets, remembering a child's bed. She lay in the darkness with her eyes open, wondering at last where she was and how she had gotten here: first the bus and then the truck, and now she lay in the darkness and no one knew where she was or what was to become of her. She had only her suitcase and a little money in her pocketbook; she did not know where she was. She was very tired and she thought that perhaps the sleeping pill she had taken much earlier had still not quite worn off; perhaps the sleeping pill had been affecting all her actions, since she had been following docilely, bemused, wherever she was taken; in the morning, she told herself sleepily, I'll show them I can make decisions for myself.

The noise downstairs which had been a jukebox and adolescent laughter faded softly into a distant melody; my mother is singing in the drawing room, Miss Harper thought, and the com-

pany is sitting on the stiff little chairs listening; my father is playing the piano. She could not quite distinguish the song, but it was
one she had heard her mother sing many times; I could creep out
to the top of the stairs and listen, she thought, and then became
aware that there was a rustling in the closet, but the closet was
on the wrong side, on the right instead of the left. It is more a
rattling than rustling, Miss Harper thought, wanting to listen to
her mother singing, it is as though something wooden were being shaken around. Shall I get out of bed and quiet it so I can hear
the singing? Am I too warm and comfortable, am I too sleepy?

The closet was on the wrong side, but the rattling continued,
just loud enough to be irritating, and at last, knowing she would
never sleep until it stopped, Miss Harper swung her legs over the
side of the bed and, sleepily, padded barefoot over to the closet
door, reminding herself to go to the right instead of the left.

"What are you doing in there?" she asked aloud, and opened
the door. There was just enough light for her to see that it was a
wooden snake, head lifted, stirring and rattling itself against the
other toys. Miss Harper laughed. "It's my snake," she said aloud,
"it's my old snake, and it's come alive." In the back of the closet
she could see her old toy clown, bright and cheerful, and as she
watched, enchanted, the toy clown flopped languidly forward
and back, coming alive. At Miss Harper's feet the snake moved
blindly, clattering against a doll house where the tiny people inside stirred, and against a set of blocks, which fell and crashed.
Then Miss Harper saw the big beautiful doll sitting on a small
chair, the doll with long golden curls and wide-lashed blue eyes
and a stiff organdy party dress; as Miss Harper held out her hands
in joy the doll opened her eyes and stood up.

"Rosabelle," Miss Harper cried out, "Rosabelle, it's me."

The doll turned, looking widely at her, smile painted on. The
red lips opened and the doll quacked, outrageously, a flat slapping voice coming out of that fair mouth. "Go away, old lady,"
the doll said, "go away, old lady, go away."

Miss Harper backed away, staring. The clown tumbled and
danced, mouthing at Miss Harper, the snake flung its eyeless head
viciously at her ankles, and the doll turned, holding her skirts,

and her mouth opened and shut. "Go away," she quacked, "go away, old lady, go away."

The inside of the closet was all alive; a small doll ran madly from side to side, the animals paraded solemnly down the gangplank of Noah's ark, a stuffed bear wheezed asthmatically. The noise was louder and louder, and then Miss Harper realized that they were all looking at her hatefully and moving toward her. The doll said "Old lady, old lady," and stepped forward; Miss Harper slammed the closet door and leaned against it. Behind her the snake crashed against the door and the doll's voice went on and on. Crying out, Miss Harper turned and fled, but the closet was on the wrong side and she turned the wrong way and found herself cowering against the far wall with the door impossibly far away while the closet door slowly opened and the doll's face, smiling, looked for her.

Miss Harper fled. Without stopping to look behind she flung herself across the room and through the door, down the hall and on down the wide lovely stairway. "Mommy," she screamed, "Mommy, Mommy."

Screaming, she fled out the door. "Mommy," she cried, and fell, going down and down into darkness, turning, trying to catch onto something solid and real, crying.

"Look, lady," the bus driver said. "I'm not an alarm clock. Wake up and get off the bus."

"You'll be sorry," Miss Harper said distinctly.

"Wake up," he said, "wake up and get off the bus."

"I intend to report you," Miss Harper said. Pocketbook, gloves, hat, suitcase.

"I'll certainly report you," she said, almost crying.

"This is as far as you go," the driver said.

The bus lurched, moved, and Miss Harper almost stumbled in the driving rain, her suitcase at her feet, under the sign reading RICKET'S LANDING.

THE

FRIENDS

OF THE FRIENDS

Henry James

I find, as you prophesied, much that's interesting, but little that helps the delicate question—the possibility of publication. Her diaries are less systematic than I hoped; she only had a blessed habit of noting and narrating. She summarized, she saved; she appears seldom indeed to have let a good story pass without catching it on the wing. I allude of course not so much to things she heard as to things she saw and felt. She writes sometimes of herself, sometimes of others, sometimes of the combination. It's under this last rubric that she's usually most vivid. But it's not, you'll understand, when she's most vivid that she's always most publishable. To tell the truth she's fearfully indiscreet, or has at least all the material for making *me* so. Take as an instance the fragment I send you after dividing it for your convenience into several small chapters. It's the contents of a thin blank-book which I've had copied out and which has the merit of being nearly enough a rounded thing, an intelligible whole. These pages evidently date from years ago. I've read with the liveliest wonder the statement they so circumstantially make and done my best to swallow the prodigy they leave to be inferred. These things would be striking, wouldn't they? to any reader; but can you imagine for a moment my placing such a document before the world, even though, as if she herself had desired the world should have the benefit of it, she has given her friends neither name nor initials? Have you any sort of clue to their identity? I leave her the floor.

I

I know perfectly of course that I brought it upon myself; but that doesn't make it any better. I was the first to speak of her to him— he had never even heard her mentioned. Even if I had happened not to speak some one else would have made up for it: I tried afterwards to find comfort in that reflexion. But the comfort of reflexions is thin: the only comfort that counts in life is not to have been a fool. That's a beatitude I shall doubtless never enjoy. "Why you ought to meet her and talk it over" is what I immediately said. "Birds of a feather flock together." I told him who she was and that they were birds of a feather because if he had had in youth a strange adventure she had had about the same time just such another. It was well known to her friends—an incident she was constantly called on to describe. She was charming clever pretty unhappy; but it was none the less the thing to which she had originally owed her reputation.

Being at the age of eighteen somewhere abroad with an aunt she had had a vision of one of her parents at the moment of death. The parent was in England hundreds of miles away and so far as she knew neither dying nor dead. It was by day, in the museum of some great foreign town. She had passed alone, in advance of her companions, into a small room containing some famous work of art and occupied at that moment by two other persons. One of these was an old custodian; the second, before observing him, she took for a stranger, a tourist. She was merely conscious that he was bareheaded and seated on a bench. The instant her eyes rested on him however she beheld to her amazement her father, who, as if he had long waited for her, looked at her in singular distress and an impatience that was akin to reproach. She rushed to him with a bewildered cry, "Papa, what *is* it?" but this was followed by an exhibition of still livelier feeling when on her movement he simply vanished, leaving the custodian and her relations, who were by that time at her heels, to gather round her in dismay. These persons, the official, the aunt, the cousins, were therefore in a manner witnesses of the fact— the fact at least of the impression made on her; and there was the further testimony of a doctor who was attending one of the party and to whom it was immediately afterwards communicated. He gave her a remedy for hysterics, but said to the aunt privately: "Wait and see if something doesn't happen at home." Something *had* happened—the poor father, suddenly and violently seized, had died that morning. The aunt, the mother's sister, received before the day was out a telegram announcing the event and requesting her to prepare her niece for it. Her niece was already prepared, and the girl's sense of this visitation remained of course indelible. We had all, as her friends, had it conveyed to us and had conveyed it creepily to each other. Twelve years had elapsed, and as a woman who had made an unhappy marriage and lived apart from her husband she had become interesting from other sources; but since the name she now bore was a name frequently borne, and since moreover her judicial separation, as things were going, could hardly count as a distinction, it was usual to qualify her as "the one, you know, who saw her father's ghost."

As for him, dear man, he had seen his mother's—so there you are! I had never heard of that till this occasion on which our closer, our pleasanter acquaintance led him, through some turn of the subject of our talk, to mention it and to inspire me in so doing with the impulse to let him know that he had a rival in the field—a person with whom he could compare notes. Later on his story became for him, perhaps because of my unduly repeating it, likewise a convenient worldly label: but it hadn't a year before been the ground on which he was introduced to me. He had other merits, just as she, poor thing, had others. I can honestly say that I was quite aware of them from the first—I discovered them sooner than he discovered mine. I remember how it struck me even at the time that his sense of mine was quickened by my having been able to match, though not indeed straight from my own experience, his curious anecdote. It dated, this anecdote, as hers did, from some dozen years before—a year in which, at Oxford, he had for some reason of his own been staying on into the "Long." He had been in the August afternoon on the river. Coming back into his room while it was still distinct daylight he found his mother standing there as if her eyes had been fixed on the door. He had had a letter from her that morning out of Wales, where she was staying with her father. At the sight of him she smiled with extraordinary radiance and extended her arms to him, and then as he sprang forward and joyfully opened his own she vanished from the place. He wrote to her that night, telling her what had happened; the letter had been carefully preserved. The next morning he heard of her death. He was through this chance of our talk extremely struck with the little prodigy I was able to produce for him. He had never encountered another case. Certainly they ought to meet, my friend and he; certainly they would have something in common. I would arrange this, wouldn't I?—if *she* didn't mind; for himself he didn't mind in the least. I had promised to speak to her of the matter as soon as possible, and within the week I was able to do so. She "minded" as little as he; she was perfectly willing to see him. And yet no meeting was to occur—as meetings are commonly understood.

II

That's just half my tale—the extraordinary way it was hindered. This was the fault of a series of accidents; but the accidents, persisting for years, became, to me and to others, a subject of mirth with either party. They were droll enough at first, then they grew rather a bore. The odd thing was that both parties were amenable: it wasn't a case of their being indifferent, much less of their being indisposed. It was one of the caprices of chance, aided I suppose by some rather settled opposition of their interests and habits. His were centered in his office, his eternal inspectorship, which left him small leisure, constantly calling him away and making him break engagements. He liked society, but he found it everywhere and took it at a run. I never knew at a given moment where he was, and there were times when for months together I never saw him. She was on her side practically suburban: she lived at Richmond and never went "out." She was a woman of distinction, but not of fashion, and felt, as people said, her situation. Decidedly proud and rather whimsical, she lived her life as she had planned it. There were things one could do with her, but one couldn't make her come to one's parties. One went indeed a little more than seemed quite convenient to hers, which consisted of her cousin, a cup of tea and the view. The tea was good; but the view was familiar, though perhaps not, like the cousin—a disagreeable old maid who had been of the group at the museum and with whom she now lived—offensively so. This connection with an inferior relative, which had partly an economic motive—she proclaimed her companion a marvelous manager—was one of the little perversities we had to forgive her. Another was her estimate of the proprieties created by her rupture with her husband. That was extreme—many persons called it even morbid. She made no advances; she cultivated scruples; she suspected, or I should perhaps rather say she remembered, slights: she was one of the few women I've known whom that particular predicament had rendered modest rather than bold. Dear thing, she had some delicacy! Especially marked were the limits she had set to possible attentions from men: it was always her thought that her husband only waited to pounce on her. She discouraged if she didn't forbid the visits of male persons not senile: she said she could never be too careful.

When I first mentioned to her that I had a friend whom fate had distinguished in the same weird way as herself I put her quite at liberty to say "Oh bring him out to see me!" I should probably have been able to bring him, and a situation perfectly innocent or at any rate comparatively simple would have been created. But she uttered no such word; she only said: "I must meet him certainly; yes, I shall look out for him!" That caused the first delay, and meanwhile various things happened. One of them was that as time went on she made, charming as she was, more and more friends, and that it regularly befell that these friends were sufficiently also friends of his to bring him up in conversation. It was odd that without belonging, as it were, to the same world or, according to the horrid term, the same set, my baffled pair should have happened in so many cases to fall in with the same people and make them join in the droll chorus. She had friends who didn't know each other but who inevitably and punctually recommended *him*. She had also the sort of originality, the intrinsic interest, that led her to be kept by each of us as a private resource, cultivated jealously, more or less in secret, as a person whom one didn't meet in society, whom it was not for every one—whom it was not for the vulgar—to approach, and with whom therefore acquaintance was particularly difficult and particularly precious. We saw her separately, with appointments and conditions, and found it made on the whole for harmony not to tell each other. Somebody had always had a note from her still later than somebody else. There was some silly woman who for a long time, among the unprivileged, owed to three simple visits to Richmond a reputation for being intimate with "lots of awfully clever out-of-the-way people."

Every one has had friends it has seemed a happy thought to bring together, and every one remembers that his happiest thoughts have not been his greatest successes; but I doubt if there was ever a case in which the failure was in such direct proportion to the quantity of influence set in motion. It's really perhaps here the quantity of influence that was most remarkable. My lady and my gentleman each pronounced it to me and others quite a subject for a roaring farce. The reason first given had with time dropped out of sight and fifty better ones flourished on top of it. They were so awfully alike: they had the same ideas and tricks and tastes, the same prejudices and superstitions and heresies; they said the same things and sometimes did them; they liked and disliked the same persons and places, the same books, authors and styles; there were touches of resemblance even in their looks and features. It established much of a propriety that they were in common parlance equally "nice" and almost equally handsome. But the great sameness, for wonder and chatter, was their rare perversity in regard to being photographed. They were the only persons ever heard of who had never been "taken" and who had a passionate objection to it. They just *wouldn't* be—no, not for anything any one could say. I had loudly complained of this; him in particular I had so vainly desired to be able to show on my drawing-room chimney-piece in a Bond Street frame. It was at any rate the very liveliest of all the reasons why they ought to know each other—all the lively reasons reduced to naught by the strange law that had made them bang so many doors in each other's face, made them the buckets in the well, the two ends of the see-saw, the two parties in the State, so that when one was up the other was down, when one was out the other was in; neither by any possibility entering a house till the other had left it or leaving it all unawares till the other was at hand. They only arrived when they had been given up, which was precisely also when they departed. They were in a word alternate and incompatible; they missed each other with an inveteracy that could be explained only by its being preconcerted. It was however so far from preconcerted that it had ended—literally after several years—by disappointing and annoying them. I don't think their curiosity was lively till it had been proved utterly vain. A great deal was of course done to help them, but it merely laid wires for them to trip. To give examples I should have to have taken notes; but I happen to remember that neither had ever been able to dine on the right occasion. The right occasion for each was the occasion that would be wrong for the other. On the wrong one they were most punctual, and there were never any but wrong ones. The very elements conspired and the constitution of man reinforced them. A cold, a headache, a bereavement, a storm, a fog, an earthquake, a cataclysm, infallibly intervened. The whole business was beyond a joke.

Yet as a joke it had still to be taken, though one couldn't help feeling that the joke had made the situation serious, had produced on the part of each a consciousness, an awkwardness, a positive dread of the last accident of all, the only one with any freshness left, the accident that *would* bring them together. The final effect of its predecessors had been to kindle this instinct. They were quite ashamed—perhaps even a little of each other. So much preparation, so much frustration: what indeed could be good enough for it all to lead up to? A mere meeting would be mere flatness. Did I see them at the end of years, they often asked, just stupidly confronted? If they were bored by the joke they might be worse bored by something else. They made exactly the same reflexions, and each in some manner was sure to hear of the other's. I really think it was this peculiar diffidence that finally controlled the situation. I mean that if they had failed for the first year or two because they couldn't help it, they kept up the habit because they had—what shall I call it. —grown nervous. It really took some lurking volition to account for anything both so regular and so ridiculous.

III

When to crown our long acquaintance I accepted his renewed off of marriage it was humorously said, I know, that I had made the gift of his photograph a condition. This was so far true that I had refused to give him mine without it. At any rate I had him at last, in his high distinction, on the chimney-piece, where the day she called to congratulate me she came nearer than she had ever done to seeing him. He had in being taken set her an example that I invited her to follow; he had sacrificed his perversity— wouldn't she sacrifice hers? She too must give me something on my engagement—wouldn't she give me the companion-piece? She laughed and shook her head; she had headshakes whose impulse seemed to come from as far away as the breeze that stirs a flower. The companion-piece to the portrait of my future husband was the portrait of his future wife. She had taken her stand—she could depart from it as little as she could explain it. It was a prejudice, an *entêtement,* a vow—she would live and die unphotographed. Now too she was alone in that state: this was what she liked; it made her so much more original. She rejoiced in the fall of her late associate and looked a long time at his picture, about which she made no memorable remark, though she even turned it over to see the back. About our engagement she was charming—full of cordiality and sympathy. "You've known him even longer than I've *not,*" she said, "and that seems a very long time." She understood how we had jogged together over hill and dale and how inevitable it was that we should now rest together. I'm definite about all this because what followed is so strange that it's a kind of relief to me to mark the point up to which our relations were as natural as ever. It was I myself who in a sudden madness altered and destroyed them. I see now that she gave me no pretext and that I only found one in the way she looked at the fine face in the Bond Street frame. How then would I have had her look at it? What I had wanted from the first was to make her care for him. Well, that was what I still wanted—up to the moment of her having promised me she would on this occasion really aid me to break the silly spell that had kept them asunder. I had arranged with him to do his part if she would as triumphantly do hers. I was on a different footing now—I was on a footing to answer for him. I would positively engage that at five on the following Saturday he should be on that spot. He was out of town on pressing business, but, pledged to keep his promise to the letter, would return on purpose and in abundant time. "Are you perfectly sure?" I remember she asked, looking grave and considering: I thought she had turned a little pale. She was tired, she was indisposed: it was a pity he was to see her after all at so poor a moment. If he only *could* have seen her five years before! However, I replied that this time I was sure and that success therefore depended simply on herself. At five o'clock on the Saturday she would find him in a particular chair I pointed out, the one in which he usually sat and in which—though this I didn't mention—he had been sitting when, the week before, he put the question of our future to me in the way that had brought me round. She looked at it in silence, just as she had looked at the photograph, while I repeated for the twentieth time that it was too preposterous one shouldn't somehow succeed in introducing to one's dearest friend one's second self. "*Am* I your dearest friend?" she asked with a smile that for a moment brought back her beauty. I replied by pressing her to my bosom; after which she said: "Well, I'll come. I'm extraordinarily afraid, but you may count on me."

When she had left me I began to wonder what she was afraid of, for she had spoken as if she fully meant it. The next day, late in the afternoon, I had three lines from her: she found on getting home the announcement of her husband's death. She hadn't seen him for seven years, but she wished me to know it in this way before I should hear of it in another. It made however in her life, strange and sad to say, so little difference that she would scrupulously keep her appointment. I rejoiced for her—I supposed it would make at least the difference of her having more money; but even in this diversion, far from forgetting she had said she was afraid, I seemed to catch sight of a reason for her being so. Her fear, as the evening went on, became contagious, and the contagion took in my breast the form of a sudden panic. It wasn't jealousy—it just was the dread of jealousy. I called myself a fool for not having been quiet till we were man and wife. After that I should somehow feel secure. It was only a question of waiting another month—a trifle surely for people who had waited so long. It had been plain enough she was nervous, and now she was free her nervousness wouldn't be less. What was it therefore but a sharp foreboding? She had been hitherto the victim of interference, but it was quite possible she would henceforth be the source of it. The victim in that case would be my simple self. What had the interference been but the finger of Providence pointing out a danger? The danger was of course for poor *me*. It had been kept at bay by a series of accidents unexampled in their frequency; but the reign of accident was now visibly at an end. I had an intimate conviction that both parties would keep the tryst. It was more and more impressed on me that they were approaching, converging. They were like the seekers for the hidden object in the game of blindfold; they had one and the other begun to "burn." We had talked about breaking the spell; well, it would be effectually broken—unless indeed it should merely take another form and overdo their encounters as it had overdone their escapes. This was something I couldn't sit still for thinking of: it kept me awake—at midnight I was full of unrest. At last I felt there was only one way of laying the ghost. If the reign of accident was over I must just take up the succession. I sat down and wrote a hurried note which would meet him on his return and which as the servants had gone to bed I sallied forth bareheaded into the empty gusty street to drop into the nearest pillar-box. It was to tell him that I shouldn't be able to be at home in the afternoon as I had hoped and that he must postpone his visit till dinner-time. This was an implication that he would find me alone.

IV

When accordingly at five she presented herself I naturally felt false and base. My act had been a momentary madness, but I had at least, as they say, to live up to it. She remained an hour; he of course never came; and I could only persist in my perfidy. I had thought it best to let her come: singular as this now seems to me I held it diminished my guilt. Yet as she sat there so visibly white and weary, stricken with a sense of everything her husband's death had opened up, I felt a really piercing pang of pity and remorse. If I didn't tell her on the spot what I had done it was because I was too ashamed. I feigned astonishment—I feigned it to the end; I protested that if ever I had had confidence I had had it that day. I blush as I tell my story—I take it as my penance. There was nothing indignant I didn't say about him; I invented suppositions, attenuations; I admitted in stupefaction, as the hands of the clock traveled, that their luck hadn't turned. She smiled at this vision of their "luck," but she looked anxious—she looked unusual; the only thing that kept me up was the fact that, oddly enough, she wore mourning—no great depths of crape, but simple and scrupulous black. She had in her bonnet three small black feathers. She carried a little muff of astrachan. This put me, by the aid of some acute reflexion, a little in the right. She had written to me that the sudden event made no difference for her, but apparently it made as much difference as that. If she was inclined to the usual forms why didn't she observe that of not going the first day or two out to tea? There was some one she wanted so much to see that she couldn't wait till her husband was buried. Such a betrayal of eagerness made me hard and cruel enough to practise my odious deceit, though at the same time, as the hour waxed and waned, I suspected in her something deeper still than disappointment and somewhat less successfully concealed. I mean a strange underlying relief, the soft low emission of the breath that comes when a danger is past. What happened as she spent her barren hour with me was that at last she gave him up. She let him go for ever. She made the most graceful joke of it that I've ever seen made of anything; but it was for all that a great date in her life. She spoke with her mild gaiety of all the other vain times, the long game of hide-and-seek, the unprecedented queerness of such a relation. For it *was,* or had been, a relation, wasn't it, hadn't it? That was just the absurd part of it. When she got up to go I said to her that it was more a relation than ever, but that I hadn't the face after what had occurred to propose to her for the present another opportunity. It was plain that the only valid opportunity would be my accomplished marriage. Of course she would be at my wedding? It was even to be hoped that *he* would.

"If *I* am, he won't be!"—I remember the high quaver and the little break of her laugh. I admitted there might be something in that. The thing was therefore to get us safely married first. "That won't help us. Nothing will help us!" she said as she kissed me farewell. "I shall never, never see him!" It was with those words she left me.

I could bear her disappointment as I've called it; but when a couple of hours later I received him at dinner I discovered I couldn't bear his. The way my maneuver might have affected him hadn't been particularly present to me; but the result of it was the first word of reproach that had ever yet dropped from him. I say "reproach" because that expression is scarcely too strong for the terms in which he conveyed to me his surprise that under the extraordinary circumstances I shouldn't have found some means not to deprive him of such an occasion. I might really have managed either not to be obliged to go out or to let their meeting take place all the same. They would probably have got on, in my drawing-room, well enough without me. At this I quite broke down—I confessed my iniquity and the miserable reason of it. I hadn't put her off and I hadn't gone out; she had been there and, after waiting for him an hour, had departed in the belief that he had been absent by his own fault.

"She must think me a precious brute!" he exclaimed. "Did she say of me"—and I remember the just perceptible catch of breath in his pause—"what she had a right to say?"

"I assure you she said nothing that showed the least feeling. She looked at your photograph, she even turned round the back of it, on which your address happens to be inscribed. Yet it provoked her to no demonstration. She doesn't care so much as all that."

"Then why are you afraid of her?"

"It wasn't of her I was afraid. It was of you."

"Did you think I'd be so sure to fall in love with her? You never alluded to such a possibility before," he went on as I remained silent. "Admirable person as you pronounced her, that wasn't the light in which you showed her to me."

"Do you mean that if it *had* been you'd have managed by this time to catch a glimpse of her? I didn't fear things then," I added. "I hadn't the same reason."

He kissed me at this, and when I remembered that she had done so an hour or two before I felt for an instant as if he were taking from my lips the very pressure of hers. In spite of kisses the incident had shed a certain chill, and I suffered horribly from the sense that he had seen me guilty of a fraud. He had seen it only through my frank avowal, but I was as unhappy as if I had a stain to efface. I couldn't get over the manner of his looking at me when I spoke of her apparent indifference to his not having come. For the first time since I had known him he seemed to have expressed a doubt of my word. Before we parted I told him that I'd undeceive her—start the first thing in the morning for Richmond and there let her know he had been blameless. At this he kissed me again. I'd expiate my sin, I said; I'd humble myself in the dust; I'd confess and ask to be forgiven. At this he kissed me once more.

V

In the train the next day this struck me as a good deal for him to have consented to; but my purpose was firm enough to carry me on. I mounted the long hill to where the view begins, and then I knocked at her door. I was a trifle mystified by the fact that her blinds were still drawn, reflecting that if in the stress of my compunction I had come early I had certainly yet allowed people time to get up.

"At home, mum? She has left home for ever."

I was extraordinarily startled by this announcement of the elderly parlor-maid. "She has gone away?"

"She's dead, mum, please." Then as I gasped at the horrible word: "She died last night."

The loud cry that escaped me sounded even in my own ears like some harsh violation of the hour. I felt for the moment as if I had killed her; I turned faint and saw through a vagueness that woman hold out her arms to me. Of what next happened I've no recollection, nor of anything but my friend's poor stupid cousin, in a darkened room, after an interval that I suppose very brief, sobbing at me in a smothered accusatory way. I can't say how long it took me to understand, to believe and then to press back with an immense effort that pang of responsibility which, superstitiously, insanely, had been at first almost all I was conscious of. The doctor, after the fact, had been superlatively wise and clear: he was satisfied of a long-latent weakness of the heart, determined probably years before by the agitations and terrors to which her marriage had introduced her. She had had in those days cruel scenes with her husband, she had been in fear of her life. All emotion, everything in the nature of anxiety and suspense had been after that to be strongly deprecated, as in her marked cultivation of a quiet life she was evidently well aware; but who could say that any one, especially a "real lady," might be successfully protected from *every* little rub? She had had one a day or two before in the news of her husband's death—since there were shocks of all kinds, not only those of grief and surprise. For that matter she had never dreamed of so near a release: it had looked uncommonly as if he would live as long as herself. Then in the evening, in town, she had manifestly had some misadventure: something must have happened there that it would be imperative to clear up. She had come back very late—it was past eleven o'clock, and on being met in the hall by her cousin, who was extremely anxious, had allowed she was tired and must rest a moment before mounting the stairs. They had passed together into the dining-room, her companion proposing a glass of wine and bustling to the sideboard to pour it out. This took but a moment, and when my informant turned round our poor friend had not had time to seat herself. Suddenly, with a small moan that was barely audible, she dropped upon the sofa. She was dead. What unknown "little rub" had dealt her the blow? What concussion, in the name of wonder, *had* awaited her in town? I mentioned immediately the one thinkable ground of disturbance— her having failed to meet at my house, to which by invitation for the purpose she had come at five o'clock, the gentleman I was to be married to, who had been accidentally kept away and with whom she had no acquaintance whatever. This obviously counted for little; but something else might easily have occurred: nothing in the London streets was more possible than an accident, especially an accident in those desperate cabs. What had she done, where had she gone on leaving my house? I had taken for granted she had gone straight home. We both presently remembered that in her excursions to town she sometimes, for convenience, for refreshment, spent an hour or two at the "Gentlewomen," the quiet little ladies' club, and I promised that it should be my first care to make at that establishment an earnest appeal. Then we entered the dim and dreadful chamber where she lay locked up in death and where, asking after a little to be left alone with her, I remained for half an hour. Death had made her, had kept her beautiful; but I felt above all, as I knelt at her bed, that it had made her, had kept her silent. It had turned the key on something I was concerned to know.

On my return from Richmond and after another duty had been performed I drove to his chambers. It was the first time, but I had often wanted to see them. On the staircase, which, as the house contained twenty sets of rooms, was unrestrictedly public, I met his servant, who went back with me and ushered me in. At the sound of my entrance he appeared in the doorway of a further room, and the instant we were alone I produced my news: "She's dead!"

"Dead?" He was tremendously struck, and I noticed he had no need to ask whom, in this abruptness, I meant.

"She died last evening—just after leaving me."

He stared with the strangest expression, his eyes searching mine as for a trap. "Last evening—after leaving you?" He repeated my words in stupefaction. Then he brought out, so that it was in stupefaction I heard, "Impossible! I saw her."

"You 'saw' her?"

"On that spot—where you stand."

This called back to me after an instant, as if to help me to take it in, the great wonder of the warning of his youth. "In the hour of death—I understand: as you so beautifully saw your mother."

"Ah *not* as I saw my mother—not that way, not that way!" He was deeply moved by my news—far more moved, it was plain, than he would have been the day before: it gave me a vivid sense that, as I had then said to myself, there was indeed a relation between them and that he had actually been face to face with her. Such an idea, by its reassertion of his extraordinary privilege, would have suddenly presented him as painfully abnormal hadn't he vehemently insisted on the difference. "I saw her living. I saw her to speak to her. I saw her as I see you now."

It's remarkable that for a moment, though only for a moment, I found relief in the more personal, as it were, but also the more natural, of the two odd facts. The next, as I embraced this image of her having come to him on leaving me and of just what it accounted for in the disposal of her time, I demanded with a shade of harshness of which I was aware: "What on earth did she come for?"

He had now had a minute to think—to recover himself and judge of effects, so that if it was still with excited eyes he spoke he showed a conscious redness and made an inconsequent attempt to smile away the gravity of his words. "She came just to see me. She came—after what had passed at your house—so that we *should,* nevertheless at last meet. The impulse seemed to me exquisite, and that was the way I took it."

I looked round the room where she had been—where *she* had

been and I never had till now. "And was the way you took it the way she expressed it?"

"She only expressed it by being here and by letting me look at her. That was enough!" he cried with an extraordinary laugh.

I wondered more and more. "You mean she didn't speak to you?"

"She said nothing. She only looked at me as I looked at her."

"And you didn't speak either?"

He gave me again his painful smile. "I thought of *you.* The situation was every way delicate. I used the finest tact. But she saw she had pleased me." He even repeated his dissonant laugh.

"She evidently 'pleased' you!" Then I thought a moment. "How long did she stay?"

"How can I say? It seemed twenty minutes, but it was probably a good deal less."

"Twenty minutes of silence!" I began to have my definite view and now in fact quite to clutch at it. "Do you know you're telling me a thing positively monstrous?"

He had been standing with his back to the fire; at this, with a pleading look, he came to me. "I beseech you, dearest, to take it kindly."

I could take it kindly, and I signified as much; but I couldn't somehow, as he rather awkwardly opened his arms, let him draw me to him. So there fell between us for an appreciable time the discomfort of a great silence.

VI

He broke it by presently saying: "There's absolutely no doubt of her death?"

"Unfortunately none. I've just risen from my knees by the bed where they've laid her out."

He fixed his eyes hard on the floor; then he raised them to mine. "How does she look?"

"She looks—at peace."

He turned away again while I watched him: but after a moment he began: "At what hour then—?"

"It must have been near midnight. She dropped as she reached her house—from an affection of the heart which she knew herself and her physician knew her to have, but of which, patiently, bravely, she had never spoken to me."

He listened intently and for a minute was unable to speak. At last he broke out with an accent of which the almost boyish confidence, the really sublime simplicity, rings in my ears as I write: "Wasn't she *wonderful!*" Even at the time I was able to do it justice enough to answer that I had always told him so; but the next minute, as if after speaking he had caught a glimpse of what he might have made me feel, he went on quickly: "You can easily understand that if she didn't get home till midnight—"

I instantly took him up. "There was plenty of time for you to have seen her? How so," I asked, "when you didn't leave my house till late? I don't remember the very moment—I was preoccupied. But you know that though you said you had lots to do you sat for some time after dinner. She, on her side, was all the evening at the 'Gentlewomen,' I've just come from there—I've ascertained. She had tea there; she remained a long long time."

"What was she doing all the long long time?"

I saw him eager to challenge at every step my account of the matter; and the more he showed this the more I was moved to emphasize that version, to prefer with apparently perversity an explanation which only deepened the marvel and the mystery, but which, of the two prodigies it had to choose from, my reviving jealousy found easiest to accept. He stood there pleading with a candor that now seems to me beautiful for the privilege of having in spite of supreme defeat known the living woman; while I, with a passion I wonder at to-day, though it still smolders in a manner in its ashes, could only reply that, through a strange gift shared by her with his mother and on her own side likewise hereditary, the miracle of his youth had been renewed for him, the miracle of hers for her. She had been to him—yes, and by an impulse as charming as he liked; but oh she hadn't been in the body! It was a simple question of evidence. I had had, I maintained, a definite statement of what she had done—most of the time—at the little club. The place was almost empty, but the servants had noticed her. She had sat motionless in a deep chair by the drawing-room fire; she had leaned back her head, she had closed her eyes, she had seemed softly to sleep.

"I see. But till what o'clock?"

"There," I was obliged to answer, "the servants fail me a little. The portress in particular is unfortunately a fool, even though she too is supposed to be a Gentlewoman. She was evidently at that period of the evening, without a substitute and against regulations, absent for some little time from the cage in which it's her business to watch the comings and goings. She's muddled, she palpably prevaricates; so I can't positively, from her observation, give you an hour. But it was remarked toward half-past ten that our poor friend was no longer in the club."

It suited him down to the ground. "She came straight here, and from here she went straight to the train."

"She couldn't have run it so close," I declared. "That was a thing she particularly never did."

"There was no need of running it close, my dear—she had plenty of time. Your memory's at fault about my having left you late: I left you, as it happens, unusually early. I'm sorry my stay with you seemed long, for I was back here by ten."

"To put yourself into your slippers," I retorted, "and fall asleep in your chair. You slept till morning—you saw her in a dream!" He looked at me in silence and with somber eyes—eyes that showed me he had some irritation to repress. Presently I went on "You had a visit, at an extraordinary hour, from a lady—*soit:* nothing in the world's more probable. But there are ladies and ladies. How in the name of goodness, if she was unannounced and dumb and you had into the bargain never seen the least portrait of her—how could you identify the person we're talking of?"

"Haven't I to absolute satiety heard her described? I'll describe her for you in every particular."

"Don't!" I cried with a promptness that made him laugh once more, I colored at this, but I continued: "Did your servant introduce her?"

"He wasn't here—he's always away when he's wanted. One of

the features of this big house is that from the street-door the different floors are accessible practically without challenge. My servant makes love to a young person employed in the rooms above these, and he had a long bout of it last evening. When he's out on that job he leaves my outer door, on the staircase, so much ajar as to enable him to slip back without a sound. The door then only requires a push. She pushed it—that simply took a little courage."

"A little? It took tons! And it took all sorts of impossible calculations."

"Well, she had them—she made them. Mind you, I don't deny for a moment," he added "that it was very very wonderful!"

Something in his tone kept me a time from trusting myself to speak. At last I said: "How did she come to know where you live?"

"By remembering the address on the little label the shop-people happily left sticking to the frame I had had made for my photograph."

"And how was she dressed?"

"In mourning, my own dear. No great depths of crape, but simple and scrupulous black. She had in her bonnet three small black feathers. She carried a little muff of astrachan. She has near the left eye," he continued, "a tiny vertical scar—"

I stopped him short. "The mark of a caress from her husband." Then I added: "How close you must have been to her!" He made no answer to this, and I thought he blushed, observing which I broke straight off. "Well, good-bye."

"You won't stay a little?" He came to me again tenderly, and this time I suffered him. "Her visit had its beauty," he murmured as he held me, "but yours has a greater one."

I let him kiss me, but I remembered, as I had remembered the day before, that the last kiss she had given, as I supposed, in this world had been for the lips he touched. "I'm life, you see," I answered. "What you saw last night was death."

"It was life—it was life!"

He spoke with a soft stubbornness—I disengaged myself. We stood looking at each other hard. "You describe the scene—so far as you describe it all—in terms that are incomprehensible. She was in the room before you knew it?''

"I looked up from my letter-writing—at that table under the lamp I had been wholly absorbed in it—and she stood before me.''

"Then what did you do?''

"I sprang up with an ejaculation, and she, with a smile, laid her finger, ever so warningly, yet with a sort of delicate dignity, to her lips. I knew it meant silence, but the strange thing was that it seemed immediately to explain and to justify her. We at any rate stood for a time that, as I've told you, I can't calculate, face to face. It was just as you and I stand now.''

"Simply staring?''

He shook an impatient head. "Ah! *we're* not staring!''

"Yes, but we're talking.''

"Well, *we* were—after a fashion.'' He lost himself in the memory of it. "It was as friendly as this.'' I had on my tongue's end to ask if that was saying much for it, but I made the point instead that what they had evidently done was to gaze in mutual admiration. Then I asked if his recognition of her had been immediate. "Not quite,'' he replied, "for of course I didn't expect her; but it came to me long before she went who she was—who only she could be.''

I thought a little. "And how did she at last go?''

"Just as she arrived. The door was open behind her and she passed out.''

"Was she rapid—slow?''

"Rather quick. But looking behind her,'' he smiled to add. "I let her go, for I perfectly knew I was to take it as she wished.''

I was conscious of exhaling a long vague sigh. "Well, you must take it now as *I* wish—you must let *me* go.''

At this he drew near me again, detaining and persuading me, declaring with all due gallantry that I was a very different matter. I'd have given anything to have been able to ask him if he had touched her, but the words refused to form themselves: I knew to the last tenth of a tone how horrid and vulgar they'd sound. I said something else—I forget exactly what: it was feebly tortuous and intended, meanly enough, to make him tell me without my putting the question. But he didn't tell me; he only repeated, as from a glimpse of the propriety of soothing and consoling me, the sense of his declaration of some minutes before—the assurance that she was indeed exquisite, as I had always insisted, but that I was his "real" friend and his very own for ever. This led me to reassert, in the spirit of my previous rejoinder, that I had at least the merit of being alive; which in turn drew from him again the flash of contradiction I dreaded. "Oh *she* was alive! She was, she was!"

"She was dead, she was dead!" I asseverated with an energy, a determination it should *be* so, which comes back to me now almost as grotesque. But the sound of the word as it rang out filled me suddenly with horror, and all the natural emotion the meaning of it might have evoked in other conditions gathered and broke in a flood. It rolled over me that here was a great affection quenched and how much I had loved and trusted her. I had a vision at the same time of the lonely beauty of her end. "She's gone—she's lost to us for ever!" I burst into sobs.

"That's exactly what I feel," he exclaimed, speaking with extreme kindness and pressing me to him for comfort. "She's gone; she's lost to us for ever: so what does it matter now?" He bent over me, and when his face had touched mine I scarcely knew if it were wet with my tears or with his own.

VII

It was my theory, my conviction, it became, as I may say, my attitude, that they had still never "met": and it was just on this ground I felt it generous to ask him to stand with me at her grave. He did so very modestly and tenderly, and I assumed, though he himself clearly cared nothing for the danger, that the solemnity of the occasion, largely made up of persons who had known them both and had a sense of the long joke, would sufficiently deprive his presence of all light association. On the question of what had happened the evening of her death little more passed between us: I had been taken by a horror of the element of evidence. On either hypothesis it was gross and prying. He on his side lacked producible corroboration—everything, that is, but a statement of his house-porter, on his own admission a most casual and intermittent personage—that between the hours of ten o'clock and midnight no less than three ladies in deep black had flitted in and out of the place. This proved far too much; we had neither of us any use for three. He knew I considered I had accounted for every fragment of her time, and we dropped the matter as settled; we abstained from further discussion. What *I* knew however was that he abstained to please me rather than because he yielded to my reasons. He didn't yield—he was only indulgent; he clung to his interpretation because he liked it better. He liked it better, I held, because it had more to say to his vanity. That, in a similar position, wouldn't have been its effect on me, though I had doubtless quite as much; but these are things for individual humor and as to which no person can judge for another. I should have supposed it more gratifying to be the subject of one of those inexplicable occurrences that are chronicled in thrilling books and disputed about at learned meetings: I could conceive, on the part of a being just engulfed in the infinite and still vibrating with human emotion, of nothing more fine and pure, more high and august, than such an impulse of reparation, of admonition, or even of curiosity. *That* was beautiful, if one would, and I should in his place have thought more of myself for being so distinguished and so selected. It was public that he had already, that he had long figured in that light, and what was such a fact in itself but almost a proof? Each of the strange visitations contributed to establish the other. He had a different feeling; but he had also, I hasten to add, an unmistakable desire not to make a stand or, as they say, a fuss about it. I might believe what I liked—the more so that the whole thing was in a manner a mystery of my producing. It was an event of my history, a puzzle of my consciousness, not of his; therefore he would take about it any tone that struck me as convenient. We had both at all events other business on hand; we were pressed with preparations for our marriage.

   Mine were assuredly urgent, but I found as the days went on that to believe what I "liked" was to believe what I was more and more intimately convinced of. I found also that I didn't like it so much as that came to, or that the pleasure at all events was far from being the cause of my conviction. My obsession, as I may really call it and as I began to perceive, refused to be elbowed away, as I had hoped, by my sense of paramount duties. If I had a great deal to do I had still more to think of, and the moment came when my occupations were gravely menaced by my thoughts. I see it all now, I feel it, I live it over. It's terribly void of joy, it's full indeed to overflowing of bitterness; and yet I must do myself justice—I couldn't have been other than I was. The same strange impressions, had I to meet them again, would produce the same deep anguish, the same sharp doubts, the same still sharper certainties. Oh it's all easier to remember than to write, but even could I retrace the business hour by hour, could I find terms for the inexpressible, the ugliness and the pain would quickly stay my hand. Let me then note very simply and briefly that a week before our wedding-day, three weeks after her death, I knew in all my fibers that I had something very serious to look in the face and that if I was to make this effort I must make it on the spot and before another hour should elapse. My unextinguished jealousy—that was the Medusamask. It hadn't died with her death, it had lividly survived, and it was fed by suspicions unspeakable. They *would* be unspeakable to-day, that is, if I hadn't felt the sharp need of uttering them at the time. This need took possession of me—to save me, as it seemed, from my fate. When once it had done so I saw—in the urgency of the case, the diminishing hours and shrinking interval—only one issue, that of absolute promptness and frankness. I could at least not do him the wrong of delaying another day; I could at least treat my difficulty as too fine for a subterfuge. Therefore very quietly, but none the less abruptly and hideously, I put it before him on a certain evening that we must reconsider our situation and recognize that it had completely altered.

He stared bravely. "How in the world altered?"

"Another person has come between us."

He took but an instant to think. "I won't pretend not to know whom you mean." He smiled in pity for my aberration, but he meant to be kind. "A woman dead and buried!"

"She's buried, but she's not dead. She's dead for the world— she's dead for me. But she's not dead for you."

"You hark back to the different construction we put on her appearance that evening?"

"No," I answered, "I hark back to nothing. I've no need of it. I've more than enough with what's before me."

"And pray, darling, what may that be?"

"You're completely changed."

"By that absurdity?" he laughed.

"Not so much by that one as by other absurdities that have followed it."

"And what may *they* have been?"

We had faced each other fairly, with eyes that didn't flinch: but his had a dim strange light, and my certitude triumphed in his perceptible paleness. "Do you really pretend," I asked, "not to know what they are?"

"My dear child," he replied, "you describe them too sketch-ily!"

I considered a moment. "One may well be embarrassed to fin-ish the picture! But from that point of view—and from the begin-ning—what was ever more embarrassing than your idiosyn-crasy?"

He invoked his vagueness—a thing he always did beautifully. "My idiosyncrasy?"

"Your notorious, your peculiar power."

He gave a great shrug of impatience, a groan of overdone dis-dain. "Oh my peculiar power!"

"Your accessibility to forms of life," I coldly went on, "your command of impressions, appearances, contacts, closed—for our gain or our loss—to the rest of us. That was originally a part of the deep interest with which you inspired me—one of the rea-sons I was amused, I was indeed positively proud, to know you. It was a magnificent distinction; it's a magnificent distinction still. But of course I had no prevision then of the way it would operate now; and even had that been the case I should have had none of the extraordinary way of which its action would affect me."

"To what in the name of goodness," he pleadingly enquired, "are you fantastically alluding?" Then as I remained silent, gathering a tone for my charge, "How in the world *does* it operate?" he went on; "and how in the world are you affected?"

"She missed you for five years," I said, "but she never misses you now. You're making it up!"

"Making it up?" He had begun to turn from white to red.

"You see her—you see her: you see her every night!" He gave a loud sound of derision, but I felt it ring false. "She comes to you as she came that evening," I declared; "having tried it she found she liked it!" I was able, with God's help, to speak without blind passion or vulgar violence; but those were the exact words—and far from "sketchy" they then appeared to me—that I uttered. He had turned away in his laughter, clapping his hands at my folly, but in an instant he faced me again with a change of expression that struck me. "Do you dare to deny," I then asked, "that you habitually see her?"

He had taken the line of indulgence, of meeting me halfway and kindly humoring me. At all events he to my astonishment suddenly said: "Well, my dear, what if I do?"

"It's your natural right: it belongs to your constitution and to your wonderful if not perhaps quite enviable fortune. But you'll easily understand that it separates us. I unconditionally release you."

"Release me?"

"You must choose between me and her."

He looked at me hard. "I see." Then he walked away a little, as if grasping what I had said and thinking how he had best treat it. At last he turned on me afresh. "How on earth do you know such an awfully private thing?"

"You mean because you've tried so hard to hide it? It *is* awfully private, and you may believe I shall never betray you. You've done your best, you've acted your part, you've behaved, poor dear! loyally and admirably. Therefore I've watched you in silence, playing my part too; I've noted every drop in your voice, every absence in your eyes, every effort in your indifferent hand: I've waited till I was utterly sure and miserably unhappy. How *can* you hide it when you're abjectly in love with her, when you're sick almost to death with the joy of what she gives you?" I checked his quick protest with a quicker gesture. "You love her as you've *never* loved, and, passion for passion, she gives it straight back! She rules you, she holds you, she has you all! A woman, in such a case as mine, divines and feels and sees; she's not a dull dunce who has to be 'credibly informed.' You come to me mechanically, compunctiously, with the dregs of your tenderness and the remnant of your life. I can renounce you, but I can't share you: the best of you is hers, I know what it is and freely give you up to her for ever!"

He made a gallant fight, but it couldn't be patched up; he repeated his denial, he retracted his admission, he ridiculed my charge, of which I freely granted him moreover the indefensible extravagance. I didn't pretend for a moment that we were talking of common things; I didn't pretend for a moment that he and she were common people. Pray, if they *had* been, how should I ever have cared for them? They had enjoyed a rare extension of being and they had caught me up in their flight; only I couldn't breathe in such air and I promptly asked to be set down. Everything in the facts was monstrous, and most of all my lucid perception of them; the only thing allied to nature and truth was my having to act on that perception. I felt after I had spoken in this sense that my assurance was complete; nothing had been wanting to it but the sight of my effect on him. He disguised indeed the effect in a cloud of chaff, a diversion that gained him time and covered his retreat. He challenged my sincerity, my sanity, almost my humanity, and that of course widened our breach and confirmed our rupture. He did everything in short but convince me either that I was wrong or that he was unhappy: we separated and I left him to his inconceivable communion.

He never married, any more than I've done. When six years later, in solitude and silence, I heard of his death I hailed it as a direct contribution to my theory. It was sudden, it was never properly accounted for, it was surrounded by circumstances in which—for oh I took them to pieces!—I distinctly read an intention, the mark of his own hidden hand. It was the result of a long necessity, of an unquenchable desire. To say exactly what I mean, it was a response to an irresistible call.

BLUMFELD, AN ELDERLY BACHELOR

Franz Kafka

One evening Blumfeld, an elderly bachelor, was climbing up to his apartment—a laborious undertaking, for he lived on the sixth floor. While climbing up he thought, as he had so often recently, how unpleasant this utterly lonely life was: to reach his empty rooms he had to climb these six floors almost in secret, there put on his dressing gown, again almost in secret, light his pipe, read a little of the French magazine to which he had been subscribing for years, at the same time sip at a homemade kirsch, and finally, after half an hour, go to bed, but not before having completely rearranged his bedclothes which the unteachable charwoman would insist on arranging in her own way. Some companion, someone to witness these activities, would have been very welcome to Blumfeld. He had already been wondering whether he shouldn't acquire a little dog. These animals are gay and above all grateful and loyal; one of Blumfeld's colleagues has a dog of this kind; it follows no one but its master and when it hasn't seen him for a few moments it greets him at once with loud barkings, by which it is evidently trying to express its joy at once more finding that extraordinary benefactor, its master. True, a dog also has its drawbacks. However well kept it may be, it is bound to dirty the room. This just cannot be avoided; one cannot give it a hot bath each time before letting it into the room; besides, its health couldn't stand that. Blumfeld, on the other hand, can't stand dirt in his room. To him cleanliness is essential, and several times a week he is obliged to have words with his charwoman, who is unfortunately not very painstaking in this respect. Since she is hard of hearing he usually drags her by the arm to those spots in the room which he finds lacking in cleanliness. By this strict discipline he has achieved in his room a neatness more or less commensurate with his wishes. By acquiring a dog, however, he would be almost deliberately introducing into his room the dirt which hitherto he had been so careful to avoid. Fleas, the dog's constant companions, would appear. And once fleas were there, it would not be long before Blumfeld would be abandoning his comfortable room to the dog and looking for another one. Uncleanliness, however, is but one of the drawbacks of dogs. Dogs also fall ill and no one really understands dogs' diseases. Then the animal sits in a corner or limps about, whimpers, coughs, chokes from some pain; one wraps it in a rug, whistles a little melody, offers it milk—in short, one nurses it in the hope that this, as indeed is possible, is a passing sickness while it may be a serious, disgusting, and contagious disease. And even if the dog remains healthy, one day it will grow old, one won't have the heart to get rid of the faithful animal in time, and then comes the moment when one's own age peers out at one from the dog's oozing eyes. Then one has to cope with the half-blind, weak-lunged animal all but immobile with fat, and in this way pay dearly for the pleasures the dog once had given. Much as Blumfeld would like to have a dog at this moment, he would rather go on climbing the stairs alone for another thirty years than be burdened later on by such an old dog which, sighing louder than he, would drag itself up, step by step.

So Blumfeld will remain alone, after all; he really feels none of the old maid's longing to have around her some submissive living creature that she can protect, lavish her affection upon, and continue to serve—for which purpose a cat, a canary, even a goldfish would suffice—or, if this cannot be, rest content with flowers on the window sill. Blumfeld only wants a companion, an animal to which he doesn't have to pay much attention, which doesn't mind an occasional kick, which even, in an emergency, can spend the night in the street, but which nevertheless, when

Blumfeld feels like it, is promptly at his disposal with its barking, jumping, and licking of hands. This is what Blumfeld wants, but since, as he realizes, it cannot be had without serious drawbacks, he renounces it, and yet—in accordance with his thoroughgoing disposition—the idea from time to time, this evening, for instance, occurs to him again.

While taking the key from his pocket outside his room, he is startled by a sound coming from within. A peculiar rattling sound, very lively but very regular. Since Blumfeld has just been thinking of dogs, it reminds him of the sounds produced by paws pattering one after the other over a floor. But paws don't rattle, so it can't be paws. He quickly unlocks the door and switches on the light. He is not prepared for what he sees. For this is magic— two small white celluloid balls with blue stripes jumping up and down side by side on the parquet; when one of them touches the floor the other is in the air, a game they continue ceaselessly to play. At school one day Blumfeld had seen some little pellets jumping about like this during a well-known electrical experiment, but these are comparatively large balls jumping freely about in the room and no electrical experiment is being made. Blumfeld bends down to get a good look at them. They are undoubtedly ordinary balls, they probably contain several smaller balls, and it is these that produce the rattling sound. Blumfeld gropes in the air to find out whether they are hanging from some threads—no, they are moving entirely on their own. A pity Blumfeld isn't a small child, two balls like these would have been a happy surprise for him, whereas now the whole thing gives him rather an unpleasant feeling. It's not quite pointless after all to live in secret as an unnoticed bachelor, now someone, no matter who, has penetrated this secret and sent him these two strange balls.

He tries to catch one but they retreat before him, thus luring him on to follow them through the room. It's really too silly, he thinks, running after balls like this; he stands still and realizes that the moment he abandons the pursuit, they too remain on the same spot. I will try to catch them all the same, he thinks again, and hurries toward them. They immediately run away, but

Blumfeld, his legs apart, forces them into a corner of the room, and there, in front of a trunk, he manages to catch one ball. It's a small cool ball, and it turns in his hand, clearly anxious to slip away. And the other ball, too, as though aware of its comrade's distress, jumps higher than before, extending the leaps until it touches Blumfeld's hand. It beats against his hand, beats in ever faster leaps, alters its angle of attack, then, powerless against the hand which encloses the ball so completely, springs even higher and is probably trying to reach Blumfeld's face. Blumfeld could catch this ball too, and lock them both up somewhere, but at the moment it strikes him as too humiliating to take such measures against two little balls. Besides, it's fun owning these balls, and soon enough they'll grow tired, roll under the cupboard, and be quiet. Despite this deliberation, however, Blumfeld, near to anger, flings the ball to the ground, and it is a miracle that in doing so the delicate, all but transparent celluloid cover doesn't break. Without hesitation the two balls resume their former low, well-coordinated jumps.

Blumfeld undresses calmly, arranges his clothes in the wardrobe which he always inspects carefully to make sure the charwoman has left everything in order. Once or twice he glances over his shoulder at the balls, which, unpursued, seem to be pursuing him; they have followed him and are now jumping close behind him. Blumfeld puts on his dressing gown and sets out for the opposite wall to fetch one of the pipes which are hanging in a rack. Before turning around he instinctively kicks his foot out backwards, but the balls know how to get out of its way and remain untouched. As Blumfeld goes off to fetch the pipe the balls at once follow close behind him; he shuffles along in his slippers, taking irregular steps, yet each step is followed almost without pause by the sound of the balls; they are keeping pace with him. To see how the balls manage to do this, Blumfeld turns suddenly around. But hardly has he turned when the balls describe a semicircle and are already behind him again, and this they repeat every time he turns. Like submissive companions, they try to avoid appearing in front of Blumfeld. Up to the present they have evidently dared to do so only in order to introduce themselves; now, however, it seems they have actually entered into his service.

Hitherto, when faced with situations he couldn't master, Blumfeld had always chosen to behave as though he hadn't noticed anything. It had often helped and usually improved the situation. This, then, is what he does now; he takes up a position in front of the pipe rack and, puffing out his lips, chooses a pipe, fills it with particular care from the tobacco pouch close at hand, and allows the balls to continue their jumping behind him. But he hesitates to approach the table, for to hear the sound of the jumps coinciding with that of his own steps almost hurts him. So there he stands, and while taking an unnecessarily long time to fill his pipe he measures the distance separating him from the table. At last, however, he overcomes his faintheartedness and covers the distance with such stamping of feet that he cannot hear the balls. But the moment he is seated he can hear them jumping up and down behind his chair as distinctly as ever.

Above the table, within reach, a shelf is nailed to the wall on which stands the bottle of kirsch surrounded by little glasses. Beside it, in a pile, lie several copies of the French magazine. (This very day the latest issue has arrived and Blumfeld takes it down. He quite forgets the kirsch; he even has the feeling that today he is proceeding with his usual activities only to console himself, for he feels no genuine desire to read. Contrary to his usual habit of carefully turning one page after the other, he opens the magazine at random and there finds a large photograph. He forces himself to examine it in detail. It shows a meeting between the Czar of Russia and the President of France. This takes place on a ship. All about as far as can be seen are many other ships, the smoke from their funnels vanishing in the bright sky. Both Czar and President have rushed toward each other with long strides and are clasping one another by the hand. Behind the Czar as well as behind the President stand two men. By comparison with the gay faces of the Czar and the President, the faces of their attendants are very solemn, the eyes of each group focused on their master. Lower down—the scene evidently takes place on the top deck—stand long lines of saluting sailors cut off by the margin. Gradually Blumfeld contemplates the picture with more interest, then holds it a little further away and looks at it with blinking eyes. He has always had a taste for such imposing scenes. The way the chief personages clasp each other's hand so naturally, so cordially and lightheartedly, this he finds most life-like. And it's just as appropriate that the attendants—high-ranking gentlemen, of course, with their names printed beneath—express in their bearing the solemnity of the historical moment.)

And instead of helping himself to everything he needs, Blumfeld sits there tense, staring at the bowl of his still unlit pipe. He is lying in wait. Suddenly, quite unexpectedly, his numbness leaves him and with a jerk he turns around in his chair. But the balls, equally alert, or perhaps automatically following the law governing them, also change their position the moment Blumfeld turns, and hide behind his back. Blumfeld now sits with his back to the table, the cold pipe in his hand. And now the balls jump under the table and, since there's a rug there, they are less audible. This is a great advantage: only faint, hollow noises can be heard, one has to pay great attention to catch their sound. Blumfeld, however, does pay great attention, and hears them distinctly. But this is so only for the moment, in a little while he probably won't hear them anymore. The fact that they cannot make themselves more audible on the rug strikes Blumfeld as a great weakness on the part of the balls. What one has to do is lay one or even better two rugs under them and they are all but powerless. Admittedly only for a limited time, and besides, their very existence wields a certain power.

Right now Blumfeld could have made good use of a dog, a wild young animal would soon have dealt with these balls; he imagines this dog trying to catch them with its paws, chasing them from their positions, hunting them all over the room, and finally getting hold of them between its teeth. It's quite possible that before long Blumfeld will acquire a dog.

For the moment, however, the balls have no one to fear but Blumfeld, and he has no desire to destroy them just now, perhaps he lacks the necessary determination. He comes home in the evening tired from work and just when he is in need of some rest he is faced with this surprise. Only now does he realize how tired he really is. No doubt he will destroy the balls, and that in the near future, but not just yet, probably not until tomorrow. If one looks at the whole thing with an unprejudiced eye, the balls behave modestly enough. From time to time, for instance, they could jump into the foreground, show themselves, and then return again to their positions, or they could jump higher so as to beat against the tabletop in order to compensate themselves for the muffling effect of the rug. But this they don't do, they don't want to irritate Blumfeld unduly, they are evidently confining themselves to what is absolutely necessary.

Even this measured necessity, however, is quite sufficient to spoil Blumfeld's rest at the table. He has been sitting there only a few minutes and is already considering going to bed. One of his motives for this is that he can't smoke here, for he has left the matches on his bedside table. Thus he would have to fetch these matches, but once having reached the bedside table he might as well stay there and lie down. For this he has an ulterior motive: he thinks that the balls, with their mania for keeping behind him, will jump onto the bed, and that there, in lying down, on purpose or not, he will squash them. The objection that what would then remain of the balls could still go on jumping, he dismisses. Even the unusual must have its limits. Complete balls jump anyway, even if not incessantly, but fragments of balls never jump, and consequently will not jump in this case, either. "Up!" he shouts, having grown almost reckless from this reflection and, the balls still behind him, he stamps off to bed. His hope seems to be confirmed, for when he purposely takes up a position quite near the bed, one ball promptly springs onto it. Then, however, the unexpected occurs: the other ball disappears under the bed. The possibility that the balls could jump under the bed as well had not occurred to Blumfeld. He is outraged about the one ball, although he is aware how unjust this is, for by jumping under the bed the ball fulfills its duty perhaps better than the ball on the bed. Now everything depends on which place the balls decide to choose, for Blumfeld does not believe that they can work separately for any length of time. And sure enough a moment later the ball on the floor also jumps onto the bed. Now I've got them, thinks Blumfeld, hot with joy, and tears his dressing gown from his body to throw himself into bed. At that moment, however, the very same ball jumps back under the bed. Overwhelmed with disappointment, Blumfeld almost collapses. Very likely the ball just took a good look around up there and decided it didn't like it. And now the other one has followed, too, and of course remains, for it's better down there. "Now I'll have these drummers with me all night," thinks Blumfeld, biting his lips and nodding his head.

He feels gloomy, without actually knowing what harm the balls could do him in the night. He is a good sleeper, he will easily be able to ignore so slight a noise. To make quite sure of this and mindful of his past experience, he lays two rugs on the floor. It's as if he owned a little dog for which he wants to make a soft bed. And as though the balls had also grown tired and sleepy, their jumping has become lower and slower than before. As Blumfeld kneels beside the bed, lamp in hand, he thinks for a moment that the balls might come to rest on the rug—they fall so weakly, roll so slowly along. Then, however, they dutifully rise again. Yet it is quite possible that in the morning when Blumfeld looks under the bed he'll find there two quiet, harmless children's balls.

But it seems that they may not even be able to keep up their jumping until the morning, for as soon as Blumfeld is in bed he doesn't hear them anymore. He strains his ears, leans out of bed to listen—not a sound. The effect of the rugs can't be as strong as that; the only explanation is that the balls are no longer jumping, either because they aren't able to bounce themselves off the rug and have therefore abandoned jumping for the time being or, which is more likely, they will never jump again. Blumfeld could get up and see exactly what's going on, but in his relief at finding peace at last he prefers to remain where he is. He would rather not risk disturbing the pacified balls even with his eyes. Even smoking he happily renounces, turns over on his side, and promptly goes to sleep.

But he does not remain undisturbed; as usual he sleeps without dreaming, but very restlessly. Innumerable times during the night he is startled by the delusion that someone is knocking at his door. He knows quite well that no one is knocking; who would knock at night and at his lonely bachelor's door? Yet although he knows this for certain, he is startled again and again and each time glances in suspense at the door, his mouth open, eyes wide, a strand of hair trembling over his damp forehead. He tries to count how many times he has been woken but, dizzy from the huge numbers he arrives at, he falls back to sleep again. He thinks he knows where the knocking comes from; not from the door, but somewhere quite different; being heavy with sleep, however, he cannot quite remember on what his suspicions are based. All he knows is that innumerable tiny unpleasant sounds accumulate before producing the great strong knocking. He would happily suffer all the unpleasantness of the small sounds if he could be spared the actual knocking, but for some reason it's too late; he cannot interfere, the moment has passed, he can't even speak, his mouth opens but all that comes out is a silent yawn, and furious at this he thrusts his face into the pillows. Thus the night passes.

   In the morning he is awakened by the charwoman's knocking; with a sigh of relief he welcomes the gentle tap on the door whose inaudibility has in the past always been one of his sources of complaint. He is about to shout "Come in!" when he hears another lively, faint, yet all but belligerent knocking. It's the balls under the bed. Have they woken up? Have they, unlike him, gathered new strength overnight? "Just a moment," shouts Blumfeld to the charwoman, jumps out of bed, and, taking great care to keep the balls behind him, throws himself on the floor, his back still toward them; then, twisting his head over his shoulder, he glances at the balls and—nearly lets out a curse. Like children pushing away blankets that annoy them at night, the balls have apparently spent all night pushing the rugs, with tiny twitching movements, so far away from under the bed that they are now once more on the parquet, where they can continue making their noise. "Back onto the rugs!" says Blumfeld with an angry face, and only when the balls, thanks to the rugs, have become quiet again, does he call in the charwoman. While she— a fat, dull-witted, stiff-backed woman—is laying the breakfast on the table and doing the few necessary chores, Blumfeld stands motionless in his dressing gown by his bed so as to keep the balls in their place. With his eyes he follows the charwoman to see whether she notices anything. This, since she is hard of hearing, is very unlikely, and the fact that Blumfeld thinks he sees the charwoman stopping here and there, holding on to some furniture and listening with raised eyebrows, he puts down to his overwrought condition caused by a bad night's sleep. It would relieve him if he could persuade the charwoman to speed up her work, but if anything she is slower than usual. She loads herself laboriously with Blumfeld's clothes and shuffles out with them into the corridor, stays away a long time, and the din she makes beating the clothes echoes in his ears with slow, monotonous thuds. And during all this time Blumfeld has to remain on the bed, cannot move for fear of drawing the balls behind him, has to let the coffee—which he likes to drink as hot as possible—get cold, and can do nothing but stare at the drawn blinds behind which the day is dimly dawning. At last the charwoman has finished, bids him good morning, and is about to leave; but before she actually goes she hesitates by the door, moves her lips a little, and takes a long look at Blumfeld. Blumfeld is about to remonstrate when she at last departs. Blumfeld longs to fling the door open and shout after her that she is a stupid, idiotic old woman. However, when he reflects on what he actually has against her, he can only think of the paradox of her having clearly noticed nothing and yet trying to give the impression that she has. How confused his thoughts have become! And all on account of a bad night. Some explanation for his poor sleep he finds in the fact that last night he deviated from his usual habits by not smoking or drinking any schnapps. When for once I don't smoke or drink schnapps—and this is the result of his reflections—I sleep badly.

From now on he is going to take better care of his health, and he begins by fetching some cotton wool from his medicine chest which hangs over his bedside table and putting two little wads of it into his ears. Then he stands up and takes a trial step. Although the balls do follow he can hardly hear them; the addition of another wad makes them quite inaudible. Blumfeld takes a few more steps; nothing particularly unpleasant happens. Everyone for himself, Blumfeld as well as the balls, and although they are bound to one another they don't disturb each other. Only once, when Blumfeld turns around rather suddenly and one ball fails to make the countermovement fast enough, does he touch it with his knee. But this is the only incident. Otherwise Blumfeld calmly drinks his coffee; he is as hungry as though, instead of sleeping last night, he had gone for a long walk; he washes in cold, exceedingly refreshing water, and puts on his clothes. He still hasn't pulled up the blinds; rather, as a precaution, he has preferred to remain in semidarkness; he has no wish for the balls to be seen by other eyes. But now that he is ready to go he has somehow to provide for the balls in case they should dare—not that he thinks they will—to follow him into the street. He thinks of a good solution, opens the large wardrobe, and places himself with his back to it. As though divining his intention, the balls steer clear of the wardrobe's interior, taking advantage of every inch of space between Blumfeld and the wardrobe; when there's no other alternative they jump into the wardrobe for a moment, but when faced by the dark out they promptly jump again. Rather than be lured over the edge further into the wardrobe, they neglect their duty and stay by Blumfeld's side. But their little ruses avail them nothing, for now Blumfeld himself climbs backward into the wardrobe and they have to follow him. And with this their fate has been sealed, for on the floor of the wardrobe lie various smallish objects such as boots, boxes, small trunks which, although carefully arranged—Blumfeld now regrets this—nevertheless considerably hamper the balls. And when Blumfeld, having by now pulled the door almost to, jumps out of it with an enormous leap such as he has not made for years, slams the door, and turns the key, the balls are imprisoned. "Well, that worked," thinks Blumfeld, wiping the sweat from his face. What a din the balls are making in the wardrobe! It sounds as though they are desperate. Blumfeld, on the other hand, is very contented. He leaves the room and already the deserted corridor has a soothing effect on him. He takes the wool out of his ears and is enchanted by the countless sounds of the waking house. Few people are to be seen, it's still very early.

Downstairs in the hall in front of the low door leading to the charwoman's basement apartment stands that woman's ten-year-old son. The image of his mother, not one feature of the woman has been omitted in this child's face. Bandy-legged, hands in his trouser pockets, he stands there wheezing, for he already has a goiter and can breathe only with difficulty. But whereas Blumfeld, whenever the boy crosses his path, usually quickens his step to spare himself the spectacle, today he almost feels like pausing for a moment. Even if the boy has been brought into the world by this woman and shows every sign of his origin, he is nevertheless a child, the thoughts of a child still dwell in this shapeless head, and if one were to speak to him sensibly and ask him something, he would very likely answer in a bright voice, innocent and reverential, and after some inner struggle one could bring oneself to pat these cheeks. Although this is what Blumfeld thinks, he nevertheless passes him by. In the street he realizes that the weather is pleasanter than he had suspected from his room. The morning mist has dispersed and patches of blue sky have appeared, brushed by a strong wind. Blumfeld has the balls to thank for his having left his room much earlier than usual; even the paper he has left unread on the table; in any case he has saved a great deal of time and can now afford to walk slowly. It is remarkable how little he worries about the balls now that he is separated from them. So long as they were following him they could have been considered as something belonging to him, something which, in passing judgment on his person, had somehow to be taken into consideration. Now, however, they were mere toys in his wardrobe at home. And it occurs to Blumfeld that the best way of rendering the balls harmless would be to put them to their original use. There in the hall stands the boy; Blumfeld will give him the balls, not lend them, but actually present them to him, which is surely tantamount to ordering their destruction. And even if they were to remain intact they would mean even less in the boy's hands than in the wardrobe, the whole house would watch the boy playing with them, other children would join in, and the

general opinion that the balls are things to play with and in no
way life companions of Blumfeld would be firmly and irrefutably
established. Blumfeld runs back into the house. The boy has just
gone down the basement stairs and is about to open the door. So
Blumfeld has to call the boy and pronounce his name, a name
that to him seems as ludicrous as everything else connected with
the child. "Alfred! Alfred!" he shouts. The boy hesitates for a long
time. "Come here!" shouts Blumfeld, "I've got something for
you." The janitor's two little girls appear from the door opposite
and, full of curiosity, take up positions on either side of Blumfeld.
They grasp the situation much more quickly than the boy and
cannot understand why he doesn't come at once. Without taking
their eyes off Blumfeld they beckon to the boy, but cannot
fathom what kind of present is awaiting Alfred. Tortured with
curiosity, they hop from one foot to the other. Blumfeld laughs at
them as well as at the boy. The latter seems to have figured it all
out and climbs stiffly, clumsily up the steps. Not even in his gait
can he manage to belie his mother, who, incidentally, has appeared in the basement doorway. To make sure that the charwoman also understands and in the hope that she will supervise
the carrying out of his instructions, should it be necessary,
Blumfeld shouts excessively loud. "Up in my room," says
Blumfeld, "I have two lovely balls. Would you like to have them?"
Not knowing how to behave, the boy simply screws up his
mouth, turns around, and looks inquiringly down at his mother.
The girls, however, promptly begin to jump around Blumfeld and
ask him for the balls. "You will be allowed to play with them
too," Blumfeld tells them, but waits for the boy's answer. He
could of course give the balls to the girls, but they strike him as
too unreliable and for the moment he has more confidence in the
boy. Meanwhile, the latter, without having exchanged a word,
has taken counsel with his mother and nods his assent to
Blumfeld's repeated question. "Then listen," says Blumfeld, who
is quite prepared to receive no thanks for his gift. "Your mother
has the key of my door, you must borrow it from her. But here is
the key of my wardrobe, and in the wardrobe you will find the
balls. Take good care to lock the wardrobe and the room again.

But with the balls you can do what you like and you don't have to bring them back. Have you understood me?" Unfortunately, the boy has not understood. Blumfeld has tried to make everything particularly clear to this hopelessly dense creature, but for this very reason has repeated everything too often, has in turn too often mentioned keys, room, and wardrobe, and as a result the boy stares at him as though he were rather a seducer than his benefactor. The girls, on the other hand, have understood everything immediately, press against Blumfeld, and stretch out their hands for the key. "Wait a moment," says Blumfeld, by now annoyed with them all. Time, moreover, is passing, he can't stand about much longer. If only the mother would say that she has understood him and take matters in hand for the boy! Instead of which she still stands down by the door, smiles with the affectation of the bashful deaf, and is probably under the impression that Blumfeld up there has suddenly fallen for the boy and is hearing him his lessons. Blumfeld on the other hand can't very well climb down the basement stairs and shout into the charwoman's ear to make her son for God's sake relieve him of the balls! It had required enough of his self-control as it was to entrust the key of his wardrobe for a whole day to this family. It is certainly not in order to save himself trouble that he is handing the key to the boy rather than himself leading the boy up and there giving him the balls. But he can't very well first give the balls away and then immediately deprive the boy of them by—as would be bound to happen—drawing them after him as his followers. "So you still don't understand me?" asks Blumfeld almost wistfully after having started a fresh explanation which, however, he immediately interrupts at sight of the boy's vacant stare. So vacant a stare renders one helpless. It could tempt one into saying more than one intends, if only to fill the vacancy with sense. Whereupon "We'll fetch the balls for him!" shout the girls. They are shrewd and have realized that they can obtain the balls only through using the boy as an intermediary, but that they themselves have to bring about this mediation. From the janitor's room a clock strikes, warning Blumfeld to hurry. "Well, then, take the key," says Blumfeld, and the key is more snatched from his hand than given by him. He would have handed it to the boy with infinitely more confidence. "The key to the room you'll have to get from the woman," Blumfeld adds. "And when you return with the balls you must hand both keys to her." "Yes, yes!" shout the girls and run down the steps. They know everything, absolutely everything; and as though Blumfeld were infected by the boy's denseness, he is unable to understand how they could have grasped everything so quickly from his explanations.

Now they are already tugging at the charwoman's skirt but, tempting as it would be, Blumfeld cannot afford to watch them carrying out their task, not only because it's already late, but also because he has no desire to be present at the liberation of the balls. He would in fact far prefer to be several streets away when the girls first open the door of his room. After all, how does he know what else he might have to expect from these balls! And so for the second time this morning he leaves the house. He has one last glimpse of the charwoman defending herself against the girls, and of the boy stirring his bandy legs to come to his mother's assistance. It's beyond Blumfeld's comprehension why a creature like this servant should prosper and propagate in this world.

While on his way to the linen factory, where Blumfeld is employed, thoughts about his work gradually get the upper hand. He quickens his step and, despite the delay caused by the boy, he is the first to arrive in his office. This office is a glass-enclosed room containing a writing desk for Blumfeld and two standing desks for the two assistants subordinate to him. Although these standing desks are so small and narrow as to suggest they are meant for schoolchildren, this office is very crowded and the assistants cannot sit down, for then there would be no place for Blumfeld's chair. As a result they stand all day, pressed against their desks. For them of course this is very uncomfortable, but it also makes it very difficult for Blumfeld to keep an eye on them. They often press eagerly against their desks not so much in order to work as to whisper to one another or even to take forty winks. They give Blumfeld a great deal of trouble; they don't help him sufficiently with the enormous amount of work that is imposed on him. This work involves supervising the whole distribution of fabrics and cash among the women homeworkers who are employed by the factory for the manufacture of certain fancy commodities. To appreciate the magnitude of this task an intimate knowledge of the general conditions is necessary. But since Blumfeld's immediate superior has died some years ago, no one any longer possesses this knowledge, which is also why Blumfeld cannot grant anyone the right to pronounce an opinion on his work. The manufacturer, Herr Ottomar, for instance, clearly underestimates Blumfeld's work; no doubt he recognizes that in the course of twenty years Blumfeld has deserved well of the factory, and this he acknowledges not only because he is obliged to, but also because he respects Blumfeld as a loyal, trustworthy person.—He underestimates his work, nevertheless, for he believes it could be conducted by methods more simple and therefore in every respect more profitable than those employed by Blumfeld. It is said, and it is probably not incorrect, that Ottomar shows himself so rarely in Blumfeld's department simply to spare himself the annoyance that the sight of Blumfeld's working methods causes him. To be so unappreciated is undoubtedly sad for Blumfeld, but there is no remedy, for he cannot very well compel Ottomar to spend let us say a whole month on end in Blumfeld's department in order to study the great variety of work being accomplished there, to apply his own allegedly better methods, and to let himself be convinced of Blumfeld's soundness by the collapse of the department—which would be the inevitable result. And so Blumfeld carries on his work undeterred as before, gives a little start whenever Ottomar appears after a long absence, then with the subordinate's sense of duty makes a feeble effort to explain to Ottomar this or that arrangement, whereupon the latter, his eyes lowered and giving a silent nod, passes on. But what worries Blumfeld more than this lack of appreciation is the thought that one day he will be compelled to leave his job, the immediate consequence of which will be pandemonium, a confusion no one will be able to straighten out because so far as he knows there isn't a single soul in the factory capable of replacing him and of carrying on his job in a manner that could be relied upon to prevent months of the most serious interruptions. Needless to say, if the boss underestimates an employee the latter's colleagues try their best to surpass him in this respect. In consequence everyone underestimates Blumfeld's work; no one considers it necessary to spend any time training in Blumfeld's department, and when new employees are hired not one of them is ever assigned to Blumfeld. As a result Blumfeld's department lacks a younger generation to carry on. When Blumfeld, who up to then had been managing the entire department with the help of only one servant, demanded an assistant, weeks of bitter fighting ensued. Almost every day Blumfeld appeared in Ottomar's office and explained to him calmly and in minute detail why an assistant was needed in his department. He was needed not by any means because Blumfeld wished to spare himself, Blumfeld had no intention of sparing himself, he was doing more than his share of work and this he had no desire to change, but would Herr Ottomar please consider how in the course of time the business had grown, how every department had been correspondingly enlarged, with the exception of Blumfeld's department, which was invariably forgotten! And would he consider too how the work had increased just there! When Blumfeld had entered the firm, a time Herr Ottomar probably could not remember, they had employed some ten seamstresses, today the number varied between fifty and sixty. Such a job requires great energy; Blumfeld could guarantee that he was completely wearing himself out in this work, but that he will continue to master it completely he can henceforth no longer guarantee. True, Herr Ottomar had never flatly refused Blumfeld's requests, this was something he could not do to an old employee, but the manner in which he hardly listened, in which he talked to others over Blumfeld's head, made halfhearted promises and had forgotten everything in a few days—this behavior was insulting, to say the least. Not actually to Blumfeld, Blumfeld is no romantic, pleasant as honor and recognition may be, Blumfeld can do without them, in spite of everything he will stick to his desk as long as it is at all possible, in any case he is in the right, and right, even though on occasion it may take a long time, must prevail in the end. True, Blumfeld has at last been given two assistants, but what assistants! One might have thought Ottomar had realized he could express his contempt for the department even better by granting rather than by refusing it these assistants. It was even possible that Ottomar had kept Blumfeld waiting so long because he was looking for two assistants just like these, and—as may be imagined—took a long time to find them. And now of course Blumfeld could no longer complain; if he did, the answer could easily be foreseen: after all, he had asked for one assistant and had been given two, that's how cleverly Ottomar had arranged things. Needless to say, Blumfeld complained just the same, but only because his predicament all but forced him to do so, not because he still hoped for any redress. Nor did he complain emphatically, but only by the way, whenever the occasion arose. Nevertheless, among his spiteful colleagues the rumor soon spread that someone had asked Ottomar if it were really possible that Blumfeld, who after all had been given such unusual aid, was still complaining. To which Ottomar answered that this was correct, Blumfeld was still complaining, and rightly so. He, Ottomar, had at last realized this and he intended gradually to assign to Blumfeld one assistant for each seamstress, in other words some sixty in all. In case this number should prove insufficient, however, he would let him have even more and would not cease until the bedlam, which had been developing for years in Blumfeld's department, was complete. Now it cannot be denied that in this remark Ottomar's manner of speech had been cleverly imitated, but Blumfeld had no doubts whatever that Ottomar would not dream of speaking about him in such a way. The whole thing was a fabrication of the loafers in the offices on the first floor. Blumfeld ignored it—if only he could as calmly have ignored the presence of the assistants! But there they stood, and could not be spirited away. Pale, weak children. According to their credentials they had already passed school age, but in reality this was difficult to believe. In fact their rightful place was so clearly at their mother's knee that one would hardly have dared to entrust them to a teacher. They still couldn't even move properly; standing up for any length of time tired them inordinately, especially when they first arrived. When left to themselves they promptly doubled up in their weakness, standing hunched and crooked in their corner. Blumfeld tried to point out to them that if they went on giving in to their indolence they would become cripples for life. To ask the assistants to make the slightest move was to take a risk; once when one of them had been ordered to carry something a short distance, he had run so eagerly that he had banged his knee against a desk. The room had been full of seamstresses, the desks covered in merchandise, but Blumfeld had been obliged to neglect everything and take the sobbing assistant into the office and there bandage his wound. Yet even this zeal on the part of the assistant was superficial; like actual children they tried once in a while to excel, but far more often—indeed almost always—they tried to divert their superior's attention and to cheat him. Once, at a time of the most intensive work, Blumfeld had rushed past them, dripping with sweat, and had observed them secretly swapping stamps among the bales of merchandise. He had felt like banging them on the head with his fists, it would have been the only possible punishment for such behavior, but they were after all only children and Blumfeld could not very well knock children down. And so he continued to put up with them. Originally he had imagined that the assistants would help him with the essential chores which at the moment of the distribution of goods required so much effort and vigilance. He had imagined himself standing in the center behind his desk, keeping an eye on everything, and making the entries in the books while the assistants ran to and fro, distributing everything according to his orders. He had imagined that his supervision, which, sharp as it was, could not cope with such a crowd, would be complemented by the assistants' attention; he had hoped that these assistants would gradually acquire experience, cease depending entirely on his orders, and finally learn to discriminate on their own between the seamstresses as to their trustworthiness and requirements. Blumfeld soon realized that all these hopes had been in vain and that he could not afford to let them even talk to the seamstresses. From the beginning they had ignored some of the seamstresses, either from fear or dislike; others to whom they felt partial they would sometimes run to meet at the door. To them the assistants would bring whatever the women wanted, pressing it almost secretly into their hands, although the seamstresses were perfectly entitled to receive it, would collect on a bare shelf for these favorites various cuttings, worthless remnants, but also a few still useful odds and ends, waving them blissfully at the women behind Blumfeld's back and in return having sweets popped into their mouths. Blumfeld of course soon put an end to this mischief and the moment the seamstresses arrived he ordered the assistants back into their glass-enclosed cubicles. But for a long time they considered this to be a grave injustice, they sulked, willfully broke their nibs, and sometimes, although not daring to raise their heads, even knocked loudly against the glass panes in order to attract the seamstresses' attention to the bad treatment that in their opinion they were suffering at Blumfeld's hands.

The wrong they do themselves the assistants cannot see. For instance, they almost always arrive late at the office. Blumfeld, their superior, who from his earliest youth has considered it natural to arrive half an hour before the office opens—not from ambition or an exaggerated sense of duty but simply from a certain feeling of decency—often has to wait more than an hour for his assistants. Chewing his breakfast roll he stands behind his desk, looking through the accounts in the seamstresses' little books. Soon he is immersed in his work and thinking of nothing else when suddenly he receives such a shock that his pen continues to tremble in his hand for some while afterwards. One of the assistants has dashed in, looking as though he is about to collapse; he is holding on to something with one hand while the other is pressed against his heaving chest. All this, however, simply means that he is making excuses for being late, excuses so absurd that Blumfeld purposely ignores them, for if he didn't he would have to give the young man a well-deserved thrashing. As it is, he just glances at him for a moment, points with outstretched hand at the cubicle, and turns back to his work. Now one really might expect the assistant to appreciate his superior's kindness and hurry to his place. No, he doesn't hurry, he dawdles about, he walks on tiptoe, slowly placing one foot in front of the other. Is he trying to ridicule his superior? No. Again it's just that mixture of fear and self-complacency against which one is powerless. How else explain the fact that even today Blumfeld, who has himself arrived unusually late in the office and now after a long wait—he doesn't feel like checking the books—sees, through the clouds of dust raised by the stupid servant with his broom, the two assistants sauntering peacefully along the street? Arm in arm, they appear to be telling one another important things which, however, are sure to have only the remotest and very likely irreverent connections with the office. The nearer they approach the glass door, the slower they walk. One of them seizes the door handle but fails to turn it; they just go on talking, listening, laughing. "Hurry out and open the door for our gentlemen!" shouts Blumfeld at the servant, throwing up his hands. But when the assistants come in, Blumfeld no longer feels like quarreling, ignores their greetings, and goes to his desk. He starts doing his accounts, but now and again glances up to see what his assistants are up to. One of them seems to be very tired and rubs his eyes. When hanging up his overcoat he takes the opportunity to lean against the wall. On the street he seemed lively enough, but the proximity of work tires him. The other assistant, however, is eager to work, but only work of a certain kind. For a long time it has been his wish to be allowed to sweep. But this is work to which he is not entitled; sweeping is exclusively the servant's job; in itself Blumfeld would have nothing against the assistant sweeping, let the assistant sweep, he can't make a worse job of it than the servant, but if the assistant wants to sweep then he must come earlier, before the servant begins to sweep, and not spend on it time that is reserved exclusively for office work. But since the young man is totally deaf to any sensible argument, at least the servant—that half-blind old buffer whom the boss would certainly not tolerate in any department but Blumfeld's and who is still alive only by the grace of the boss and God—at least the servant might be sensible and hand the broom for a moment to the young man who, being clumsy, would soon lose his interest and run after the servant with the broom in order to persuade him to go on sweeping. It appears, however, that the servant feels especially responsible for the sweeping; one can see how he, the moment the young man approaches him, tries to grasp the broom more firmly with his trembling hands; he even stands still and stops sweeping so as to direct his full attention to the ownership of the broom. The assistant doesn't actually plead in words, for he is afraid of Blumfeld, who is ostensibly doing his accounts; moreover, ordinary speech is useless, since the servant can be made to hear only by excessive shouting. So at first the assistant tugs the servant by the sleeve. The servant knows, of course, what it is about, glowers at the assistant, shakes his head, and pulls the broom nearer, up to his chest. Whereupon the assistant folds his hands and pleads. Actually, he has no hope of achieving anything by pleading, but the pleading amuses him and so he pleads. The other assistant follows the goings-on with low laughter and seems to think, heaven knows why, that Blumfeld can't hear him. The pleading makes not the slightest impression on the servant, who turns around and thinks he can safely use the broom again. The assistant, however, has skipped after him on tiptoe and, rubbing his hands together imploringly, now pleads from another side. This turning of the one and skipping of the other is repeated several times. Finally the servant feels cut off from all sides and realizes—something which, had he been slightly less stupid, he might have realized from the beginning— that he will be tired out long before the assistant. So, looking for help elsewhere, he wags his finger at the assistant and points at Blumfeld, suggesting that he will lodge a complaint if the assistant refuses to desist. The assistant realizes that if he is to get the broom at all he'll have to hurry, so he impudently makes a grab for it. An involuntary scream from the other assistant heralds the imminent decision. The servant saves the broom once more by taking a step back and dragging it after him. But now the assistant is up in arms: with open mouth and flashing eyes he leaps forward, the servant tries to escape, but his old legs wobble rather than run, the assistant tugs at the broom and though he doesn't succeed in getting it he nevertheless causes it to drop and in this way it is lost to the servant. Also apparently to the assistant for, the moment the broom falls, all three, the two assistants and the servant, are paralyzed, for now Blumfeld is bound to discover everything. And sure enough Blumfeld at his peephole glances up as though taking in the situation only now. He stares at each one with a stern and searching eye, even the broom on the floor does not escape his notice. Perhaps the silence has lasted too long or perhaps the assistant can no longer suppress his desire to sweep, in any case he bends down—albeit very carefully, as though about to grab an animal rather than a broom—seizes it, passes it over the floor, but, when Blumfeld jumps up and steps out of his cubicle, promptly casts it aside in alarm. "Both of you back to work! And not another sound out of you!" shouts Blumfeld, and with an outstretched hand he directs the two assistants back to their desks. They obey at once, but not shamefaced or with low-ered heads, rather they squeeze themselves stiffly past Blumfeld, staring him straight in the eye as though trying in this way to stop him from beating them. Yet they might have learned from experi-ence that Blumfeld on principle never beats anyone. But they are overapprehensive, and without any tact keep trying to protect their real or imaginary rights.

—Translated by Tania and James Stern

"THEY"

Rudyard Kipling

One view called me to another; one hill top to its fellow, half across the county, and since I could answer at no more trouble than the snapping forward of a lever, I let the country flow under my wheels. The orchid-studded flats of the East gave way to the thyme, ilex, and grey grass of the Downs; these again to the rich cornland and fig-trees of the lower coast, where you carry the beat of the tide on your left hand for fifteen level miles; and when at last I turned inland through a huddle of rounded hills and woods I had run myself clean out of my known marks. Beyond that precise hamlet which stands godmother to the capital of the United States, I found hidden villages where bees, the only things awake, boomed in eighty-foot lindens that overhung grey Norman churches; miraculous brooks diving under stone bridges built for heavier traffic than would ever vex them again; tithe-barns larger than their churches, and an old smithy that cried out aloud how it had once been a hall of the Knights of the Temple. Gypsies I found on a common where the gorse, bracken, and heath fought it out together up a mile of Roman road; and a little farther on I disturbed a red fox rolling dog-fashion in the naked sunlight.

As the wooded hills closed about me I stood up in the car to take the bearings of that great Down whose ringed head is a landmark for fifty miles across the low countries. I judged that the lie of the country would bring me across some westward running road that went to his feet, but I did not allow for the confusing veils of the woods. A quick turn plunged me first into a green cutting brimful of liquid sunshine, next into a gloomy tunnel where last year's dead leaves whispered and scuffled about my tires. The strong hazel stuff meeting overhead had not been cut for a couple of generations at least, nor had any axe helped the moss-cankered oak and beech to spring above them. Here the road changed frankly into a carpeted ride on whose brown velvet spent primrose-clumps showed like jade, and a few sickly, white-stalked blue-bells nodded together. As the slope favored I shut off the power and slid over the whirled leaves, expecting every moment to meet a keeper; but I only heard a jay, far off, arguing against the silence under the twilight of the trees.

Still the track descended. I was on the point of reversing and working my way back on the second speed ere I ended in some swamp, when I saw sunshine through the tangle ahead and lifted the brake.

It was down again at once. As the light beat across my face my forewheels took the turf of a great still lawn from which sprang horsemen ten feet high with leveled lances, monstrous peacocks, and sleek round-headed maids of honor—blue, black, and glistening—all of clipped yew. Across the lawn—the marshalled woods besieged it on three sides—stood an ancient house of lichened and weather-worn stone, with mullioned windows and roofs of rose-red tile. It was flanked by semi-circular walls, also rose-red, that closed the lawn on the fourth side, and at their feet a box hedge grew man-high. There were doves on the roof about the slim brick chimneys, and I caught a glimpse of an octagonal dove-house behind the screening wall.

Here, then, I stayed; a horseman's green spear laid at my breast; held by the exceeding beauty of that jewel in that setting.

"If I am not packed off for a trespasser, or if this knight does not ride a wallop at me," thought I, "Shakespeare and Queen Elizabeth at least must come out of that half-open garden door and ask me to tea."

A child appeared at an upper window, and I thought the little thing waved a friendly hand. But it was to call a companion, for presently another bright head showed. Then I heard a laugh among the yew-peacocks, and turning to make sure (till then I had been watching the house only) I saw the silver of a fountain behind a hedge thrown up against the sun. The doves on the roof cooed to the cooing water; but between the two notes I caught the utterly happy chuckle of a child absorbed in some light mischief.

The garden door—heavy oak sunk deep in the thickness of the wall—opened further: a woman in a big garden hat set her foot slowly on the time-hollowed stone step and as slowly walked across the turf. I was forming some apology when she lifted up her head and I saw that she was blind.

"I heard you," she said. "Isn't that a motor car?"

"I'm afraid I've made a mistake in my road. I should have turned off up above—I never dreamed"—I began.

"But I'm very glad. Fancy a motor car coming into the garden! It will be such a treat—" She turned and made as though looking about her. "You—you haven't seen any one have you—perhaps?"

"No one to speak to, but the children seemed interested at a distance."

"Which?"

"I saw a couple up at the window just now, and I think I heard a little chap in the grounds."

"Oh, lucky you!" she cried, and her face brightened. "I hear them, of course, but that's all. You've seen them and heard them?"

"Yes," I answered. "And if I know anything of children one of them's having a beautiful time by the fountain yonder. Escaped, I should imagine."

"You're fond of children?"

I gave her one or two reasons why I did not altogether hate them.

"Of course, of course," she said. "Then you understand. Then you won't think it foolish if I ask you to take your car through the gardens, once or twice—quite slowly. I'm sure they'd like to see it. They see so little, poor things. One tries to make their life pleasant, but—" she threw out her hands towards the woods. "We're so out of the world here."

"That will be splendid," I said. "But I can't cut up your grass."

She faced to the right. "Wait a minute," she said. "We're at the South gate, aren't we? Behind those peacocks there's a flagged path. We call it the Peacock's Walk. You can't see it from here, they tell me, but if you squeeze along by the edge of the wood you can turn at the first peacock and get on to the flags."

It was a sacrilege to wake that dreaming house-front with the clatter of machinery, but I swung the car to clear the turf, brushed along the edge of the wood and turned in on the broad stone path where the fountain-basin lay like a star-sapphire.

"May I come too?" she cried. "No, please don't help me. They'll like it better if they see me."

She felt her way lightly to the front of the car, and with one foot on the step she called: "Children, oh, children! Look and see what's going to happen!"

The voice would have drawn lost souls from the Pit, for the yearning that underlay its sweetness, and I was not surprised to hear an answering shout behind the yews. It must have been the child by the fountain, but he fled at our approach, leaving a little toy boat in the water. I saw the glint of his blue blouse among the still horsemen.

Very disposedly we paraded the length of the walk and at her request backed again. This time the child had got the better of his panic, but stood far off and doubting.

"The little fellow's watching us," I said. "I wonder if he'd like a ride."

"They're very shy still. Very shy. But, oh, lucky you to be able to see them! Let's listen."

I stopped the machine at once, and the humid stillness, heavy with the scent of box, cloaked us deep. Shears I could hear where some gardener was clipping; a mumble of bees and broken voices that might have been the doves.

"Oh, unkind!" she said wearily.

"Perhaps they're only shy of the motor. The little maid at the window looks tremendously interested."

"Yes?" She raised her head. "It was wrong of me to say that. They are really fond of me. It's the only thing that makes life worth living—when they're fond of you, isn't it? I daren't think what the place would be without them. By the way, is it beautiful?"

"I think it is the most beautiful place I have ever seen."

"So they all tell me. I can feel it, of course, but that isn't quite the same thing."

"Then have you never—?" I began, but stopped abashed.

"Not since I can remember. It happened when I was only a few months old, they tell me. And yet I must remember something, else how could I dream about colors. I see light in my dreams, and colors, but I never see *them*. I only hear them just as I do when I'm awake."

"It's difficult to see faces in dreams. Some people can, but most of us haven't the gift," I went on, looking up at the window where the child stood all but hidden.

"I've heard that too," she said. "And they tell me that one never sees a dead person's face in a dream. Is that true?"

"I believe it is—now I come to think of it."

"But how is it with yourself—yourself?" The blind eyes turned towards me.

"I have never seen the faces of my dead in any dream," I answered.

"Then it must be as bad as being blind."

The sun had dipped behind the woods and the long shades were possessing the insolent horsemen one by one. I saw the light die from off the top of a glossy-leaved lance and all the brave hard green turn to soft black. The house, accepting another day at end, as it had accepted an hundred thousand gone, seemed to settle deeper into its rest among the shadows.

"Have you ever wanted to?" she said after the silence.

"Very much sometimes," I replied. The child had left the window as the shadows closed upon it.

"Ah! So've I, but I don't suppose it's allowed. . . . Where d'you live?"

"Quite the other side of the county—sixty miles and more, and I must be going back. I've come without my big lamp."

"But it's not dark yet. I can feel it."

"I'm afraid it will be by the time I get home. Could you lend me someone to set me on my road at first? I've utterly lost myself."

"I'll send Madden with you to the cross-roads. We are so out of the world, I don't wonder you were lost! I'll guide you round to the front of the house; but you will go slowly, won't you, till you're out of the grounds? It isn't foolish, do you think?"

"I promise you I'll go like this," I said, and let the car start herself down the flagged path.

We skirted the left wing of the house, whose elaborately cast lead guttering alone was worth a day's journey; passed under a great rose-grown gate in the red wall, and so round to the high front of the house which in beauty and stateliness as much excelled the back as that all others I had seen.

"Is it so very beautiful?" she said wistfully when she heard my raptures. "And you like the lead-figures too? There's the old azalea garden behind. They say that this place must have been made for children. Will you help me out, please? I should like to come with you as far as the cross-roads, but I mustn't leave them. Is that you, Madden? I want you to show this gentleman the way to the cross-roads. He has lost his way but—he has seen them."

A butler appeared noiselessly at the miracle of old oak that must be called the front door, and slipped aside to put on his hat. She stood looking at me with open blue eyes in which no sight lay, and I saw for the first time that she was beautiful.

"Remember," she said quietly, "if you are fond of them you will come again," and disappeared within the house.

The butler in the car said nothing till we were nearly at the lodge gates, where catching a glimpse of a blue blouse in a shrubbery I swerved amply lest the devil that leads little boys to play should drag me into child-murder.

"Excuse me," he asked of a sudden, "but why did you do that, Sir?"

"The child yonder."

"Our young gentleman in blue?"

"Of course."

"He runs about a good deal. Did you see him by the fountain, Sir?"

"Oh, yes, several times. Do we turn here?"

"Yes, Sir. And did you 'appen to see them upstairs too?"

"At the upper window? Yes."

"Was that before the mistress come out to speak to you, Sir?"

"A little before that. Why d'you want to know?"

He paused a little. "Only to make sure that—that they had seen the car, Sir, because with children running about, though I'm sure you're driving particularly careful, there might be an accident. That was all, Sir. Here are the cross-roads. You can't miss your way from now on. Thank you, Sir, but that isn't *our* custom, not with—"

"I beg your pardon," I said, and thrust away the British silver.

"Oh, it's quite right with the rest of 'em as a rule. Goodbye, Sir."

He retired into the armor-plated conning tower of his caste and walked away. Evidently a butler solicitous for the honor of his house, and interested, probably through a maid, in the nursery.

Once beyond the signposts at the cross-roads I looked back, but the crumpled hills interlaced so jealously that I could not see where the house had lain. When I asked its name at a cottage along the road, the fat woman who sold sweetmeats there gave me to understand that people with motor cars had small right to live—much less to "go about talking like carriage folk." They were not a pleasant-mannered community.

When I retraced my route on the map that evening I was little wiser. Hawkin's Old Farm appeared to be the survey title of the place, and the old *County Gazeteer*, generally so ample, did not allude to it. The big house of those parts was Hodnington Hall, Georgian with early Victorian embellishments, as an atrocious steel engraving attested. I carried my difficulty to a neighbor—a deep-rooted tree of that soil—and he gave me a name of a family which conveyed no meaning.

A month or so later—I went again, or it may have been that my car took the road of her own volition. She over-ran the fruitless Downs, threaded every turn of the maze of lanes below the hills, drew through the high-walled woods, impenetrable in their full leaf, came out at the cross-roads where the butler had left me, and a little further on developed an internal trouble which forced me to turn her in on a grass way-waste that cut into a summer-silent hazel wood. So far as I could make sure by the sun and a six-inch Ordnance map, this should be the road flank of that wood which I had first explored from the heights above. I made a mighty serious business of my repairs and a glittering shop of my repair kit, spanners, pump, and the like, which I spread out orderly upon a rug. It was a trap to catch all childhood, for on such a day, I argued, the children would not be far off. When I paused in my work I listened, but the wood was so full of the noises of summer (though the birds had mated) that I could not at first distinguish these from the tread of small cautious feet stealing across the dead leaves. I rang my bell in an alluring manner, but the feet fled, and I repented, for to a child a sudden noise is very real terror. I must have been at work half an hour when I heard in the wood the voice of the blind woman crying: "Children, oh children, where are you?" and the stillness made slow to close on the perfection of that cry. She came towards me, half feeling her way between the tree boles, and though a child it seemed clung to her skirt, it swerved into the leafage like a rabbit as she drew nearer.

"Is that you?" she said, "from the other side of the county?"

"Yes, it's me from the other side of the county."

"Then why didn't you come through the upper woods? They were there just now."

"They were here a few minutes ago. I expect they knew my car had broken down, and came to see the fun."

"Nothing serious, I hope? How do cars break down?"

"In fifty different ways. Only mine has chosen the fifty first."

She laughed merrily at the tiny joke, cooed with delicious laughter, and pushed her hat back.

"Let me hear," she said.

"Wait a moment," I cried, "and I'll get you a cushion."

She set her foot on the rug all covered with spare parts, and stooped above it eagerly. "What delightful things!" The hands through which she saw glanced in the checkered sunlight. "A box here—another box! Why you've arranged them like playing shop!"

"I confess now that I put it out to attract them. I don't need half those things really."

"How nice of you! I heard your bell in the upper wood. You say they were here before that?"

"I'm sure of it. Why are they so shy? That little fellow in blue who was with you just now ought to have got over his fright. He's been watching me like a Red Indian."

"It must have been your bell," she said. "I heard one of them go past me in trouble when I was coming down. They're shy—so shy even with me." She turned her face over her shoulder and cried again: "Children! Oh, children! Look and see!"

"They must have gone off together on their own affairs," I suggested, for there was a murmur behind us of lowered voices broken by the sudden squeaking giggles of childhood. I returned to my tinkerings and she leaned forward, her chin on her hand, listening interestedly.

"How many are they?" I said at last. The work was finished, but I saw no reason to go.

Her forehead puckered a little in thought. "I don't quite know," she said simply. "Sometimes more—sometimes less. They come and stay with me because I love them, you see."

"That must be very jolly," I said, replacing a drawer, and as I spoke I heard the inanity of my answer.

"You—you aren't laughing at me," she cried. "I—I haven't any of my own. I never married. People laugh at me sometimes about them because—because—"

"Because they're savages," I returned. "It's nothing to fret for. That sort laugh at everything that isn't in their own fat lives."

"I don't know. How should I? I only don't like being laughed at about *them*. It hurts; and when one can't see. . . . I don't want to seem silly," her chin quivered like a child's as she spoke, "but we blindies have only one skin, I think. Everything outside hits straight at our souls. It's different with you. You've such good defenses in your eyes—looking out—before anyone can really pain you in your soul. People forget that with us.''

I was silent reviewing that inexhaustible matter—the more than inherited (since it is also carefully taught) brutality of the Christian peoples, beside which the mere heathendom of the West Coast nigger is clean and restrained. It led me a long distance into myself.

''Don't do that!'' she said of a sudden, putting her hands before her eyes.

''What?''

She made a gesture with her hand.

''That! It's—it's all purple and black. Don't! That color hurts.''

''But, how in the world do you know about colors?'' I exclaimed, for here was a revelation indeed.

''Colors as colors?'' she asked.

''No. *Those* Colors which you saw just now.''

''You know as well as I do,'' she laughed, ''else you wouldn't have asked that question. They aren't in the world at all. They're in *you*—when you went so angry.''

''D'you mean a dull purplish patch, like port-wine mixed with ink?'' I said.

''I've never seen ink or port-wine, but the colors aren't mixed. They are separate—all separate.''

''Do you mean black streaks and jags across the purple?''

She nodded. ''Yes—if they are like this,'' and zig-zagged her finger again, ''but it's more red than purple—that bad color.''

''And what are the colors at the top of the—whatever you see?''

Slowly she leaned forward and traced on the rug the figure of the Egg itself.

''I see them so,'' she said, pointing with a grass stem, ''white, green, yellow, red, purple, and when people are angry or bad, black across the red—as you were just now.''

''Who told you anything about it—in the beginning?'' I demanded.

''About the colors? No one. I used to ask what colors were when I was little—in table-covers and curtains and carpets, you see—because some colors hurt me and some made me happy. People told me; and when I got older that was how I saw people." Again she traced the outline of the Egg which it is given to very few of us to see.

"All by yourself?" I repeated.

"All by myself. There wasn't anyone else. I only found out afterwards that other people did not see the Colors."

She leaned against the tree-bole plaiting and unplaiting chance-plucked grass stems. The children in the wood had drawn nearer. I could see them with the tail of my eye frolicking like squirrels.

"Now I am sure you will never laugh at me," she went on after a long silence. "Nor at *them.*"

"Goodness! No!" I cried, jolted out of my train of thought. "A man who laughs at a child—unless the child is laughing too—is a heathen!"

"I didn't mean that of course. You'd never laugh *at* children, but I thought—I used to think—that perhaps you might laugh about *them.* So now I beg your pardon. . . . What are you going to laugh at?"

I had made no sound, but she knew.

"At the notion of your begging my pardon. If you had done your duty as a pillar of the state and a landed proprietress you ought to have summoned me for trespass when I barged through your woods the other day. It was disgraceful of me—inexcusable."

She looked at me, her head against the tree trunk—long and steadfastly—this woman who could see the naked soul.

"How curious," she half whispered. "How very curious."

"Why, what have I done?"

"You don't understand . . . and yet you understood about the Colors. Don't you understand?"

She spoke with a passion that nothing had justified, and I faced her bewilderedly as she rose. The children had gathered themselves in a roundel behind a bramble bush. One sleek head bent over something smaller, and the set of the little shoulders told me that fingers were on lips. They too, had some child's tremendous secret. I alone was hopelessly astray there in the broad sunlight.

"No," I said, and shook my head as though the dead eyes could note. "Whatever it is, I don't understand yet. Perhaps I shall later—if you'll let me come again."

"You will come again," she answered. "You will surely come again and walk in the wood."

"Perhaps the children will know me well enough by that time to let me play with them—as a favor. You know what children are like."

"It isn't a matter of favor but of right," she replied, and while I wondered what she meant, a disheveled woman plunged round the bend of the road, loose-haired, purple, almost lowing with agony as she ran. It was my rude, fat friend of the sweetmeat shop. The blind woman heard and stepped forward. "What is it, Mrs. Madehurst?" she asked.

The woman flung her apron over her head and literally groveled in the dust, crying that her grandchild was sick to death, that the local doctor was away fishing, that Jenny the mother was at her wit's end, and so forth, with repetitions and bellowings.

"Where's the next nearest doctor?" I asked between paroxysms.

"Madden will tell you. Go round to the house and take him with you. I'll attend to this. Be quick!" She half-supported the fat woman into the shade. In two minutes I was blowing all the horns of Jericho under the front of the House Beautiful, and Madden, in the pantry, rose to the crisis like a butler and a man.

A quarter of an hour at illegal speeds caught us a doctor five miles away. Within the half-hour we had decanted him, much interested in motors, at the door of the sweetmeat shop, and drew up the road to await the verdict.

"Useful things cars," said Madden, all man and no butler. "If I'd had one when mine took sick she wouldn't have died."

"How was it?" I asked.

"Croup. Mrs. Madden was away. No one knew what to do. I drove eight miles in a tax cart for the doctor. She was choked when we came back. This car 'd ha' saved her. She'd have been close on ten now."

"I'm sorry," I said. "I thought you were rather fond of children from what you told me going to the cross-roads the other day."

"Have you seen 'em again, Sir—this mornin'?"

"Yes, but they're well broke to cars. I couldn't get any of them within twenty yards of it."

He looked at me carefully as a scout considers a stranger—not as a menial should lift his eyes to his divinely appointed superior.

"I wonder why," he said just above the breath that he drew.

We waited on. A light wind from the sea wandered up and down the long lines of the woods, and the wayside grasses, whitened already with summer dust, rose and bowed in sallow waves.

A woman, wiping the suds off her arms, came out of the cottage next the sweetmeat shop.

"I've be'n listenin' in de back-yard," she said cheerily. "He says Arthur's unaccountable bad. Did ye hear him shruck just now? Unaccountable bad. I reckon t'will come Jenny's turn to walk in de wood nex' week along Mr. Madden."

"Excuse me, Sir, but your lap-robe is slipping," said Madden deferentially. The woman started, dropped a curtsey, and hurried away.

"What does she mean by 'walking in the wood'?" I asked.

"It must be some saying they use hereabouts. I'm from Norfolk myself," said Madden. "They're an independent lot in this county. She took you for a chauffeur, Sir."

I saw the Doctor come out of the cottage followed by a draggle-tailed wench who clung to his arm as though he could make treaty for her with Death. "Dat sort," she wailed—"dey're just as much to us dat has 'em as if dey was lawful born. Just as much—just as much! An' God he'd be just as pleased if you saved 'un, Doctor. Don't take it from me. Miss Florence will tell ye de very same. Don't leave 'im, Doctor!"

"I know. I know," said the man, "but he'll be quiet for a while now. We'll get the nurse and the medicine as fast as we can." He signaled me to come forward with the car, and I strove not to be privy to what followed; but I saw the girl's face, blotched and frozen with grief, and I felt the hand without a ring clutching at my knees when we moved away.

The Doctor was a man of some humor, for I remember he claimed my car under the Oath of Æsculapius, and used it and me without mercy. First we convoyed Mrs. Madehurst and the blind woman to wait by the sick bed till the nurse should come. Next we invaded a neat county town for prescriptions (the Doctor said the trouble was cerebro-spinal meningitis), and when the County Institute, banked and flanked with scared market cattle, reported itself out of nurses for the moment we literally flung ourselves loose upon the county. We conferred with the owners of great houses—magnates at the ends of overarching avenues whose big-boned womenfolk strode away from their tea-tables to listen to the imperious Doctor. At last a whitehaired lady sitting under a cedar of Lebanon and surrounded by a court of magnificent Borzois—all hostile to motors—gave the Doctor, who received them as from a princess, written orders which we bore many miles at top speed, through a park, to a French nunnery, where we took over in exchange a pallid-faced and trembling Sister. She knelt at the bottom of the tonneau telling her beads without pause till, by short cuts of the Doctor's invention, we had her to the sweet-meat shop once more. It was a long afternoon crowded with mad episodes that rose and dissolved like the dust of our wheels; cross-sections of remote and incomprehensible lives through which we raced at right angles; and I went home in the dusk, wearied out, to dream of the clashing horns of cattle; round-eyed nuns walking in a garden of graves; pleasant tea-parties beneath shaded trees; the carbolic-scented, grey-painted corridors of the County Institute; the steps of shy children in the wood, and the hands that clung to my knees as the motor began to move.

I had intended to return in a day or two, but it pleased Fate to hold me from that side of the county, on many pretexts, till the elder and the wild rose had fruited. There came at last a brilliant day, swept clear from the south-west, that brought the hills within hand's reach—a day of unstable airs and high filmy clouds. Through no merit of my own I was free, and set the car for the third time on that known road. As I reached the crest of the Downs I felt the soft air change, saw it glaze under the sun; and, looking down at the sea, in that instant beheld the blue of the Channel turn through polished silver and dulled steel to dingy pewter. A laden collier hugging the coast steered outward for deeper water and, across copper-colored haze, I saw sails rise one by one on the anchored fishing-fleet. In a deep dene behind me an eddy of sudden wind drummed through sheltered oaks, and spun aloft the first day sample of autumn leaves. When I reached the beach road the sea-fog fumed over the brickfields, and the side was telling all the groins of the gale beyond Ushant. In less than an hour summer England vanished in chill grey. We were again the shut island of the North, all the ships of the world bellowing at our perilous gates; and between their outcries ran the piping of bewildered gulls. My cap dripped moisture, the folds of the rug held it in pools or sluiced it away in runnels, and the salt-rime stuck to my lips.

Inland the smell of autumn loaded the thickened fog among the trees, and the drip became a continuous shower. Yet the late flowers—mallow of the wayside, scabious of the field, and dahlia of the garden—showed gay in the midst, and beyond the sea's breath there was little sign of decay in the leaf. Yet in the villages the house doors were all open, and bare-legged, bare-headed children sat at ease on the damp doorsteps to shout "pip-pip" at the stranger.

I made bold to call at the sweetmeat shop, where Mrs. Madehurst met me with a fat woman's hospitable tears. Jenny's child, she said, had died two days after the nun had come. It was, she felt, best out of the way, even though insurance offices, for reasons which she did not pretend to follow, would not willingly insure such stray lives. "Not but what Jenny didn't tend to Arthur as though he'd come all proper at de end of de first year—like Jenny herself." Thanks to Miss Florence, the child had been buried with a pomp which, in Mrs. Madehurst's opinion, more than covered the small irregularity of its birth. She described the coffin, within and without, the glass hearse, and the evergreen lining of the grave.

"But how's the mother?" I asked.

"Jenny? Oh, she'll get over it. I've felt dat way with one or two o' my own. She'll get over. She's walkin' in de wood now."

"In this weather?"

Mrs. Madehurst looked at me with narrowed eyes across the counter.

"I dunno but it opens de 'eart like. Yes, it opens de 'eart. Dat's where losin' and bearin' comes so alike in de long run, we do say."

Now the wisdom of the old wives is greater than that of all the Fathers, and this last oracle sent me thinking so extendedly as I went up the road, that I nearly ran over a woman and a child at the wooded corner by the lodge gates of the House Beautiful.

"Awful weather!" I cried, as I slowed dead for the turn.

"Not so bad," she answered placidly out of the fog. "Mine's used to 'un. You'll find yours indoors, I reckon."

Indoors, Madden received me with professional courtesy, and kind inquiries for the health of the motor, which he would put under cover.

I waited in a still, nut-brown hall, pleasant with late flowers and warmed with a delicious wood fire—a place of good influence and great peace. (Men and women may sometimes, after great effort, achieve a creditable lie; but the house, which is their temple, cannot say anything save the truth of those who have lived in it.) A child's cart and a doll lay on the black-and-white floor, where a rug had been kicked back. I felt that the children had only just hurried away—to hide themselves, most like—in the many turns of the great adzed staircase that climbed statelily out of the hall, or to crouch at gaze behind the lions and roses of the carven gallery above. When I heard her voice above me, singing as the blind sing—from the soul:—

In the pleasant orchard-closes.

And all my early summer came back at the call.

In the pleasant orchard-closes,
    God bless all our gains say we—

But may God bless all our losses,
Better suits with our degree.

She dropped the marring fifth line, and repeated—

Better suits with our degree!

I saw her lean over the gallery, her linked hands white as pearl against the oak.

"Is that you—from the other side of the county?" she called.

"Yes, me—from the other side of the county," I answered laughing.

"What a long time before you had to come here again." She ran down the stairs, one hand lightly touching the broad rail. "It's two months and four days. Summer's gone!"

"I meant to come before, but Fate prevented."

"I knew it. Please do something to that fire. They won't let me play with it, but I can feel it's behaving badly. Hit it!"

I looked on either side of the deep fireplace, and found but a half-charred hedge-stake with which I punched a black log into flame.

"It never goes out, day or night," she said, as though explaining. "In case any one comes in with cold toes, you see."

"It's even lovelier inside than it was out," I murmured. The red light poured itself along the age-polished dusky panels till the Tudor roses and lions of the gallery took color and motion. An old eagle-topped convex mirror gathered the picture into its mysterious heart, distorting afresh the distorted shadows, and curving the gallery lines into the curves of a ship. The day was shutting down in half a gale as the fog turned to stringy scud. Through the uncurtained mullions of the broad window I could see valiant horsemen of the lawn rear and recover against the wind that taunted them with legions of dead leaves.

"Yes, it must be beautiful," she said. "Would you like to go over it? There's still light enough upstairs."

I followed her up the unflinching, wagon-wide staircase to the gallery whence opened the thin fluted Elizabethan doors.

"Feel how they put the latch low down for the sake of the children." She swung a light door inward.

"By the way, where are they?" I asked. "I haven't even heard them to-day."

She did not answer at once. Then, "I can only hear them," she replied softly. "This is one of their rooms—everything ready, you see."

She pointed into a heavily-timbered room. There were little low gate tables and children's chairs. A doll's house, its hooked front half open, faced a great dappled rocking-horse, from whose padded saddle it was but a child's scramble to the broad window-seat overlooking the lawn. A toy gun lay in a corner beside a gilt wooden cannon.

"Surely they've only just gone," I whispered. In the failing light a door creaked cautiously. I heard the rustle of a frock and the patter of feet—quick feet through a room beyond.

"I heard that," she cried triumphantly. "Did you? Children. O children, where are you?"

The voice filled the walls that held it lovingly to the last perfect note, but there came no answering shout such as I had heard in the garden. We hurried on from room to oak-floored room; up a step here, down three steps there; among a maze of passages; always mocked by our quarry. One might as well have tried to work an unstopped warren with a single ferret. There were bolt-holes innumerable—recesses in walls, embrasures of deep slitten windows now darkened, whence they could start up behind us; and abandoned fireplaces, six feet deep in the masonry, as well as the tangle of communicating doors. Above all, they had the twilight for their helper in our game. I had caught one or two joyous chuckles of evasion, and once or twice had seen the silhouette of a child's frock against some darkening window at the end of a passage; but we returned empty-handed to the gallery, just as a middle-aged woman was setting a lamp in its niche.

"No, I haven't seen her either this evening, Miss Florence," I heard her say, "but that Turpin he says he wants to see you about his shed."

"Oh, Mr. Turpin must want to see me very badly. Tell him to come to the hall, Mrs. Madden."

I looked down into the hall whose only light was the dulled fire, and deep in the shadow I saw them at last. They must have slipped down while we were in the passages, and now thought themselves perfectly hidden behind an old gilt leather screen. By child's law, my fruitless chase was as good as an introduction, but since I had taken so much trouble I resolved to force them to come forward later by the simple trick, which children detest, of pretending not to notice them. They lay close, in a little huddle, no more than shadows except when a quick flame betrayed an outline.

"And now we'll have some tea," she said. "I believe I ought to have offered it you at first, but one doesn't arrive at manners somehow when one lives alone and is considered—h'm—peculiar." Then with very pretty scorn, "would you like a lamp to see to eat by?"

"The firelight's much pleasanter, I think." We descended into that delicious gloom and Madden brought tea.

I took my chair in the direction of the screen ready to surprise or be surprised as the game should go, and at her permission, since a hearth is always sacred, bent forward to play with the fire.

"Where do you get these beautiful short faggots from?" I asked idly. "Why, they are tallies!"

"Of course," she said. "As I can't read or write I'm driven back on the early English tally for my accounts. Give me one and I'll tell you what it meant."

I passed her an unburned hazel-tally, about a foot long, and she ran her thumb down the nicks.

"This is the milk-record for the home farm for the month of April last year, in gallons," said she. "I don't know what I should have done without tallies. An old forester of mine taught me the system. It's out of date now for every one else; but my tenants respect it. One of them's coming now to see me. Oh, it doesn't matter. He has no business here out of office hours. He's a greedy, ignorant man—very greedy or—he wouldn't come here after dark."

"Have you much land then?"

"Only a couple of hundred acres in hand, thank goodness. The other six hundred are nearly all let to folk who knew my folk before me, but this Turpin is quite a new man—and a highway robber."

"But are you sure I sha'n't be—?"

"Certainly not. You have the right. He hasn't any children."

"Ah, the children!" I said, and slid my low chair back till it nearly touched the screen that hid them. "I wonder whether they'll come out for me."

There was a murmur of voices—Madden's and a deeper note— at the low, dark side door, and a ginger-headed, canvas-gaitered giant of the unmistakable tenant farmer type stumbled or was pushed in.

"Come to the fire, Mr. Turpin," she said.

"If—if you please, Miss, I'll—I'll be quite as well by the door." He clung to the latch as he spoke like a frightened child. Of a sudden I realized that he was in the grip of some almost overpowering fear.

"Well?"

"About that new shed for the young stock—that was all. These first autumn storms settin' in . . . but I'll come again, Miss." His teeth did not chatter much more than the door latch.

"I think not," she answered levelly. "The new shed—m'm. What did my agent write you on the 15th?"

"I—fancied p'raps that if I came to see you—ma—man to man like, Miss. But—"

His eyes rolled into every corner of the room wide with horror. He half opened the door through which he had entered, but I noticed it shut again—from without and firmly.

"He wrote what I told him," she went on. "You are overstocked already. Dunnett's Farm never carried more than fifty bullocks—even in Mr. Wright's time. And *he* used cake. You've sixty-seven and you don't cake. You've broken the lease in that respect. You're dragging the heart out of the farm."

"I'm—I'm getting some minerals—superphosphates—next week. I've as good as ordered a truck-load already. I'll go down to the station to-morrow about 'em. Then I can come and see you man to man like, Miss, in the daylight. . . . That gentleman's not going away, is he?" He almost shrieked.

I had only slid the chair a little further back, reaching behind me to tap on the leather of the screen, but he jumped like a rat.

"No. Please attend to me, Mr. Turpin." She turned in her chair and faced him with his back to the door. It was an old and sordid little piece of scheming that she forced from him—his plea for the new cowshed at his landlady's expense, that he might with the covered manure pay his next year's rent out of the valuation after, as she made clear, he had bled the enriched pastures to the bone. I could not but admire the intensity of his greed, when I saw him out-facing for its sake whatever terror it was that ran wet on his forehead.

I ceased to tap the leather—was, indeed, calculating the cost of the shed—when I felt my relaxed hand taken and turned softly between the soft hands of a child. So at last I had triumphed. In a moment I would turn and acquaint myself with those quick-footed wanderers. . . .

The little brushing kiss fell in the center of my palm—as a gift on which the fingers were, once, expected to close: as the all faithful half-reproachful signal of a waiting child not used to neglect even when grown-ups were busiest—a fragment of the mute code devised very long ago.

Then I knew. And it was as though I had known from the first day when I looked across the lawn at the high window.

I heard the door shut. The woman turned to me in silence, and I felt that she knew.

What time passed after this I cannot say. I was roused by the fall of a log, and mechanically rose to put it back. Then I returned to my place in the chair very close to the screen.

"Now you understand," she whispered, across the packed shadows.

"Yes, I understand—now. Thank you."

"I—I only hear them." She bowed her head in her hands. "I have no right, you know—no other right. I have neither borne nor lost—neither borne nor lost!"

"Be very glad then," said I, for my soul was torn open within me.

"Forgive me!"

She was still, and I went back to my sorrow and my joy.

"It was because I loved them so," she said at last, brokenly. *"That* was why it was, even from the first—even before I knew that they—they were all I should ever have. And I loved them so!"

She stretched out her arms to the shadows and the shadows within the shadow.

"They came because I loved them—because I needed them. I—I must have made them come. Was that wrong, think you?"

"No—no."

"I—I grant you that the toys and—and all that sort of thing were nonsense, but—but I used to so hate empty rooms myself when I was little." She pointed to the gallery. "And the passages all empty. . . . And how could I ever bear the garden door shut? Suppose—"

"Don't! For pity's sake, don't!" I cried. The twilight had brought a cold rain with gusty squalls that plucked at the leaded windows.

"And the same thing with keeping the fire in all night. *I* don't think it so foolish—do you?"

I looked at the broad brick hearth, saw, through tears I believe, that there was no unpassable iron on or near it, and bowed my head.

"I did all that and lots of other things—just to make believe. Then they came. I heard them, but I didn't know that they were not mine by right till Mrs. Madden told me—"

"The butler's wife? What?"

"One of them—I heard—she saw. And knew. Hers! *Not* for me. I didn't know at first. Perhaps I was jealous. Afterwards, I began to understand that it was only because I loved them, not because— . . . Oh, you *must* bear or lose," she said piteously. "There is no other way—and yet they love me. They must! Don't they?"

There was no sound in the room except the lapping voices of

the fire, but we two listened intently, and she at least took comfort from what she heard. She recovered herself and half rose. I sat still in my chair by the screen.

"Don't think me a wretch to whine about myself like this, but—but I'm all in the dark, you know, and *you* can see."

In truth I could see, and my vision confirmed me in my resolve, though that was like the very parting of spirit and flesh. Yet a little longer I would stay since it was the last time.

"You think it is wrong, then?" she cried sharply, though I had said nothing.

"Not for you. A thousand times no. For you it is right. . . . I am grateful to you beyond words. For me it would be wrong. For me only. . . ."

"Why?" she said, but passed her hand before her face as she had done at our second meeting in the wood. "Oh, I see," she went on simply as a child. "For you it would be wrong." Then with a little indrawn laugh, "and, d'you remember, I called you lucky—once—at first. You who must never come here again!"

She left me to sit a little longer by the screen, and I heard the sound of her feet die out along the gallery above.

THE
HIGHBOY

Alison Lurie

Even before I knew more about that piece of furniture I wouldn't have wanted it in my house. For a valuable antique, it wasn't particularly attractive: with that tall stack of dark mahogany drawers and those long spindly bowed legs, it looked not only heavy but top-heavy. But then Clark and I have never cared much for Chippendale; we prefer simple lines and light woods. The carved bonnet top of the highboy was too elaborate for my taste, and the surface had been polished till it glistened a deep blackish brown, the color of canned prunes.

Still, I could understand why the piece meant so much to Clark's sister-in-law, Buffy Stockwell. It mattered to her that she had what she called "really good things": that her antiques were genuine and her china was Spode. She never made a point of how superior her "things" were to most people's, but one was always aware of it. And besides, the highboy was an heirloom; it had been in her family for years. I could easily see why she was disappointed and cross when her aunt left it to Buffy's brother.

"I don't want to sound ungrateful, Janet, honestly," Buffy told me over lunch at the country club. "I realize Jack's carrying on the family name and I'm not. And of course I was glad to have Aunt Betsy's Tiffany coffee service. I suppose it's worth more than the highboy actually, but it just doesn't have any past. It's got no personality, if you know what I mean."

Buffy giggled, but I barely smiled. My sister-in-law was given to anthropomorphizing her possessions, speaking of them as if they had almost human traits: "A dear little Paul Revere sugar spoon." "It's lively, even kind of aggressive, for a wicker plant stand—but I think it'll be really happy on the sun porch." Whenever their washer or sit-down mower or VCR wasn't working properly she'd say it was "ill." I'd thought the habit endearing once, but by now it had begun to rather bore me.

"I don't understand it really," Buffy said, digging her little dessert fork into the lemon cream tart that she always ordered at the club after declaring—quite rightly—that she shouldn't. "After all, I'm the one who was named for Aunt Betsy, and she knew how interested I was in family history. I always thought I was her favorite. Well, live and learn." She giggled again in that rather self-consciously girlish way she had and took another bite, leaving a fleck of whipped cream on her short, pouting upper lip.

You mustn't get me wrong. Buffy and her husband Bobby, Clark's brother, were both dears, and as affectionate and reliable and nice as anyone could possibly be. But even Clark and I had to admit that they'd never quite grown up. Bobby was sixty-one and a vice president of his company, but his life still centered around golf and tennis.

Buffy, who was nearly his age, didn't play anymore because of her heart. But she still favored yellow and shocking-pink sportswear with rather silly designs. She kept her hair blonde and wore it in all-over curls, and maintained her girlish manner. Then of course she had these bouts of childlike whimsicality: she attributed opinions to their pets, and named their automobiles. As long as it was alive, she had insisted that their poodle Suzy didn't like the mailman because he was a Democrat, and for years she had had a series of Plymouth Valiant wagons called Prince.

The next time the subject of the highboy came up was at a big dinner party about a month later, after Buffy'd been to see her brother in Connecticut. "It wasn't all that successful a visit," she reported. "You know my Aunt Betsy Lumpkin left Jack her Newport highboy, that I was hoping would come to me. I think I told you."

I agreed that she had.

"Well, it's in his house in Stonington now," Buffy said. "But it's completely out of place there, among all that pickled walnut imitation French-provincial furniture that Jack's new wife chose, and those boring fashion plates. It looked so *uncomfortable.*" She sighed and accepted another helping of roast potatoes.

"It really makes me sad," she went on. "I could tell right away that Jack and his wife don't appreciate Aunt Betsy's highboy, the way they've shoved it into a corner behind the door to the patio." She helped herself to gravy. "Jack says it's because he can't get it to stand steady, and the drawers always stick."

"Well, perhaps they do," I said. "After all, the piece must be over two hundred years old."

But Buffy wouldn't agree. Aunt Betsy had never had that sort of trouble, she told me. If the highboy wobbled it was probably because the floors of Jack's contemporary house were subsiding; you couldn't trust architects these days.

It was true, her aunt had said that the highboy was temperamental. Usually the drawers would slide open as smoothly as butter, but now and then they seized up. It probably had something to do with the humidity, I thought; but according to Buffy her Aunt Betsy, who seems to have had the same sort of childish imagination as her niece, used to say that the highboy was sulking; someone had been rough with it, she would suggest, or it hadn't been polished lately.

"I'm sure Jack's wife doesn't know how to take care of good furniture properly either," Buffy went on after the salad had been served. "She's too busy with her high-powered executive job." Buffy had never worked a day in her life.

"Honestly, Janet, it's true," she said, mistaking my smile for skepticism. "When I was there last week the finish was already beginning to look dull, almost soapy. Aunt Betsy always used to polish it once a week with beeswax, to keep the patina. I mentioned that twice, but I could see Jack's wife wasn't paying any attention. Not that she ever pays any attention to me." Buffy gave a little nervous giggle, more of a hiccup really. Her brother's wife wasn't the only one of the family who thought of her as a light-weight, and she wasn't too silly to know it.

"What I suspect is, Janet, I suspect she's letting her cleaning lady spray it with that awful synthetic no-rub polish they make now," Buffy went on, frowning across the glazed damask. "I found a can of the stuff under her sink. Full of awful chemicals you can't pronounce. Anyhow, I'm sure the climate in Stonington can't be good for old furniture; not with all that nasty salt and damp in the air."

There was a lull in the conversation then, and at the other end of the table Buffy's husband heard her and gave a kind of guffaw. "Say, Clark," he called to my husband. "I wish you'd tell Buffy to forget about that dumb highboy of her aunt's."

Well, naturally Clark was not going to do anything of the sort. But he turned and listened patiently to Buffy's story, and then he suggested that she ask her brother if he'd be willing to exchange the highboy for her aunt's coffee service.

I thought this was a good idea, and so did Buffy. She wrote off to her brother, and the following Sunday evening, before she'd even expected an answer, Jack phoned to say that was fine by him. He was sick of the thing; no matter how he tried to prop up the legs it still wobbled.

Besides, the day before he'd gone to get out some maps for a trip they were planning, and the whole thing just kind of seized up. He'd stopped trying to free the top drawer with a screwdriver and was working on one of the lower ones, when he got a hell of a crack on the head. He must have loosened something some-how, he told Buffy, so that when he pulled on the lower drawer the upper one slid out noiselessly above him. And when he stood up, bingo.

It was Saturday, and their doctor was off call, so Jack's wife had to drive him ten miles to the Westerly emergency room; he was too dizzy and confused to drive himself. There wasn't any concus-sion, according to the X rays, but he had a lump on his head the size of a plum and a headache the size of a football. He'd be happy to ship that goddamned piece of furniture out of his house as soon as it was convenient, he told Buffy, and she could take her time about sending along the coffee service.

Two weeks later when I went over to Buffy's for tea her aunt's highboy had arrived. She was so happy that I bore with her when she started being silly about how it appreciated the care she was taking of it. "When I rub in the beeswax I can almost feel it purring under my hand like a big cat," she insisted, giggling.

I glanced at the highboy again. I thought I'd never seen a less agreeable-looking piece of furniture. Its pretentious high-arched bonnet top resembled a clumsy mahogany Napoleon hat, and the ball-and-claw feet made the thing look as if it were up on tiptoe. If it was a big cat, it was a cat with bird's legs—a sort of gryphon.

"I know it's grateful to be here," Buffy told me. "The other day I couldn't find my reading glasses anywhere; but then, as I was standing in the sitting room, at my wit's end, I heard a little creak, or maybe it was more sort of a pop. I looked round and one of the top drawers of the highboy was out about an inch. Well, I went to shut it, and there were my glasses! Now what do you make of that?"

I made nothing of it, but humored her. "Quite a coincidence."

"Oh, more than that." Buffy gave another rippling giggle. "And it's completely steady now. Try and see."

I put a hand on one side of the highboy and gave the thing a little push, and she was perfectly right. It stood solid and heavy against the cream and yellow Colonial Williamsburg wallpaper, as if it had been in Buffy's house for centuries. The prune-dark mahogany was waxy to the touch, and colder than I would have expected.

"And the drawers don't stick in the least." Buffy slid them open and shut to demonstrate. "I know it's going to be happy here."

It was early spring when the highboy arrived, and whether or not it was happy, it gave no trouble until that summer. Then in July we had a week of drenching thunderstorms, and the drawers began to jam. I saw it happen one Sunday when Clark and I were over and Bobby tried to get out the slides of their recent trip to Quebec. He started shaking the thing and swore a bit, and Buffy had to go and help him.

"There's nothing at all wrong with the highboy," she whispered to me afterward. "Bobby just doesn't understand how to treat it. You mustn't force the drawers open like that; you have to be gentle."

After we'd sat through the slides, Bobby went over to the highboy again to put them away.

"Careful, darling," Buffy warned him.

"Okay, okay," Bobby said; but it was clear he wasn't listening seriously. He yanked the drawer open without much trouble; but when he slammed it shut he let out a frightful howl: he'd shut his right thumb inside.

"Christ, will you look at that!" he shouted, holding out his stubby red hand to show us a deep dented gash below the knuckle. "I think the damn thing's broken."

Well, Bobby's thumb wasn't broken; but it was bruised rather badly, as things turned out. His hand was swollen for over a week, so that he couldn't play in the golf tournament at the club, which meant a lot to him.

Buffy and I were sitting on the clubhouse terrace that day, and Bobby was moseying about by the first tee in a baby-blue golf shirt, with his hand still wadded up in bandages.

"Poor darling, he's so cross," Buffy said.

"Cross?" I asked; in fact Bobby didn't look cross, only foolish and disconsolate.

"He's furious at the highboy, you know, Janet," she said. "And what I've decided is, there's no point any longer in trying to persuade him to treat it right. After what happened last week, I realized it would be better to keep them apart. So I've simply moved all his things out of the drawers, and now I'm using them for my writing paper and tapestry wools."

This time, perhaps because it was such a sticky hot day and there were too many flies on the terrace, I felt more than usually impatient with Buffy's whimsy. "Really, dear, you mustn't let your imagination run away with you," I said, squeezing more lemon into my iced tea. "Your aunt's highboy doesn't have any quarrel with Bobby. It isn't a human being, it's a piece of furniture."

"But that's just it," Buffy insisted. "That's why it matters so much. I mean, you and I, and everybody else." She waved her plump little freckled hand at the other people under their pink and white umbrellas, and the golfers scattered over the rolling green plush of the course. "We all know we've got to die sooner or later, no matter how careful we are. Isn't that so?"

"Well, yes," I admitted.

"But furniture and things can be practically immortal, if they're lucky. A heirloom piece like Aunt Betsy's highboy—I really feel I've got an obligation to preserve it, you know."

"For the children and grandchildren, you mean."

"Oh, that too, certainly. But they're just temporary themselves, you know." Buffy took a gulp of the hot summer air. "You see, from our point of view we own our things. But really, as far as they're concerned we're only looking after them for a while. We're just caretakers, like poor old Billy here at the club." She giggled.

"He's retiring this year, I heard," I said, hoping to change the subject.

"Yes. But they'll hire someone else, you know, and if he's competent it won't make much difference to us. Well, it's the same with our things, Janet. Naturally they want to do whatever they can to preserve themselves, and to find the best possible caretakers. They don't ask much: just to be polished regularly, and not to have their drawers wrenched open and slammed shut. And of course they don't want to get cold or wet or dirty, or have lighted cigarettes put down on them, or drinks or houseplants."

"It sounds like quite a lot to ask," I said.

"But Janet, it's so important for them!" Buffy cried. "Of course it was naughty of the highboy to give Bobby such a bad pinch, but I think it was understandable. He was being awfully rough, and it got frightened."

"Now, Buffy," I said, stirring my iced tea so that the cubes clinked impatiently. "You can't possibly believe that we're all in danger of being injured by our possessions."

"Oh no," she said, with another little rippling giggle. "Most of them don't have the strength to do any serious damage. But I'm not worried anyhow. I have a lovely relationship with all my nice things: they know I have their best interests at heart."

I didn't scold Buffy anymore; it was too hot, and I realized there wasn't any point. My sister-in-law was fifty-six years old, and if she hadn't grown up by then, she probably never would. Anyhow, I heard no more about the highboy until about a month later, when Buffy's grandchildren were staying with her. One hazy damp afternoon in August I drove over to the house with a basket of surplus tomatoes and zucchini. The children were building with blocks, and Buffy was sitting near them working on a gros-point cushion-cover design from the Metropolitan Museum. After a while she needed more pink wool; so she asked her grandson, who was about six, to run over to the highboy and fetch it.

He got up and went at once—he's really a very nice little boy. But when he pulled on the bottom drawer it wouldn't come out, and he gave the bird leg a little kick. It was nothing serious, but Buffy screamed and leapt up as if she had been stung, spilling her canvas and colored wools.

"Jamie!" Really, she was almost shrieking. "You must never, never do that!" And she grabbed him by the arm and dragged him away roughly.

Well naturally the child was shocked and upset; he cast a terri-fied look at Buffy and burst into tears. That brought her to her senses. She hugged him and explained that Grandma wasn't an-gry; but he must be very, very careful of the highboy, because it was so old and valuable.

I thought Buffy had overreacted terribly, and when she went out to the kitchen to fix gin and tonics, and milk and peanut butter cookies for the children, "to settle us all down," I followed her in and told her so. Surely, I said, she cared more for her grandchildren than she did for her furniture.

Buffy gave me an odd look; then she pushed the swing door shut.

"You don't understand, Janet," she said in a low voice, as if someone might hear. "Jamie really mustn't annoy the highboy. It's been rather difficult lately, you see." She tried to open a bottle of tonic, but couldn't—I had to take it from her.

"Oh, thank you," she said distractedly. "It's just—Well, for instance. The other day Mary Lee was playing house under the highboy: she'd made a kind of nest for herself with the sofa pillows, and she had some of her dolls in there. I don't know what happened exactly, but I think one of the claw feet gave her that nasty-looking scratch on her leg." Buffy looked over her shoulder apprehensively and spoke even lower. "And there've been other incidents—Oh, never mind." She sighed, then giggled. "I know you think it's all perfect nonsense, Janet. Would you like lime or lemon?"

I was disturbed by this conversation, and that evening I told Clark so; but he made light of it. "Darling, I wouldn't worry. It's just Buffy's usual sort of whimsy."

"Well, but this time she was carrying the joke too far," I said. "She really frightened those children. And even if she was partly fooling, I think she cares far too much about her old furniture. Really, it made me cross."

"I think you should feel sorry for Buffy," Clark remarked. "You know what we've said so often: now that she's had to give up sports, she doesn't have enough to do. I expect she's just trying to add a little interest to her life."

I said that perhaps he was right. And then I had an idea: I'd get Buffy elected secretary of the Historical Society, to fill out the term of the woman who'd just resigned. I knew it wouldn't be easy, because she had no experience and a lot of people thought she was a little flighty. But I was sure she could do it; she'd always run that big house perfectly, and she knew lots about local history and genealogy and antiques.

First I had to convince the Historical Society board that they wanted her, and then I had to convince Buffy; but I managed. I was quite proud of myself. And I was even prouder as time went on and she not only did the job beautifully, she seemed to have forgotten all that nonsense about the highboy. That whole fall and winter she didn't mention it even once.

It wasn't until early the following spring that Buffy phoned one morning, in what was obviously rather a state, and asked me to come over. I found her waiting in the front hall, wearing her white quilted parka. Her fine blonde-tinted curls were all over the place, her eyes unnaturally round and bright, and the tip of her snub nose pink; she looked like a distracted rabbit.

"Don't take off your coat yet, Janet," she told me almost breathlessly. "Come out into the garden; I must show you something."

I was surprised, because it was a cold blowy day in March. Apart from a few snowdrops and frozen-looking white crocus scattered over the lawn, there was nothing to see. But it wasn't the garden Buffy had on her mind.

"You know that woman from New York, that Abigail Jones, who spoke on 'Decorating with Antiques' yesterday at the Society?" she asked as we stood between two beds of spaded earth and sodden compost.

"Mm," I agreed.

"Well, I was talking to her after the lecture, and I invited her to come for brunch this morning and see the house."

"Mm? And how did that go?"

"It was awful, Janet. I don't mean—" Buffy hunched her shoulders against the damp wind and swallowed as if she were about to sob. "I mean, Mrs. Jones was very pleasant. She admired my Hepplewhite table and chairs; and she was very nice about the canopy bed in the blue room too, though I felt I had to tell her that one of the posts wasn't original. But what she liked best was Aunt Betsy's highboy."

"Oh yes?"

"She thought it was a really fine piece. I told her we'd always believed it was made in Newport, but Mrs. Jones thought Salem was more likely. Well, that naturally made me uneasy."

"What? I mean, why?"

"Because of the witches, you know." Buffy gave her nervous

giggle. "Then she said she hoped I was taking good care of it. So of course I told her I was. Mrs. Jones said she could see that, but what I should realize was that my highboy was quite unique, with the carved feathering of the legs, and what looked like all the original hardware. It really ought to be in a museum, she said. I tried to stop her, because I could tell the highboy was getting upset."

"Upset?" I laughed, because I still assumed—or hoped—that it was a joke. "Why should it be upset? I should think it would be pleased to be admired by an expert."

"But don't you see, Janet?" Buffy almost wailed. "It didn't know about museums before. It didn't realize that there were places where it could be well taken care of and perfectly safe for, well, almost forever. It wouldn't know about them, you see, because when pieces of furniture go to a museum they don't come back to tell the others. It's like our going to heaven, I suppose. But now the highboy knows, that's what it will want."

"But a piece of furniture can't force you to send it to a museum," I protested, thinking how crazy this conversation would sound to anyone who didn't know Buffy.

"Oh, can't it." She brushed her wispy curls out of her face. "You don't know what it can do, Janet. None of us does. There've been things I didn't tell you about—But never mind that. Only in fairness I must say I'm beginning to have a different idea of why Aunt Betsy didn't leave the highboy to me in the first place. I don't think it was because of the Lumpkin name at all. I think she was trying to protect me." She giggled again, with a sound like ice cracking.

"Really, Buffy—" Wearily, warily, I played along. "If it's as clever as you say, the highboy must know Mrs. Jones was just being polite. She didn't really mean—"

"But she did, you see. She said that if I ever thought of donating the piece to a museum, where it could be really well cared for, she hoped I would let her know. I tried to change the subject, but I couldn't. She went on telling me how there was always the danger of fire or theft in a private home. She said home instead of house, that's the kind of woman she is." Buffy giggled again. "Then she started to talk about tax deductions, and said she knew of several places that would be interested. I didn't know what to do; I told her that if I did ever decide to part with the highboy I'd probably give it to our Historical Society."

"Well, of course you could," I suggested. "If you felt—"

"But it doesn't matter now," Buffy interrupted, putting a small cold plump hand on my wrist. "I was weak for a moment, but I'm not going to let it push me around. I've worked out what to do to protect myself: I'm changing my will. I called Toni Stevenson already, and I'm going straight over to her office after you leave."

"You're willing the highboy to the Historical Society?" I asked.

"Well, maybe eventually, if I have to. Not outright; heavens, no. That would be fatal. For the moment I'm going to leave it to Bobby's nephew Fred. But only in case of my accidental death." Behind her distracted wisps of hair, Buffy gave a very peculiar little smile.

"Death!" I swallowed. "You don't really think—"

"I think that highboy is capable of absolutely anything. It has no feelings, no gratitude at all. I suppose that's because from its point of view I'm going to die so soon anyway."

"But, Buffy—" The hard wind whisked away the rest of my words, but I doubt if she would have heard them.

"Anyhow, what I'd like you to do now, Janet, is come in with me and be a witness when I tell it what I've planned."

I was almost sure then that Buffy had gone a bit mad; but of course I went back indoors with her.

"Oh, I wanted to tell you, Janet," she said in an unnaturally loud, clear voice when we reached the sitting room. "Now that I know how valuable Aunt Betsy's highboy is, I've decided to leave it to the Historical Society. I put it in my will today. That's if I die of natural causes, of course. But if it's an accidental death, then I'm giving it to my husband's nephew, Fred Turner." She paused and took a loud breath.

"Really," I said, feeling as if I were in some sort of absurdist play.

"I realize the highboy may feel a little out of place in Fred's house," Buffy went on relentlessly, "because he and his wife have all that weird modern canvas and chrome furniture. But I don't really mind about that. And of course Fred's a little careless sometimes. Once when he was here he left a cigarette burning on the cherry pie table in the study; that's how it got that ugly scorch mark, you know. And he's rather thoughtless about wet glasses and coffee cups too." Though Buffy was still facing me, she kept glancing over my left shoulder toward the highboy.

I turned to follow her gaze, and suddenly for a moment I shared her delusion. The highboy had not moved; but now it looked heavy and sullen, and it seemed to have developed a kind of vestigial face. The brass pulls of the two top drawers formed the half-shut eyes of this face, and the fluted column between them was its long thin nose; the ornamental brass keyhole of the full-length drawer below supplied a pursed, tight mouth. Under its curved mahogany tricorn hat, it had a mean, calculating expression, like some hypocritical New England Colonial merchant.

"I know exactly what you're thinking," Buffy said, abandoning the pretense of speaking to me. "And if you don't behave yourself, I might give you to Fred and Roo right now. They have children too. Very active children, not nice quiet ones like Jamie and Mary Lee." Her giggle had a chilling fragmented sound now; ice shivering into shreds.

"None of that was true about Bobby's nephew, you know," Buffy confided as she walked me to my car. "They're not really careless, and neither of them smokes. I just wanted to frighten it."

"You rather frightened me," I told her.

Which was no lie, as I said to Clark that evening. It wasn't just the strength of Buffy's delusion, but the way I'd been infected by it. He laughed and said he'd never known she could be so convincing. Also he asked if I was sure she hadn't been teasing me.

Well, I had to admit I wasn't. But I was still worried. Didn't he think we should do something?

"Do what?" Clark said. And he pointed out that even if Buffy hadn't been teasing, he didn't imagine I'd have much luck trying to get her to a therapist; she thought psychologists were completely bogus. He said we should just wait and see what happened.

All the same, the next time I saw Buffy I couldn't help inquiring about the highboy. "Oh, everything's fine now," she said, laughing lightly. "Right after I saw you I signed the codicil. I put a copy in one of the drawers to remind it, and it's been as good as gold ever since."

Several months passed, and Buffy never mentioned the subject again. When I finally asked how the highboy was, she said, "What? Oh, fine, thanks," in an uninterested way that suggested she'd forgotten her obsession—or tired of her joke.

The irritating thing was that now that I'd seen the unpleasant face of the highboy, it was there every time I went to the house. I would look from it to Buffy's round pink-nosed face, and wonder if she had been laughing at me all along.

Finally, though, I began to forget the whole thing. Then one day late that summer Clark's nephew's wife Roo was at our house. She's a photographer, quite a successful one, and she'd come to take a picture of me.

As many photographers do, Roo always kept up a more or less mindless conversation with her subjects as she worked; trying to prevent them from getting stiff and self conscious, I suppose.

"I like your house, you know, Janet," she said. "You have such simple, great-looking things. Could you turn slowly to the right a little? . . . Good. Hold it. . . . Now over at Uncle Bobby's— Hold it. . . . The garden's great of course, but I don't care much for their furniture. Lower your chin a little, please . . . You know that big dark old chest of drawers, that Buffy's left to Fred."

"The highboy," I said.

"Right. Let's move those roses over a little. That's better. . . . It's supposed to be so valuable, but I think it's hideous. I told Fred I didn't want it around. Hold it. Okay."

"And what did he say?" I asked.

"Huh? Oh, he feels the same as I do. He said that if he did inherit the thing he was going to give it to a museum."

"A museum?" I have to admit that my voice rose. "Where was Fred when he told you this?"

"Don't move, please. Okay. . . . What? I think we were in Buffy's sitting room; but she wasn't there, of course. You don't have to worry, Janet. Fred wouldn't say anything like that in front of his aunt; he knows it would sound awfully ungrateful."

Well, my first impulse was to pick up the phone and warn my sister-in-law as soon as Roo left. But then I thought that would sound ridiculous. It was crazy to imagine that Buffy was in danger from a chest of drawers. Especially long after she'd gotten over the idea herself, if she'd ever really had it in the first place.

Buffy might even laugh at me, I thought; she wasn't anywhere near as whimsical as she had been. She'd become more and more involved in the Historical Society, and it looked as if she'd be reelected automatically next year. Besides, if by chance she hadn't been kidding, and I reminded her of her old delusion and seemed to share it, the delusion might come back and it would be my fault.

So I didn't do anything. I didn't even mention the incident to Clark.

Two days later, while I was writing letters in the study, Clark burst in. I knew something awful had happened as soon as I saw his face.

Bobby had just called from the hospital, he told me. Buffy was in intensive care, and the prognosis was bad. She had a broken hip and a concussion, but the real problem was the shock to her weak heart. Apparently, he said, some big piece of furniture had fallen on her when she tried to pull open a drawer.

I didn't wait to ask what piece of furniture that was. I drove straight to the hospital with him; but by the time we got there Buffy was in a coma.

Though she was nearer plump than slim, she seemed horribly small in that room, on that high flat bed—like a kind of faded child. Her head was in bandages, and there were tubes and wires all over her like mechanical snakes; her little freckled hands lay in weak fists on the white hospital sheet. You could see right away that it was all over with her, though in fact they managed to keep her alive, if you can use that word, for nearly three days more.

Fred Turner, just as he had promised, gave the highboy to a New York museum. I went to see it there recently. Behind its maroon velvet rope it looked exactly the same: tall, glossy, top-heavy, bird-legged and claw-footed.

"You wicked, selfish, ungrateful thing," I told it. "I hope you get termites. I hope some madman comes in here and attacks you with an axe."

The highboy did not answer me, of course. But under its mahogany Napoleon hat, it seemed to wear a little self-satisfied smile.

THE

GHOSTS

OF AUGUST

Gabriel García Márquez

We reached Arezzo a little before noon, and spent more than two hours looking for the Renaissance castle that the Venezuelan writer Miguel Otero Silva had bought in that idyllic corner of the Tuscan countryside. It was a burning, bustling Sunday in early August, and it was not easy to find anyone who knew anything in the streets teeming with tourists. After many useless attempts, we went back to the car and left the city by a road lined with cypresses but without any signs, and an old woman tending geese told us with precision where the castle was located. Before saying good-bye she asked us if we planned to sleep there, and we replied that we were going only for lunch, which was our original intention.

"That's just as well," she said, "because the house is haunted."

My wife and I, who do not believe in midday phantoms, laughed at her credulity. But our two sons, nine and seven years old, were overjoyed at the idea of meeting a ghost in the flesh.

Miguel Otero Silva, who was a splendid host and a refined gourmet as well as a good writer, had an unforgettable lunch waiting for us. Because we arrived late, we did not have time to see the inside of the castle before sitting down at the table, but there was nothing frightening about its external appearance, and any uneasiness was dissipated by our view of the entire city from the flower-covered terrace where we ate lunch. It was difficult to believe that so many men of lasting genius had been born on that hill crowded with houses with barely enough room for ninety thousand people.

Miguel Otero Silva, however, said with his Caribbean humor that none of them was the most renowned native of Arezzo.

"The greatest of all," he declared, "was Ludovico."

Just like that, with no family names: Ludovico, the great patron of the arts and of war, who had built this castle of his affliction, and about whom Miguel spoke all during lunch. He told us of Ludovico's immense power, his troubled love, his dreadful death. He told us how it was that in a moment of heart's madness he stabbed his lady in the bed where they had just made love, turned his ferocious fighting dogs on himself, and was torn to pieces. He assured us, in all seriousness, that after midnight the ghost of Ludovico walked the dark of the house trying to find peace in his purgatory of love.

The castle really was immense and gloomy. But in the light of day, with a full stomach and a contented heart, Miguel's tale seemed only another of the many diversions with which he entertained his guests. After our siesta we walked without foreboding through the eighty-two rooms that had undergone all kinds of alterations by a succession of owners. Miguel had renovated the entire first floor and built a modern bedroom with marble floors, a sauna, and exercise equipment, as well as the terrace covered with brilliant flowers where we had eaten lunch. The second story, the one most used over the centuries, consisted of characterless rooms with furnishings from different periods which had been abandoned to their fate. But on the top floor we saw a room, preserved intact, that time had forgotten to visit—the bedchamber of Ludovico.

The moment was magical. There stood the bed, its curtains embroidered in gold thread, the bedspread and its prodigies of passementerie still stiff with the dried blood of his sacrificed lover. There was the fireplace with its icy ashes and its last log turned to stone, the armoire with its weapons primed, and, in a gold frame, the oil portrait of the pensive knight, painted by some Florentine master who did not have the good fortune to survive his time. What affected me most, however, was the unexplainable scent of fresh strawberries that hung over the entire bedroom.

The days of summer are long and unhurried in Tuscany, and the horizon stays in its place until nine at night. When we finished walking through the castle it was after five, but Miguel insisted on taking us to see the frescoes by Piero della Francesca in the Church of San Francesco. Then we lingered over coffee beneath the arbors on the square, and when we came back for our suitcases we found a meal waiting for us. And so we stayed for supper.

While we ate under a mauve sky with a single star, the boys took flashlights from the kitchen and set out to explore the darkness on the upper floors. From the table we could hear the gallop of wild horses on the stairs, the lamenting doors, the joyous shouts calling for Ludovico in the gloomy rooms. They were the ones who had the wicked idea of sleeping there. A delighted Miguel Otero Silva supported them, and we did not have the social courage to tell them no.

Contrary to what I had feared, we slept very well, my wife and I in a first-floor bedroom and the children in one adjoining ours. Both rooms had been modernized and there was nothing gloomy about them. As I waited for sleep I counted the twelve insomniac strokes of the pendulum clock in the drawing room, and I remembered the fearsome warning of the woman tending geese. But we were so tired that we soon fell into a dense, unbroken slumber, and I woke after seven to a splendid sun shining through the climbing vines at the window. Beside me my wife sailed the calm sea of the innocent. "What foolishness," I said to myself, "to still believe in ghosts in this day and age." Only then was I shaken by the scent of fresh strawberries, and I saw the fireplace with its cold ashes and its final log turned to stone, and the portrait of the melancholy knight in the gold frame looking at us over a distance of three centuries. For we were not in the first-floor bedroom where we had fallen asleep the night before, but in the bedchamber of Ludovico, under the canopy and the dusty curtains and the sheets soaked with still-warm blood of his accursed bed.

—Translated by Edith Grossman

THE
DOLL

Joyce Carol Oates

Many years ago a little girl was given, for her fourth birthday, an antique dolls' house of unusual beauty and complexity, and size: for it seemed large enough, almost, for a child to crawl into.

The dolls' house was said to have been built nearly one hundred years before, by a distant relative of the little girl's mother. It had come down through the family and was still in excellent condition: with a steep gabled roof, many tall, narrow windows fitted with real glass, dark green shutters that closed over, three fireplaces made of stone, mock lightning rods, mock shingleboard siding (white), a veranda that nearly circled the house, stained glass at the front door and at the first floor landing, and even a cupola whose tiny roof lifted miraculously away. In the master bedroom there was a canopied bed with white organdy flounces and ruffles; there were tiny window boxes beneath most of the windows; the furniture—all of it Victorian, of course—was uniformly exquisite, having been made with the most fastidious care and affection. The lampshades were adorned with tiny gold fringes, there was a marvelous old tub with claw feet, and nearly every room had a chandelier. When she first saw the dolls' house on the morning of her fourth birthday the little girl was so astonished she could not speak: for the present was unexpected, and uncannily "real." It was to be the great present, and the great memory, of her childhood.

Florence had several dolls which were too large to fit into the house, since they were average-sized dolls, but she brought them close to the house, facing its open side, and played with them there. She fussed over them, and whispered to them, and scolded them, and invented little conversations between them. One day, out of nowhere, came the name *Bartholomew*—the name of the family who owned the dolls' house. Where did you get that name from, her parents asked, and Florence replied that those were the people who lived in the house. Yes, but where did the name come from? they asked.

The child, puzzled and a little irritated, pointed mutely at the dolls.

One was a girl-doll with shiny blond ringlets and blue eyes that were thickly lashed, and almost too round; another was a red-haired freckled boy in denim coveralls and a plaid shirt. It was obvious that they were sister and brother. Another was a woman-doll, perhaps a mother, who had bright red lips and who wore a hat cleverly made of soft gray-and-white feathers. There was even a baby-doll, made of the softest rubber, hairless and expression-less, and oversized in relationship to the other dolls; and a span-iel, about nine inches in length, with big brown eyes and a quizzi-cal upturned tail. Sometimes one doll was Florence's favorite, sometimes another. There were days when she preferred the blond girl, whose eyes rolled in her head, and whose complexion was a lovely pale peach. There were days when the mischievous red-haired boy was obviously her favorite. Sometimes she ban-ished all the human dolls and played with the spaniel, who was small enough to fit into most of the rooms of the dolls' house.

Occasionally Florence undressed the human dolls, and washed them with a tiny sponge. How strange they were, without their clothes . . . ! Their bodies were poreless and smooth and blank, there was nothing secret or nasty about them, no crevices for dirt to hide in, no trouble at all. Their faces were unperturb-able, as always. Calm wise fearless staring eyes that no harsh words or slaps could disturb. But Florence loved her dolls very much, and rarely felt the need to punish them.

Her treasure was, of course, the dolls' house with its steep Victorian roof and its gingerbread trim and its many windows and that marvelous veranda, upon which little wooden rocking chairs, each equipped with its own tiny cushion, were set. Visitors—friends of her parents or little girls her own age—were always astonished when they first saw it. They said: Oh, isn't it beautiful! They said: Why, it's almost the size of a real house, isn't it?—though of course it wasn't, it was only a dolls' house, a little less than thirty-six inches high.

Nearly four decades later while driving along East Fainlight Avenue in Lancaster, Pennsylvania, a city she had never before visited, and about which she knew nothing, Florence Parr was astonished to see, set back from the avenue, at the top of a stately elm-shaded knoll, her old dolls' house—that is, the replica of it. The house. The house itself.

She was so astonished that for the passage of some seconds she could not think what to do. Her most immediate reaction was to brake her car—for she was a careful, even fastidious driver; at the first sign of confusion or difficulty she always brought her car to a stop.

A broad handsome elm- and plane tree-lined avenue, in a charming city, altogether new to her. Late April: a fragrant, even rather giddy spring, after a bitter and protracted winter. The very air trembled, rich with warmth and color. The estates in this part of the city were as impressive, as stately, as any she had ever seen: the houses were really mansions, boasting of wealth, their sloping, elegant lawns protected from the street by brick walls, or wrought-iron fences, or thick evergreen hedges. Everywhere there were azaleas, that most gorgeous of spring flowers—scarlet and white and yellow and flamey-orange, almost blindingly beautiful. There were newly cultivated beds of tulips, primarily red; and exquisite apple blossoms, and cherry blossoms, and flowering trees Florence recognized but could not identify by name. *Her* house was surrounded by an old-fashioned wrought-iron fence, and in its enormous front yard were red and yellow tulips that had pushed their way through patches of weedy grass.

She found herself on the sidewalk, at the front gate. Like the unwieldy gate that was designed to close over the driveway, this gate was not only open but its bottom spikes had dug into the ground; it had not been closed for some time and could probably not be dislodged. Someone had put up a hand-lettered sign in black, not long ago: 1377 EAST FAINLIGHT. But no name, no family name. Florence stood staring up at the house, her heart beating rapidly. She could not quite believe what she was seeing. Yes, there it was, of course—yet it *could* not be, not in such detail.

The antique dolls' house. *Hers.* After so many years. There was the steep gabled roof, in what appeared to be slate; the old lightning rods; the absurd little cupola that was so charming; the veranda; the white shingleboard siding (which was rather weathered and gray in the bright spring sunshine); most of all, most striking, the eight tall, narrow windows, four to each floor, with their dark shutters. Florence could not determine if the shutters were painted a very dark green, or black. What color had they been on the dolls' house . . . She saw that the gingerbread trim was badly rotted.

The first wave of excitement, almost of vertigo, that had overtaken her in the car had passed; but she felt, still, an unpleasant sense of urgency. Her old dolls' house. Here on East Fainlight Avenue in Lancaster, Pennsylvania. Glimpsed so suddenly, on this warm spring morning. And what did it mean . . . ? Obviously there was an explanation. Her distant uncle, who had built the house for his daughter, had simply copied this house, or another just like it; no doubt there were many houses like this one. Florence knew little about Victorian architecture but she supposed that there were many duplications, even in large, costly houses. Unlike contemporary architects, the architects of that era must have been extremely limited, forced to use again and again certain basic structures, and certain basic ornamentation—the cupolas, the gables, the complicated trim. What struck her as so odd, so mysterious, was really nothing but a coincidence. It would make an interesting story, an amusing anecdote, when she returned home; though perhaps it was not even worth mentioning. Her parents might have been intrigued but they were both dead. And she was always careful about dwelling upon herself, her private life, since she halfway imagined that her friends and acquaintances and colleagues would interpret nearly anything she said of a personal nature according to their vision of her as a public person, and she wanted to avoid that.

There was a movement at one of the upstairs windows that caught her eye. It was then transmitted, fluidly, miraculously, to the other windows, flowing from right to left. . . . But no, it was only the reflection of clouds being blown across the sky, up behind her head.

She stood motionless. It was unlike her, it was quite uncharacteristic of her, yet there she stood. She did not want to walk up to the veranda steps, she did not want to ring the doorbell, such a gesture would be ridiculous, and anyway there was no time: she really should be driving on. They would be expecting her soon. Yet she could not turn away. Because it *was* the house. Incredibly, it was her old dolls' house. (Which she had given away, of course, thirty—thirty-five?—years ago. And had rarely thought about since.) It was ridiculous to stand here, so astonished, so slow-witted, so perversely vulnerable . . . yet what other attitude was appropriate, what other attitude would not violate the queer sense of the sacred, the otherworldly, that the house had evoked?

She would ring the doorbell. And why not? She was a tall, rather wide-shouldered, confident woman, tastefully dressed in a cream-colored spring suit; she was rarely in the habit of apologizing for herself, or feeling embarrassment. Many years ago, perhaps, as a girl, a shy, silly, self-conscious girl: but no longer. Her wavy graying hair had been brushed back smartly from her wide, strong forehead. She wore no makeup, had stopped bothering with it years ago, and with her naturally high-colored, smooth complexion, she was a handsome woman, especially attractive when she smiled and her dark staring eyes relaxed. She *would* ring the doorbell, and see who came to the door, and say whatever flew into her head. She was looking for a family who lived in the neighborhood, she was canvassing for a school millage vote, she was inquiring whether they had any old clothes, old furniture, for . . .

Halfway up the walk she remembered that she had left the keys in the ignition of her car, and the motor running. And her purse on the seat.

She found herself walking unusually slowly. It was unlike her, and the disorienting sense of being unreal, of having stepped into another world, was totally new. A dog began barking somewhere near: the sound seemed to pierce her in the chest and bowels. An attack of panic. An involuntary fluttering of the eyelids. . . . But it was nonsense of course. She would ring the bell, someone would open the door, perhaps a servant, perhaps an elderly woman, they would have a brief conversation, Florence would glance behind her into the foyer to see if the circular staircase looked the same, if the old brass chandelier was still there, if the "marble" floor remained. Do you know the Parr family, Florence would ask, we've lived in Cummington, Massachusetts, for generations, I think it's quite possible that someone from my family visited you in this house, of course it was a very long time ago. I'm sorry to disturb you but I was driving by and I saw your striking house and I couldn't resist stopping for a moment out of curiosity. . . .

There were the panes of stained glass on either side of the oak door! But so large, so boldly colored. In the dolls' house they were hardly visible, just chips of colored glass. But here they were each about a foot square, starkly beautiful: reds, greens, blues. Exactly like the stained glass of a church.

I'm sorry to disturb you, Florence whispered, but I was driving by and . . .

I'm sorry to disturb you but I am looking for a family named Bartholomew, I have reason to think that they live in this neighborhood. . . .

But as she was about to step onto the veranda the sensation of panic deepened. Her breath came shallow and rushed, her thoughts flew wildly in all directions, she was simply terrified and could not move. The dog's barking had become hysterical.

When Florence was angry or distressed or worried she had a habit of murmuring her name to herself, Florence Parr, Florence Parr, it was soothing, it was mollifying, Florence Parr, it was often vaguely reproachful, for after all she *was* Florence Parr and that carried with it responsibility as well as authority. She named herself, identified herself. It was usually enough to bring her undisciplined thoughts under control. But she had not experienced an attack of panic for many years. All the strength of her body seemed to have fled, drained away; it terrified her to think that she might faint here. What a fool she would make of herself. . . .

As a young university instructor she had nearly succumbed to panic one day, mid-way through a lecture on the metaphysical poets. Oddly, the attack had come not at the beginning of the semester but well into the second month, when she had come to believe herself a thoroughly competent teacher. The most extraordinary sensation of fear, unfathomable and groundless fear, which she had never been able to comprehend afterward. . . . One moment she had been speaking of Donne's famous image in "The Relic"—a bracelet of "bright hair about the bone"—and the next moment she was so panicked she could hardly catch her breath. She wanted to run out of the classroom, wanted to run out of the building. It was as if a demon had appeared to her. It breathed into her face, shoved her about, tried to pull her under. She would suffocate: she would be destroyed. The sensation was possibly the most unpleasant she had ever experienced in her life though it carried with it no pain and no specific images. Why she was so frightened she could not grasp. Why she wanted nothing more than to run out of the classroom, to escape her students' curious eyes, she was never to understand.

But she did not flee. She forced herself to remain at the podium. Though her voice faltered she did not stop; she continued with the lecture, speaking into a blinding haze. Surely her students must have noticed her trembling . . . ? But she was stubborn, she was really quite tenacious for a young woman of twenty-four, and by forcing herself to imitate herself, to imitate her normal tone and mannerisms, she was able to overcome the attack. As it lifted, gradually, and her eyesight strengthened, her heartbeat slowed, she seemed to know that the attack would never come again in a classroom. And this turned out to be correct.

But now she could not overcome her anxiety. She hadn't a

podium to grasp, she hadn't lecture notes to follow, there was no
one to imitate, she was in a position to make a terrible fool of
herself. And surely someone was watching from the house. . . .
It struck her that she had no reason, no excuse, for being here.
What on earth could she say if she rang the doorbell? How would
she explain herself to a skeptical stranger? I simply must see the
inside of your house, she would whisper, I've been led up this
walk by a force I can't explain, please excuse me, please humor
me, I'm not well, I'm not myself this morning, I only want to see
the inside of your house to see if it *is* the house I remember. . . .
I had a house like yours. It was yours. But no one lived in my
house except dolls; a family of dolls. I loved them but I always
sensed that they were blocking the way, standing between me
and something else. . . .

The barking dog was answered by another, a neighbor's dog.
Florence retreated. Then turned and hurried back to her car,
where the keys were indeed in the ignition, and her smart leather
purse lay on the seat where she had so imprudently left it.

So she fled the dolls' house, her poor heart thudding. What a
fool you are, Florence Parr, she thought brutally, a deep hot blush
rising into her face.

The rest of the day—the late afternoon reception, the dinner
itself, the after-dinner gathering—passed easily, even routinely,
but did not seem to her very real; it was not very convincing.
That she was Florence Parr, the president of Champlain College,
that she was to be a featured speaker at this conference of administrators of small private liberal arts colleges: it struck her for
some reason as an imposture, a counterfeit. The vision of the
dolls' house kept rising in her mind's eye. How odd, how very
odd the experience had been, yet there was no one to whom she
might speak about it, even to minimize it, to transform it into an
amusing anecdote. . . . The others did not notice her discomfort. In fact they claimed that she was looking well, they were
delighted to see her and to shake her hand. Many were old acquaintances, men and women, but primarily men, with whom
she had worked in the past at one college or another; a number

were strangers, younger administrators who had heard of her heroic effort at Champlain College, and who wanted to be introduced to her. At the noisy cocktail hour, at dinner, Florence heard her somewhat distracted voice speaking of the usual matters: declining enrollments, building fund campaigns, alumni support, endowments, investments, state and federal aid. Her remarks were met with the same respectful attention as always, as though there were nothing wrong with her.

For dinner she changed into a linen dress of pale blue and dark blue stripes which emphasized her tall, graceful figure, and drew the eye away from her wide shoulders and her stolid thighs; she wore her new shoes with the fashionable three-inch heel, though she detested them. Her haircut was becoming, she had manicured and even polished her nails the evening before, and she supposed she looked attractive enough, especially in this context of middle-aged and older people. But her mind kept drifting away from the others, from the handsome though rather dark colonial dining room, even from the spirited, witty after-dinner speech of a popular administrator and writer, a retired president of Williams College, and formerly—a very long time ago, now—a colleague of Florence's at Swarthmore. She smiled with the others, and laughed with the others, but she could not attend to the courtly, white-haired gentlemen's astringent witticisms; her mind kept drifting back to the dolls' house, out there on East Fainlight Avenue. It was well for her that she hadn't rung the doorbell, for what if someone who was attending the conference had answered the door; it was, after all, being hosted by Lancaster College. What an utter fool she would have made of herself. . . .

She went to her room in the fieldstone alumni house shortly after ten, though there were people who clearly wished to talk with her, and she knew a night of insomnia awaited. Once in the room with its antique furniture and its self-consciously quaint wallpaper she regretted having left the ebullient atmosphere downstairs. Though small private colleges were in trouble these days, and though most of the administrators at the conference were having serious difficulties with finances, and faculty morale, there was nevertheless a spirit of camaraderie, of heartiness. Of course it was the natural consequence of people in a social gathering. One simply cannot resist, in such a context, the droll remark, the grateful laugh, the sense of cheerful complicity in even an unfortunate fate. How puzzling the human personality is, Florence thought, preparing for bed, moving uncharacteristically slowly, when with others there is a public self, alone there is a private self, and yet both are real. . . . Both are experienced as real. . . .

She lay sleepless in the unfamiliar bed. There were noises in the distance; she turned on the air conditioner, the fan only, to drown them out. Still she could not sleep. The house on East Fainlight Avenue, the dolls' house of her childhood, she lay with her eyes open, thinking of absurd, disjointed things, wondering now why she had *not* pushed her way through that trivial bout of anxiety to the veranda steps, and to the door, after all she was Florence Parr, she had only to imagine people watching her—the faculty senate, students, her fellow administrators—to know how she should behave, with what alacrity and confidence. It was only when she forgot who she was, and imagined herself utterly alone, that she was crippled by uncertainty and susceptible to fear.

The luminous dials of her watch told her it was only 10:35. Not too late, really, to dress and return to the house and ring the doorbell. Of course she would only ring it if the downstairs was lighted, if someone was clearly up. . . . Perhaps an elderly gentleman lived there, alone, someone who had known her grandfather, someone who had visited the Parrs in Cummington. For there *must* be a connection. It was very well to speak of coincidences, but she knew, she knew with a deep, unshakable conviction, that there was a connection between the dolls' house and the house here in town, and a connection between her childhood and the present house. . . . When she explained herself to whoever opened the door, however, she would have to be casual, conversational. Years of administration had taught her diplomacy; one must not appear to be *too* serious. Gravity in leaders is disconcerting, what is demanded is the light, confident touch, the air of private and even secret knowledge. People do not want equality with their leaders: they want, they desperately need, them to be superior. The superiority must be tacitly communicated, however, or it becomes offensive. . . .

Suddenly she was frightened: it seemed to her quite possible that the panic attack might come upon her the next morning, when she gave her address ("The Future of the Humanities in American Education"). She was scheduled to speak at 9:30, she would be the first speaker of the day, and the first real speaker of the conference. And it was quite possible that that disconcerting weakness would return, that sense of utter, almost infantile help-lessness. . . .

She sat up, turned on the light, and looked over her notes. They were handwritten, not typed, she had told her secretary not to bother typing them, the address was one she'd given before in different forms, her approach was to be conversational rather than formal though of course she would quote the necessary statistics. . . . But it had been a mistake, perhaps, not to have the notes typed. There were times when she couldn't decipher her own handwriting.

A drink might help. But she couldn't very well go over to the Lancaster Inn, where the conference was to be held, and where there was a bar; and of course she hadn't anything with her in the room. As a rule she rarely drank. She never drank alone. . . . However, if a drink would help her sleep: would calm her wild racing thoughts.

The dolls' house had been a present for her birthday. Many years ago. She could not recall how many. And there were her dolls, her little family of dolls, which she had not thought of for a lifetime. She felt a pang of loss, of tenderness. . . .

Florence Parr who suffered quite frequently from insomnia. But of course no one knew.

Florence Parr who had had a lump in her right breast removed, a cyst really, harmless, absolutely harmless, shortly after her thirty-eighth birthday. But none of her friends at Champlain knew. Not even her secretary knew. And the ugly little thing turned out to be benign: absolutely harmless. So it was well that no one knew.

Florence Parr of whom it was said that she was distant, even guarded, at times. You can't get close to her, someone claimed. And yet it was often said of her that she was wonderfully warm and open and frank and totally without guile. A popular president. Yet she had the support of her faculty. There might be individual jealousies here and there, particularly among the vice presidents and deans, but in general she had everyone's support and she knew it and was grateful for it and intended to keep it.

It was only that her mind worked, late into the night. Raced. Would not stay still.

Should she surrender to her impulse, and get dressed quickly and return to the house? It would take no more than ten minutes. And quite likely the downstairs lights would *not* be on, the inhabitants would be asleep, she could see from the street that the visit was totally out of the question, she would simply drive on past. And be saved from her audacity.

If I do this, the consequence will be. . . .

If I fail to do this. . . .

She was not, of course, an impulsive person. Nor did she admire impulsive "spontaneous" people: she thought them immature, and frequently exhibitionistic. It was often the case that they were very much aware of their own spontaneity. . . .

She would defend herself against the charge of being calculating. Of being overly cautious. Her nature was simply a very pragmatic one. She took up tasks with extreme interest, and absorbed herself deeply in them, one after another, month after month and year after year, and other considerations simply had to be shunted to the side. For instance, she had never married. The surprise would have been not that Florence Parr had married, but that she had had time to cultivate a relationship that would end in marriage. I am not opposed to marriage for myself, she once said, with unintentional naiveté, but it would take so much time to become acquainted with a man, to go out with him, and talk. . . . At Champlain where everyone liked her, and shared anecdotes about her, it was said that she'd been even as a younger woman so oblivious to men, even to attentive men, that she had failed to recognize a few years later a young linguist whose carrel at the Widener Library had been next to hers, though the young man claimed to have said hello to her every day, and to have asked her out for coffee occasionally. (She had always refused, she'd been far too busy.) When he turned up at Champlain, married, the author of a well-received book on linguistic theory, an associate professor in the Humanities division, Florence had not only been unable to recognize him but could not remember him at all, though he remembered her vividly, and even amused the gathering by recounting to Florence the various outfits she had worn that winter, even the colors of her knitted socks. She had been deeply embarrassed, of course, and yet flattered, and amused. It was proof, after all, that Florence Parr was always at all times Florence Parr.

Afterward she was somewhat saddened, for the anecdote meant, did it not, that she really *had* no interest in men. She was not a spinster because no one had chosen her, not even because she had been too fastidious in her own choosing, but simply because she had no interest in men, she did not even "see" them when they presented themselves before her. It was said, it was irrefutable. She was an ascetic not through an act of will but through temperament.

It was at this point that she pushed aside the notes of her talk, her heart beating wildly as a girl's. She had no choice, she *must* satisfy her curiosity about the house, if she wanted to sleep, if she wanted to remain sane.

As the present of the dolls' house was the great event of her childhood, so the visit to the house on East Fairnlight Avenue was to be the great event of her adulthood: though Florence Parr was never to allow herself to think of it, afterward.

It was a mild, quiet night, fragrant with blossoms, not at all intimidating. Florence drove to the avenue, to the house, and was consoled by the numerous lights burning in the neighborhood: of course it wasn't late, of course there was nothing extraordinary about what she was going to do.

Lights were on downstairs. Whoever lived there was up, in the living room. Waiting for her.

Remarkable, her calmness. After so many foolish hours of inde-
cision.

She ascended the veranda steps, which gave slightly beneath
her weight. Rang the doorbell. After a minute or so an outside
light went on: she felt exposed: began to smile nervously. One
smiled, one soon learned how. There was no retreating.

She saw the old wicker furniture on the porch. Two rocking
chairs, a settee. Once painted white but now badly weathered.
No cushions.

A dog began barking angrily.

Florence Parr, Florence Parr. She knew who she was, but there
was no need to tell *him*. Whoever it was, peering out at her
through the dark stained glass, an elderly man, someone's left-
behind grandfather. Still, owning this house in this part of town
meant money and position: you might sneer at such things but
they do have significance. Even to pay the property taxes, the
school taxes. . . .

The door opened and a man stood staring out at her, half smiling, quizzical. He was not the man she expected, he was not
elderly, but of indeterminate age, perhaps younger than she.
"Yes? Hello? What can I do for . . . ?" he said.

She heard her voice, full-throated and calm. The rehearsed
question. Questions. An air of apology beneath which her confidence held firm. ". . . driving in the neighborhood earlier today,
staying with friends. . . . Simply curious about an old connection between our families. . . . Or at any rate between my family
and the people who built this. . . ."

Clearly he was startled by her presence, and did not quite grasp
her questions. She spoke too rapidly, she would have to repeat
herself.

He invited her in. Which was courteous. A courtesy that struck
her as unconscious, automatic. He was very well mannered. Puzzled but not suspicious. Not unfriendly. Too young for this house,
perhaps—for so old and shabbily elegant a house. Her presence
on his doorstep, her bold questions, the bright strained smile that
stretched her lips must have baffled him but he did not think her
odd: he respected her, was not judging her. A kindly, simple

person. Which was of course a relief. He might even be a little simple-minded. Slow-thinking. He certainly had nothing to do with . . . with whatever she was involved in, in this part of the world. He would tell no one about her.

". . . a stranger to the city? . . . staying with friends?"

"I only want to ask: does the name Parr mean anything to you?"

A dog was barking, now frantically. But kept its distance.

Florence was being shown into the living room, evidently the only lighted room downstairs. She noted the old staircase, grace-ful as always. But they had done something awkward with the wainscoting, painted it a queer slate blue. And the floor was no longer of marble but a poor imitation, some sort of linoleum tile. . . .

"The chandelier," she said suddenly.

The man turned to her, smiling his amiable quizzical worn smile.

"Yes . . . ?"

"It's very attractive," she said. "It must be an antique."

In the comfortable orangish light of the living room she saw that he had sandy red hair, thinning at the crown. But boyishly frizzy at the sides. He might have been in his late thirties but his face was prematurely lined and he stood with one shoulder slightly higher than the other, as if he were very tired. She began to apologize again for disturbing him. For taking up his time with her impulsive, probably futile curiosity.

"Not at all," he said. "I usually don't go to bed until well past midnight."

Florence found herself sitting at one end of an overstuffed sofa. Her smile was strained but as wide as ever, her face had begun to grow very warm. Perhaps he would not notice her blushing.

". . . insomnia?"

"Yes. Sometimes."

"I too . . . sometimes."

He was wearing a green-and-blue plaid shirt, with thin red stripes. A flannel shirt. The sleeves rolled up to his elbows. And what looked like work-trousers. Denim. A gardener's outfit perhaps. Her mind cast about desperately for something to say and she heard herself asking about his garden, his lawn. So many lovely tulips. Most of them red. And there were plane trees, and several elms. . . .

He faced her, leaning forward with his elbows on his knees. A faintly sunburned face. A redhead's complexion, somewhat freckled.

The chair he sat in did not look familiar. It was an ugly brown, imitation brushed velvet. Florence wondered who had bought it: a silly young wife perhaps.

". . . Parr family?"

"From Lancaster?"

"Oh no. From Cummington, Massachusetts. We've lived there for many generations."

He appeared to be considering the name, frowning at the carpet.

". . . *does* sound familiar. . . ."

"Oh, does it? I had hoped. . . ."

The dog approached them, no longer barking. Its tail wagged and thumped against the side of the sofa, the leg of an old-fashioned table, nearly upsetting a lamp. The man snapped his fingers at the dog and it came no further; it quivered, and made a half growling, half sighing noise, and lay with its snout on its paws and its skinny tail outstretched, a few feet from Florence. She wanted to placate it, to make friends. But it was such an ugly creature—partly hairless, with scruffy white whiskers, a naked sagging belly.

"If the dog bothers you . . ."

"Oh no, no. Not at all."

"He only means to be friendly."

"I can see that," Florence said, laughing girlishly. ". . . He's very handsome."

"Hear that?" the man said, snapping his fingers again. "The lady says you're very handsome! Can't you at least stop drooling, don't you have any manners at all?"

"I haven't any pets of my own. But I like animals."

She was beginning to feel quite comfortable. The living room was not exactly what she had expected but it was not *too* bad. There was the rather low, overstuffed sofa in which she sat, the cushions made of a silvery-white, silvery-gray material, with a feathery sheen, plump, immense, like bellies or breasts, a monstrous old piece of furniture yet nothing one would want to sell: for certainly it had come down in the family, it must date from the turn of the century. There was the Victorian table with its coy ornate legs, and its tasseled cloth, and its extraordinary over-sized lamp: the sort of thing Florence would smile at in an antique shop, but which looked fairly reasonable here. In fact she should comment on it, since she was staring at it so openly.

". . . antique? European?"

"I think so, yes," the man said.

"Is it meant to be fruit, or a tree, or . . ."

Bulbous and flesh-colored, peach-colored. With a tarnished brass stand. A dust-dimmed golden lampshade with embroidered blue trim that must have been very pretty at one time.

They talked of antiques. Of old houses. Families.

A queer odor defined itself. It was not unpleasant, exactly.

"Would you like something to drink?"

"Why yes I—"

"Excuse me just a moment."

Alone she wondered if she might prowl about the room. But it was long and narrow and poorly lighted at one end: in fact, one end dissolved into darkness. A faint suggestion of furniture there, an old spinet piano, a jumble of chairs, a bay window that must look out onto the garden. She wanted very much to examine a portrait above the mantel of the fireplace but perhaps the dog would bark, or grow excited, if she moved.

It had crept closer to her feet, shuddering with pleasure.

The redheaded man, slightly stooped, brought a glass of something dark to her. In one hand was his own drink, in the other hand hers.

"Taste it. Tell me what you think."

"It seems rather strong. . . ."

Chocolate. Black and bitter. And thick.

"It should really be served hot," the man said.

"Is there a liqueur of some kind in it?"

"Is it too strong for you?"

"Oh no. No. Not at all."

Florence had never tasted anything more bitter. She nearly gagged.

But a moment later it was all right: she forced herself to take a second swallow, and a third. And the prickling painful sensation in her mouth faded.

The redheaded man did not return to his chair, but stood before her, smiling. In the other room he had done something hurried with his hair: had tried to brush it back with his hands, perhaps. A slight film of perspiration shone on his high forehead.

"Do you live alone here?"

"The house does seem rather large, doesn't it?—for a person to live in it alone."

"Of course you have your dog. . . ."

"Do *you* live alone now?"

Florence sat the glass of chocolate down. Suddenly she remembered what it reminded her of: a business associate of her father's, many years ago, had brought a box of chocolates back from a trip to Russia. The little girl had popped one into her mouth and had been dismayed by their unexpectedly bitter taste.

She had spat the mess out into her hand. While everyone stared.

As if he could read her thoughts the redheaded man twitched, moving his jaw and his right shoulder jerkily. But he continued smiling as before and Florence did not indicate that she was disturbed. In fact she spoke warmly of the living room's furnishings, and repeated her admiration for handsome old houses like this one. The man nodded, as if waiting for her to say more.

". . . a family named Bartholomew? Of course it was many years ago."

"Bartholomew? Did they live in this neighborhood?"

"Why yes I think so. That's the real reason I stopped in. I once knew a little girl who—"

"Bartholomew, Bartholomew," the man said slowly, frowning. His face puckered. One corner of his mouth twitched with the effort of his concentration: and again his right shoulder jerked. Florence was afraid he would spill his chocolate drink.

Evidently he had a nervous ailment of some kind. But she could not inquire.

He murmured the name *Bartholomew* to himself, his expression grave, even querulous. Florence wished she had not asked the question because it was a lie, after all. She rarely told lies. Yet it had slipped from her, it had glided smoothly out of her mouth.

She smiled guiltily, ducking her head. She took another swallow of the chocolate drink.

Without her having noticed, the dog had inched forward. His great head now rested on her feet. His wet brown eyes peered up at her, oddly affectionate. A baby's eyes. It was true that he was drooling, in fact he was drooling on her ankles, but of course he could not help it. . . . Then she noted that he had wet on the carpet. Only a few feet away. A dark stain, a small puddle.

Yet she could not shrink away in revulsion. After all, she was a guest and it was not time for her to leave.

". . . Bartholomew. You say they lived in this neighborhood?"

"Oh yes."

"But when?"

"Why I really don't . . . I was only a child at the. . . ."

"But when was this?"

He was staring oddly at her, almost rudely. The twitch at the corner of his mouth had gotten worse. He moved to set his glass down and the movement was jerky, puppet-like. Yet he stared at her all the while. Florence knew people often felt uneasy because of her dark over-large staring eyes: but she could not help it. She did not *feel* the impetuosity, the reproach, her expression suggested. So she tried to soften it by smiling. But sometimes the smile failed, it did not deceive anyone at all.

Now that her host had stopped smiling she could see that he was really quite mocking. His tangled sandy eyebrows lifted ironically.

"You said you were a stranger to this city, and now you're saying you've been here. . . ."

"But it was so long ago, I was only a . . ."

He drew himself up to his full height. He was not a tall man, nor was he solidly built. In fact his waist was slender, for a man's—and he wore odd trousers, or jeans, tight-fitting across his thighs and without zipper or snaps, crotchless. They fit him tightly in the crotch, which was smooth, seamless. His legs were rather short for his torso and arms.

He began smiling at Florence. A sly accusing smile. His head jerked mechanically, indicating something on the floor. He was trying to point with his chin and the gesture was clumsy.

"You did something nasty on the floor there. On the carpet."

Florence gasped. At once she drew herself away from the dog, at once she began to deny it. "I didn't—It wasn't—"

"Right on the carpet there. For everyone to see. To smell."

"I certainly did not," Florence said, blushing angrily. "You know very well it was the—"

"Somebody's going to have to clean it up and it isn't going to be *me,*" the man said, grinning.

But his eyes were still angry.

He did not like her at all: she saw that. The visit was a mistake, but how could she leave, how could she escape, the dog had crawled up to her again and was nuzzling and drooling against her ankles and the redheaded man who had seemed so friendly was now leaning over her, his hands on his slim hips, grinning rudely.

As if to frighten her, as one might frighten an animal or a child, he clapped his hands smartly together. Florence blinked at the sudden sound. And then he leaned forward and clapped his hands together again, right before her face. She cried out for him to leave her alone, her eyes smarted with tears, she was leaning back against the cushions, her head back as far as it would go, and then he clapped his hands once again, hard, bringing them against her burning cheeks, slapping both her cheeks at once, and a sharp thin white-hot sensation ran through her body, from her face and throat to her belly, to the pit of her belly, and from the pit of her belly up into her chest, into her mouth, and even down into her stiffened legs. She screamed for the redheaded man to stop, and twisted convulsively on the sofa to escape him.

"Liar! Bad girl! Dirty girl!" someone shouted.

She wore her new reading glasses, with their attractive plastic frames. And a spring suit, smartly styled, with a silk blouse in a floral pattern. And the tight but fashionable shoes.

Her audience, respectful and attentive, could not see her trembling hands behind the podium, or her slightly quivering knees. They would have been astonished to learn that she hadn't been able to eat breakfast that morning—that she felt depressed and exhausted though she had managed to fall asleep the night before, probably around two, and had evidently slept her usual dreamless sleep.

She cleared her throat several times in succession, a habit she detested in others.

But gradually her strength flowed back into her. The morning was so sunny, so innocent. These people were, after all, her colleagues and friends: they certainly wished her well, and even appeared to be genuinely interested in what she had to say about the future of the humanities. Perhaps Dr. Parr knew something they did not, perhaps she would share her professional secrets with them. . . .

As the minutes passed Florence could hear her voice grow richer and firmer, easing into its accustomed rhythms. She began to relax. She began to breathe more regularly. She was moving into familiar channels, making points she had made countless times before, at similar meetings, with her deans and faculty chairmen at Champlain, with other educators. A number of people applauded heartily when she spoke of the danger of small private colleges competing unwisely with one another; and again when she made a point, an emphatic point, about the need for the small private school in an era of multiversities. Surely these were remarks anyone might have made, there was really nothing original about them, yet her audience seemed extremely pleased to hear them from her. They *did* admire Florence Parr—that was clear.

She removed her reading glasses. Smiled, spoke without needing to glance at her notes. This part of her speech—an amusing summary of the consequences of certain experimental programs at Champlain, initiated since she'd become president—was more specific, more interesting, and of course she knew it by heart.

The previous night had been one of her difficult nights. At least initially. Her mind racing in that way she couldn't control, those flame-like pangs of fear, insomnia. And no help for it. And no way out. She'd fallen asleep while reading through her notes and awakened suddenly, her heart beating erratically, body drenched in perspiration—and there she was, lying twisted back against the headboard, neck stiff and aching and her left leg numb beneath her. She'd been dreaming she'd given in and driven out to see the dolls' house; but of course she had not, she'd been in her hotel room all the time. *She'd never left her hotel room.*

She'd never left her hotel room but she'd fallen asleep and dreamt she had but she refused to summon back her dream, not that dream nor any others; in fact she rather doubted she did dream, she never remembered afterward. Florence Parr was one of those people who, as soon as they awake, are *awake*. And eager to begin the day.

At the conclusion of Florence's speech everyone applauded enthusiastically. She'd given speeches like this many times before and it had been ridiculous of her to worry.

Congratulations, handshakes. Coffee was being served.

Florence was flushed with relief and pleasure, crowded about by well-wishers. This was her world, these people her colleagues, they knew her, admired her. Why does one worry about anything! Florence thought, smiling into these friendly faces, shaking more hands. These were all good people, serious professional people, and she liked them very much.

At a distance a faint fading jeering cry *Liar! Dirty girl!* but Florence was listening to the really quite astute remarks of a youngish man who was a new dean of arts at Vassar. How good the hot, fresh coffee was. And a thinly layered apricot brioche she'd taken from a proffered silver tray.

The insult and discomfort of the night were fading; the vision of the dolls' house was fading, dying. She refused to summon it back. She would not give it another thought. Friends—acquaintances—well-wishers were gathering around her, she knew her skin was glowing like a girl's, her eyes were bright and clear and hopeful; at such times, buoyed by the presence of others as by waves of applause, you forget your age, your loneliness—the very perimeters of your soul.

Day is the only reality. She'd always known.

Though the conference was a success, and colleagues at home heard that Florence's contribution had been particularly well received, Florence began to forget it within a few weeks. So many conferences!—so many warmly applauded speeches! Florence was a professional woman who, by nature more than design, pleased both women and men; she did not stir up controversy, she "stimulated discussion." Now she was busily preparing for her first major conference, to be held in London in September: "The Role of the Humanities in the 21st Century." Yes, she was apprehensive, she told friends—"But it's a true challenge."

When a check arrived in the mail for five hundred dollars, an honorarium for her speech in Lancaster, Pennsylvania, Florence was puzzled at first—not recalling the speech, nor the circumstances. How odd! She'd never been there, had she? Then, to a degree, as if summoning forth a dream, she remembered: the beautiful Pennsylvania landscape, ablaze with spring flowers; a small crowd of well-wishers gathered around to shake her hand. Why, Florence wondered, had she ever worried about her speech?—her public self? Like an exquisitely precise clockwork mechanism, a living mannequin, she would always do well: you'll applaud too, when you hear her.

WOLFIE

For Elinor P. Cubbage

Robert Phillips

After their sheep farm failed, the couple moved from the country to the city ninety miles away. It wasn't a great city, but he had been offered a steady job there, and a steady income was what they needed now. For too long they had depended upon the uncertainties of taking a prize for breeding at a sheep fair, receiving stud fees, breeding the ewes, and fluctuating market prices for the wool, milk, and chops. They raised Hampshires, and loved the large, hornless, dark-faced animals. Their best ewe they named Maybelline, because of her long dark, seemingly mascaraed eyelashes. The Hampshires yielded superior mutton, but not much wool. It was a hard life, but neither minded—not getting up before dawn to do the chores, not the constant smell of ammonia in the barn, not burying the miscarried. It was a plague of Brucellosis that did them in. Milk production all but stopped, lambs were aborted or stillborn, ewes died in large numbers. Every day he was digging a trench to bury more. They fell behind on the mortgage. The bank wanted to foreclose.

If their boy missed the sheep and the farm, he didn't say so. What he missed was Shep, his collie, who worked as a herd dog in the farm's fields, rounding up the strays at night, nudging them toward the barn. He was sturdy and agile and very affectionate. The boy and the collie used to romp the fields together, the collie nipping at his heels. But the couple could not imagine a dog as big as a collie in a small two-bedroom apartment in the city. So they gave Shep to the neighboring farm couple, whose children had been playmates of their son and who promised to take good care of the dog. When the family left their farm for the last time, he and she up front in the car, the boy in back, the boy whimpered softly, quietly, saying only, "Shep, Shep," over and over. The boy was five.

As they approached the city two hours later, the boy had long since quieted down and fallen asleep, and the couple discussed their good fortune in having been offered a new lease on life. He was to become an automobile salesman on the floor of a Dodge agency. The owner had liked his straightforward, country ways. He was, the owner said, like Andy Griffith in "Matlock." Customers would feel they could trust him. He would wear a suit and tie every day. The agency's doors did not open until nine a.m. It was a total change from the farm. A change for the better, they thought—though they both were naive about depending upon commissions from auto sales. It was, if anything, as unpredictable as marketing sheep. But they had hopes. And neither felt they were in disgrace, despite the loss of the farm. There was a certain dignity to their failure: It was open, unvarnished, and complete. Everyone knew, and everyone knew it was beyond their ability to stop what happened. It was a clean closed chapter, with no tinges of remorse. They realized enough from selling the farm equipment to begin a new life.

The apartment, from the first time they'd seen it, seemed to suit their needs. It was in a small apartment house set before a gas plant at the end of a dead-end street. The boy could play outside without undue worry about traffic. On one side of the building a black iron fire escape exerted itself like a stitched-up appendix scar. There was a bedroom for the parents and one for the child. In the autumn, when school began, there was a public school nearby. A few things were unsatisfactory: The walls were painted a deep mustard shade, which the wife loathed. It reminded her, she said, of baby poop. She planned to wallpaper the flat with cheery floral patterns. Something along the line of cabbage roses would brighten things up. The previous tenants seemed to have left in a great hurry. When the realtor had first shown them the flat, it smelled musty, almost animal-like. "From being shut up so long," the realtor said. There had been a dead decorated Christmas tree still standing in the corner of the unfurnished living room—and it was the month of July! The limbs of the tree were bedraggled and drooped, of course, with yellow needles dropped all over the floor. And on the mustard-colored polyester carpet were several piles of what appeared to be desiccated dog feces. The realtor lady was most apologetic, and promised to have the tree and droppings of both sorts removed. Weeks later, when they took possession of the flat, the couple found the dried-out Christmas tree was indeed gone, the carpet had been vacuumed. But the polyester carpet stubbornly retained traces of the dog excrement. "Well, we'll just get another carpet soon," the wife sighed. "And completely air out the place," he added.

The boy liked his room. It faced onto the dead-end street below, and they placed his bed next to the window. Since it was June, it was still daylight when he went to bed, and when he wasn't exhausted, he spent hours leaning against the windowsill, peering up at the moon overhead, or down at the cars parking and unparking at the curb, people walking their dogs, or occasional fire trucks and police cars going down the street at the end of the block. Nothing like that was to be seen back on the farm. Once the sheep had been put up for the night and Shep fed, there had been only the television, which they allowed him to watch sparingly.

After some weeks in the apartment, the couple became aware that the boy had begun talking to himself in his bedroom after he had been kissed goodnight and tucked in and the door closed. They weren't fooled; they knew he rarely stayed "tucked-in" for long. Rather, he crawled out of the brightly colored sheets and leaned on his little elbows, peering out the window. They didn't mind. He always fell asleep when he was tired enough. But when he started to talk behind the door, they wondered a bit. Was he pretending to talk to the pedestrians below? To the moon above? They couldn't make out just what it was he said.

One morning at breakfast they asked him. The man was just

about to leave for the Dodge agency—where already he had sold three cars, and thereby gained a false sense of security and confidence—when he looked over at his young son and inquired, "We hear you talking in your room night after night. You never did that on the farm. Who are you talking to? Yourself?"

The boy's blue eyes opened wide with pleasure. "Oh no. Not myself." He was a charming child. His ears stuck out like jug handles, his only imperfection. His hair was blond, his nose pert and freckled.

"Who is it, then?" his father persisted.

The boy stabbed his spoon into his bowl of cereal, sending a jet of milk onto the breakfast table. "Wolfie," he said.

"Who?" the mother joined in.

"Wolfie. I talk to Wolfie."

"And who is Wolfie?" they both asked at once.

"I'll show you," the youngster said importantly. He climbed down from his chair and proceeded through the hall toward his room. The door was open, it being morning, and he walked to the center of the bedroom. There he raised his right hand and pointed directly overhead.

In unison both parents raised their eyes. There, in the center of the ceiling, hung a light fixture. They had seen it countless times, of course, but had paid it no attention.

Staring at it now, it seemed commonplace, in need of dusting. Inside was a single bulb covered by a convex, snout-shaped glass shade. The opaque glass was tan, held in place by three screws at equidistant points. After an embarrassed silence, his father said, "That's Wolfie?"

"Yah!" the little boy said. "Come over here, you can see him better." The boy clambered onto his bed and lay with his head on the pillow. When his father hesitated, the boy urged him on. "Over here," he said patting the pillow.

"Really, I have to get to work. I'll be late—"

"Just a minute? Please?" the boy said.

So the father lay down on the little bed and looked toward the ceiling. And, yes, he could see it. The shade of the overhead light was shaped rather like an animal's head, the head of a dog or wolf. The three screws completed the illusion, forming two eyes and a dot for a mouth. The convex shade formed the snout or nose.

"See him? See him?"

"Well, yes—" the father laughed. "I see something that looks like—"

"—like Wolfie! That's Wolfie!" the boy cried with glee.

"Let *me* see," the mother said, and the parents exchanged places. After a moment on the child's bed she said, "I don't see anything. Just a dirty old lamp shade, which I must get up on a ladder and dust today. There's even a dead fly or two in there."

"It's Wolfie, Wolfie," the boy insisted.

"Is it a dog or a wolf?" his father asked good-naturedly.

"I'm not sure yet. Sometimes he's a dog, sometimes I think he might be a wolf. It's how he acts."

"Well, when you find out for sure, let us know," the father said with a laugh. But out in the hallway, kissing his wife good-bye for the day, he asked her, "Do you think it's okay?"

"Do I think what's okay?"

"Him imagining the ceiling lamp is an animal? Wolfie?"

It was her turn to laugh. "Of course it's okay. It's only a game. He has an extremely active imagination, that's all. Besides, it's rather an affectionate name. That's what Mozart's wife called him, 'Wolfie'." She had had two years of college.

"It is?"

"From Wolfgang Amadeus Mozart!" she added brightly.

"And our son is supposed to know that, of course," he said dryly.

"You never know. He's a bright little kid." She patted her husband playfully on the behind and said, "Now you go out and sell some cars."

"I will. One good thing about this job, if a deal dies on me, I don't have to bury it in the field."

Every night after that they heard the boy talking in his room. The doggy, almost feral, smell in the apartment never seemed to leave, despite the fact she had replaced the soiled living room carpet and aired all the rooms. She even used Airwick room freshener spray in the new Potpourri fragrance. Still the flat smelled doggy and mildewy. "Maybe it comes from the gas factory," he offered. "Fumes or something."

"I don't think so," she said.

Once they put their ears against the bedroom door and heard the boy say, "Nice Wolfie. Down, Wolfie, down. That's a good boy." He almost caught them eavesdropping, which would have embarrassed them dreadfully, despite his young age. They felt very strongly about mutual respect and trust. They had just left their positions kneeling by his door when it opened and he came out wearing his circus pajamas.

"Have to go to the bathroom?" she asked.

"No," he said, carefully closing the door behind him. "I want to get Wolfie a treat. He's been such a good dog."

"Oh, so you decided he is a dog?" his father asked.

"I think so. He looks like a dog. He even smells like a dog," the boy laughed.

"Then maybe you should give him a bath."

"Not tonight," the boy said.

"Well," the mother offered, "let's see what there is in the way of a treat." In the refrigerator she found some leftover hamburger. "Will this do?" she asked the boy.

"Probably. Everybody likes hamburger. Specially with catsup on it."

She put the meat on a plate and he pounded the bottom of the catsup bottle until a thick layer came out. Then he solemnly carried the plate to his room. Pausing before the door, his father asked, "May I come in and see Wolfie?"

"Not now," the boy said firmly. "He's hungry and you might scare him away."

"I see."

The door closed behind the five-year-old.

In the morning his mother found the plate on the floor beside the bed. The hamburger was all gone.

"Wolfie *liked* it," the boy beamed.

"What do you make of that?" she later asked her husband, brandishing the empty plate.

"So the boy got hungry and ate it himself. Clever way to get a snack out of us." They kissed in the hallway by the elevator.

Every night after that the boy took food on a plate into the room and closed the door. And soon it was not just sounds of the boy talking aloud they heard, but also growls—small, friendly, guttural growls.

"So now he's imitating a dog as well," the mother said. "Isn't this going too far?"

"The poor kid's just lonely. He's left the farm and all his playmates. Haven't you made any friends on the street or in the building yet?"

"No one his age. One little girl we see when we go down to the laundry room. But he thinks she's a baby."

"Well, once school starts, he'll make new friends."

"That's still a long way off. Maybe we should do more things together. As a family."

So they took him to a carnival that came to the city. It pitched its tents on the side of the river, and the three of them wandered beneath brightly colored lights strung overhead. There was a merry-go-round, a Ferris wheel, bumper cars, pop corn, and cotton candy—they thought he would be enchanted. Instead, he began to whimper.

"What is it?" they asked.

"Wolfie. I miss Wolfie."

Eventually they left the carnival and returned to the apartment. He searched the refrigerator for the "dog's" dinner. His mother put a hot dog on a plate.

"I'm not sure he likes hot dogs," the boy said doubtfully.

"Try it, he may like it," she said, rolling her eyes toward her husband.

"Got to have lots of catsup, then," he said, reaching for the Heinz bottle.

Once the boy was out of earshot, she said, "I think it's time we got him a dog. A real dog. Obviously he's overcompensating like crazy. We never should have separated him from Shep."

"I thought we agreed this place was too small for a dog."

"For a collie, it is. But not for a little Pekinese or cocker span-
iel."

"I *hate* little yip-yip dogs. Little lap dogs are totally unmanly.
No son of mine is going to have a Pekinese, for God's sake."

"All right, a beagle, then. Whatever, you pick it out. But I want
a dog—a real dog—in this place soon."

"It will have to be walked and groomed."

"It will be good for him. Give him something to do. Something
instead of all this make-believe."

It was not the best of times to buy a pet. The father had not
sold a car in three weeks. He was beginning to realize the difference between the car business and the sheep business: When a
Dodge didn't sell, you couldn't slaughter it and have the satisfaction of eating it.

Nevertheless, they bought a beagle. It was a little brown, black,
and white puppy and it cost two-hundred dollars. When the father wrote out the check, he wondered if it would clear—he had
no idea. The boy was thrilled with the puppy, but not for the
reason the couple had thought: "Now Wolfie will have a play-
mate!" he crowed.

They looked at one another uneasily.

"What should I name him?" the boy asked in the car on the
way home, petting the puppy a bit too vigorously.

"Anything you want," the man said.

"I'll name him Shep!" the boy said.

"Well," the father hesitated. "He's not a sheep-herding dog,
you know."

The boy fell silent for a moment. Then he said, "I could name
him Wolfie."

It was the mother's turn to answer. "But there already is a
Wolfie . . . isn't there?"

"Oh yeah. That's right," the boy said.

"What about Spot?" the mother volunteered.

"That's a dumb name," the father said.

"Spot, Spot, Spot!" the boy repeated, petting the dog even
harder.

"Spot!" the father mumbled. "Who arc we, Dick and Jane?" He shot his wife a look of contempt.

"It's only a puppy's name," she said.

"Goddamn ridiculous. Spot! Where's baby Sally?" he said, recalling a grade-school reader.

But the boy hugged his new puppy with love.

When they reached the apartment they placed newspapers on the kitchen floor to teach the puppy where to do its business. They put down a plate and emptied some dog food from a can. Then they themselves ate dinner. In a new attempt at economy, she served left-over meatloaf. Neither knew when he would sell his next car.

After dinner the boy said, "Spot wants to play with Wolfie," and carried the plump puppy into his bedroom and closed the door.

"I thought the new puppy was supposed to make him forget that nonsense," the father said.

"It will, in time," she said, feeling wise.

For several hours the couple watched television: "The Cosby Show" and "Cheers" and "Adam Smith's Money World" and a Lucy rerun. They heard occasional outbursts of joy from the boy's room—boy-joy and puppy-joy combined. They smiled at one another, aware they had done the right thing. At one point the boy emerged and asked for a bowl. "Spot wants water!" he proclaimed, though how he knew the puppy wanted water was moot. After Johnny Carson went off the air, the couple went to bed, having looked in and found both the boy and the puppy asleep across his bed.

It was in the middle of the night that they heard the blood-curdling sounds of a ferocious dog fight. At first they thought the cries were coming from the street. Then they realized they came from the boy's room. Together they ran toward him, and as they did, the dog fight seemed to get even worse. The father hesitated with his hand on the door, doubtless in fear. Then he turned the knob and threw the door open.

On the floor the puppy lay dying. His throat was ripped wide open like a flap. Blood was everywhere—spattered on the walls, the carpet, the white chenille bedspread. And where was the boy? He was not in the bed. Further inspection revealed he was not in the closet. A low whimper indicated he was under the bed, flat on his stomach in his circus pajamas. Doubtless he had crawled there to seek safety from the fighting dogs.

The dogs. There was the puppy. And what other? No dog could climb up to their floor in the apartment house. The boy could not tell them where the other dog had come from or gone. He was, in fact, struck speechless, and despite endless consultations over the years with doctors, psychiatrists, and speech therapists, he was never to speak again. He remained silent for hours in his room, which is unchanged to this day with one exception: His father has removed the ceiling lamp and broken it into hundreds of glass shards with a hammer.

A

SPIRITUALIST

Jean Rhys

"I assure you," said the Commandant, "that I adore women—that without a woman in my life I cannot exist."

"But one must admit that one has deceptions. They are frankly disappointing, or else they exact so much that the day comes when, inevitably, one asks oneself: Is it worth while?"

"In any case it cracks. It always cracks."

He fixed his monocle more firmly into his eye to look at a passing lady, with an expression like that of an amiable and cynical old fox.

"And it is my opinion, Madame, that that is the fault of the woman. All the misunderstandings, all the quarrels! It is astonishing how gentle, how easily fooled most men are. Even an old Parisian like myself, Madame. . . . I assure you that of all men the Parisians are the most sentimental. And it is astonishing how lacking in calm and balance is the most clever woman, how prone to weep at a wrong moment—in a word, how exhausting!"

"For instance: A few months ago I was obliged to break with a most charming little friend whom I passionately adored. Because she exaggerated her eccentricity. One must be in the movement, even though one may regret in one's heart the more agreeable epoch that has vanished. A little eccentricity is permissible. It is indeed *chic*. Yes, it is now chic to be eccentric. But when it came to taking me to a chemist and forcing me to buy her ether, which she took at once in the restaurant where we dined: and then hanging her legs out of the taxi window in the middle of the Boulevard: you will understand that I was *gêné:* that I found that she exaggerated. In the middle of the Boulevard!"

"Most unfortunately one can count no longer on women, even Frenchwomen, to be dignified, to have a certain *tenue.* I remember the time when things were different. And more agreeable, I think."

The Commandant gazed into the distance, and his expression became sentimental. His eyes were light blue. He even blushed.

"Once I was happy with a woman. Only once. I will tell you about it. Her name was Madeleine, and she was a little dancer whom some *sale individu* had deserted when she was without money and ill. She was the most sweet and gentle woman I have ever met. I knew her for two years, and we never quarrelled once or even argued. Never. For Madeleine gave way in everything. . . . And to think that my wife so often accused me of having a *sale caractère. . . .*"

He mused for a while.

"A *sale caractère. . . .* Perhaps I have. But Madeleine was of a sweetness . . . ah, well, she died suddenly after two years. She was only twenty-eight."

"When she died I was sad as never in my life before. The poor little one. . . . Only twenty-eight!"

"Three days after the funeral her mother, who was a very good woman, wrote to me saying that she wished to have the clothes and the effects, you understand, of her daughter. So in the afternoon I went to her little flat, Place de L'Odéon, fourth floor. I took my housekeeper with me, for a woman can be useful with her advice on these occasions."

"I went straight into the bedroom and I began to open the cupboards and arrange her dresses. I wished to do that myself. I had the tears in my eyes, I assure you, for it is sad to see and to touch the dresses of a dead woman that one has loved. My housekeeper, Gertrude, she went into the kitchen to arrange the household utensils."

"Well, suddenly, there came from the closed sitting-room a very loud, a terrible crash. The floor shook."

"Gertrude and I both called out at the same time. What is that? And she ran to me from the kitchen saying that the noise had come from the salon. I said: Something has fallen down, and I opened quickly the sitting-room door."

"You must understand that it was a flat on the fourth floor; all the windows of the sitting-room were tightly shut, naturally, and the blinds were drawn as I had left them on the day of the funeral. The door into the hall was locked, the other led into the bedroom where I was."

"And, there, lying right in the middle of the floor was a block of white marble, perhaps fifty centimeters square."

"Gertrude said: *Mon Dieu,* Monsieur, look at that. How did that get here?—Her face was pale as death.—It was not there, she said, when we came."

"As for me, I just looked at the thing, stupefied."

"Gertrude crossed herself and said: I am going. Not for anything: for nothing in the world would I stay here longer. There is something strange about this flat."

"She ran. I—well, I did not run. I walked out, but very quickly. You understand, I have been a soldier for twenty-five years, and, God knows, I had nothing to reproach myself with with regard to the poor little one. But it shakes the nerves—something like that."

The Commandant lowered his voice.

"The fact was, I understood. I knew what she meant."

"I had promised her a beautiful, white marble tombstone, and I had not yet ordered it. Not because I had not thought of it. Oh, no—but because I was too sad, too tired. But the little one doubtless thought that I had forgotten. It was her way of reminding me."

I looked hard at the Commandant. His eyes were clear and as naïve as a child's: a little dim with emotion. . . . Silence. . . . He lit a cigarette.

"Well, to show how strange women are: I recounted this to a

lady I knew, not long ago. And she laughed. Laughed! You understand. . . . *Un fou rire.* . . . And do you know what she said:

"She said: How furious that poor Madeleine must have been
that she missed you!"

"Now can you imagine the droll ideas that women can have!"

OWL

Elizabeth Spencer

What was she doing at the window?

She had just been sleeping. Lying pencil straight in the narrow guest room bed, had she heard it only once, or so it seemed. Once was all that got through. Drawn up, she had gone to the window and stood looking out, or trying to. She knew what it was: Owl.

On that moonless night, the second floor window revealed only the dark presence of trees outside, branches of elm and sycamore, melted indistinctly together.

It spoke again. *Oooo.* . . . Deep sound drawn up out of feathers. Feathery deep . . . then a rustle. She thought she could make out a large moving shape and could hear a rustle in the branches. The motion stopped. There had been something clumsy about it, as though the wings were too large for the spaces between branches. Then a righting, a folding down, suspended silence. It was all so near.

Ooooo. . . .

Wendy was alone. Two children grown, moved away, married, husband away. She never minded the empty house, even after the cat had got run over and the dog had died of age. She had things to do. Guy's trips never lasted long, his fishing, golfing, hunting, out with the "club." Club was his word; she thought of it as "the gang." But not resentfully. Life was easy for this older woman on this late spring night.

Owls were large and grey, a sort of striated grey, a very dark stippled edge, next a stripe of medium dark, then a paler one still, and start again. There was the tiny curved beak, set dead center under glowing golden eyes, dark-seeing. Could it see her?

I wish I could see you, she thought. She whispered it. "Why can't we see each other?" She leaned closer to the screen, peering, and then began to raise it. But what a blunder that was, for she at once heard the branches shake, a whoosh of wings, a large shadow and a presence fled. Which direction? It seemed to have gone straight up.

Night silence.

Had she dreamed it? Drowsy back in bed she was tumbling into sleep when a chill, glacial in the warm night, a thought-shadow, close to palbable, fell across her. Owl call meant death. She had heard that from childhood. So their cook had told her often. And three times. It could only mean three days. Nonsense. Childish nonsense.

But grey and feathery, the presence lingered and so did the exact, seeking sound of the call. A call was meant to say something to some other being. Person? Bird? Beast? Another owl? Who was to know?

Sleep, returning, tumbled her like surf.

Wendy did accounts for a local charity and one afternoon a week kept the desk at a shelter for the homeless. She served on committees and talked to friends. Her daughter urged her to get a regular job. She said she didn't want to.

"Guy's coming back next week," she told a caller. "They're playing several courses in Florida."

That was the first day. She read obituaries, but found no name she knew.

On the second an entire family of friends she had not seen in twenty years called while passing through. She asked them to stop by. The husband and wife, getting grey and over-cheerful, had brought their daughter with two grandchildren. They had been travelling in the mountains.

As they sat at the dining table with coffee, Cokes, and cookies,

the little girl bent double with a terrible stomach pain. The visit
ended in the emergency room at the hospital where Wendy sat in
a row with the family, trying to amuse the little boy. He wanted
to be sick, too, finding it interesting. She thought of the owl.
Appendicitis? Even so, there was no real danger. Unless peritoni-
tis. . . .   The doctor called them in. Acute gastritis. Take these.
The trouble passed.

Alone again in a night so silent, the silence seemed a presence
she might speak to. She leaned to the window. Nothing was
there.

The third day. She kept a lunch date with a friend. The friend
was tearful. Her little spaniel had had a fierce fight with a neighbor's doberman and was now at the vet. He might not survive
"Why, that's terrible," said Wendy. Back home in the afternoon,
she left her chores to telephone. Great news. The dog was im-
proving. It wouldn't have to be "put down." That awful phrase.

Restless, she finished dinner alone and telephoned her children. Everybody was well. "He's coming back early next week,"
she said. Another still twilight faded toward another silent night.
She locked up the house and went to a movie.

On the drive home a thin scythe of moon was just shyly showing over the treetops. She lowered the window to breathe night
air. The glare of headlights appeared very close in the rear view
mirror. A man in a white tee shirt was driving the car behind. It
kept pressing nearer. The face was expressionless, pale, nonde-
script. The bumper touched hers, a jolt like a shudder.

For the first time, she thought: *Maybe it meant me.*

She did not want to lead him home with no one there. She
spun out to the highway. He followed close behind. She knew
what the next move should be—the police station, sitting outside
and honking out a call. The empty highway climbed. The frail
moon looked coolly toward a far horizon. Abruptly, the pursuer
swung left, crossed the meridian and vanished into a side road,
thick with dark trees.

She drove some minutes longer, but he did not return.

Entering her house from the driveway, she saw she had left a
light on in the kitchen.

When she entered, Guy stood from searching the refrigerator to greet her. "Got rained out. Should have called. Hey, what's the matter?" She had almost screamed. "You look like you've seen a ghost."

She sank in a chair. "I feel like it."

His face was florid. His bourbon sat half-empty on the table. His booming voice filled the room. "Not one yet, sweetheart. You'll have to wait awhile." He squeezed her hand and planted a kiss.

Once he was asleep and snoring happily, she returned to the guest room window and searched the darkness. "Where are you?" she whispered, as though to a friend. "Come back. You're nothing bad, nothing bad. Only let me hear you once again."

A

GRACIOUS

RAIN

Christopher Tilghman

One early summer evening, Stanley Harris, a family man with a wife named Beth, sat on his porch and looked out idly as two clergymen went about their separate and competing duties among their parishioners on Raymond Street. To Stanley's eyes it was a pleasant scene. The red sun brought colors out of the brown lawns and weathered clapboards, and the low shafts of light played and wound through the repetition of porches, stoops, and gables. In the evening, the rich smells of frying pork and fresh dinner rolls replaced the dust of midday and the chaff from the grain elevator. Stanley listened to the sharp yips of the children playing, and the low mumble of their parents sharing their days, and he reflected that, considering the choices, he could have met a worse fate than to live and die on a back street in Cookestown, Maryland.

This evening's pastoral duties, performed by Father William Francis, pastor of Immaculate Conception, and Dr. Emmett Daggett, of the Second Baptist, could not be called momentous. Father Francis helped Gladys Foster into the car for a visit to her sister Ethel in the hospital, and then walked quickly to the Smarts' to discuss, Stanley was sure, altar flowers. Dr. Daggett ran gamely to field a wild pitch, clutching his glasses, cross, and pocketful of change, but otherwise seemed to have little on his schedule. It was enough for him to stand there, gold teeth shining in his black face like the cross on his dark suit, reminding his flock of the Word. Stanley and his family were Episcopalians, "Anglicans," his mother used to say, tracing an alleged lineage back to families fleeing from Oliver Cromwell. But he had no quarrel with Father Francis or Dr. Daggett, even if he found the Catholic a little stiff for his taste. He rather liked the feeling that Raymond Street attracted this kind of attention, like the occasional pass down the street by Officer Stapleton that made him feel noticed and well served.

When Stanley was in the Army, in Germany during the Johnson buildup, he'd often been struck with much the same feeling. Most of the Army seemed dedicated to feeding him, maintaining his very nice teeth, entertaining him with movies and occasional USO shows; that the cooks and dentists and musicians avoided their share of all-night field exercises didn't strike him as unfair given the gifts of a hot meal and a painless mouth to eat it with. Even in the field the Army was thoughtful enough to supply cigarettes in the K rations; though Stanley didn't smoke, he had traded the Marlboros for canned peaches.

Stanley worked as a machinist at the Jones Machine Tool plant in Easton, and often came home with feathery spirals of stainless steel caught in his hair. He knew enough to appreciate this job, in a plant that had landed as if from nowhere in a played-out cornfield. Why would a company that big put a plant in Easton? How would they know Easton existed? He was proud to walk into his shop every morning under a banner that read *The Jap invasion stops here.*

In fact, when the rector of their church, the Reverend James Broadhurst, said that, even as Christ had, we would all die feeling forsaken, Stanley could not help but take silent and prayerful issue. Stanley admired Mr. Broadhurst's words, but the priest always wore a rather whipped-dog look on his frail brow, and seemed eager to hear of his flock's deepest doubts. Maybe it was because the still-young preacher had no wife and lived alone in an old huntsman's cottage at the tip of Spears Neck. The sound of all those geese in the winter would drive anyone crazy. So when Mr. Broadhurst preached about the universal fear that God would forget us, Stanley listened gravely but saved his real fear for himself: that God would remember him all too well, that He already had blessed him. But why? Why would He bother?

"What you thinking about so hard there," asked Beth, who'd come out for a cigarette and breather. She liked to lean against the porch rail with her back to the last cusp of sun, the fires of daylight turning brilliant on the distant waters of the Bay. Stanley had always thought the homes of Raymond Street, built by a mill gang in the thirties, looked like houseboats, one by one, long and narrow, with overhanging roofs to keep the sun off vacationers. In the dim light, Stanley could see Beth, thicker now after her pregnancies but still fit, her straight brown hair in the same bob she'd worn since high school, and he saw her leaning over the rail of a houseboat, like girls in the travel ads of the *Register.* Susan, Timmie, and Molly were in the bath. Behind Beth, Delia Bagwell was calling the kids to bed, and behind Bagwells' was McCready, and Twyford, and Pusey. Stanley and Dickie Bagwell had little to say to each other, but Delia and Beth were best friends, close as high-schoolers and so often seen shopping together that newcomers in town mistook them for sisters.

"Nothing," he said. "I was just setting, darlin."

Whenever Stanley tried to explain his deepest thoughts, even to himself, he ended up close to blasphemy, which made him nervous. Yet whenever a feeling of meaninglessness nagged at him, the more he felt chosen to bear witness that life had a reason and a reward, that life was a blessing. At the plant, during coffee, he sometimes tried to interrupt the bitching of his friends with a few words of moderation, and Bobby and Frank were sharp and quick enough to call him "Preacher" because of it. It was not that Stanley didn't complain now and again about the way Beth kept house or the new shop rules. But though he tried, he never could see why the things that didn't work in his life should be so much more important than the things that did. He couldn't seem to lose his temper about any of it, a lack of passion that earned him a reputation as something of a marshmallow when it came to sticking up for his rights. Because he was well liked, he had once been nominated from the floor for union shop steward, a suggestion that was hooted down by his best friends with a lot of fun all around. For a few days after that he worried that maybe it was true, maybe he was a pushover. But in the end, Stanley decided that there was a part of him that sometimes, like tonight, filled his soul with questions so deep that he felt graced to think of them at all. It was a gift, something that he didn't understand very well, and maybe no one would, and maybe it was something that was simply beyond his brain power to grasp or express.

"Night, Dad." Eight-year-old Timmie had come out, clean and sleepy, the way Stanley loved his children best. The last red glow was fading from the horizon. Stanley gathered him in, rubbed his cheek on the boy's soft, aromatic head, and patted his skinny bottom through the spaceman pajamas.

"Say your prayers."

"I hate Susan," said Timmie. Stanley had heard snatches of a fight a few minutes earlier, and he had to admit that Susan, thirteen just last week, was quickly becoming impossible.

"Okay. God will get up and down with Susan," he said, and gave him a final shove back in the door.

It was dark now on Raymond Street: the special restfulness of dusk had ended as the mumble and murmur of games and conversations hushed into individual voices. A baby cried at the west end, probably little Emlen Paggin; and from the other end of the street he heard the sharp bark of a man's "Shit on you," and a door slamming. All over Cookestown, people were drawing away from the dark and dew and into the false light of the houses. Stanley could picture, up and down the street, the husbands and wives grinding toward rapid and silent climax, toward the emptiness of the first hours before dawn. Stanley feared emptiness, the eternal dark, just like everybody. Inside, Beth was beginning the dishes, and he would soon slip in beside her to dry. She would need stories about his day, and though this duty fatigued him more than anything he could imagine, he would do his best. Raymond Street was on its own now: no clergy, no police, just Stanley turning for a final look from the door with the dying wonder of the gift that was his, and was not.

* * *

The following morning Stanley woke up feeling not bad, but different. He dressed and ate with a sense of change coming, most likely the beginning of a cold or possibly another bout with his slipped disc. He told himself that this was part of being over forty, the sense that the body was telegraphing its minor disturbances and pains. But no sooner had he punched in at the plant and settled at his lathe than his heart ruptured along an unsuspected family fault line, and he died without catching his breath.

Two hours later, in the white light of mid-morning, when the asphalt and rooftops of Raymond Street were soft, and the dogs under the porches wore fixed grins and boiling eyes, Beth Harris glanced up from folding her laundry as if someone had called her, and looked out the front window. She saw Mr. Broadhurst and Officer Stapleton climbing out of the cruiser. She fell down where she was, in front of the screen door, and the men had to run around back to let themselves in through the kitchen. They rushed over to her, but as they knelt down she jumped up swinging, and nearly connected with Mr. Broadhurst's jaw, and he backed off until he fell into a brown Morris chair.

"So it's yours now," screamed Beth. "It's God's?"

And it took Mr. Broadhurst a few moments to realize she was talking about the chair, but by this time Delia Bagwell had come running with an undiapered baby under one arm, and little Molly began shrieking from her crib. Beth ran to the bedroom while Delia, still holding her own baby on her hip, called Beth's mother, who lived in Chestertown and had no car. At the door appeared a couple of the Paggin girls, one of whom was wearing a purple T-shirt with *Spittle* written on it, and they reached into the room to snatch Molly out of Beth's arms and take her down to the other end of the street. And as all this carried forth Frank Stapleton looked at the clergyman in amazement and said, "Neither of us never said a word."

By two in the afternoon, the Benefits Office had arranged for Stanley to be brought to Lee and Evans Funeral Home, and Beth and her mother went to see him. Beth's cousin Harold, the surliest gas-station attendant in the county, drove her mother over from Chestertown in his Dodge Charger, and despite the occa-

sion laid a patch of rubber on Raymond Street as he left. Her
mother was wearing a light blue pantsuit and had brought her
white leather purse, but Beth hadn't changed from her jeans and
sweatshirt. She borrowed Delia's car, and they passed through
town with a procession of clanks, down Raymond Street to Ches-
ter, to the courthouse square with its fragrant lines of box
bushes, and down past the low whitewashed brick office buildings of Lawyers' Row. She didn't know if Stanley had a will; she
didn't know who would know, or if it would ever matter. They
stopped at the corner by the school, and Beth began to cry.
Timmie and Susan were there, for the annual two-week summer
camp organized by the Cookestown United Church Council.
"They don't know yet, Mama," she said. "They're in there playing, thinking everything's fine, and their daddy's dead."

Her mother couldn't say anything right, so she told Beth the
light was green.

"Shouldn't we stop for flowers or something?" asked Beth suddenly as they drove to a space in front of the Victorian home of
Lee and Evans. "I don't know what to do."

The pink stucco building was hooded with striped awnings on
every window. Beth remembered the sign that used to hang on
the movie theater marquee: COME ON IN. IT'S COOOOL INSIDE. That
was their first date: she wore a yellow muumuu, a tube-like fashion her mother had copied from a picture of Jackie Kennedy, and
they saw *Blue Hawaii,* with Elvis.

"Now don't worry about what you do or don't do," said her
mother. "Phil Evans said to leave everything to him."

Beth had been schoolmates with Sally Pingree Evans. "It's like
she won this time for good."

"Shush. To think of childhood quarrels at a time like this."

"I always had Stan," she said, and she reached into her purse
and took out a Kleenex, a comb, and a piece of gum.

Phil Evans met them at the door. To Beth, he had always
seemed a little light, a "fairy," but today she found his manner
surprisingly soothing. The voice, the eyes, the familiarity—they
reminded her that people die all the time, even die young like
Stan, and there was no use being ashamed of it. He led them

through the offices and past the floral arrangements just delivered for the evening wakes, and into a simple, windowless room where a body lay under a sheet. Phil paused to see whether both women were composed, and pulled back the cover.

And there was Stanley. She reached out immediately, and her hand, by accident, fell right on the long scar from the corner of his left eye. She gasped and pulled her hand back, but whether what shocked her was touching his scar or the unfamiliar feeling of cold flesh, she could not be sure. Some days she'd have to force herself not to look at this blemish when she talked to him: it now seemed so necessary, an identifying mark, as the police said. She didn't know whether she was going to cry or not. Right then, for a second—a flicker as long as the heart attack that killed him—she had to search in her heart to find the love she felt for him, to find the sharp part of it. He had such a good jaw, with those fine teeth that she could see through his slightly parted mouth. Beth used to look at him during sermons, down at the other end of the family pew, and his jaw made him seem so intelligent, as if Mr. Broadhurst were speaking only for him. Beth had never learned how to concentrate on the sermons; by the time one child had reached the age where he or she could be depended upon to sit quietly, another came along. He'd missed a place, that very morning, shaving, and there was a small square of whisker under his chin. Maybe it was only mistakes that outlived people, she thought. He seemed so dead; Beth couldn't help using the word to describe the way his body and limbs looked. Beth could see that the funeral home had already put some powder on his face; it still bore the trace of pain, but the mouth and eyebrows had started to relax as he went down, and the last suffocated breath left him looking strangely content. It was a martyr's face, she thought. It was, she suddenly realized, a message to her from Stan, and at that, tears did begin to come.

"It was very quick," said Phil. "He could not have been in pain."

"I still don't understand," she sobbed. "It was a weak heart or something?"

"You'll have to ask Dr. Peters, Elizabeth." Phil still held the sheet high above Stanley and his arms began to quiver and drop. He did feel professionally competent to add, "His rest is now complete."

"You can put your arms down now," she said, composed again. "It's Stanley."

"Of course," said Phil.

"No," said Beth, looking one last time at that satisfied brow, "I mean, this is how Stanley would have wanted to look."

She left her mother to make arrangements, and retraced her steps back to the front door. Outside she paused to take three or four deep breaths, and to look both ways to make sure no one was coming toward her. Except for the funeral home, no one she knew well would have reason to be in this neighborhood: the cooks and cleaning ladies were all from Corsica Hollow. She began walking toward town, crackling the brittle sheets of plane tree bark that peeled all summer. There weren't any trees on Raymond Street—just a few scrubby privet hedges overgrown with honeysuckle. She'd never lived on a street with trees and now she never would. Not that getting or being rich was anything she and Stanley had thought much about. At the beginning, her mother had argued against Stanley. I don't see much ambition in the boy, said her mother, and she was right if all there was to ambition was wanting something you didn't have. That was fine for Stanley now, but Beth began to worry how long Timmie's sneakers would last and whether his coat from last year would still fit. She couldn't remember if she'd bought underpants for Susan at the Kmart yesterday, and if she had, whether Susan would demand some different kind—colored bikinis, maybe— now that she had so many opinions. Molly would be in Susan's hand-me-downs for years, that was okay, but there was no way they could afford Pampers anymore and no way they'd ever see a washing machine in their house, so she just better plan now to be spending a lot more time in the BestClean.

By now she was standing on the hot concrete of the school entrance, a set of stairs rising like bunkers out of the worn brown grass. The building faced the courthouse and was often mistaken for the county jail. Beth was tired now, her legs felt spongy and her breath kept dropping out of the bottom of her lungs. She sat on the steps and lit a cigarette, and listened to the muffled voices of the children playing inside, and the sound farther off of the tomato trucks, loaded to the axles, downshifting into Fox's canning, and then, way in the distance, the faint whine of Route 50, almost bumper to bumper on hot days all the way from the Bay Bridge to Ocean City. She didn't feel like herself, sitting here only seven or so hours after Stanley had died: she felt she was watching all this from above, as in the movies, as if she had died too and some stand-in was breaking the news to the kids.

At last there was activity from inside the door, a final shout in the hall before the birds flew, and at just the same moment Beth's mother pulled up to the curb in the Bagwells' Dodge. So when Susan came out first, acting so sophisticated with her friends Meg and Tiffany, what she saw was her mother climbing to her feet from the steps, and her grandmother, dressed in a suit with her white purse, getting out of the Bagwells' car, and Susan's bright smooth look was replaced with a scowl, because even as she understood something very bad had happened, she realized also that her afternoon plans were now ruined. But when Timmie ran out a few moments later, his maroon hat pulled over his scarlet hair, his eyes darted from his mother to his grandmother to Susan, and he kept looking for a second for the other person who should have been there given the totally unexpected presence of his mother and grandmother, and he dropped his tin lunch box, and cried out, "Where's Daddy!" And by this time Susan's friends had taken several steps beyond her, and she gave one last look at them as if she had somehow been expelled from the group, and then ran to lead Timmie, whimpering now like a puppy, into their mother's arms.

They drove back to Raymond Street with Beth in the back seat holding the children, but at the top of the street Beth waved her mother on and they headed out onto the flat of Route 50 and turned south. They all cried a good bit, even Beth's mother as she drove along slowly, mostly in the breakdown lane. Beth watched the trucks thundering by, and looked out at the road crews and farmers deep in their fields, and saw all these workingmen, with wives at home, all still alive. Soon they reached the Bay Bridge, a heaving backbone hunched over the silent water, and Beth tapped her mother on the shoulder. They turned and were nearing their exit when Beth tapped again, and her mother understood and drove into Frostee's Ice Cream. They took a booth, and for a moment all four of them sat in front of their sundaes topped with sharp spirals of whipped cream and they cried once again, as if saying grace.

"Are they sure?" said Timmie finally.

"Yes, hon. Grandma and I saw him."

Timmie picked up his spoon and started on his ice cream, and then asked, "Is he in heaven?"

Beth hesitated, and asked herself what Mr. Broadhurst would say.

"Of course he is," said her mother, glowering at Beth's delay. "He's watching over us right now."

"Oh, Grandma," said Susan.

"Shush," said her grandmother.

They all picked at their sundaes. But it had been the right move, to come into this air-conditioned world surrounded by orange and purple plastic. Everyone there, except for Beth and her mother, was so young, the counter girls not much older than Susan, their round adolescent bottoms straining in the purple short-shorts of the Frostee's uniform.

"Are you going to stay tonight?" Susan asked her grandmother.

Beth glared: Susan was asking whether she would have to sleep on the couch. "We don't know what's going to happen just yet. Eat your sundae."

They all made a last attempt to finish, and then left. From the averted looks Susan got from the high school girls, Beth knew the word had traveled through town. This time when they reached the head of Raymond Street, the light now the burnished yellow of a closing day, there was nothing left but to drive down the center, between the porches. Normally the children would be out by now, darting through the evening like fireflies. But the baseball games of the boys and the curbside Pony and Pound Puppy parties of the girls were off for the night. Instead, there

were cars bunched at the middle of the street in front of their
house, several strollers—Beth read each of them like name tags—
on the lawn, and Nancy Paggin was disappearing in their front
door carrying a casserole dish and a bag of groceries topped by a
flowering of celery leaves.

A parking space had been left for them at the front, and as the
four of them headed up the oyster-shell walk to the house, Beth
had the sensation that she was carrying something, like a new
television in a big cardboard box, that she wished she could keep
private from the neighbors. She took little notice of all the familiar faces. Considering the number of people in their small house,
there was surprisingly little noise, but the hot air was fluid and
heavy with sweat. They were spread all over the house, into the
hall and back to her bedroom, the cousins, the Puseys, Mc-
Creadys, and Twyfords.

The family walked in, and one by one they were peeled off,
until Beth ended up alone in the kitchen with Delia. Both women
burst into tears as they started to hug, and as Beth sobbed she felt
the comfort of Delia's breasts and the warmth of Delia's cheek on
hers, a softness without whiskers or the smell of work, and she
wondered if ever again a man would hold her, or if she wanted it
to happen, ever again. At length they parted, and made the apologetic faces two friends make when their cheeks are stained with
tears, and Delia turned to stir the chicken stew that had been
simmering on the stove all day.

Beth took a moment to herself on the back steps, and then
worked forward into the front room. From the doorway she saw
Mr. Broadhurst standing quite uncomfortably beside the floor
lamp. None of Stanley and her friends on Raymond Street was an
Episcopalian, and the day for the parish visit would come later,
yet she couldn't help but observe that the one person who
should have known what to do looked like the one person someone should send home.

"It's real nice of you to come," she said to him.

He was holding a Dixie cup and had worked his little finger up
through the bottom. He blushed slightly as he pulled his hands

free, and made a show of crumpling the cup, as if to prove to Beth that he had drunk some wine just to be sociable.

He said, "My place is at your side, Elizabeth," and he reached out for her hand awkwardly, without stepping closer to her, his own hand now unencumbered.

Beth thanked him, for what she wasn't entirely sure, and began to greet the people who had come into her house. The men were still in their work clothes, but most of the wives, unlike Beth, had changed into skirts, put on makeup, and done their hair. The white and black faces mingled comfortably, which was something that might not really happen except for times like this, but could happen anytime, and was comforting to Beth because Stanley would have been pleased. All these people in her house, even the children and babies, all of them would die one day, that was the point; all of them, like Stanley, would go. That's the message, anyway, that Beth took from them. Before she knew it, she had begun to think of each new face she greeted, each new body that embraced her, almost as a corpse. And when she realized this she thought she might faint, and asked Hugh Twyford to take her out for some air.

The day had now cooled into early evening. Susan was already out there sitting with the Paggin girls, and the three of them were playing with Molly. Beth picked up the baby and stood for a long time holding her firm little body, the warmth of her tufted head. "Where's Timmie, sweetheart?" she asked Susan.

Susan didn't know, so Beth sent her off to find him, and a minute or two later she came back to say he was in the bedroom with Mr. Broadhurst.

"What are they doing?" Beth asked.

"They're playing Clue, I think. Something." Susan looked embarrassed. "Timmie was telling Mr. Broadhurst that Daddy's in heaven."

"What did Mr. Broadhurst say?"

"Mom," Susan whined.

"I just want to know whether Timmie needs me."

"Well, I don't know. He's fine." Beth reached out and patted

Susan on the head; there just wasn't enough room in there for her father's death, not today anyway.

They fed all the children first, the mothers, some holding babies, standing behind the chairs of the little ones, reaching forward to catch a plastic cup of milk before it flooded the table, and then sent the children out into the sweet dusk of summer with ice cream bars. The adults sat on chairs brought from other houses, in front of dishes and silverware brought from other kitchens. They quieted for Mr. Broadhurst's prayer, which contained a line that we will know God "not by reason but by fire," and as the conversation resumed, Beth heard old Mr. McCready announce that this thought was "too deep by a fathom for me." Then one by one, and family by family, they gathered their things, bid goodbye and courage to Beth, and left. A light rain had begun to fall, and they dashed to the ends of Raymond Street with their chairs and utensils held over their heads. Delia took her place in the kitchen, where she would remain for the next few days, and Beth and her mother put everyone to bed. Susan would sleep with Beth, on Stanley's side, and Beth knew if they woke in the middle of the night they could talk, perhaps even go out to the porch together in their nightgowns and watch the sun rise. She could not have borne Timmie lying there, already such a little male, with his father's sharp features, but she went to his room and lay beside him while he cried, and curled up onto him as he fell asleep.

When all this was done Beth came back out into the quiet house, and was surprised and annoyed to see Mr. Broadhurst's brooding presence leaning against the rail out on the porch. She wasn't sure why he assumed the right to be the last to leave. But Stanley would have wanted this conversation, so she opened the screen door as silently as possible and leaned against the rail on the other side, with Stanley's empty chair between them.

"That was real nice of you to play with Timmie," she said.

"He will do fine. He's very sure his father has been gathered into the fellowship of saints."

"I know," said Beth.

"Stanley was a man of great faith. He had . . . faith . . ." Mr. Broadhurst's thought trailed off.

It was a black night. "Can I get you some coffee?" asked Beth.

"Oh no, Elizabeth. I must be going, of course."

But he didn't go, and Beth was by now fatigued and perplexed. Searching around in her mind for something suitable, she said, "Stanley always loved the line where Jesus says—of course I can't really say it—but he says, 'If it wasn't true I wouldn't say so.' "

"Oh yes. John 14:1–6. 'In my Father's house . . .' "

"He liked it because it seemed so matter-of-fact."

"Yes," said Mr. Broadhurst, but the whole conversation seemed to have depressed him even further. Beth said nothing more, and they both stared out into the darkness of Raymond Street until finally, not a moment before she felt she would simply have to say good night and leave him there, he announced that he must go. He straightened, and then had to maneuver slightly around Stanley's empty chair so that he could draw close to her and once more take her hand, and he held on to it as he said, "We would all like to know the truth, wouldn't we, Elizabeth?"

"The truth?" asked Beth. He still had her hand.

"When it's a man as young as Stanley . . ."

Beth did not understand what he was saying, but she did understand that he wasn't really speaking to her. "I'm sorry," she said finally.

He waved off her sympathy with a joyless smile. "Please remember what I said inside. I am always here for you, and," he added, "the children." Finally he let go and walked quickly through the rain out to his car, and when he turned the key, the radio came alive at the volume he had set on the way over, and it blasted forth a line or two of an advertisement for discount clothing, before he could hastily turn it down.

And Stanley looked on all this with a sense of distance that, under the circumstances, hardly surprised him. He felt extremely bad for Beth, it having fallen to her to deal with Mr. Broadhurst very much as one spouse occasionally must spend a terrible evening with the drunken best friend of the other. If Stanley had thought it mattered, he would have warned her earlier about Mr. Broadhurst's darker side, for his sermons were full of it, full of disciples losing heart, full of the loneliness of Gethsemane. He would do better tomorrow, buttressed by the presence of the vestry and the parish children; he'd be too busy to brood.

On this matter of the hand-holding, however, Stanley was as surprised as Beth. He never would have guessed that Mr. Broadhurst harbored feelings for her, even though, from the inner peace of his current viewpoint, Stanley found Beth almost impossibly lovely in every way. It would be a mistake from the start, not that Beth would make it. But poor old Mr. Broadhurst would: even now, as he drove out Route 16 to his empty cottage on Spears Neck, awash with embarrassment, tormented by something the living called guilt but which Stanley recognized now was the very fire of mortality. He could only follow his headlights, straight ahead into the darkness beyond their reach. From above, Stanley could see the route, out all the way to the cottage, all the way beyond into the Corsica River and out onto the Bay. Mr. Broadhurst would keep driving till he drowned at this rate: she was too much for him, Stanley figured.

Stanley had certainly believed, all his life—he was just getting used to the real meaning of the phrase—that she was too much for *him.* He'd asked her on their first date because Delia Bagwell ordered him to, and they went to the Palace and saw Elvis in *King Creole,* but Stanley had been so nervous he couldn't remember a single frame of the show. He had come home from the Army expecting bad news—he wasn't much of a letter writer—and there she was waiting for him, as he had always believed she would be, against odds that Stanley more than anyone judged overwhelming. Because in that abyss, when all he could picture was her saying "I do" to a hundred more suitable men, a more unlikely and perhaps impossible image grew even more radiant. Hope had kept him going, but it was the doubt that gave him joy.

Stanley, it was true, wished Beth hadn't taken a swing at Mr. Broadhurst, and he found it disappointing that, if only for a moment, she had thought back to her long-running competition with Sally Pingree. On the other hand, he did have to admit to himself that he felt a deep irony when his body ended up on Phil Evans's slab. The man had been patronizing him for years, and actively avoided him on the streets of Cookestown. Who was he to tell Beth that "his rest was now complete"? He was wrong in every way, as if rest was ever anything Stanley had sought anyway. And who was he to tell Beth that a fatal heart attack is painless? He wouldn't want Beth to know it, of course, but the feeling of a mortal organ virtually splitting in two made childbirth and kidney stones look like a day at the beach. A millisecond of that was enough for eternity.

He wasn't really surprised to see her staring blankly at his body when Phil Evans pulled back the sheet. He might have hoped for a more tender moment, but he had from time to time in the past wondered whether he would cry freely and unselfconsciously if Beth died. Perhaps it had something to do with vanity, a condition, he recognized now, that found expression in the flesh but was not entirely restricted to it. If he had still had his body it would have stiffened when Beth's hand landed on his scar, a jagged blemish that went from the corner of his eye into his hairline. It had bothered him almost from the day Lee McCready did it with a brick when they were eight, an accident that nearly cost Stanley his vision on one side. Sometimes, meeting new people, he had to force himself not to consciously present his good side, keeping the other in a kind of shame. He wondered now, in fact, even after he had left his body behind, whether he would still be known as the "guy with the scar," or maybe, more accurately, as "the guy who used to have the scar."

But it was such a small matter, such an odd little detail, that it did nothing more than give resonance to the thing. In the meantime, he had so much more to think about. Beth. The kids. Yes, those wonderful, sweet children. He was delighted to hear Timmie lecture Mr. Broadhurst that he was in heaven; Stanley was also glad that Timmie would lose his certainty as he aged, because there would be no savor in his life without questions. As Stanley had, Timmie would sit on his porch in the evenings, and wonder. And Susan. Oh, where had the glorious idea for adolescence come from, that magnificent rush, the body searing itself in fullness onto the flesh? If he could, he would have kissed her when she asked Beth's mother whether she was staying for the night; he would carry the image of her frown at the schoolyard forever, even as she grew into womanhood and finally into the decrepitude of age. And could humankind ever condemn itself, could a man find fault with his species once having known a single two-year-old? Molly in some sense that Stanley knew he'd have to figure out, was the Resurrection.

Yes, everything was going fairly much as he might have imagined, except for one large detail: the communion of saints, as he had tried to picture it when reciting the Apostle's Creed, was not exactly complete. In fact, when Mr. Broadhurst had talked about "the eternal fear that God would forget us," he was more correct than he knew. Because everyone around Stanley seemed, just as before, to be waiting, and searching. The babel of complaints and jealousies had survived death. In fact, the major source of common dissatisfaction centered on death itself: those who had died young, like Stanley, talked constantly about plans gone awry, ambitions unfulfilled, children's lives still not set; those who had died old wailed about the miseries of age, the pain and indignity of long decline.

The truth, after all, was that little had changed. He had expected to have so much answered by now, either in the darkness of the void or in the light of eternity. Instead, it was dusk again, a lazy summer evening. Yet that, Stanley already understood, was the ultimate good fortune. The quest was not over. He had been spared once again, spared the end of doubt, preserved from eternal rest. Life, in other words, went on. With this discovery, Stanley found himself back in his accustomed place on the porch. He had often thought, as he sat in his old chair, that he could remain there for days; now, perhaps, he would be there forever. Raymond Street was quiet, the houses firm and solid in a line, under a gracious rain falling lightly onto a resting land.

MRS. ACLAND'S
GHOSTS

William Trevor

Mr. Mockler was a tailor. He carried on his business in a house that after twenty-five years of mortgage arrangements had finally become his: 22 Juniper Street, S W 17. He had never married and since he was now sixty-three it seemed likely that he never would. In a old public house, the Charles the First, he had a drink every evening with his friends Mr. Uprichard and Mr. Tile, who were tailors also. He lived in his house in Juniper Street with his cat Sam, and did his own cooking and washing and cleaning: he was not unhappy.

On the morning of 19 October 1972, Mr. Mockler received a letter that astonished him. It was nearly written in a pleasantly rounded script that wasn't difficult to decipher. It did not address him as "Dear Mr. Mockler," nor was it signed, nor conventionally concluded. But his name was used repeatedly, and from its contents it seemed to Mr. Mockler that the author of the letter was a Mrs. Acland. He read the letter in amazement and then read it again and then, more slowly, a third time:

Dr. Scott-Rowe is dead, Mr. Mockler. I know he is dead because a new man is here, a smaller, younger man, called Dr. Friendman. He looks at us, smiling, with his unblinking eyes. Miss Acheson says you can tell at a glance that he has practiced hypnosis.

They're so sure of themselves, Mr. Mockler: beyond the limits

405

of their white-coated world they can accept nothing. I am a woman imprisoned because I once saw ghosts. I am paid for by the man who was my husband, who writes out monthly checks for the peaches they bring to my room, and the beef olives and the marrons glacés. *"She must above all things be happy," I can imagine the stout man who was my husband saying, walking with Dr. Scott-Rowe over the sunny lawns and among the rose-beds. In this house there are twenty disturbed people in private rooms, cosseted by luxury because other people feel guilty. And when we walk ourselves on the lawns and among the rose-beds we murmur at the folly of those who have so expensively com-mitted us, and at the greater folly of the medical profession: you can be disturbed without being mad. Is this the letter of a luna-tic, Mr. Mockler?*

I said this afternoon to Miss Acheson that Dr. Scott-Rowe was dead. She said she knew. All of us would have Dr. Friendman now, she said, with his smile and his tape-recorders, "May Dr. Scott-Rowe rest in peace," said Miss Acheson: it was better to be dead than to be like Dr. Friendman. Miss Acheson is a very old lady, twice my age exactly: I am thirty-nine and she is seventy-eight. She was committed when she was eighteen, in 1913, a year before the First World War. Miss Acheson was disturbed by visions of St. Olaf of Norway and she still is. Such visions were an embarrassment to Miss Acheson's family in 1913 and so they quietly slipped her away. No one comes to see her now, no one has since 1927.

"You must write it all down," Miss Acheson said to me when I told her, years ago, that I'd been committed because I'd seen ghosts and that I could prove the ghosts were real because the Rachels had seen them too. The Rachels are living some normal existence somewhere, yet they were terrified half out of their wits at the time and I wasn't frightened at all. The trouble nowadays, Miss Acheson says and I quite agree, is that if you like having ghosts near you people think you're round the bend.

I was talking to Miss Acheson about all this yesterday and she said why didn't I do what Sarah Crookham used to do? There's nothing the matter with Sarah Crookham, any more than there is with Miss Acheson or myself: all that Sarah Crookham suffers from is a broken heart. "You must write it all down," Miss Acheson said to her when she first came here, weeping, poor thing, every minute of the day. So she wrote it down and posted it to A. J. Rawson, a person she found in the telephone directory. But Mr. Rawson never came, nor another person Sarah Crookham wrote to. I have looked you up in the telephone directory, Mr. Mockler. It is nice to have a visitor.

"You must begin at the beginning," Miss Acheson says, and so I am doing that. The beginning is back a bit, in January 1949, when I was fifteen. We lived in Richmond then, my parents and one brother, George, and my sisters Alice and Isabel. On Sundays, after lunch, we used to walk all together in Richmond Park with our dog, a Dalmatian called Salmon. I was the oldest and Alice was next, two years younger, and George was eleven and Isabel eight. It was lovely walking together in Richmond Park and then going home to Sunday tea. I remember the autumns and winters best, the coziness of the coal fire, hot sponge cake and special Sunday sandwiches, and little buns that Alice and I always helped to make on Sunday mornings. We played Monopoly by the fire, and George would always have the ship and Anna the hat and Isabel the racing-car and Mummy the dog. Daddy and I would share the old boot. I really loved it.

I loved the house: 17 Lorelei Avenue, an ordinary suburban house built some time in the early 1920s, when Miss Acheson was still quite young. There were bits of stained glass on either side of the hall door and a single stained-glass pane. Moses in the bulrushes, in one of the landing windows. At Christmas especially it was lovely: we'd have the Christmas tree in the hall and always on Christmas Eve, as long as I can remember, there'd be a party. I can remember the parties quite vividly. There'd be people standing round drinking punch and the children would play hide-and-seek upstairs, and nobody could ever find George. It's George, Mr. Mockler, that all this is about. And Alice, of course, and Isabel.

When I first described them to Dr. Scott-Rowe he said they sounded marvelous, and I said I thought they probably were, but I suppose a person can be prejudiced in family matters of that kind. Because they were, after all, my brother and my two sisters and because, of course, they're dead now. I mean, they were probably ordinary, just like any children. Well, you can see what you think, Mr. Mockler.

George was small for his age, very wiry, dark-haired, a darting kind of boy who was always laughing, who had often to be reprimanded by my father because his teachers said he was the most mischievous boy in his class. Alice, being two years older, was just the opposite: demure and silent, but happy in her quiet way, and beautiful, far more beautiful than I was. Isabel wasn't beautiful at all. She was all freckles, with long pale plaits and long legs that sometimes could run as fast as George's. She and George were as close as two persons can get, but in a way we were all close: there was a lot of love in 17 Lorelei Avenue.

I had a cold the day it happened, a Saturday it was. I was cross because they kept worrying about leaving me in the house on my own. They'd bring me back Black Magic chocolates, they said, and my mother said she'd buy a bunch of daffodils if she saw any. I heard the car crunching over the gravel outside the garage, and then their voices telling Salmon not to put his paws on the upholstery. My father blew the horn, saying goodbye to me, and after that the silence began. I must have known even then, long before it happened, that nothing would be the same again.

When I was twenty-two, Mr. Mockler, I married a man called Acland, who helped me to get over the tragedy. George would have been eighteen, and Anna twenty and Isabel fifteen. They would have liked my husband because he was a good-humored and generous man. He was very plump, many years older than I was, with a fondness for all food. "You're like a child," I used to say to him and we'd laugh together. Cheese in particular he liked, and ham and every kind of root vegetable, parsnips, turnips, celeriac, carrots, leeks, potatoes. He used to come back to the house and take four or five pounds of gammon from the car, and chops, and blocks of ice cream, and biscuits, and two or even three McVitie's fruitcakes. He was very partial to McVi-tie's fruitcakes. At night, at nine or ten o'clock, he'd make cocoa for both of us and we'd have it while we were watching the television, with a slice or two of fruitcake. He was such a kind man in those days. I got quite fat myself, which might surprise you, Mr. Mockler, because I'm on the thin side now.

My husband was, and still is, both clever and rich. One led to the other: he made a fortune designing metal fasteners for the aeroplane industry. Once, in May 1960, he drove me to a house in Worchestershire. "I wanted it to be a surprise," he said, stopping his mustard-colored Alfa-Romero in front of this quite extensive Victorian façade. "There," he said, embracing me, reminding me that it was my birthday. Two months later we went to live there.

We had no children. In the large Victorian house I made my life with the man I'd married and once again, as in 17 Lorelei Avenue, I was happy. The house was near a village but otherwise remote. My husband went away from it by day, to the place where his aeroplane fasteners were manufactured and tested. There were—and still are—aeroplanes in the air which would have fallen to pieces if they hadn't been securely fastened by the genius of my husband.

The house had many rooms. There was a large square drawing-room with a metal ceiling—beaten tin, I believe it was. It had patterns like wedding-cake icing on it. It was painted white and blue, and gave, as well as the impression of a wedding-cake, a Wedgewood effect. People remarked on this ceiling and my husband used to explain that metal ceilings had once been very popular, especially in the large houses of Australia. Well-to-do Australians, apparently, would have them shipped from Birmingham in colonial imitation of an English fashion. My husband and I, arm in arm, would lead people about the house, pointing out the ceiling or the green wallpaper in our bedroom or the portraits hung on the stairs.

The lighting was bad in the house. The long first-floor landing was a gloomy place by day and lit by a single wall-light at night. At the end of this landing another flight of stairs, less grand than the stairs that led from the hall, wound upwards to the small rooms that had once upon a time been servants' quarters, and another flight continued above them to attics and store-rooms. The bathroom was on the first floor, tiled in green Victorian tiles, and there was a lavatory next door to it, encased in mahogany.

In the small rooms that had once been the servants' quarters lived Mr. and Mrs. Rachels. My husband had had a kitchen and a bathroom put in for them so that their rooms were quite self-contained. Mr. Rachels worked in the garden and his wife cleaned the house. It wasn't really necessary to have them at all: I could have cleaned the house myself and even done the gardening, but my husband insisted in his generous way. At night I could hear the Rachels moving about above me. I didn't like this and my husband asked them to move more quietly.

In 1962 my husband was asked to go to Germany, to explain his airplane fasteners to the German aircraft industry. It was to be a prolonged trip, three months at least, and I was naturally unhappy when he told me. He was unhappy himself, but on March 4th he flew to Hamburg, leaving me with the Rachels.

They were a pleasant enough couple, somewhere in their fifties I would think, he rather silent, she inclined to talk. The only thing that worried me about them was the way they used to move about at night above my head. After my husband had gone to Germany I gave Mrs. Rachels money to buy slippers, but I don't think she ever did because the sounds continued just as before. I naturally didn't make a fuss about it.

On the night of March 7th I was awakened by a band playing in the house. The tune was an old tune of the fifties called, I believe, "Looking for Henry Lee." The noise was very loud in my bedroom and I lay there frightened, not knowing why this noise should be coming to me like this, Victor Silvester in strict dance tempo. Then a voice spoke, a long babble of French, and I realized that I was listening to a radio program. The wireless was across the room, on a table by the windows. I put on my bedside light and got up and switched it off. I drank some or-

ange juice and went back to sleep. It didn't even occur to me to wonder who had turned it on.

The next day I told Mrs. Rachels about it, and it was she, in fact, who made me think that it was all rather stranger than it seemed. I definitely remembered turning the wireless off myself before going to bed, and in any case I was not in the habit of listening to French stations, so that even if the wireless had somehow come on of its own accord it should not have been tuned in to a French station.

Two days later I found the bath half-filled with water and the towels all rumpled and damp, thrown about on the floor. The water in the bath was tepid and dirty: someone, an hour or so ago, had had a bath.

I climbed the stairs to the Rachels' flat and knocked on their door. "Is your bathroom out of order?" I said when Mr. Rachels came to the door, not wearing any slippers I'd given them money for. I said I didn't at all mind their using mine, only I'd be grateful if they'd remember to let the water out and to bring down their own towels. Mr. Rachels looked at me in the way people have sometimes, as though you're insane. He called his wife and all three of us went down to look at my bathroom. They denied emphatically that either of them had had a bath.

When I came downstairs the next morning, having slept badly, I found the kitchen table had been laid for four. There was a tablecloth on the table, which was something I never bothered about, and a kettle was boiling on the Aga. Beside it, a large brown teapot, not the one I normally used, was heating. I made some tea and sat down, thinking about the Rachels. Why should they behave like this? Why should they creep into my bedroom in the middle of the night and turn the wireless on? Why should they have a bath in my bathroom and deny it? Why should they lay the breakfast table as though we had overnight guests? I left the table just as it was. Butter had been rolled into pats. Marmalade had been placed in two china dishes. A silver toast-rack that an aunt of my husband had given us as a wedding present was waiting for toast.

"Thank you for laying the table," I said to Mrs. Rachels when she entered the kitchen an hour later.

She shook her head. She began to say that she hadn't laid the table but then she changed her mind. I could see from her face that she and her husband had been discussing the matter of the bath the night before. She could hardly wait to tell him about the breakfast table. I smiled at her.

"A funny thing happened the other night," I said. "I woke up to find Victor Silvester playing a tune called 'Looking for Henry Lee'."

"Henry Lee?" Mrs. Rachels said, turning around from the sink. Her face, usually blotched with pink, like the skin of an apple, was white.

"It's an old song of the fifties."

It was while saying that that I realized what was happening in the house. I naturally didn't say anything to Mrs. Rachels, and I at once began to regret that I'd said anything in the first place. It had frightened me, finding the bathroom like that, and clearly it must have frightened the Rachels. I didn't want them to be frightened because naturally there was nothing to be frightened about. George and Alice and Isabel wouldn't hurt anyone, not unless death had changed them enormously. But even so I knew I couldn't ever explain that to the Rachels.

"Well, I suppose I'm just getting absent-minded," I said. "People do, so they say, when they live alone." I laughed to show I wasn't worried or frightened, to make it all seem ordinary.

"You mean, you laid the table yourself?" Mrs. Rachels said. "And had a bath?"

"And didn't turn the wireless off properly. Funny," I said, "how these things go in threes. Funny, how there's always an explanation." I laughed again and Mrs. Rachels had to laugh too.

After that it was lovely, just like being back in 17 Lorelei Avenue. I bought Black Magic chocolates and bars of Fry's and Cadbury's Milk, all the things we'd liked. I often found bathwater left in and the towels crumpled, and now and again I came down in the morning to find the breakfast table laid. On the first-floor landing, on the evening of March 11th, I caught a glimpse of George, and in the garden, three days later, I saw Isabel and Alice.

On March 15th the Rachels left. I hadn't said a word to them about finding the bathroom used again or the breakfast laid or actually seeing the children. I'd been cheerful and smiling whenever I met them. I'd talked about how Brasso wasn't as good as it used to be to Mrs. Rachels, and had asked her husband about the best kinds of soil for bulbs.

"We can't stay a minute more," Mrs. Rachels said, her face all white and tight in the hall, and then to my astonishment they attempted to persuade me to go also.

"The house isn't fit to live in," Mr. Rachels said.

"Oh now, that's nonsense," I began to say, but they both shook their heads.

"There's children here," Mrs. Rachels said. "There's three children appearing all over the place."

"Come right up to you," Mr. Rachels said. "Laugh at you sometimes."

They were trembling, both of them. They were so terrified I thought they might die, that their hearts would give out there in the hall and they'd just drop down. But they didn't. They walked out of the hall door with their three suitcases, down the drive to catch a bus. I never saw them again.

I suppose, Mr. Mockler, you have to be frightened of ghosts: I suppose that's their way of communicating. I mean, it's no good being like me, delighting in it all, being happy because I wasn't lonely in that house any more. You have to be like the Rachels, terrified half out of your wits. I think I knew that as I watched the Rachels go: I think I knew that George and Isabel and Alice would go with them, that I was only a kind of go-between, that the Rachels were what George and Isabel and Alice could really have fun with. I almost ran after the Rachels, but I knew it would be no good.

Without the Rachels and my brother and my two sisters, I was frightened myself in that big house. I moved everything into the kitchen: the television set and the plants I kept in the drawing-room, and a camp-bed to sleep on. I was there, asleep in the camp-bed, when my husband returned from Germany; he had changed completely. He raved at me, not listening to a word I said. There were cups of tea all over the house, he said, and bits of bread and biscuits and cake and chocolates. There were notes in envelopes, and messages scrawled in my hand-writing on the wallpaper in various rooms. Everywhere was dusty. Where, he wanted to know, were the Rachels?

He stood there with a canvas bag in his left hand, an airline bag that had the word Lufthansa *on it. He'd put on at least a stone, I remember thinking, and his hair was shorter than before.*

"Listen," I said. "I would like to tell you." And I tried to tell him, as I've told you, Mr. Mockler, about George and Isabel and Alice in 17 Lorelei Avenue and how we all went together for a walk with our dog, every Sunday afternoon in Richmond Park, and how on Christmas Eve my mother always gave a party. I told him about the stained-glass pane in the window, Moses in the bulrushes, and the hide-and-seek we played, and how my father and I always shared the old boot in Monopoly. I told him about the day of the accident, how the tire on the lorry suddenly exploded and how the lorry went whizzing around on the road and then just tumbled over on top of them. I'd put out cups of tea, I said, and biscuits and cake and the little messages, just in case they came back again—not for them to eat or to read particularly, but just as a sign. They'd given me a sign first, I explained: George had turned on my wireless in the middle of the night and Isabel had had baths and Alice had laid the breakfast table. But then they'd gone because they'd been more interested in annoying the Rachels than in comforting me. I began to weep, telling him how lonely I'd been without them, how lonely I'd been ever since the day of the accident, how the silence had been everywhere. I couldn't control myself: tears came out of my eyes as though they'd never stop. I felt sickness all over my body, paining me in my head and my chest, sour in my stomach. I wanted to die because the loneliness was too much. Loneliness was the worst thing in the world, I said, gasp-

ing out words, with spit and tears going cold on my face. People were only shadows, I tried to explain, when you had loneliness and silence like that, like a shroud around you. You couldn't reach out of the shroud sometimes, you couldn't connect because shadows are hard to connect with and it's frightening when you try because everyone is looking at you. But it was lovely, I whispered, when the children came back to annoy the Rachels. My husband replied by telling me I was insane.

The letter finished there, and Mr. Mockler was more astonished each time he read it. He had never in his life received such a document before, nor did he in fact very often receive letters of any kind, apart from bills and, if he was fortunate, checks in settlement. He shook his head over the letter and placed it in the inside pocket of his jacket.

That day, as he stitched and measured, he imagined the place Mrs. Acland wrote of, the secluded house with twenty female inmates, and the lawn and the rose-beds. He imagined the other house, 17 Lorelei Avenue in Richmond, and the third house, the Victorian residence in the Worcestershire countryside. He imagined Mrs. Acland's obese husband with his short hair and his airplane fasteners, and the children who had been killed in a motor-car accident, and Mr. and Mrs. Rachels whom they had haunted. All day long the faces of these people flitted through Mr. Mockler's mind, with old Miss Acheson and Sarah Crookham and Dr. Scott-Rowe and Dr. Friendman. In the evening, when he met his friends Mr. Tile and Mr. Uprichard in the Charles the First, he showed them the letter before even ordering them drinks.

"Well, I'm beggared," remarked Mr. Uprichard, a man known locally for his gentle nature. "That poor creature."

Mr. Tile, who was not given to expressing himself, shook his head.

Mr. Mockler asked Mr. Uprichard if he should visit this Mrs. Acland. "Poor creature," Mr. Uprichard said again, and added that without a doubt Mrs. Acland had written to a stranger because of the loneliness she mentioned, the loneliness like a shroud around her.

Some weeks later Mr. Mockler, having given the matter further thought and continuing to be affected by the contents of the letter, took a Green Line bus out of London to the address that Mrs. Acland had given him. He made inquiries, feeling quite adventurous, and was told that the house was three-quarters of a mile from where the bus had dropped him, down a side road. He found it without further difficulty. It was a house surrounded by a high brick wall in which large, black wrought-iron gates were backed with sheets of tin so that no one could look through the ornamental scrollwork. The gates were locked. Mr. Mockler rang a bell in the wall.

"Yes?" a man said, opening the gate that was on Mr. Mockler's left.

"Well," said Mr. Mockler and found it difficult to proceed.

"Yes?" the man said.

"Well, I've had a letter. Asking me to come, I think. My name's Mockler."

The man opened the gate a little more and Mr. Mockler stepped through.

The man walked ahead of him and Mr. Mockler saw the lawns that had been described, and the rose-beds. The house he considered most attractive: a high Georgian building with beautiful windows. An old woman was walking slowly by herself with the assistance of a stick: Miss Acheson, Mr. Mockler guessed. In the distance he saw other women, walking slowly on leaf-strewn paths.

Autumn was Mr. Mockler's favorite season and he was glad to be in the country on this pleasantly autumnal day. He thought of remarking on this to the man who led him towards the house, but since the man did not incline towards conversation he did not do so.

In the yellow waiting-room there were no magazines and no pictures on the walls and no flowers. It was not a room in which Mr. Mockler would have cared to wait for long, and in fact he did not have to. A woman dressed as a nurse except that she wore a green cardigan came in. She smiled briskly at him and said that

Dr. Friendman would see him. She asked Mr. Mockler to follow her.

"How very good of you to come," Dr. Friendman said, smiling at Mr. Mockler in the way that Mrs. Acland had described in her letter. "How very humane," said Dr. Friendman.

"I had a letter, from a Mrs. Acland."

"Quite so, Mr. Mockler. Mr. Mockler, could I press you towards a glass of sherry?"

Mr. Mockler, surprised at this line of talk, accepted the sherry, saying it was good of Dr. Friendman. He drank the sherry while Dr. Friendman read the letter. When he'd finished, Dr. Friendman crossed to the window of the room and pulled aside a curtain and asked Mr. Mockler if he'd mind looking out.

There was a courtyard, small and cobbled, in which a gardener was sweeping leaves into a pile. At the far end of it, sitting on a tapestry-backed dining-chair in the autumn sunshine, was a woman in a blue dress. "Try these," said Dr. Friendman and handed Mr. Mockler a pair of binoculars.

It was a beautiful face, thin and seeming fragile, with large blue eyes and lips that were now slightly parted, smiling in the sunshine. Hair the color of corn was simply arranged, hanging on either side of the face and curling in around it. The hair shone in the sunlight, as though it was for ever being brushed.

"I find them useful," Dr. Friendman said, taking the binoculars from Mr. Mockler's hands. "You have to keep an eye, you know."

"That's Mrs. Acland?" Mr. Mockler asked.

"That's the lady who wrote to you: the letter's a bit inaccurate, Mr. Mockler. It wasn't quite like that in 17 Lorelei Avenue."

"Not quite like it?"

"She cannot forget Lorelei Avenue. I'm afraid she never will. That beautiful woman, Mr. Mockler, was a beautiful girl, yet she married the first man who asked her, a widower thirty years older than her, a fat designer of aircraft fasteners. He pays her bills just as she says in her letter, and even when he's dead they'll go on being paid. He used to visit her at first, but he found it too painful. He stood in this very room one day, Mr. Mockler, and said to Dr. Scott-Rowe that no man had ever been appreciated by a woman as much as he had by her. And all because he'd been kind to her in the most ordinary ways."

Mr. Mockler said he was afraid that he didn't know what Dr. Friendman was talking about. As though he hadn't heard this quiet protest, Dr. Friendman smiled and said:

"But it was, unfortunately, too late for kindness. 17 Lorelei Avenue had done its damage, like a cancer in her mind: she could not forget her childhood."

"Yes, she says in her letter. George and Alice and Isabel—"

"All her childhood, Mr. Mockler, her parents did not speak to one another. They didn't quarrel, they didn't address each other in any way whatsoever. When she was five they'd come to an agreement: that they should both remain in 17 Lorelei Avenue because neither would ever have agreed to give up an inch of the child they'd between them caused to be born. In the house there was nothing, Mr. Mockler, for all her childhood years: nothing except silence."

"But there was George and Alice and Isabel—"

"No, Mr. Mockler. There was no George and no Alice and no Isabel. No hide-and-seek or parties on Christmas Eve, no Monopoly on Sundays by the fire. Can you imagine 17 Lorelei Avenue, Mr. Mockler, as she is now incapable of imagining it? Two people so cruel to one another that they knew that either of them could be parted from the child in some divorce court. A woman bitterly hating the man whom once she'd loved, and he returning each evening, hurrying back from an office in case his wife and the child were having a conversation. She would sit, Mr. Mockler, in a room with them, with the silence heavy in the air, and their hatred for one another. All three of them would sit down to a meal and no one would speak. No other children came to that house, no other people. She used to hide on the way back from school: she'd go down the area steps of other houses and crouch beside dustbins."

"Dustbins?" repeated Mr. Mockler, more astonished than ever. *"Dustbins?"*

"Other children didn't take to her. She couldn't talk to them.

She'd never learned to talk to anyone. He was a patient man, Mr. Acland, when he came along, a good and patient man.''

Mr. Mockler said that the child's parents must have been monsters, but Dr. Friendman shook his head. No one was a monster, Dr. Friendman said in a professional manner, and in the circumstances Mr. Mockler didn't feel he could argue with him. But the people called Rachels were real, he did point out, as real as the fat designer of aircraft fasteners. Had they left the house, he asked, as it said in the letter? And if they had, what had they been frightened of?

Dr. Friendman smiled again. "I don't believe in ghosts," he said, and he explained at great length to Mr. Mockler that it was Mrs. Acland herself who had frightened the Rachels, turning on a wireless in the middle of the night and running baths and laying tables for people who weren't there. Mr. Mockler listened and was interested to note that Dr. Friendman used words that were not easy to understand, and quoted from experts who were in Dr. Friendman's line of business but whose names meant nothing to Mr. Mockler.

Mr. Mockler, listening to all of it, nodded but was not convinced. The Rachels had left the house, just as the letter said: he knew that, he felt it in his bones and it felt like the truth. The Rachels had been frightened of Mrs. Acland's ghosts even though they'd been artificial ghosts. They'd been real to her, and they'd been real to the Rachels because she'd made them so. Shadows had stepped out of her mind because in her loneliness she'd wished them to. They'd laughed and played, and frightened the Rachels half out of their wits.

"There's always an explanation," said Dr. Friendman.

Mr. Mockler nodded, profoundly disagreeing.

"She'll think you're Mr. Rachels," said Dr. Friendman, "come to say he saw the ghosts. If you wouldn't mind saying you did, it keeps her happy."

"But it's the truth," Mr. Mockler cried with passion in his voice. "Of course it's the truth: there can be ghosts like that, just as there can be in any other way."

"Oh, come now," murmured Dr. Friendman with his sad, humane smile.

Mr. Mockler followed Dr. Friendman from the room. They crossed a landing and descended a back staircase, passing near a kitchen in which a chef with a tall chef's hat was beating pieces of meat. "Ah, Wiener schnitzel," said Dr. Friendman.

In the cobbled courtyard the gardener had finished sweeping up the leaves and was wheeling them away in a wheelbarrow. The woman was still sitting on the tapestry-backed chair, still smiling in the autumn sunshine.

"Look," said Dr. Friendman, "a visitor."

The woman rose and went close to Mr. Mockler. "They didn't mean to frighten you," she said, "even though it's the only way ghosts can communicate. They were only having fun, Mr. Rachels."

"I think Mr. Rachels realizes that now," Dr. Friendman said.

"Yes, of course," said Mr. Mockler.

"No one ever believed me, and I kept on saying, "When the Rachels come back, they'll tell the truth about poor George and Alice and Isabel." You saw them, didn't you, Mr. Rachels?"

"Yes," Mr. Mockler said. "We saw them."

She turned and walked away, leaving the tapestry-backed chair behind her.

"You're a humane person," Dr. Friendman said, holding out his right hand, which Mr. Mockler shook. The same man led him back through the lawns and the rose-beds, to the gates.

It was an experience that Mr. Mockler found impossible to forget. He measured and stitched, and talked to his friends Mr. Uprichard and Mr. Tile in the Charles the First; he went for a walk morning and evening, and no day passed during which he did not think of the woman whom people looked at through binoculars. Somewhere in England, or at least somewhere in the world, the Rachels were probably still alive, and had Mr. Mockler been a younger man he might even have set about looking for them. He would have liked to bring them to the secluded house where the woman now lived, to have been there himself when they told the truth to Dr. Friendman. It seemed a sadness, as he once remarked to Mr. Uprichard, that on top of everything else a woman's artificial ghosts should not be honored, since she had brought them into being and given them life, as other women give children life.

THE
LEAF-SWEEPER

Muriel Spark

Behind the town hall there is a wooded parkland which, towards the end of November, begins to draw a thin blue cloud right into itself; and as a rule the park floats in this haze until mid-February. I pass every day, and see Johnnie Geddes in the heart of this mist, sweeping up the leaves. Now and again he stops, and jerking his long head erect, looks indignantly at the pile of leaves, as if it ought not to be there; then he sweeps on. This business of leaf-sweeping he learnt during the years he spent in the asylum; it was the job they always gave him to do; and when he was discharged the town council gave him the leaves to sweep. But the indignant movement of the head comes naturally to him, for this has been one of his habits since he was the most promising and buoyant and vociferous graduate of his year. He looks much older than he is, for it is not quite twenty years ago that Johnnie founded the Society for the Abolition of Christmas.

Johnnie was living with his aunt then. I was at school, and in the Christmas holidays Miss Geddes gave me her nephew's pamphlet, *How to Grow Rich at Christmas.* It sounded very likely, but it turned out that you grow rich at Christmas by doing away with Christmas, and so pondered Johnnie's pamphlet no further.

But it was only his first attempt. He had, within the next three years, founded his society of Abolitionists. His new book, *Abolish Christmas or We Die,* was in great demand at the public library, and my turn for it came at last. Johnnie was really convincing, this time, and most people were completely won over until after they had closed the book. I got an old copy for sixpence the other day, and despite the lapse of time it still proves conclusively that Christmas is a national crime. Johnnie demonstrates that every human-unit in the kingdom faces inevitable starvation within a period inversely proportional to that in which one in every six industrial-productivity units, if you see what he means, stops producing toys to fill the stockings of the educational-intake units. He cites appalling statistics to show that 1.024 per cent of the time squandered each Christmas in reckless shopping and thoughtless churchgoing brings the nation closer to its doom by five years. A few readers protested, but Johnnie was able to demolish their muddled arguments, and meanwhile the Society for the Abolition of Christmas increased. But Johnnie was troubled. Not only did Christmas rage throughout the kingdom as usual that year, but he had private information that many of the Society's members had broken the Oath of Abstention.

He decided, then, to strike at the very roots of Christmas. Johnnie gave up his job on the Drainage Supply Board; he gave up all his prospects, and, financed by a few supporters, retreated for two years to study the roots of Christmas. Then, all jubilant, Johnnie produced his next and last book, in which he established, either that Christmas was an invention of the Early Fathers to propitiate the pagans, or it was invented by the pagans to placate the Early Fathers, I forget which. Against the advice of his friends, Johnnie entitled it *Christmas and Christianity*. It sold eighteen copies. Johnnie never really recovered from this; and it happened, about that time, that the girl he was engaged to, an ardent Abolitionist, sent him a pullover she had knitted, for Christmas; he sent it back, enclosing a copy of the Society's rules, and she sent back the ring. But in any case, during Johnnie's absence, the Society had been undermined by a moderate faction. These moderates finally became more moderate, and the whole thing broke up.

Soon after this, I left the district, and it was some years before I saw Johnnie again. One Sunday afternoon in summer, I was idling among the crowds who were gathered to hear the speakers at

Hyde Park. One little crowd surrounded a man who bore a banner marked "Crusade against Christmas"; his voice was frightening; it carried an unusually long way. This was Johnnie. A man in the crowd told me Johnnie was there every Sunday, very violent about Christmas, and that he would soon be taken up for insulting language. As I saw in the papers, he was soon taken up for insulting language. And a few months later I heard that poor Johnnie was in a mental home, because he had Christmas on the brain and couldn't stop shouting about it.

After that I forgot all about him until three years ago, in December, I went to live near the town where Johnnie had spent his youth. On the afternoon of Christmas Eve I was walking with a friend, noticing what had changed in my absence, and what hadn't. We passed a long, large house, once famous for its armory, and I saw that the iron gates were wide open.

"They used to be kept shut," I said.

"That's an asylum now," said my friend; "they let the mild cases work in the grounds, and leave the gates open to give them a feeling of freedom."

"But," said my friend, "they lock everything inside. Door after door. The lift as well; they keep it locked."

While my friend was chattering, I stood in the gateway and looked in. Just beyond the gate was a great bare elm-tree. There I saw a man in brown corduroys, sweeping up the leaves. Poor soul, he was shouting about Christmas.

"That's Johnnie Geddes," I said. "Has he been here all these years?"

"Yes," said my friend as we walked on. "I believe he gets worse at this time of year."

"Does his aunt see him?"

"Yes. And she sees nobody else."

We were, in fact, approaching the house where Miss Geddes lived. I suggested we call on her. I had known her well.

"No fear," said my friend.

I decided to go in, all the same, and my friend walked on to the town.

Miss Geddes had changed, more than the landscape. She had

been a solemn, calm woman, and now she moved about quickly, and gave short agitated smiles. She took me to her sitting-room, and as she opened the door she called to someone inside,

"Johnnie, see who's come to see us!"

A man, dressed in a dark suit, was standing on a chair, fixing holly behind a picture. He jumped down.

"Happy Christmas," he said. "A Happy and a Merry Christmas indeed. I do hope," he said, "you're going to stay for tea, as we've got a delightful Christmas cake, and at this season of goodwill I would be cheered indeed if you could see how charmingly it's decorated; it has 'Happy Christmas' in red icing, and then there's a robin and—"

"Johnnie," said Miss Geddes, "you're forgetting the carols."

"The carols," he said. He lifted a gramophone record from a pile and put it on. It was "The Holly and the Ivy."

"It's 'The Holly and the Ivy,'" said Miss Geddes. "Can't we have something else? We had that all morning."

"It is sublime," he said, beaming from his chair, and holding up his hand for silence.

While Miss Geddes went to fetch the tea, and he sat absorbed in his carol, I watched him. He was so like Johnnie, that if I hadn't seen poor Johnnie a few moments before, sweeping up the asylum leaves, I would have thought he really was Johnnie. Miss Geddes returned with the tray, and while he rose to put on another record, he said something that startled me.

"I saw you in the crowd that Sunday when I was speaking at Hyde Park."

"What a memory you have!" said Miss Geddes.

"It must be ten years ago," he said.

"My nephew has altered his opinion of Christmas," she explained. "He always comes home for Christmas now, and don't we have a jolly time, Johnnie?"

"Rather!" he said. "Oh, let me cut the cake."

He was very excited about the cake. With a flourish he dug a large knife into the side. The knife slipped, and I saw it run deep into his finger. Miss Geddes did not move. He wrenched his cut finger away, and went on slicing the cake.

"Isn't it bleeding?" I said.

He held up his hand. I could see the deep cut, but there was no blood.

Deliberately, and perhaps desperately, I turned to Miss Geddes.

"That house up the road," I said, "I see it's a mental home now. I passed it this afternoon."

"Johnnie," said Miss Geddes, as one who knows the game is up, "go and fetch the mince-pies."

He went, whistling a carol.

"You passed the asylum," said Miss Geddes wearily.

"Yes," I said.

"And you saw Johnnie sweeping up the leaves."

"Yes."

We could still hear the whistling of the carol.

"Who is *he?*" I said.

"That's Johnnie's ghost," she said. "He comes home every Christmas.

"But," she said, "I don't like him. I can't bear him any longer, and I'm going away tomorrow. I don't want Johnnie's ghost, I want Johnnie in flesh and blood."

I shuddered, thinking of the cut finger that could not bleed. And I left, before Johnnie's ghost returned with the mince-pies.

Next day, as I had arranged to join a family who lived in the town, I started walking over about noon. Because of the light mist, I didn't see at first who it was approaching. It was a man, waving his arm to me. It turned out to be Johnnie's ghost.

"Happy Christmas. What do you think," said Johnnie's ghost, "my aunt has gone to London. Fancy, on Christmas day, and I thought she was at church, and here I am without anyone to spend a jolly Christmas with, and, of course, I forgive her, as it's the season of goodwill, but I'm glad to see you, because now I can come with you, wherever it is you're going, and we can all have a Happy . . ."

"Go away," I said, and walked on.

It sounds hard. But perhaps you don't know how repulsive and loathsome is the ghost of a living man. The ghosts of the dead may be all right, but the ghost of mad Johnnie gave me the creeps.

"Clear off," I said.

He continued walking beside me. "As it's the time of goodwill, I make allowances for your tone," he said. "But I'm coming."

We had reached the asylum gates, and there, in the grounds, I saw Johnnie sweeping the leaves. I suppose it was his way of going on strike, working on Christmas day. He was making a noise about Christmas.

On a sudden impulse I said to Johnnie's ghost, "You want company?"

"Certainly," he replied. "It's the season of . . ."

"Then you shall have it," I said.

I stood in the gateway. "Oh, Johnnie," I called.

He looked up.

"I've brought your ghost to see you, Johnnie."

"Well, well," said Johnnie, advancing to meet his ghost. "Just imagine it!"

"Happy Christmas," said Johnnie's ghost.

"Oh, really?" said Johnnie.

I left them to it. And when I looked back, wondering if they would come to blows, I saw that Johnnie's ghost was sweeping the leaves as well. They seemed to be arguing at the same time. But it was still misty, and really, I can't say whether, when I looked a second time, there were two men or one man sweeping the leaves.

Johnnie began to improve in the New Year. At least, he stopped shouting about Christmas, and then he never mentioned it at all; in a few months, when he had almost stopped saying anything, they discharged him.

The town council gave him the leaves of the park to sweep. He seldom speaks, and recognizes nobody. I see him every day at the late end of the year, working within the mist. Sometimes, if there is a sudden gust, he jerks his head up to watch a few leaves falling behind him, as if amazed that they are undeniably there, although, by rights, the falling of leaves should be stopped.

POMEGRANATE
SEED

Edith Wharton

Charlotte Ashby paused on her doorstep. Dark had descended on the brilliancy of the March afternoon, and the grinding, rasping street life of the city was at its highest. She turned her back on it, standing for a moment in the old-fashioned, marble-flagged vestibule before she inserted her key in the lock. The sash curtains drawn across the panes of the inner door softened the light within to a warm blur through which no details showed. It was the hour when, in the first months of her marriage to Kenneth Ashby, she had most liked to return to that quiet house in a street long since deserted by business and fashion. The contrast between the soulless roar of New York, its devouring blaze of lights, the oppression of its congested traffic, congested houses, lives, minds and this veiled sanctuary she called home, always stirred her profoundly. In the very heart of the hurricane she had found her tiny islet—or thought she had. And now, in the last months, everything was changed, and she always wavered on the doorstep and had to force herself to enter.*

While she stood there she called up the scene within: the hall hung with old prints, the ladder-like stairs, and on the left her husband's long shabby library, full of books and pipes and worn

* Persephone, daughter of Demeter, goddess of fertility, was abducted and taken to Hades by Pluto, the god of the underworld. Her mother begged Jupiter to intercede, and he did so. But Persephone had broken her vow of abstinence in Hades by eating some pomegranate seeds. She was therefore required to spend a certain number of months each year—essentially the winter months—with Pluto.

armchairs inviting to meditation. How she had loved that room! Then, upstairs, her own drawing room, in which, since the death of Kenneth's first wife, neither furniture nor hangings had been changed, because there had never been money enough, but which Charlotte had made her own by moving furniture about and adding more books, another lamp, a table for the new reviews. Even on the occasion of her only visit to the first Mrs. Ashby—a distant, self-centered woman, whom she had known very slightly—she had looked about her with an innocent envy, feeling it to be exactly the drawing room she would have liked for herself; and now for more than a year it had been hers to deal with as she chose—the room to which she hastened back at dusk on winter days, where she sat reading by the fire, or answering notes at the pleasant roomy desk, or going over her stepchildren's copybooks, till she heard her husband's step.

Sometimes friends dropped in; sometimes—oftener—she was alone; and she liked that best, since it was another way of being with Kenneth, thinking over what he had said when they parted in the morning, imagining what he would say when he sprang up the stairs, found her by herself and caught her to him.

Now, instead of this, she thought of one thing only—the letter she might or might not find on the hall table. Until she had made sure whether or not it was there, her mind had no room for anything else. The letter was always the same—a square grayish envelope with "Kenneth Ashby, Esquire," written on it in bold but faint characters. From the first it had struck Charlotte as peculiar that anyone who wrote such a firm hand should trace the letters so lightly; the address was always written as though there were not enough ink in the pen, or the writer's wrist were too weak to bear upon it. Another curious thing was that, in spite of its masculine curves, the writing was so visibly feminine. Some hands are sexless, some masculine, at first glance; the writing on the gray envelope, for all its strength and assurance, was without a doubt a woman's. The envelope never bore anything but the recipient's name; no stamp, no address. The letter was presumably delivered by hand—but whose? No doubt it was slipped into the letter box, whence the parlormaid, when she closed the shut-

ters and lit the lights, probably extracted it. At any rate, it was
always in the evening, after dark, that Charlotte saw it lying there.
She thought of the letter in the singular, as "it," because, though
there had been several since her marriage—seven, to be exact—
they were so alike in appearance that they had become merged
in one another in her mind, become one letter, become "it."

The first had come the day after their return from their honeymoon—a journey prolonged to the West Indies, from which they
had returned to New York after an absence of more than two
months. Re-entering the house with her husband, late on that
first evening—they had dined at his mother's—she had seen,
alone on the hall table, the gray envelope. Her eye fell on it
before Kenneth's, and her first thought was: "Why, I've seen that
writing before"; but where she could not recall. The memory
was just definite enough for her to identify the script whenever it
looked up at her faintly from the same pale envelope; but on that
first day she would have thought no more of the letter if, when
her husband's glance lit on it, she had not chanced to be looking
at him. It all happened in a flash—his seeing the letter, putting
out his hand for it, raising it to his shortsighted eyes to decipher
the faint writing, and then abruptly withdrawing the arm he had
slipped through Charlotte's, and moving away to the hanging
light, his back turned to her. She had waited—waited for a sound,
an exclamation; waited for him to open the letter; but he had
slipped it into his pocket without a word and followed her into
the library. And there they had sat down by the fire and lit their
cigarettes, and he had remained silent, his head thrown back
broodingly against the armchair, his eyes fixed on the hearth, and
presently had passed his hand over his forehead and said: "Wasn't
it unusually hot at my mother's tonight? I've got a splitting head.
Mind if I take myself off to bed?"

That was the first time. Since then Charlotte had never been
present when he had received the letter. It usually came before
he got home from his office, and she had to go upstairs and leave
it lying there. But even if she had not seen it, she would have
known it had come by the change in his face when he joined
her—which, on those evenings, he seldom did before they met

for dinner. Evidently, whatever the letter contained, he wanted to be by himself to deal with it; and when he reappeared he looked years older, looked emptied of life and courage, and hardly conscious of her presence. Sometimes he was silent for the rest of the evening; and if he spoke, it was usually to hint some criticism of her household arrangements, suggest some change in the domestic administration, to ask, a little nervously, if she didn't think Joyce's nursery governess was rather young and flighty, or if she herself always saw to it that Peter—whose throat was delicate—was properly wrapped up when he went to school. At such times Charlotte would remember the friendly warnings she had received when she became engaged to Kenneth Ashby: "Marrying a heartbroken widower! Isn't that rather risky? You know Elsie Ashby absolutely dominated him"; and how she had jokingly replied: "He may be glad of a little liberty for a change." And in this respect she had been right. She had needed no one to tell her, during the first months, that her husband was perfectly happy with her. When they came back from their protracted honeymoon the same friends said: "What have you done to Kenneth? He looks twenty years younger"; and this time she answered with careless joy: "I suppose I've got him out of his groove."

But what she noticed after the gray letters began to come was not so much his nervous tentative faultfinding—which always seemed to be uttered against his will—as the look in his eyes when he joined her after receiving one of the letters. The look was not unloving, not even indifferent; it was the look of a man who had been so far away from ordinary events that when he returns to familiar things they seem strange. She minded that more than the faultfinding.

Though she had been sure from the first that the handwriting on the gray envelope was a woman's, it was long before she associated the mysterious letters with any sentimental secret. She was too sure of her husband's love, too confident of filling his life, for such an idea to occur to her. It seemed far more likely that the letters—which certainly did not appear to cause him any sentimental pleasure—were addressed to the busy lawyer than to the private person. Probably they were from some tiresome client—women, he had often told her, were nearly always tiresome as clients—who did not want her letters opened by his secretary and therefore had them carried to his house. Yes; but in that case the unknown female must be unusually troublesome, judging from the effect her letters produced. Then again, though his professional discretion was exemplary, it was odd that he had never uttered an impatient comment, never remarked to Charlotte, in a moment of expansion, that there was a nuisance of a woman who kept badgering him about a case that had gone against her. He had made more than one semiconfidence of the kind—of course without giving names or details; but concerning this mysterious correspondent his lips were sealed.

There was another possibility: what is euphemistically called an "old entanglement." Charlotte Ashby was a sophisticated woman. She had few illusions about the intricacies of the human heart; she knew that there were often old entanglements. But when she had married Kenneth Ashby, her friends, instead of hinting at such a possibility, had said: "You've got your work cut out for you. Marrying a Don Juan is a sinecure to it. Kenneth's never looked at another woman since he first saw Elsie Corder. During all the years of their marriage he was more like an unhappy lover than a comfortably contented husband. He'll never let you move an armchair or change the place of a lamp; and whatever you venture to do, he'll mentally compare with what Elsie would have done in your place."

Except for an occasional nervous mistrust as to her ability to manage the children—a mistrust gradually dispelled by her good humor and the children's obvious fondness for her—none of these forebodings had come true. The desolate widower, of whom his nearest friends said that only his absorbing professional interests had kept him from suicide after his first wife's death, had fallen in love, two years later, with Charlotte Gorse, and after an impetuous wooing had married her and carried her off on a tropical honeymoon. And ever since he had been as tender and lover-like as during those first radiant weeks. Before asking her to marry him he had spoken to her frankly of his great love for his first wife and his despair after her sudden death; but even then he had assumed no stricken attitude, or implied that life offered no possibility of renewal. He had been perfectly simple and natural, and had confessed to Charlotte that from the beginning he had hoped the future held new gifts for him. And when, after their marriage, they returned to the house where his twelve years with his first wife had been spent, he had told Charlotte at once that he was sorry he couldn't afford to do the place over for her, but that he knew every woman had her own views about furniture and all sorts of household arrangements a man would never notice, and had begged her to make any changes she saw fit without bothering to consult him. As a result, she made as few as possible; but his way of beginning their new life in the old setting was so frank and unembarrassed that it put her immediately at her ease, and she was almost sorry to find that the portrait of Elsie Ashby, which used to hang over the desk in his library, had been transferred in their absence to the children's nursery. Knowing herself to be the indirect cause of this banishment, she spoke of it to her husband; but he answered: "Oh, I thought they ought to grow up with her looking down on them." The answer moved Charlotte, and satisfied her; and as time went by she had to confess that she felt more at home in her house, more at ease and in confidence with her husband, since that long coldly beautiful face on the library wall no longer followed her with guarded eyes. It was as if Kenneth's love had penetrated to the secret she hardly acknowledged to her own heart—her passionate need to feel herself the sovereign even of his past.

With all this stored-up happiness to sustain her, it was curious that she had lately found herself yielding to a nervous apprehension. But there the apprehension was; and on this particular afternoon—perhaps because she was more tired than usual, or because of the trouble of finding a new cook or, for some other ridiculously trivial reason, moral or physical—she found herself unable to react against the feeling. Latchkey in hand, she looked back down the silent street to the whirl and illumination of the great thoroughfare beyond, and up at the sky already aflare with the city's nocturnal life. "Outside there," she thought, "skyscrapers, advertisements, telephones, wireless, airplanes, movies, motors, and all the rest of the twentieth century; and on the other side of the door something I can't explain, can't relate to them. Something as old as the world, as mysterious as life. . . . Nonsense! What am I worrying about? There hasn't been a letter for three months now—not since the day we came back from the country after Christmas. . . . Queer that they always seem to come after our holidays! . . . Why should I imagine there's going to be one tonight!"

No reason why, but that was the worst of it—one of the worst!—that there were days when she would stand there cold and shivering with the premonition of something inexplicable, intolerable, to be faced on the other side of the curtained panes; and when she opened the door and went in, there would be nothing; and on other days when she felt the same premonitory chill, it was justified by the sight of the gray envelope. So that ever since the last had come she had taken to feeling cold and premonitory every evening, because she never opened the door without thinking the letter might be there.

Well, she'd had enough of it: that was certain. She couldn't go on like that. If her husband turned white and had a headache on the days when the letter came, he seemed to recover afterward; but she couldn't. With her the strain had become chronic, and the reason was not far to seek. Her husband knew from whom the letter came and what was in it; he was prepared beforehand for whatever he had to deal with, and master of the situation, however bad; whereas she was shut out in the dark with her conjectures.

"I can't stand it! I can't stand it another day!" she exclaimed aloud, as she put her key in the lock. She turned the key and went in; and there, on the table, lay the letter.

II

She was almost glad of the sight. It seemed to justify everything, to put a seal of definiteness on the whole blurred business. A letter for her husband; a letter from a woman—no doubt another vulgar case of "old entanglement." What a fool she had been ever to doubt it, to rack her brains for less obvious explanations! She took up the envelope with a steady contemptuous hand, looked closely at the faint letters, held it against the light and just discerned the outline of the folded sheet within. She knew now she would have no peace till she found out what was written on that sheet.

Her husband had not come in; he seldom got back from his office before half-past six or seven, and it was not yet six. She would have time to take the letter up to the drawing room, hold it over the tea kettle which at that hour always simmered by the fire in expectation of her return, solve the mystery and replace the letter where she had found it. No one would be the wiser, and her gnawing uncertainty would be over. The alternative, of course, was to question her husband; but to do that seemed even more difficult. She weighed the letter between thumb and finger, looked at it again under the light, started up the stairs with the envelope—and came down again and laid it on the table.

"No, I evidently can't," she said disappointed.

What should she do, then? She couldn't go up alone to that warm welcoming room, pour out her tea, look over her correspondence, glance at a book or review—not with that letter lying below and the knowledge that in a little while her husband would come in, open it and turn into the library alone, as he always did on the days when the gray envelope came.

Suddenly she decided. She would wait in the library and see for herself; see what happened between him and the letter when they thought themselves unobserved. She wondered the idea had never occurred to her before. By leaving the door ajar, and sitting in the corner behind it, she could watch him unseen. . . . Well, then, she would watch him! She drew a chair into the corner, sat down, her eyes on the crack, and waited.

As far as she could remember, it was the first time she had ever tried to surprise another person's secret, but she was conscious of no compunction. She simply felt as if she were fighting her way through a stifling fog that she must at all costs get out of.

At length she heard Kenneth's latchkey and jumped up. The impulse to rush out and meet him had nearly made her forget why she was there; but she remembered in time and sat down again. From her post she covered the whole range of his movements—saw him enter the hall, draw the key from the door and take off his hat and overcoat. Then he turned to throw his gloves on the hall table, and at that moment he saw the envelope. The light was full on his face, and what Charlotte first noted there was a look of surprise. Evidently he had not expected the letter—had not thought of the possibility of its being there that day. But though he had not expected it, now that he saw it he knew well enough what it contained. He did not open it immediately, but stood motionless, the color slowly ebbing from his face. Apparently he could not make up his mind to touch it; but at length he put out his hand, opened the envelope, and moved with it to the light. In doing so he turned his back on Charlotte, and she saw only his bent head and slightly stooping shoulders. Apparently all the writing was on one page, for he did not turn the sheet but continued to stare at it for so long that he must have reread it a dozen times—or so it seemed to the woman breathlessly watching him. At length she saw him move; he raised the letter still closer to his eyes, as though he had not fully deciphered it. Then he lowered his head, and she saw his lips touch the sheet.

"Kenneth!" she exclaimed, and went on out into the hall.

The letter clutched in his hand, her husband turned and looked at her. "Where were you?" he said, in a low bewildered voice, like a man waked out of his sleep.

"In the library, waiting for you." She tried to steady her voice: "What's the matter! What's in that letter? You look ghastly."

Her agitation seemed to calm him, and he instantly put the envelope into his pocket with a slight laugh. "Ghastly? I'm sorry. I've had a hard day in the office—one or two complicated cases. I look dog-tired, I suppose."

"You didn't look tired when you came in. It was only when you opened that letter—"

He had followed her into the library, and they stood gazing at each other. Charlotte noticed how quickly he had regained his self-control; his profession had trained him to rapid mastery of face and voice. She saw at once that she would be at a disadvan-

tage in any attempt to surprise his secret, but at the same moment she lost all desire to maneuver, to trick him into betraying
anything he wanted to conceal. Her wish was still to penetrate
the mystery, but only that she might help him to bear the burden
it implied. "Even if it *is* another woman," she thought.

"Kenneth," she said, her heart beating excitedly, "I waited
here on purpose to see you come in. I wanted to watch you while
you opened that letter."

His face, which had paled, turned to dark red; then it paled
again. "That letter? Why especially that letter?"

"Because I've noticed that whenever one of those letters
comes it seems to have such a strange effect on you."

A line of anger she had never seen before came out between
his eyes, and she said to herself: "The upper part of his face is too
narrow; this is the first time I ever noticed it."

She heard him continue, in the cool and faintly ironic tone of
the prosecuting lawyer making a point: "Ah, so you're in the
habit of watching people open their letters when they don't
know you're there?"

"Not in the habit. I never did such a thing before. But I had to
find out what she writes to you, at regular intervals, in those gray
envelopes."

He weighed this for a moment; then: "The intervals have not
been regular," he said.

"Oh, I dare say you've kept a better account of the dates than I
have," she retorted, her magnanimity vanishing at his tone. "All I
know is that every time that woman writes to you—"

"Why do you assume it's a woman?"

"It's a woman's writing. Do you deny it?"

He smiled. "No, I don't deny it. I asked only because the writing is generally supposed to look more like a man's."

Charlotte passed this over impatiently. "And this woman—
what does she write to you about?"

Again he seemed to consider a moment. "About business."

"Legal business?"

"In a way, yes. Business in general."

"You look after her affairs for her?"

"Yes."

"You've looked after them for a long time?"

"Yes. A very long time."

"Kenneth, dearest, won't you tell me who she is?"

"No. I can't." He paused, and brought out, as if with a certain hesitation: "Professional secrecy."

The blood rushed from Charlotte's heart to her temples. "Don't say that—don't!"

"Why not?"

"Because I saw you kiss the letter."

The effect of the words was so disconcerting that she instantly repented having spoken them. Her husband, who had submitted to her cross-questioning with a sort of contemptuous composure, as though he were humoring an unreasonable child, turned on her a face of terror and distress. For a minute he seemed unable to speak; then, collecting himself, with an effort, he stammered out: "The writing is very faint; you must have seen me holding the letter close to my eyes to try to decipher it."

"No; I saw you kissing it." He was silent. "Didn't I see you kissing it?"

He sank back into indifference. "Perhaps."

"Kenneth! You stand there and say that—to me?"

"What possible difference can it make to you? The letter is on business, as I told you. Do you suppose I'd lie about it? The writer is a very old friend whom I haven't seen for a long time."

"Men don't kiss business letters, even from women who are very old friends, unless they have been their lovers, and still regret them."

He shrugged his shoulders slightly and turned away, as if he considered the discussion at an end and were faintly disgusted at the turn it had taken.

"Kenneth!" Charlotte moved toward him and caught hold of his arm.

He paused with a look of weariness and laid his hand over hers. "Won't you believe me?" he asked gently.

"How can I? I've watched these letters come to you—for months now they've been coming. Ever since we came back from the West Indies—one of them greeted me the very day we arrived. And after each one of them I see their mysterious effect on you, I see you disturbed, unhappy, as if someone were trying to estrange you from me."

"No, dear; not that. Never!"

She drew back and looked at him with passionate entreaty. "Well, then, prove it to me, darling. It's so easy!"

He forced a smile. "It's not easy to prove anything to a woman who's once taken an idea into her head."

"You've only got to show me the letter."

His hand slipped from hers and he drew back and shook his head.

"You won't?"

"I can't."

"Then the woman who wrote it is your mistress."

"No, dear. No."

"Not now, perhaps. I suppose she's trying to get you back, and you're struggling, out of pity for me. My poor Kenneth!"

"I swear to you she never was my mistress."

Charlotte felt the tears rushing to her eyes. "Ah, that's worse, then—that's hopeless! The prudent ones are the kind that keep their hold on a man. We all know that." She lifted her hands and hid her face in them.

Her husband remained silent; he offered neither consolation nor denial, and at length, wiping away her tears, she raised her eyes almost timidly to his.

"Kenneth, think! We've been married such a short time. Imagine what you're making me suffer. You say you can't show me this letter. You refuse even to explain it."

"I've told you the letter is on business. I will swear to that too."

"A man will swear to anything to screen a woman. If you want me to believe you, at least tell me her name. If you'll do that, I promise you I won't ask to see the letter."

There was a long interval of suspense, during which she felt her heart beating against her ribs in quick admonitory knocks, as if warning her of the danger she was incurring.

"I can't," he said at length.

"Not even her name?"

"No."

"You can't tell me anything more?"

"No."

Again a pause; this time they seemed both to have reached the end of their arguments and to be helplessly facing each other across a baffling waste of incomprehension.

Charlotte stood breathing rapidly, her hands against her breast. She felt as if she had run a hard race and missed the goal. She had meant to move her husband and had succeeded only in irritating him; and this error of reckoning seemed to change him into a stranger, a mysterious incomprehensible being whom no argument or entreaty of hers could reach. The curious thing was that she was aware in him of no hostility or even impatience, but only of a remoteness, an inaccessibility, far more difficult to overcome. She felt herself excluded, ignored, blotted out of his life. But after a moment or two, looking at him more calmly, she saw that he was suffering as much as she was. His distant guarded face was drawn with pain; the coming of the gray envelope, though it always cast a shadow, had never marked him as deeply as this discussion with his wife.

Charlotte took heart; perhaps, after all, she had not spent her last shaft. She drew nearer and once more laid her hand on his arm. "Poor Kenneth! If you knew how sorry I am for you—"

She thought he winced slightly at this expression of sympathy, but he took her hand and pressed it.

"I can think of nothing worse than to be incapable of loving long," she continued, "to feel the beauty of a great love and to be too unstable to bear its burden."

He turned on her a look of wistful reproach. "Oh, don't say that of me. Unstable!"

She felt herself at last on the right track, and her voice trembled with excitement as she went on: "Then what about me and this other woman? Haven't you already forgotten Elsie twice within a year?"

She seldom pronounced his first wife's name; it did not come naturally to her tongue. She flung it out now as if she were flinging some dangerous explosive into the open space between them, and drew back a step, waiting to hear the mine go off.

Her husband did not move; his expression grew sadder, but showed no resentment. "I have never forgotten Elsie," he said.

Charlotte could not repress a faint laugh. "Then, you poor dear, between the three of us—"

"There are not—" he began; and then broke off and put his hand to his forehead.

"Not what?"

"I'm sorry; I don't believe I know what I'm saying. I've got a blinding headache." He looked wan and furrowed enough for the statement to be true, but she was exasperated by his evasion.

"Ah, yes; the gray envelope headache!"

She saw the surprise in his eyes. "I'd forgotten how closely I've been watched," he said coldly. "If you'll excuse me, I think I'll go up and try an hour in the dark, to see if I can get rid of this neuralgia."

She wavered; then she said, with desperate resolution: "I'm sorry your head aches. But before you go I want to say that sooner or later this question must be settled between us. Someone is trying to separate us, and I don't care what it costs me to find out who it is." She looked him steadily in the eyes. "If it costs me your love, I don't care! If I can't have your confidence I don't want anything from you."

He still looked at her wistfully. "Give me time."

"Time for what? It's only a word to say."

"Time to show you that you haven't lost my love or my confidence."

"Well, I'm waiting."

He turned toward the door, and then glanced back hesitatingly. "Oh, do wait, my love," he said, and went out of the room.

She heard his tired step on the stairs and the closing of his bedroom door above. Then she dropped into a chair and buried her face in her folded arms. Her first movement was one of compunction; she seemed to herself to have been hard, unhuman, unimaginative. "Think of telling him that I didn't care if my insistence cost me his love! The lying rubbish!" She started up to follow him and unsay the meaningless words. But she was checked by a reflection. He had had his way, after all; he had eluded all attacks on his secret, and now he was shut up alone in his room, reading that other woman's letter.

III

She was still reflecting on this when the surprised parlormaid came in and found her. No, Charlotte said, she wasn't going to dress for dinner; Mr. Ashby didn't want to dine. He was very tired and had gone up to his room to rest; later she would have something brought on a tray to the drawing room. She mounted the stairs to her bedroom. Her dinner dress was lying on the bed, and at the sight of the quiet routine of her daily life took hold of her and she began to feel as if the strange talk she had just had with her husband must have taken place in another world, between two beings who were not Charlotte Gorse and Kenneth Ashby, but phantoms projected by her fevered imagination. She recalled the year since her marriage—her husband's constant devotion; his persistent, almost too insistent tenderness; the feeling he had given her at times of being too eagerly dependent on her, too searchingly close to her, as if there were not air enough between her soul and his. It seemed preposterous, as she recalled all this, that a few moments ago she should have been accusing him of an intrigue with another woman! But, then, what—

Again she was moved by the impulse to go up to him, beg his pardon and try to laugh away the misunderstanding. But she was restrained by the fear of forcing herself upon his privacy. He was troubled and unhappy, oppressed by some grief or fear; and he had shown her that he wanted to fight out his battle alone. It would be wiser, as well as more generous, to respect his wish. Only, how strange, how unbearable, to be there, in the next room to his, and feel herself at the other end of the world! In her nervous agitation she almost regretted not having had the courage to open the letter and put it back on the hall table before he came in. At least she would have known what his secret was, and the bogy might have been laid. For she was beginning now to think of the mystery as something conscious, malevolent: a secret persecution before which he quailed, yet from which he could not free himself. Once or twice in his evasive eyes she thought she had detected a desire for help, an impulse of confession, instantly restrained and suppressed. It was as if he felt she could have helped him if she had known, and yet had been unable to tell her!

There flashed through her mind the idea of going to his mother. She was very fond of old Mrs. Ashby, a firm-fleshed clear-eyed old lady, with an astringent bluntness of speech which re-sponded to the forthright and simple in Charlotte's own nature. There had been a tacit bond between them ever since the day when Mrs. Ashby Senior, coming to lunch for the first time with her new daughter-in-law, had been received by Charlotte down-stairs in the library, and glancing up at the empty wall above her son's desk, had remarked laconically: "Elsie gone, eh?" adding, at Charlotte's murmured explanation: "Nonsense. Don't have her back. Two's company." Charlotte, at this reading of her thoughts, could hardly refrain from exchanging a smile of complicity with her mother-in-law; and it seemed to her now that Mrs. Ashby's almost uncanny directness might pierce to the core of this new mystery. But here again she hesitated, for the idea almost sug-gested a betrayal. What right had she to call in anyone, even so close a relation, to surprise a secret which her husband was try-ing to keep from her? "Perhaps, by and by, he'll talk to his mother of his own accord," she thought, and then ended: "But what does it matter? He and I must settle it between us."

She was still brooding over the problem when there was a knock on the door and her husband came in. He was dressed for dinner and seemed surprised to see her sitting there, with her evening dress lying unheeded on the bed.

"Aren't you coming down?"

"I thought you were not well and had gone to bed," she faltered.

He forced a smile. "I'm not particularly well, but we'd better go down." His face, though still drawn, looked calmer than when he had fled upstairs an hour earlier.

"There it is; he knows what's in the letter and has fought his battle out again, whatever it is," she reflected, "while I'm still in darkness." She rang and gave a hurried order that dinner should be served as soon as possible—just a short meal, whatever could be got ready quickly, as both she and Mr. Ashby were rather tired and not very hungry.

Dinner was announced, and they sat down to it. At first neither seemed able to find a word to say; then Ashby began to make conversation with an assumption of ease that was more oppressive than his silence. "How tired he is! How terribly overtired!" Charlotte said to herself, pursuing her own thoughts while he rambled on about municipal politics, aviation, an exhibition of modern French painting, the health of an old aunt and the installing of the automatic telephone. "Good heavens, how tired he is!"

When they dined alone they usually went into the library after dinner, and Charlotte curled herself up on the divan with her knitting while he settled down in his armchair under the lamp and lit a pipe. But this evening, by tacit agreement, they avoided the room in which their strange talk had taken place, and went up to Charlotte's drawing room.

They sat down near the fire, and Charlotte said: "Your pipe?" after he had put down his hardly tasted coffee.

He shook his head. "No, not tonight."

"You must go to bed early; you look terribly tired. I'm sure they overwork you at the office."

"I suppose we all overwork at times."

She rose and stood before him with sudden resolution. "Well, I'm not going to have you use up your strength slaving in that way. It's absurd. I can see you're ill." She bent over him and laid her hand on his forehead. "My poor old Kenneth. Prepare to be taken away soon on a long holiday."

He looked up at her, startled. "A holiday?"

"Certainly. Didn't you know I was going to carry you off at Easter? We're going to start in a fortnight on a month's voyage to somewhere or other. On any one of the big cruising steamers."

She paused and bent closer, touching his forehead with her lips. "I'm tired, too, Kenneth."

He seemed to pay no heed to her last words, but sat, his hands on his knees, his head drawn back a little from her caress, and looked up at her with a stare of apprehension. "Again? My dear, we can't; I can't possibly go away."

"I don't know why you say 'again,' Kenneth; we haven't taken a real holiday this year."

"At Christmas we spent a week with the children in the country."

"Yes, but this time I mean away from the children, from servants, from the house. From everything that's familiar and fatiguing. Your mother will love to have Joyce and Peter with her."

He frowned and slowly shook his head. "No, dear; I can't leave them with my mother."

"Why, Kenneth, how absurd! She adores them. You didn't hesitate to leave them with her for over two months when we went to the West Indies."

He drew a deep breath and stood up uneasily. "That was different."

"Different? Why?"

"I mean, at that time I didn't realize—" He broke off as if to choose his words and then went on: "My mother adores the children, as you say. But she isn't always very judicious. Grandmothers always spoil children. And sometimes she talks before them without thinking." He turned to his wife with an almost pitiful gesture of entreaty. "Don't ask me to, dear."

Charlotte mused. It was true that the elder Mrs. Ashby had a fearless tongue, but she was the last woman in the world to say or hint anything before her grandchildren at which the most scrupulous parent could take offense. Charlotte looked at her husband in perplexity.

"I don't understand."

He continued to turn on her the same troubled and entreating gaze. "Don't try to," he muttered.

"Not try to?"

"Not now—not yet." He put up his hands and pressed them

against his temples. "Can't you see that there's no use in insisting? I can't go away, no matter how much I might want to."

Charlotte still scrutinized him gravely. "The question is, *do* you want to?"

He returned her gaze for a moment; then his lips began to tremble, and he said, hardly above his breath: "I want—anything you want."

"And yet—"

"Don't ask me. I can't leave—I can't!"

"You mean that you can't go away out of reach of those letters!"

Her husband had been standing before her in an uneasy half-hesitating attitude; now he turned abruptly away and walked once or twice up and down the length of the room, his head bent, his eyes fixed on the carpet.

Charlotte felt her resentfulness rising with her fears. "It's that," she persisted. "Why not admit it? You can't live without them."

He continued his troubled pacing of the room; then he stopped short, dropped into a chair and covered his face with his hands. From the shaking of his shoulders, Charlotte saw that he was weeping. She had never seen a man cry, except her father after her mother's death, when she was a little girl; and she remembered still how the sight had frightened her. She was frightened now; she felt that her husband was being dragged away from her into some mysterious bondage, and that she must use up her last atom of strength in the struggle for his freedom, and for hers.

"Kenneth—Kenneth!" she pleaded, kneeling down beside him. "Won't you listen to me? Won't you try to see what I'm suffering? I'm not unreasonable, darling, really not. I don't suppose I should ever have noticed the letters if it hadn't been for their effect on you. It's not my way to pry into other people's affairs; and even if the effect had been different—yes, yes, listen to me—if I'd seen that the letters made you happy, that you were watching eagerly for them, counting the days between their coming, that you wanted them, that they gave you something I haven't known how to give—why, Kenneth, I don't say I shouldn't have suffered from that, too; but it would have been in a different way, and I should have had the courage to hide what I felt, and the hope that someday you'd come to feel about me as you did about the writer of the letters. But what I can't bear is to see how you dread them, how they make you suffer, and yet how you can't live without them and won't go away lest you should miss one during your absence. Or perhaps," she added, her voice breaking into a cry of accusation—"perhaps it's because she's actually forbidden you to leave. Kenneth, you must answer me! Is that the reason? Is it because she's forbidden you that you won't go away with me?"

She continued to kneel at his side, and raising her hands, she drew his gently down. She was ashamed of her persistence, ashamed of uncovering that baffled disordered face, yet resolved that no such scruples should arrest her. His eyes were lowered, the muscles of his face quivered; she was making him suffer even more than she suffered herself. Yet this no longer restrained her.

"Kenneth, is it that? She won't let us go away together?"

Still he did not speak or turn his eyes to her; and a sense of defeat swept over her. After all, she thought, the struggle was a losing one. "You needn't answer. I see I'm right," she said.

Suddenly, as she rose, he turned and drew her down again. His hands caught hers and pressed them so tightly that she felt her rings cutting into her flesh. There was something frightened, convulsive in his hold; it was the clutch of a man who felt himself slipping over a precipice. He was staring up at her now as if salvation lay in the face she bent above him. "Of course we'll go away together. We'll go wherever you want," he said in a low confused voice; and putting his arm about her, he drew her close and pressed his lips on hers.

IV

Charlotte had said to herself: "I shall sleep tonight," but instead she sat before her fire into the small hours, listening for any sound that came from her husband's room. But he, at any rate, seemed to be resting after the tumult of the evening. Once or twice she stole to the door and in the faint light that came in from the street through his open window she saw him stretched out in heavy sleep—the sleep of weakness and exhaustion. "He's ill," she thought—"he's undoubtedly ill. And it's not overwork; it's this mysterious persecution."

She drew a breath of relief. She had fought through the weary fight and the victory was hers—at least for the moment. If only they could have started at once—started for anywhere! She knew it would be useless to ask him to leave before the holidays; and meanwhile the secret influence—as to which she was still so completely in the dark—would continue to work against her, and she would have to renew the struggle day after day till they started on their journey. But after that everything would be different. If once she could get her husband away under other skies, and all to herself, she never doubted her power to release him from the evil spell he was under. Lulled to quiet by the thought, she too slept at last.

When she woke, it was long past her usual hour, and she sat up in bed surprised and vexed at having overslept herself. She always liked to be down to share her husband's breakfast by the library fire; but a glance at the clock made it clear that he must have started long since for his office. To make sure, she jumped out of bed and went into his room, but it was empty. No doubt he had looked in on her before leaving, seen that she still slept, and gone downstairs without disturbing her; and their relations were sufficiently lover-like for her to regret having missed their morning hour.

She rang and asked if Mr. Ashby had already gone. Yes, nearly an hour ago, the maid said. He had given orders that Mrs. Ashby should not be waked and that the children should not come to her till she sent for them. . . . Yes, he had gone up to the nursery himself to give the order. All this sounded usual enough, and Charlotte hardly knew why she asked: "And did Mr. Ashby leave no other message?"

Yes, the maid said, he did; she was so sorry she'd forgotten. He'd told her, just as he was leaving, to say to Mrs. Ashby that he was going to see about their passages, and would she please be ready to sail tomorrow?

Charlotte echoed the woman's "Tomorrow," and sat staring at her incredulously. "Tomorrow—you're sure he said to sail tomorrow?"

"Oh, ever so sure, ma'am. I don't know how I could have forgotten to mention it."

"Well, it doesn't matter. Draw my bath, please." Charlotte sprang up, dashed through her dressing, and caught herself singing at her image in the glass as she sat brushing her hair. It made her feel young again to have scored such a victory. The other woman vanished to a speck on the horizon, as this one, who ruled the foreground, smiled back at the reflection of her lips and eyes. He loved her, then—he loved her as passionately as ever. He had divined what she had suffered, had understood that their happiness depended on their getting away at once, and finding each other again after yesterday's desperate groping in the fog. The nature of the influence that had come between them did not much matter to Charlotte now; she had faced the phantom and dispelled it. "Courage—that's the secret! If only people who are in love weren't always so afraid of risking their happiness by looking it in the eyes." As she brushed back her light abundant hair it waved electrically above her head, like the palms of victory. Ah, well, some women knew how to manage men, and some didn't—and only the fair—she gaily paraphrased—deserve the brave! Certainly she was looking very pretty.

The morning danced along like a cockleshell on a bright sea—such a sea as they would soon be speeding over. She ordered a particularly good dinner, saw the children off to their classes, had her trunks brought down, consulted with the maid about getting out summer clothes—for of course they would be heading for heat and sunshine—and wondered if she oughtn't to take Kenneth's flannel suits out of camphor. "But how absurd," she reflected, "that I don't yet know where we're going!" She looked at the clock, saw that it was close on noon, and decided to call him up at his office. There was a slight delay; then she heard his secretary's voice saying that Mr. Ashby had looked in for a mo-

ment early, and left again almost immediately. . . . Oh, very
well; Charlotte would ring up later. How soon was he likely to be
back? The secretary answered that she couldn't tell; all they knew
in the office was that when he left he had said he was in a hurry
because he had to go out of town.

Out of town! Charlotte hung up the receiver and sat blankly
gazing into new darkness. Why had he gone out of town? And
where had he gone? And of all days, why should he have chosen
the eve of their suddenly planned departure? She felt a faint
shiver of apprehension. Of course he had gone to see that
woman—no doubt to get her permission to leave. He was as
completely in bondage as that; and Charlotte had been fatuous
enough to see the palms of victory on her forehead. She burst
into a laugh and, walking across the room, sat down again before
her mirror. What a different face she saw! The smile on her pale
lips seemed to mock the rosy vision of the other Charlotte. But
gradually her color crept back. After all, she had a right to claim
the victory, since her husband was doing what she wanted, not
what the other woman exacted of him. It was natural enough, in
view of his abrupt decision to leave the next day, that he should
have arrangements to make, business matters to wind up; it was
not even necessary to suppose that his mysterious trip was a visit
to the writer of the letters. He might simply have gone to see a
client who lived out of town. Of course they would not tell Charlotte at the office; the secretary had hesitated before imparting
even such meager information as the fact of Mr. Ashby's absence.
Meanwhile she would go on with her joyful preparations, content
to learn later in the day to what particular island of the blest she
was to be carried.

The hours wore on, or rather were swept forward on a rush of
eager preparations. At last the entrance of the maid who came to
draw the curtains roused Charlotte from her labors, and she saw
to her surprise that the clock marked five. And she did not yet
know where they were going the next day! She rang up her
husband's office and was told that Mr. Ashby had not been there
since the early morning. She asked for his partner, but the partner could add nothing to her information, for he himself, his

suburban train having been behind time, had reached the office after Ashby had come and gone. Charlotte stood perplexed; then she decided to telephone to her mother-in-law. Of course Kenneth, on the eve of a month's absence, must have gone to see his mother. The mere fact that the children—in spite of his vague objections—would certainly have to be left with old Mrs. Ashby, made it obvious that he would have all sorts of matters to decide with her. At another time Charlotte might have felt a little hurt at being excluded from their conference, but nothing mattered now but that she had won the day, that her husband was still hers and not another woman's. Gaily she called up Mrs. Ashby, heard her friendly voice, and began: "Well, did Kenneth's news surprise you? What do you think of our elopement?"

Almost instantly, before Mrs. Ashby could answer, Charlotte knew what her reply would be. Mrs. Ashby had not seen her son, she had had no word from him and did not know what her daughter-in-law meant. Charlotte stood silent in the intensity of her surprise. "But then, where *has* he been?" she thought. Then, recovering herself, she explained their sudden decision to Mrs. Ashby, and in doing so, gradually regained her own self-confidence, her conviction that nothing could ever again come between Kenneth and herself. Mrs. Ashby took the news calmly and approvingly. She, too, had thought that Kenneth looked worried and overtired, and she agreed with her daughter-in-law that in such cases change was the surest remedy. "I'm always so glad when he gets away. Elsie hated traveling; she was always finding pretexts to prevent his going anywhere. With you, thank goodness, it's different." Nor was Mrs. Ashby surprised at his not having had time to let her know of his departure. He must have been in a rush from the moment the decision was taken; but no doubt he'd drop in before dinner. Five minutes' talk was really all they needed. "I hope you'll gradually cure Kenneth of his mania for going over and over a question that could be settled in a dozen words. He never used to be like that, and if he carried the habit into his professional work he'd soon lose all his clients. . . . Yes, do come in for a minute, dear, if you have time; no doubt he'll turn up while you're here." The tonic ring of Mrs.

Ashby's voice echoed on reassuringly in the silent room while Charlotte continued her preparations.

Toward seven the telephone rang, and she darted to it. Now she would know! But it was only from the conscientious secretary, to say that Mr. Ashby hadn't been back, or sent any word, and before the office closed she thought she ought to let Mrs. Ashby know. "Oh, that's all right. Thanks a lot!" Charlotte called out cheerfully, and hung up the receiver with a trembling hand. But perhaps by this time, she reflected, he was at his mother's. She shut her drawers and cupboards, put on her hat and coat and called up to the nursery that she was going out for a minute to see the children's grandmother.

Mrs. Ashby lived nearby, and during her brief walk through the cold spring dusk Charlotte imagined that every advancing figure was her husband's. But she did not meet him on the way, and when she entered the house she found her mother-in-law alone. Kenneth had neither telephoned nor come. Old Mrs. Ashby sat by her bright fire, her knitting needles flashing steadily through her active old hands, and her mere bodily presence gave reassurance to Charlotte. Yes, it was certainly odd that Kenneth had gone off for the whole day without letting any of them know; but, after all, it was to be expected. A busy lawyer held so many threads in his hands that any sudden change of plan would oblige him to make all sorts of unforeseen arrangements and adjustments. He might have gone to see some client in the suburbs and been detained there; his mother remembered his telling her that he had charge of the legal business of a queer old recluse somewhere in New Jersey, who was immensely rich but too mean to have a telephone. Very likely Kenneth had been stranded there.

But Charlotte felt her nervousness gaining on her. When Mrs. Ashby asked her at what hour they were sailing the next day and she had to say she didn't know—that Kenneth had simply sent her word he was going to take their passages—the uttering of the words again brought home to her the strangeness of the situation. Even Mrs. Ashby conceded that it was odd; but she immediately added that it only showed what a rush he was in.

"But, mother, it's nearly eight o'clock! He must realize that I've got to know when we're starting tomorrow."

"Oh, the boat probably doesn't sail till evening. Sometimes they have to wait till midnight for the tide. Kenneth's probably counting on that. After all, he has a level head."

Charlotte stood up. "It's not that. Something has happened to him."

Mrs. Ashby took off her spectacles and rolled up her knitting. "If you begin to let yourself imagine things—"

"Aren't you in the least anxious?"

"I never am till I have to be. I wish you'd ring for dinner, my dear. You'll stay and dine? He's sure to drop in here on his way home."

Charlotte called up her own house. No, the maid said, Mr. Ashby hadn't come in and hadn't telephoned. She would tell him as soon as he came that Mrs. Ashby was dining at his mother's. Charlotte followed her mother-in-law into the dining room and sat with parched throat before her empty plate, while Mrs. Ashby dealt calmly and efficiently with a short but carefully prepared repast. "You'd better eat something, child, or you'll be as bad as Kenneth. . . . Yes, a little more asparagus, please, Jane."

She insisted on Charlotte's drinking a glass of sherry and nibbling a bit of toast; then they returned to the drawing room, where the fire had been made up, and the cushions in Mrs. Ashby's armchair shaken out and smoothed. How safe and familiar it all looked; and out there, somewhere in the uncertainty and mystery of the night, lurked the answer to the two women's conjectures, like an indistinguishable figure prowling on the threshold.

At last Charlotte got up and said: "I'd better go back. At this hour Kenneth will certainly go straight home."

Mrs. Ashby smiled indulgently. "It's not very late, my dear. It doesn't take two sparrows long to dine."

"It's after nine." Charlotte bent down to kiss her. "The fact is, I can't keep still."

Mrs. Ashby pushed aside her work and rested her two hands

on the arms of her chair. "I'm going with you," she said, helping herself up.

Charlotte protested that it was too late, that it was not necessary, that she would call up as soon as Kenneth came in, but Mrs. Ashby had already rung for her maid. She was slightly lame, and stood resting on her stick while her wraps were brought. "If Mr. Kenneth turns up, tell him he'll find me at his own house," she instructed the maid as the two women got into the taxi which had been summoned. During the short drive Charlotte gave thanks that she was not returning home alone. There was something warm and substantial in the mere fact of Mrs. Ashby's nearness, something that corresponded with the clearness of her eyes and the texture of her fresh firm complexion. As the taxi drew up she laid her hand encouragingly on Charlotte's. "You'll see; there'll be a message."

The door opened at Charlotte's ring and the two entered. Charlotte's heart beat excitedly; the stimulus of her mother-in-law's confidence was beginning to flow through her veins.

"You'll see—you'll see," Mrs. Ashby repeated.

The maid who opened the door said no, Mr. Ashby had not come in, and there had been no message from him.

"You're sure the telephone's not out of order?" his mother suggested; and the maid said, well, it certainly wasn't half an hour ago; but she'd just go and ring up to make sure. She disappeared, and Charlotte turned to take off her hat and cloak. As she did so her eyes lit on the hall table, and there lay a gray envelope, her husband's name faintly traced on it. "Oh!" she cried out, suddenly aware that for the first time in months she had entered her house without wondering if one of the gray letters would be there.

"What is it, my dear?" Mrs. Ashby asked with a glance of surprise.

Charlotte did not answer. She took up the envelope and stood staring at it as if she could force her gaze to penetrate to what was within. Then an idea occurred to her. She turned and held out the envelope to her mother-in-law.

"Do you know that writing?" she asked.

Mrs. Ashby took the letter. She had to feel with her other hand for her eyeglasses, and when she had adjusted them she lifted the envelope to the light. "Why!" she exclaimed; and then stopped. Charlotte noticed that the letter shook in her usually firm hand. "But this is addressed to Kenneth," Mrs. Ashby said at length, in a low voice. Her tone seemed to imply that she felt her daughter-in-law's question to be slightly indiscreet.

"Yes, but no matter," Charlotte spoke with sudden decision. "I want to know—do you know the writing?"

Mrs. Ashby handed back the letter. "No," she said distinctly.

The two women had turned into the library. Charlotte switched on the electric light and shut the door. She still held the envelope in her hand.

"I'm going to open it," she announced.

She caught her mother-in-law's startled glance. "But, dearest— a letter not addressed to you? My dear, you can't!"

"As if I cared about that—now!" She continued to look intently at Mrs. Ashby. "This letter may tell me where Kenneth is."

Mrs. Ashby's glossy bloom was effaced by a quick pallor; her firm cheeks seemed to shrink and wither. "Why should it? What makes you believe—It can't possibly—"

Charlotte held her eyes steadily on that altered face. "Ah, then you *do* know the writing?" she flashed back.

"Know the writing? How should I? With all my son's correspondents. . . . What I do know is—" Mrs. Ashby broke off and looked at her daughter-in-law entreatingly, almost timidly.

Charlotte caught her by the wrist. "Mother! What do you know? Tell me! You must!"

"That I don't believe any good ever came of a woman's opening her husband's letters behind his back."

The words sounded to Charlotte's irritated ears as flat as a phrase culled from a book of moral axioms. She laughed impatiently and dropped her mother-in-law's wrist. "Is that all? No good can come of this letter, opened or unopened. I know that well enough. But whatever ill comes, I mean to find out what's in it." Her hands had been trembling as they held the envelope, but now they grew firm, and her voice also. She still gazed intently at

Mrs. Ashby. "This is the ninth letter addressed in the same hand that has come for Kenneth since we've been married. Always these same gray envelopes. I've kept count of them because after each one he has been like a man who has had some dreadful shock. It takes him hours to shake off their effect. I've told him so. I've told him I must know from whom they come, because I can see they're killing him. He won't answer my questions; he says he can't tell me anything about the letters; but last night he promised to go away with me—to get away from them."

Mrs. Ashby, with shaking steps, had gone to one of the arm-chairs and sat down in it, her head drooping forward on her breast. "Ah," she murmured.

"So now you understand—"

"Did he tell you it was to get away from them?"

"He said, to get away—to get away. He was sobbing so that he could hardly speak. But I told him I knew that was why."

"And what did he say?"

"He took me in his arms and said he'd go wherever I wanted."

"Ah, thank God!" said Mrs. Ashby. There was a silence, during which she continued to sit with bowed head, and eyes averted from her daughter-in-law. At last she looked up and spoke. "Are you sure there have been as many as nine?"

"Perfectly. This is the ninth. I've kept count."

"And he has absolutely refused to explain?"

"Absolutely."

Mrs. Ashby spoke through pale contracted lips. "When did they begin to come? Do you remember?"

Charlotte laughed again. "Remember? The first one came the night we got back from our honeymoon."

"All that time?" Mrs. Ashby lifted her head and spoke with sudden energy. "Then—yes, open it."

The words were so unexpected that Charlotte felt the blood in her temples, and her hands began to tremble again. She tried to slip her finger under the flap of the envelope, but it was so tightly stuck that she had to hunt on her husband's writing table for his ivory letter opener. As she pushed about the familiar objects his own hands had so lately touched, they sent through her the icy chill emanating from the little personal effects of someone newly dead. In the deep silence of the room the tearing of the paper as she slit the envelope sounded like a human cry. She drew out the sheet and carried it to the lamp.

"Well?" Mrs. Ashby asked below her breath.

Charlotte did not move or answer. She was bending over the page with wrinkled brows, holding it nearer and nearer to the light. Her sight must be blurred, or else dazzled by the reflection of the lamplight on the smooth surface of the paper, for, strain her eyes as she would, she could discern only a few faint strokes, so faint and faltering as to be nearly undecipherable.

"I can't make it out," she said.

"What do you mean, dear?"

"The writing's too indistinct. . . . Wait."

She went back to the table and, sitting down close to Kenneth's reading lamp, slipped the letter under a magnifying glass. All this time she was aware that her mother-in-law was watching her intently.

"Well?" Mrs. Ashby breathed.

"Well, it's no clearer. I can't read it."

"You mean the paper is an absolute blank?"

"No, not quite. There is writing on it. I can make out something like 'mine'—oh, and 'come.' It might be 'come.' "

Mrs. Ashby stood up abruptly. Her face was even paler than before. She advanced to the table and, resting her two hands on it, drew a deep breath. "Let me see," she said, as if forcing herself to a hateful effort.

Charlotte felt the contagion of her whiteness. "She knows," she thought. She pushed the letter across the table. Her mother-in-law lowered her head over it in silence, but without touching it with her pale wrinkled hands.

Charlotte stood watching her as she herself, when she had tried to read the letter, had been watched by Mrs. Ashby. The latter fumbled for her glasses, held them to her eyes, and bent still closer to the outspread page, in order, as it seemed, to avoid touching it. The light of the lamp fell directly on her old face, and Charlotte reflected what depths of the unknown may lurk under the clearest and most candid lineaments. She had never seen her mother-in-law's features express any but simple and sound emotions—cordiality, amusement, a kindly sympathy; now and again a flash of wholesome anger. Now they seemed to wear a look of fear and hatred, of incredulous dismay and almost cringing defiance. It was as if the spirits warring within her had distorted her face to their own likeness. At length she raised her head. "I can't—I can't," she said in a voice of childish distress.

"You can't make it out either?"

She shook her head, and Charlotte saw two tears roll down her cheeks.

"Familiar as the writing is to you?" Charlotte insisted with twitching lips.

Mrs. Ashby did not take up the challenge. "I can make out nothing—nothing."

"But you do know the writing?"

Mrs. Ashby lifted her head timidly; her anxious eyes stole with a glance of apprehension around the quiet familiar room. "How can I tell? I was startled at first. . . ."

"Startled by the resemblance?"

"Well, I thought—"

"You'd better say it out, mother! You knew at once it was *her* writing?"

"Oh, wait, my dear—wait."

"Wait for what?"

Mrs. Ashby looked up; her eyes, traveling slowly past Charlotte, were lifted to the blank wall behind her son's writing table.

Charlotte, following the glance, burst into a shrill laugh of accusation. "I needn't wait any longer! You've answered me now! You're looking straight at the wall where her picture used to hang!"

Mrs. Ashby lifted her hand with a murmur of warning. "Sh-h."

"Oh, you needn't imagine that anything can ever frighten me again!" Charlotte cried.

Her mother-in-law still leaned against the table. Her lips moved plaintively. "But we're going mad—we're both going mad. We both know such things are impossible."

Her daughter-in-law looked at her with a pitying stare. "I've known for a long time now that everything was possible."

"Even this?"

"Yes, exactly this."

"But this letter—after all, there's nothing in this letter—"

"Perhaps there would be to him. How can I tell? I remember his saying to me once that if you were used to a handwriting the faintest stroke of it became legible. Now I see what he meant. He *was* used to it."

"But the few strokes that I can make out are so pale. No one could possibly read that letter."

Charlotte laughed again. "I suppose everything's pale about a ghost," she said stridently.

"Oh, my child—my child—don't say it!"

"Why shouldn't I say it, when even the bare walls cry it out? What difference does it make if her letters are illegible to you and me? If even you can see her face on that blank wall, why shouldn't he read her writing on this blank paper? Don't you see that she's everywhere in this house, and the closer to him because to everyone else she's become invisible?" Charlotte dropped into a chair and covered her face with her hands. A turmoil of sobbing shook her from head to foot. At length a touch on her shoulder made her look up, and she saw her mother-in-law bending over her. Mrs. Ashby's face seemed to have grown still smaller and more wasted, but it had resumed its usual quiet look. Through all her tossing anguish, Charlotte felt the impact of that resolute spirit.

"Tomorrow—tomorrow. You'll see. There'll be some explanation tomorrow."

Charlotte cut her short. "An explanation? Who's going to give it, I wonder?"

Mrs. Ashby drew back and straightened herself heroically. "Kenneth himself will," she cried out in a strong voice. Charlotte said nothing, and the old woman went on: "But meanwhile we must act; we must notify the police. Now, without a moment's delay. We must do everything—everything."

Charlotte stood up slowly and stiffly; her joints felt as cramped as an old woman's. "Exactly as if we thought it could do any good to do anything?"

Resolutely Mrs. Ashby cried: "Yes!" and Charlotte went up to the telephone and unhooked the receiver.

NOTES ON THE AUTHORS

ILSE AICHINGER (b. 1921) is a native of Vienna, Austria. After the Second World War she studied medicine and was a reader for S. Fischer Verlag Publishing Company. She is a co-founder of the Academy of Design. Her writing is often dreamlike and presented as parables. Her works include a novel, *Herod's Children* (1948), a collection of nonfiction, *Squares and Streets* (1954), a story collection, *The Bound Man* (1956), and *Selected Poetry and Prose of Ilse Aichinger* (1976).

JOAN AIKEN (b. 1924), daughter of American poet and novelist Conrad Aiken, was born in Rye, Sussex, England. She is a prolific British author of fantasy, horror, and suspense tales for both juvenile and adult readers. She also works in a genre she calls "unhistorical romances," tales that combine humor and action with myths and fairy tales. The story in this volume was taken from *The Green Flash* (1971).

SIR MAX BEERBOHM (Henry Maximilian Beerbohm, 1872–1956) was an English writer, caricaturist, and dandy. Educated at Merton College, Oxford, he succeeded George Bernard Shaw as drama critic of the *Saturday Review*. (Shaw called him "The Incomparable Max.") His books include the novel *Zuleika Dobson*

(1911), which was ranked one of the century's best novels in English by The Modern Library; the parodic *The Christmas Garland* (1912), and a collection of stories, *Seven Men* (1919), later reissued as *Seven Men and Two Others* (1950).

ELIZABETH BOWEN (1899–1973) grew up in Dublin and in Cork, and at the age of seven was taken to England for schooling. She began to write when she was twenty and had her first volume of stories, *Encounters,* published in 1923. During a writing career that lasted another fifty years, she produced more volumes of stories and many novels, including the two classics *The House in Paris* (1935) and *The Death of the Heart* (1938). While fantasy played no part in her nine novels, it is an important element in several of her best stories.

JOHN CHEEVER (1912–1982), American, published his first short story in *The New Republic* in 1930, and his magisterial *The Short Stories of John Cheever* won the Pulitzer Prize in 1978. He was also author of five novels, including *The Wapshot Chronicle* (1957) and *The Wapshot Scandal* (1964), of which "Oh Father, Father, Why Have You Come Back?" is the third chapter. With comedy, irony, and sometimes fantasy, Cheever explored the life, manners, and morals of upper middle-class metropolitan and suburban lives. His chiseled prose is noted for its poetic effects.

KATHY CHWEDYK, a former newspaper editor, has written several short stories and novellas for fantasy and horror anthologies, including *Highwaymen: Robbers and Rogues,* edited by Jennifer Roberson. She also has published several Regency romance novels under the pseudonyms Kate Huntington and Cathryn Huntington Chadwick. She lives with her husband, Bob, a photographer, in Algonquin, Illinois.

F. MARION CRAWFORD (Francis Marion Crawford, 1854–1909) was an Italian-American novelist admired for the vividness of his characterizations and settings, which is abundantly on display in "The Upper Berth," a story Edith Wharton thought comparable to "the crawling horror of Fitz James O'Brien's wizardry." Crawford lived in both Italy and America as a youth, and his best works reflect the Italy he loved. Among them are *Saracinasca* (1887), *Sant'Ilario* (1889), and *Don Orsino* (1892).

MAX EBERTS (Gerik R. Eberts, b. 1963) is a American poet and fiction writer. The son of a USAF Colonel whose tours of duty ranged from Asia to Europe, Eberts grew up overseas and has traveled extensively. He received his bachelor degree in 1993 from Rice University, where he studied art history and ancient Mediterranean civilizations. He has won the Academy of American Poets Prize and has published work in *Poetry, Sewanee Review, Southern Poetry Review, Gulf Coast, Provincetown Arts* and the *Texas Review*. In addition to having taught English and art history at Strake Jesuit College Preparatory School, he has worked at the University of Houston the last three years. Presently he is the university's Assistant Director of Athletics for external relations.

ISAK DINESEN (Karen Christence Dinesen, Baroness Blixen-Finecke, 1885–1962), the Danish writer who wrote in English as well as her native language, and whose characteristic form was the literary tale filled with dreams and the supernatural, was a born storyteller. When Ernest Hemingway received the Nobel Prize for Literature in 1954, he announced he regretted it did not go to Dinesen. Her best-known books are the memoir *Out of Africa* (1937), *Seven Gothic Tales* (1934), *Winter's Tales* (1942), *Last Tales* (1957), and *Ancedotes of Destiny* (1958).

ELLEN GLASGOW (1873–1945), a fine American novelist whose reputation currently is in decline, produced a number of first-rate novels, especially *Barren Ground* (1925), *The Sheltered Life* (1932), and *Vein of Iron* (1935). Her works largely were studies of the social changes and contrasting social classes in the South, although, when her *Collected Stories* (1963) were gathered after her death, it became apparent she also was interested in the supernatural, and four of her ghost stories were included. Her memoirs, *The Woman Within* (1954) and her *Letters* (1958), also are of interest.

WILLIAM GOYEN (Charles William Goyen, 1915–1983) was born in Trinity, Texas, and his best work captures the cadences and rhythms of that region in a prose style with hypnotic power. His work also is frequently populated by spirits and ghosts. His first novel, *The House of Breath* (1950), was followed by four others, as well as a work of nonfiction, *A Book of Jesus* (1973). Four collections of his stories have appeared to date, including *The Collected Stories* (1975), which was nominated for the Pulitzer Prize in 1977. *William Goyen: Selected Letters from a Writer's Life,* ed. Robert Phillips, received acclaim on publication in 1995.

L. P. HARTLEY (Leslie Poles Hartley, 1895–1972) was an English novelist, short story writer, and critic. His early work examined the macabre and the fantastic, such as his collection *Night Fears* (1924). His most important work is the Eustace and Hilda Trilogy—*The Shrimp and the Anemone* (1944), *The Sixth Heaven* (1946), and *Eustace and Hilda* (1947). Other significant novels include *The Boat* (1949) and *The Go-Between* (1953). *The Collected Stories of L.P. Hartley* (1968) reveal his penchant for the psychological nuance.

JAMES LEO HERLIHY (1927–1993) was a talented American novelist, playwright and actor born in Detroit. His first book of fiction, *The Sleep of Baby Filbertson* (1959), was a collection of highly original tales. "The Astral Body of a U.S. Mail Truck" comes from his second collection, *A Story That Ends with a Scream and Eight Others* (1967). His novels include *All Fall Down* (1960) and the popular *Midnight Cowboy* (1965), both of which were made into films and *Season of the Witch* (1971). His plays include *Blue Denim,* co-authored with William Noble, *Crazy October* (1958) and *Stop. You're Killing Me* (1969). Herlihy committed suicide in Hollywood in 1993.

SHIRLEY JACKSON (Shirley Hardie Jackson, 1916–1965) was born in California, educated at Syracuse University in New York State, and died in North Bennington, Vermont, where she lived the last two decades of her life with her husband, the American literary critic Stanley Edgar Hyman. Jackson is best remembered for her Kafkaesque allegorical story, "The Lottery," which has provoked debate since its original appearance in *The New Yorker* in 1949. But her three collections of stories and six novels contain much else to admire as well, especially the novels *The Haunting of Hill House* (1959) and *We Have Always Lived in the Castle* (1962). The former was made into the film *The Haunting* and the latter was adapted into a Broadway play. Her father was an architect, and she claimed always to begin a piece of fiction with the vision of a specific house, then imagined what sort of individuals would inhabit it. Hence the hill house and the castle of her titles.

HENRY JAMES (1843–1916), an American novelist and naturalized British citizen from 1915, was a great figure in transatlantic culture. America's greatest critic-novelist, he was called "The Master." R. P. Blackmur praised his *The Art of Fiction* (1884) as "the most sustained and I think the most eloquent and original piece of literary criticism in existence." His thirteen volumes of collected tales include eighteen stories of the supernatural, including "The Turn of the Screw" and "The Jolly Corner." Among his greatest novels are *The Wings of the Dove* (1902), *The Ambassadors* (1903), and *The Golden Bowl* (1904).

FRANZ KAFKA (1883–1924), Czech-born German, wrote tales which reflected his isolation, as a Jew, from the German community in Prague. Kafka took a doctorate in 1906 and worked in the insurance business from 1907 until 1922, when he retired and moved to Berlin to concentrate full-time on his writings. His retirement lasted less than two years, as he died of tuberculosis. His stories and novels are fable-like and reflect his anxiety within modern society. The office scenes in the Kafka tale included in the present volume are a perfect example. Some of his most lasting work, including the novels *The Trial* (1921) and *The Castle* (1926), were published posthumously and in disregard of his wishes.

RUDYARD KIPLING (Joseph Rudyard Kipling, 1865–1936) was born in Bombay and died in London. These locations reflect his greatest theme, the celebration of British imperialism. After his marriage in 1892 he and his wife moved for some years to the United States, but the transition was not a comfortable one and they returned to Sussex. Kipling was an extremely popular poet in his day—partly because his poems are so easily memorized—but it is for his prose he is likely to be remembered, for his short stories and *The Man Who Would Be King* (1888) and *Captains Courageous* (1897), among others. Kipling received the Nobel Prize for Literature in 1907.

ALISON LURIE (b. 1926) is a Chicago-born author who graduated from Radcliffe College in 1947 and has taught English and children's literature at Cornell University. Her novel *Foreign Affairs* was winner of the 1985 Pulitzer Prize for fiction. She is author of seven other novels, and two nonfiction works—*The Language of Clothes* and *Don't Tell the Grownups.* A delicious book of her ghost stories, *Women and Ghosts,* appeared in 1994, and she has edited *The Oxford Book of Modern Fairy Tales* (1994). She lives in Ithaca, New York, and spends part of each year in Key West and London.

GABRIEL GARCÍA MÁRQUEZ (b. 1928) is a native of Aracataca, Colombia. He attended the University of Bogotá and later worked as a reporter for the Colombian newspaper *El Espectador* and as a foreign correspondent in Rome, Paris, Barcelona, Caracas, and New York. He is the author of many novels and collections of short stories, the most influential being the long novel *One Hundred Years of Solitude* (1970), which is written in a vein usually described as "magical realism" and allows fantasy to flower in the midst of ordinary reality. "The Ghosts of August" comes from his collection of surreal and magical tales, *Strange Pilgrims* (1993).

García Márquez says he writes for the sheer pleasure of telling a story, "which may be the human condition that most resembles levitation." He was awarded the Nobel Prize for Literature in 1982 and lives in Mexico City.

JOYCE CAROL OATES (b. 1938), reared in upstate New York, is an important American novelist, short-story writer, and playwright in the naturalist tradition. She was educated at Syracuse University and the University of Wisconsin. Her most important novels include *Them* (1969), which won the National Book Award, *You Must Remember This* (1987), *Because It is Bitter, Because It is My Heart* (1990), *What I Lived For* (1994), and *We Were the Mulvaneys* (1996). Throughout her career Oates has demonstrated fascination with tales of the grotesque, and has gathered two collections of her horror stories: *Haunted* (1994) and *The Collector of Hearts* (1998). Among her numerous awards is the Bram Stoker Lifetime Achievement Award in Horror Fiction. She lives in Princeton, New Jersey, with her husband, the editor Raymond J. Smith.

ROBERT PHILLIPS (b. 1938) grew up in the Middle Atlantic state of Delaware and was educated at Syracuse University, where he took his undergraduate and graduate degrees. He began his writing career as a poet, but his oeuvre includes collections of his short stories and numerous anthologies, books of criticism, critical editions, and works of belles lettres, in addition to six collections of poetry. His prizes include an Award in Literature from the American Academy of Arts and Letters, and he is a Councilor of the Texas Institute of Letters. He lives in Houston, where he teaches in the Creative Writing Program of the University of Houston, which he directed from 1991–1996.

JEAN RHYS (Ella Gwendolen Rees William, 1890–1979) was born in the Leeward Islands and died in Exeter, Devon, England. Encouraged and promoted by Ford Madox Ford, she enjoyed early critical success with her first book, *The Left Bank* (1927), and several novels, most notably *After Leaving Mr. MacKenzie* (1931), *Voyage in the Dark* (1934), and *Good Morning, Midnight* (1939). Then she moved to Cornwall and vanished from the public eye. For decades she was presumed dead, until her astonishing novel, *Wide Sargasso Sea,* was published in 1966. It won the W. H. Smith annual literary award and marked the most amazing literary reappearance of our time. That book was followed by two new story collections, an unfinished autobiography, *Smile, Please* (1979), her *Letters 1931-1966* (1984), and *Collected Short Stories* (1987).

ELIZABETH SPENCER (b. 1921) was born in Carrollton, Mississippi, and received her undergraduate degree from Belhaven College in Jackson, Mississippi, and her graduate degree from Vanderbilt. After working briefly as a reporter for the Nashville *Tennessean,* she taught literature and writing at the University of Mississippi. In 1953 she received a Guggenheim Fellowship that took her to New York and later to Italy, where she lived and worked for some years before moving to Canada and teaching writing at Concordia University. In 1986 she returned to the South, to Chapel Hill, North Carolina. Her many books include the highly acclaimed *The Light in the Piazza* (1960), which was nominated for the National Book Award for fiction, and *The Stories of Elizabeth Spencer* (1981), which received the Award of Merit for the Short Story from the American Academy of Arts and Letters, of which she is a member. Her memoir, *Landscapes of the Heart,* appeared in 1998.

CHRISTOPHER TILGHMAN (b. 1948) is author of the story collection *In a Father's Place* (1990) and the novel *Mason's Retreat* (1996). A former resident of the eastern shore of Maryland, he now lives in Massachusetts with his family. His awards include a grant from the Massachusetts Council for the Arts and a residency from the Virginia Center for the Creative Arts. Several of his stories have been selected for *The Best American Short Stories* anthology.

WILLIAM TREVOR (William Trevor Cox, b. 1928) was born in County Cork, Ireland, educated at Trinity College, Dublin, and worked as a teacher, sculptor, and advertising copywriter before he moved to Devon, England, to become a full-time writer. His work often is populated by eccentrics and outcasts, and the tone often is wry or macabre, though he by no means is a genre writer. An acute sense of the psychological makeup of his characters makes him one of the finest Irish story writers since Frank O'Connor and Sean O'Faolain. He has published over ten novels, three novellas, eight single story collections, a play, a book of nonfiction sketches, a selected stories in 1983, and a 1,261-page *Collected Stories* in 1992. Trevor is a member of the Irish Academy of Letters and an honorary Commander of the British Empire in recognition of his service to literature.

DAME MURIEL SPARK (Muriel Sarah Camberg, b. 1918), a native of Edinburgh, Scotland, came to the writing of fiction late. She published her first novel, *The Comforters* (1957), when she was thirty-nine. After that a flow of witty and satirical novels followed, including *Memento Mori* (1959), *The Ballad of Peckham Rye* (1960), *The Prime of Miss Jean Brodie* (1961), *The Girls of Slender Means* (1963). A later novel, *The Mandelbaum Gate* (1965), is written on uncharacteristically heavier themes. It was followed by a number of novels of a sinister bent and a political satire, *The Abbess of Crewe* (1974). Her *The Stories of Muriel Spark* (1985) contains a number of excellent ghost stories, including "Portabello Road" and "The Executor." Her autobiography covering the years 1918 to 1957, *Curriculum Vitae*, was published in 1992.

EDITH WHARTON (Edith Newbold Jones, 1862–1937) was a fiction chronicler of the upper-class New York society into which she was born. She lived in France from 1907 until her death, revisiting the States only rarely. In France and England she was friends with Henry James, who became her mentor in matters of form and ethical dilemmas, and their *Letters: 1900–1915* (ed. by Lyall H. Powers) was published in 1990. Her finest fiction includes the novels *The House of Mirth* (1905), *The Custom of the Country* (1913), *The Age of Innocence* (1920), and the novellas *Summer* (1917) and *Ethan Frome* (1911). Lovers of supernatural tales will not want to miss *The Ghost Stories of Edith Wharton* (1917), of which "Pomegranate Seed" is perhaps the finest. She won the Pulitzer Prize in 1921.